Shadows Of Dusk

Aella C Grey

The Book:

Twenty-five years after magic has disappeared from the world, a young environmental scientist named Lara Ray finds herself caught in a perilous web of lies and half-truths as she delves into her work, determined to uncover the mysteries of an incredible northern lake.

Haunted by her tragic past with her stalker and parents' murderer still at large, Lara's path crosses with that of Caspian and Darian. Caspian is abrasive, cold and uncaring but lethally attractive and Darian, his devastatingly beautiful tattooed body, heterochromatic eyes and charming smile could be the death of her alone.

The two secretive men force her to question everything she once thought she knew, as she discovers that not only is magic's return to the world imminent, but she is the key. The question is, will she survive long enough to see it?

Will she find the strength to shape her own destiny, or will her past consume her once and for all?

Discover a world where danger lurks at every turn, and the power within may be the key to survival.

The Author:

Aella C. Grey is an author hailing from Winnipeg, MB, Canada, currently residing in the sunny state of Florida. When she's not immersed in the world of writing, Aella indulges in her other passions, such as playing video games, diving into captivating books, and cherishing quality time with her beloved dog and supportive husband.

With a vivid imagination and a deep appreciation for storytelling, Aella brings her unique perspective to the realm of fiction. Her love for literature and interactive entertainment has fueled her creative endeavors, inspiring her to craft compelling narratives that transport readers to captivating worlds.

Aella's writing draws readers in with dynamic characters, intriguing plots, and a touch of magic. Whether she's exploring mystical realms or delving into the complexities of the human experience, her stories are infused with emotion, suspense, and a dash of the unexpected.

Stay connected with Aella C. Grey through her website to discover more about her upcoming works, behind-the-scenes insights, and to join her on thrilling literary adventures.

Shadows Of Dusk

Unbroken 1

by

Aella C Grey

1. Edition, 2024

Published by Aella C Grey
Aellacgrey@gmail.com

https://aellacgrey.wixsite.com/aellacgrey

Dedications

To those still healing...

May your scars be worn with pride from what you endured, and may those who brought you harm get what's coming to them.

Important Note

While Shadows of Dusk is a fictional book, many of the scenes depicted are based off of very real, very human experiences.

It's important to remember that everyone heals and copes differently, everyone copes in their own way and no two traumatic events are the same.

Shadows of Dusk is, in no way, written to downplay or degrade the experiences many people have gone through and should be read as a fictional storyline, with fictional characters who have their own personalities and relationships.

Shadows of Dusk Playlist

Next One by Britton

Lock In by Mellina Tey

Hurricane by Koastle, Talia Rose

Twisted by Missio

For Me by Mellina Tey

Cravin' by Stileto, Kendyle Paige

The Wolf In Your Darkest Room by Matthew Mayfield

Pretty Devil by Alessandra

Sickly Sweet by Kenzie, Alan Walker

Talkin' Crazy by Mellina Tey

Play With Fire by Sam Tinnesz, Yacht Money

You Put A Spell On Me by Austin Giorgio

Narcissist by Alessandra

Slow Down by Mellina Tey

In Bed With A Psycho by Layto

I Guess by Saint Levant, Playyard

Behind Closed Doors by Mack Lorén

More Than Friends by Isabel LaRosa

Worship by Ari Abdul

Daylight by David Kushner

High by Stephen Sanchez

No Mercy by Austin Giorgio

Breathe by Kansh

Can't Help Falling In Love–Dark by Tommee Profitt, Brooke

IC+B by Thomas Ng

... See the Spotify playlist for more...

Chapter 1

The musty scent of dust and mold fills the air.

A feeling of grogginess dulls my mind, adding to the sense of disorientation and panic begins to settle in my chest as I survey the familiar space with growing unease.

Not this again, not here.

My heart pounds relentlessly as if it's a wild drumbeat of fear and I tightly tuck my arms close to my body, summoning the strength to push myself up from the cold, dirty wooden floor.

A loud creak shatters the stillness, reverberating through the room and I freeze in place with my teeth clenched, stifling the whimper that threatens to escape my throat.

The ensuing silence is deafening as I strain to detect the slightest indication he's noticed my movement.

One second passes.

Two seconds.

Three-

My body jolts at the sound of heavy thuds, each one closer than the last. Panic tightens its grip on me as the rhythmic footsteps approach the sole entrance of the room. I remain frozen, still holding my breath as the doorknob clicks and turns.

Cold sweat drenches my entire body and every fiber of my being screams for me to break free, to run, to do anything to escape.

My mind is alert and aware of the impending danger, but my body feels heavy and sluggish, as if my limbs are made of lead. I forcefully propel myself upright and gasp for air, sucking in desperate breaths as I'm thrown from the dream.

Another nightmare, Lara. It's not real. Not anymore.

Memories of my past flood through my mind, unwelcome and persistent as I peel the sweat-soaked sheets from my legs and sit on the edge of the bed with my head bowed in exhaustion.

I reach for my phone, taking a deep breath to steady myself as I open the messages to find my conversation with Claire, my therapist. Typing out a two-word text before I press send.

Lara: Another nightmare.

Rubbing my eyes, half-awake and still groggy, I squint at the bright screen as the message shows delivered and sigh deeply. It takes conscious effort to gather my strength and slowly make my way out of the bedroom, navigating through the familiar surroundings.

It's been 17 long years since the brutal murder of my parents, an event that shattered my world and thrust me into witness protection. Due to my age at the time and lack of any other relatives, I was thrown into the labyrinthine system of foster care.

"This will be a fresh start." they all said.

"It'll be hard to adjust but you'll be treated well. Promise." they assured me.

In hindsight, I see now that their certainty and promises were shit.

For a decade, my life was a constant cycle of upheaval. Whenever the detective assigned to my case deemed my safety compromised, I was whisked away in a matter of minutes, relocated to a new town, and thrust into the care of a different family.

The initial weeks were typically quiet and unremarkable. I would enter a new school with a fresh identity, while maintaining my distance from others. Making friends became an impossibility as I clung to the certainty of my imminent departure.

Embracing the role of an outsider became second nature to me, shielding myself from the hurtful taunts and bullying that accompanied my status as an outcast.

Despite the constant turmoil, I somehow managed to excel academically, consistently earning exceptional grades as a quiet testament to my resilience.

As the months passed in each new location, my paranoia grew. Shadows danced under the cover of trees and buildings, triggering a constant sense of being watched. I quickly developed a habit of glancing over my shoulder, never truly at ease regardless of the fact that I'd yet to see any sign of my parents' murderer's return.

In fact, the criteria for determining when it was time to uproot my life remained a mystery to me. All I knew was that the cycle of relocation seemed to occur every twelve to eighteen months.

When not in school, my foster parents confined me to a room or a closet, sometimes a basement, or at times in the shed with the animals. Oddly enough, being housed with pets became one of my preferred situations. It wasn't just because they are better than people but moreover due to the fact that, since the foster families consistently fed them, I'd get more opportunities to eat by stealing their pets' food.

Where I was held and how I was treated would typically depend on the available space and how charitable they felt in any given moment. Any time I dared to respond with even the slightest hint of defiance or independence, I would face the consequences—beatings or worse.

For years, the overwhelming fear of death dominated my existence, gradually becoming an intrinsic part of who I was. As I got older I found myself wondering, perhaps it would be better for the man who killed my parents to finally put an end to my torment.

Yet to my surprise and despair, he never did.

It's been 7 years since I managed to escape the clutches of that wretched hellhole of a foster care system, reclaiming the name my parents gave me. Throughout this time, there has been no trace or indication that their killer is on my trail and while the constant fear of exposure initially consumed me in those early years, I've gradually learned to navigate life with caution.

Even now, amidst bustling crowds, I find myself scanning faces, always on edge, waiting for the murderer to emerge from the shadows. Although my memories of the actual crime are hazy, the haunting image of discovering my father's lifeless body and the subsequent trauma of fleeing through the dark, frozen forest alone for days, remain etched in my mind.

As if all the experiences that followed weren't traumatizing enough.

Fear, like an invisible captor, held me hostage for far longer than any physical restraints ever could. Its unrelenting grip wrapped around my thoughts and emotions, weaving a web of anxiety that seemed inescapable.

It dictated my every move, overshadowing quiet moments and imprisoned me within the confines of my own mind. The trauma I endured had carved deep scars, and fear took advantage of those vulnerable wounds.

After escaping the clutches of foster care, I enrolled in numerous self-defense classes, honing my physical abilities to protect myself from any potential threats.

Simultaneously, I attended regular therapy sessions in an attempt to unravel the layers of trauma that had haunted me for years. Sheer determination drove me to expand my horizons, and I pursued higher education as if that alone would help me escape my past.

Although I have devoted myself to self-defense, therapy, and personal growth, there are times when the tendrils of my trauma reach out to ensnare me once again. The haunting memories and their emotional aftermath cast a long shadow over me, threatening to unravel the progress I have made.

It is in these moments that I am confronted with the painful realization that the scars of my past may never completely fade away.

My dreams serve as a reminder that not all scars can be seen on the surface, and their echoes persist long after the wounds have healed. These hidden injuries, unlike the ones that adorn our bodies, cannot be easily erased or washed away, and though they may never completely vanish, their prominence seems to gradually fade with time.

Time becomes the gentle balm that eases the ache of our past, allowing us to heal and grow. Yet, I find that time can be a fickle companion, its work disrupted by the slightest disturbance in my life.

Moved? Nightmares.

New school? Nightmares.

New friends? Nightmares.

By the time I acclimate to a new routine, life throws a wrench at me, and I'm drowning in my past again.

Lost in thought, I open the fridge, stealing a glance at the microwave's time.

Five in the morning. At least that's more sleep than yesterday.

Wrapping my fingers around the half-full orange juice container, I fumble as I unscrew the lid, before taking two refreshing sips. The cold, acidic sweetness helps shake the last of the dream from my mind and bring my focus to the present.

The marble counter of the center island bites against my lower back as I glance at the windows, slightly misty from the overnight rain. The quiet patter on the roof above brings another sense of calm over me as I blow out a steadying breath.

Squaring my shoulders, I make my way to the bedroom to change to my running attire. I brush my hair into a ponytail, leaving some of my white-blonde strands hanging loose and framing my face. With my hair secured, I slip into a black tank top and gym shorts before stepping toward the front door. As I pull on my running shoes, I prepare for the day, therapeutically outlining the plans ahead of me.

Five-mile run, shower, eat breakfast, go to the office, review results of the tests, bring home supplies, happy hour with Henry and Candace, sleep.

As I step out into the gentle rain, the surrounding area is enveloped in tranquil darkness. I secure the bear spray on my belt, tuck my phone and keys safely in my pocket, and begin my run.

Running has always helped clear my mind. Focusing on breathing and the path ahead of me did more than any amount of therapy when it came to my trauma. Not that I can process what happened when I run, but instead, I can focus on the pain in my muscles rather than nightmares or memories of the past.

Despite my challenging upbringing, I never anticipated finding myself employed by the government. As a young individual with a Ph.D. in Earth Sciences & Environmental Sustainability, excelling academically, my talents did not go unnoticed by influential figures. With the abundance of grants and funding available, I would have been an idiot to throw away such an opportunity.

As I continue my run, the path gradually narrows, flanked by dense woods on either side. This is where the transformation happens — vibrant luminescent moss carpets the ground, an ever-expanding lushness in the forest, and a thriving ecosystem teeming with wildlife. The closer you get to the lake from here, the more extraordinary the environment becomes. This remarkable place remains a mystery just waiting to be uncovered.

That's where I come in.

I lead a small, dedicated group of researchers focused on unraveling this phenomenon, with the ultimate goal of harnessing its potential for agricultural purposes. But first we have the daunting task of identifying the primary cause behind such impacts which no one has been able to do thus far.

Various theories have emerged since the first reports came out. Some suggest that it could be remnants of ancient magic. A vestige of long-lost realms and beings that once had a presence on Earth but have since faded away. Others propose that it signifies a natural healing process, a gradual departure from our world's historical dependence on magic.

In either case, evaluating the impacts of residual magic becomes an insurmountable challenge when we lack the means to directly interact with it.

Magic has been gone for decades. Two and a half, to be precise.

There are times I wish I would have been old enough to witness it. To observe beings undergo incredible transformations, their bodies morphing into various animals and creatures. To see the effortless summoning and manipulation of elemental forces, as natural as drawing breath.

Then again, there are times I'm glad I wasn't witness to these events.

How could one ever adjust to the loss of such freedoms, to have the fabric of their life abruptly torn apart?

I imagine it's a lingering ache, or akin to that of a phantom limb, for those who had observed or conjured such marvels. To have known that once upon a time, such fantasy was tangible and alive, only to be painfully aware of its absence in the world we inhabit today.

That was the reality my parents grappled with. They often argued with those who thought we were better off without the supernatural with particular vehemence.

My earliest memories are intertwined with the teachings of my parents, who fervently believed magic belonged in everyday life.

They filled my young mind with stories of extraordinary beings and immense powers that once existed within our world. They instilled in me their unwavering belief that the magic would one day be restored and that this ancient power would find its way back into our lives.

They never mentioned when or how it would return, merely that someday, they were certain it would. Their tales of its awe-inspiring beauty and limitless possibilities left a bittersweet longing and an ache deep in my heart.

It was as if someone painted an intricate image only to draw the curtains on it. I could vividly imagine the vibrant colors and enchanting scenes they described, but deep down, I knew it could never compare to experiencing the real thing.

Hitting the two-and-a-half mile mark with the sun rising behind me, I pause before heading back the way I came. Having been here for a week, I've yet to explore further down the path or go to the lake itself.

I had decided early on that I'll wait until I'm ready to take samples before I sully the environment with my disruptive presence. If there's anything humans are particularly good at, it's destroying beautiful ecosystems, and I refuse to contribute to that consciously.

It's not long before the house comes into view, and with a mixture of exhaustion and satisfaction, I turn the key in the lock and step inside, closing the door behind me. The familiar click of the deadbolt brings a sense of security as I toss the keys onto the side table and glance at my phone.

A sigh escapes my lips as I stare at the missed message notification.

Claire: They won't stop until you face what happened, Lara. Let's have a session today, and we can talk more about it.

Lara: I can't today. We can meet tomorrow, I have free time after work. 5 PM.

The familiar sound of the coffee maker greets my ears as I make my way past the kitchen, its gurgles signaling the start of another morning brew. I inhale deeply, savoring the rich aroma that fills the air as if the smell alone could invigorate me. Someday, it's my hope there will be a way to infuse caffeine directly into my veins, bypassing the need for a cup altogether.

Chapter 2

The drive into town is eerily quiet, the dense forest on either side offering little comfort. Memories of the cottage, where the tragic incident took place, persistently invade my thoughts, flashing within my mind.

I can't help but wonder if it's the presence of the forest itself that fuels these unsettling visions, instead of my own reluctance to confront my past.

I snort internally.

Way to shift the blame, Lara.

As the trees dissipate and the town comes into view, breathing becomes easier and the tension in my body eases. The building our team is using for our research is a small lab that's been purchased by the government. It may not be grand, but it adequately accommodates our essential supplies and the machinery transferred from our last project.

The lake is not terribly far from town, and the population of the surrounding areas is minimal in comparison to some of the other communities we've worked in. Regardless of the fact that I'm a mere eleven miles away, it still feels like I'm in the middle of nowhere.

Parking my car in the designated spot, I can't help but roll my eyes at the nameplate staring back at me.

'Reserved for Lara Ray.'

How self-absorbed that I have a plate with my name on it in an almost completely empty lot.

With my purse in hand and coffee in tow, I make my way inside, the sound of my heels echo on the laminate flooring as I approach the reception area, offering a friendly smile to Candace.

"Good morning, any messages?"

Candace is a shorter, slightly heavier-set woman with a bubbly personality and is one hell of a spitfire. Her dark brunette hair is highlighted with blonde and curls down her shoulders. As I approach, I notice her furrowed eyebrows and her focused gaze fixed on the screen in front of her as she finishes reading something, not fully acknowledging my presence yet.

She has always been well organized and has prioritized work, particularly to her own detriment. She stays late, diligently filing reports and coordinating testing teams for anything outside our area of expertise. She is also completely head-over-heels for our coworker Henry, yet the two of them haven't dared explore the possibility of romance yet. It's been a one-sided pursuit thus far.

Poor Henry.

Candace snaps out of it and looks up from her computer with exasperation. "Well, Claire called earlier to make sure you had 5 PM open tomorrow. Outside of that, no messages."

Sighing and making a dramatic gesture in front of me, I say with a hint of annoyance. "It's like she thinks I'll cancel on her or make excuses. I'm just busy, not a procrastinator."

Candace giggles quietly in response as I continue toward my office, diving straight into reports and test results.

The day passes quickly as I methodically process through countless reports of tests conducted in the surrounding areas. The three lakes nearby all exhibit similar characteristics within the soil composition, and the water data reveals comparable results for sediment, hardness, pH, particulate matter, and temperature. Bio organism counts within the samples also demonstrate consistent patterns. With no significant anomalies detected, the final task is to test the lake near the house.

Admittedly, I'm most excited to see the bioluminescent moss that blankets the area. It's greatly out of place in comparison to everything else. I itch to examine some under a microscope and analyze it. Such a phenomenon is not native to Minnesota, making it even more intriguing.

A knock on the door breaks me out of my musing.

"Come in!"

My door creaks open, revealing Henry with a smirk as he casually leans against the frame.

Henry is slightly under six feet tall, with a slender build. He's always prioritized his passion for science and video games over amplifying physical appearance. My eyes narrow at his choice of attire—a pair of nice jeans and a classy plaid button-up shirt—with suspicion. It's a far cry from his usual worn-out pants and random Nintendo game merchandise.

"We're still going to the tavern today, yeah?" he asks, his voice a mix of apprehension and anticipation. His brown hair has been freshly cut into a fade, and his beard is neatly trimmed. He's dressed in much nicer clothes than I've seen him wear in months.

I lean back in my chair, "One might look at you and think you're actually looking forward to venturing out into the public. Are you planning to catfish some poor soul into thinking you're not a hermit?" I remark with a playful tone.

Henry chuckles in response before glancing in the direction of reception as his face falls.

"What is it?" I press, frowning at him.

"She claims she's an extrovert, but I can never get her to go out with just the two of us," he confesses, tilting his head back and releasing a deep sigh. "I'm going to talk to her tonight, but this doesn't work I may just have to give up and admit there's nothing between us."

Henry has been not-so-secretly pining after Candace for the past two years we've worked together as a team. In private, she has confided in me that she shares his feelings but is uncertain about pursuing a romantic relationship, fearing it could jeopardize their friendship. The conflict has resulted in mixed messages, and thus she resorted to maintaining a purely professional dynamic between them.

Clearly, her approach is not working because they're both miserable.

"I'm positive she likes you, Henry. These things take time. Rome wasn't built in a day." I reassure him.

His shoulders droop as he exhales, "Yeah, hopefully you're right. I guess I just need to be more patient and let this happen on her terms. See you in a bit, Lara." Henry says with resignation before he turns away, and the door closes behind him.

Poor guy. I'm afraid he'll be waiting a while if she refuses to advance further so long as they work together.

No more than a few brief moments later, Candace barges into my office without any warning. The contrast between their approach has never been more apparent, and I have to suppress a laugh but the frazzled look on Candace's face quickly turns my amusement into concern.

I have never been good at matchmaking. Hell, I haven't even had a boyfriend. Perhaps I'm not the best person to give relationship advice.

"Henry was just in here, right?" she asks, and my eyes narrow in response. "He was." I confirm.

"Did he say anything?" she asks, fidgeting and avoiding eye contact.

I raise a brow at her, "What are you worried about?"

"Um…" She nervously chews her lower lip and picks under her nail.

"Candace, you and I both know he likes you. This tension between you two isn't going to be resolved through ignorance. Are you still dead set on avoiding the conversation with him?" I tilt my head, awaiting her response.

She grimaces as my words sink in, and remains quiet for a moment.

"I think I'm going to ask him out tonight after dinner…"

My eyes widen, and my jaw drops. "Really?"

She notices my reaction and stammers out an explanation. "Y-y-yes, I mean if that's okay with y-you. I don't want to break any work rules with intimacy between coworkers or, or anything. I-I'm so sorry-"

"Candace! I'm happy about it, don't mistake my shock for disapproval." I quickly interject.

Her eyes widen and her cheeks turn a bright pink as she giggles and nods.

"Well, I better start cleaning up if we're going to get there on time," I say, glancing at the clock. We have twenty minutes to get there, and it's a ten-minute drive without any traffic.

"Oh yea! I'll close up out front. We'll meet you there?"

"Sure thing."

I watch the door close behind her as she leaves and chuckle quietly to myself.

Perhaps I'm not such a bad matchmaker after all.

Chapter 3

The tavern isn't as busy as I'd expected during happy hour.

Parking is a breeze, which is usually the worst part of going out. At our favorite pubs near our old research facilities, it was like finding a needle in a haystack, and then we would have a thirty-minute wait to get a table.

The moment I walk through the front doors, I spot Henry sitting at the bar with Candace, both of them looking smitten. There's a degree of sadness that settles into my bones witnessing them this happy. I never imagined that kind of relationship for myself, and I'm not sure if I ever will. With my traumatic childhood and formative years dating was never a priority, and I'm still not sure whether I know what romance or true intimacy is.

My footsteps click as I reach the bar and I can't help but feel a little out of place, wearing 5-inch heels in a small town tavern. At 5'3, I'm already considered short and my legs do look fabulous, so I'll embrace the stares.

"We were wondering if you got lost." Candace giggles at Henry's remark, playfully elbowing him as I sit next to her.

"If I ever get lost it'll more likely be navigating these woods rather than finding the only pub in town with good food" I toss back with a wink.

"Tell me about it. Get lost in these woods and you'll only stumble upon Bigfoot, wolves, or a grizzly bear," Henry adds, joining in the banter.

Candace gasps and turns to Henry, her eyes wide with surprise. "Did you hear about that incident? Someone was actually killed by a MOOSE in the woods just north of here! A moose! I always thought they were gentle giants."

As I order my drink from the bartender, I listen in on their conversation as more patrons file in to the dining area. The bartender returns with my glass of pinot noir, and I take a sip as they seem to debate the existence of Bigfoot.

"You know, I got pulled over two days ago and the cop said that bigfoot was spotted only four miles from town. Can you believe that?!" Candace and I exchange amused glances, trying to suppress our laughter. I turn my attention to Henry, eyeing him with suspicion.

"Wait a damn minute. You did not just casually mention that you got pulled over. Care to explain that part before we delve into the Bigfoot sighting?" I raise an eyebrow, awaiting his response.

He scratches the back of his neck nervously and tosses me a sheepish grin. "I, uh, was going a bit over the speed limit."

"How much is a bit?" I keep my face composed, my raised eyebrow is the sole indication of any malcontent.

"Only like fifteen mph. The roads were empty, there was no one around." he says as if that excuses it.

I chuckle and shake my head, rubbing my temples vigorously. "Henry, we've only been here for a few days. Your need for speed should remain in movie theaters or video games."

Candace's infectious laughter echoes through the tavern, drawing the attention of other patrons as Henry and I join in, unable to contain our amusement. The sound fills the air, mingling with the lively atmosphere of the pub.

"Here you go, Miss," the bartender says as he slides another glass of wine onto a small napkin. I hand him my credit card and request, "Thank you. Could you please put all of our orders on one tab?"

The bartender nods in acknowledgment and makes his way over to the computer to process the transaction.

As the hours pass, the tavern steadily fills with locals, creating an atmosphere buzzing with energy and lively conversations. Every seat is taken, and those who arrive later are left with no choice but to stand near the bar and order drinks.

"So when are you going to get samples of the water and soil?" Henry asks as he and Candace turn their attention to me.

"I brought all the supplies with me, so I'll be able to collect the samples tomorrow," I explain. "That said, I won't be in the office until mid-afternoon. In the meantime, I'll take some pictures of the surrounding area to document the environment. Candace, did you already order the air quality samples?"

She nods and finishes her wine, waving for another from the bartender. "They'll be here in a couple of days," she says, "They have to fly in, and there's a layover from a connecting flight."

"We should have some answers within the next two weeks then, or we will be back at square one," I say, my voice filled with tentative hope, as I gaze contemplatively at my glass of wine.

Henry and Candace fall into a quiet discussion about melting glaciers and the hypothetical scenarios of a zombie virus outbreak, their animated voices blending with the lively atmosphere of the tavern.

Finishing off the last sip of my wine, a nagging paranoia tugs at the back of my mind, making the hair at the nape of my neck stand on end. My eyes scan the faces of nearby patrons nervously as my pulse rages, but none of them are paying any attention to the three of us.

Time to go.

I gather my belongings and give them a playful smile. "I'm heading home, guys. Enjoy the rest of your night." I then turn to Henry, pointing my finger at him with mock sternness. "No more speeding."

Henry chuckles and raises his hands in surrender. "Alright, alright," he concedes, "no more high-speed adventures. I'll keep it within the legal limits, promise."

Candace giggles as she stands up to wrap her arms around me in a tight hug, "Wish me luck." she whispers.

I return the hug, squeezing her slightly. "You won't need it," I assure her.

Waking up to a slight hangover and having slept in later than anticipated, I can only be grateful I did not have to suffer any dreams.

If only alcohol could solve all my problems without any of the side effects.

It doesn't take long for me to get ready, slipping into my chosen outfit, opting for comfortable and breathable attire suitable for my expedition to the lake.

Taking a moment to gather my essentials, I tuck some cash and cards securely into my bra, ensuring they are easily accessible yet discreet. I sling my equipment over my shoulder, feeling its weight settle against my back.

By the time I get to the front door, my keys and phone find their place in my pocket that I zip closed before stepping outside. I pause to lock the door, the familiar click providing a sense of security.

The hike takes approximately an hour of following the trail until I reach dense underbrush. Mindful of the surrounding vegetation, I tread cautiously, aiming to minimize any disturbance along the way. I secure biodegradable reflective ribbons onto nearby trees at regular intervals of twenty to thirty feet, creating a visual guide in case I lose my way.

Every so often, I kneel down, collecting small samples of foliage. Methodically gathering a combination of moss, roots, soil, stems, and leaves, careful not to harm the delicate ecosystem. Occasionally, peeling off fragments of bark that catch my attention. Each specimen is meticulously stored in my pack, accompanied by clear notations to maintain their integrity and ensure accurate analysis.

After another hour of navigating the wilderness, the treeline breaks revealing a picturesque clearing. The lush greenery on the ground beneath me transitions to a soft sandy surface, extending to the gentle lapping of water as a light breeze nudges it toward the shore.

I still, allowing the serene view to wash over me. The surroundings are a testament to nature's beauty, as vibrant hues of green and various splashes of color adorn the landscape. It exudes a sense of tranquility and familiarity that resonates somewhere deep within my very being. The allure of this place is captivating, tempting me to repose in its serenity for hours on end.

The position of the sun in the sky sobers me from my trance as the afternoon nears, and I move to the water, slipping off my shoes to avoid them filling with sand. As my toes sink, the granules tickle against my skin, sending shivers up my legs to my neck. The sensation is reminiscent of when someone's singing gives you goosebumps that make your entire body shiver.

Bending down to take a sample of the sand, I steal a final glance at the peaceful environment, before submerging the tube into the lake water. Noting the name, location and date on it, I tuck it in my pack and turning back the way I came.

Thirty minutes into the return hike through the woods, the once clearly marked path now shows signs of fewer markers, and a sense of unease washes over me. I glance back, noting the remaining ribbons hanging loosely in the distance, reassuring me that I am still traveling in the right direction. The absence of the markers causes a knot to form in my stomach, a subtle hint of worry creeping into my thoughts.

They would have taken weeks to dissolve. There's no shoe prints in the moss that indicate someone was following me. Where did they go?

A twig snaps in the distance and my head jerks to the sound. The flutter of butterflies in my stomach intensifies, and a surge of adrenaline courses through my veins as I scan the forest around me.

You're not in those woods, Lara. It's, in all likelihood, a bird or something.

Pulling out my compass with a cautious glance to make sure I'm alone, I continue the hike. Regardless if I veer south or north, as long as I go west, I'll intersect the main pathway.

My hand tightly grips the bear spray at my side as I proceed cautiously, my senses on high alert. The sound of a rustling sends my pulse raging until a deer eating from a bush comes into view, seemingly unbothered by my presence.

I shake off the lingering unease, securing the bear spray back in its holster on my belt with trembling hands.

Doesn't explain the missing ribbons but the twig snapping? Possibly.

Another thirty minutes pass and my surroundings remain unfamiliar, sending a flicker of doubt creeping into my mind.

Could I have missed it?

Am I going in circles?

Before my mind can conjure up more questions, the well-defined path peeks out from between two trees in the distance, stretching north and south. Relief floods over me. It may not be the exact route I initially intended, but it will lead me out of the woods.

No rescue team needed.

With the comforting feeling of being on a recognizable trail, I let out a relieved sigh.

Time to go home.

Gently placing my pack down as I step inside, the weight of the journey lifting from my shoulders as I lock the door behind me and open my messages. I send a quick update in the group chat with Henry and Candace.

Lara: Got the samples, going to shower and get changed, I'll head in to the office soon.

Henry: Great, drive safe.

Candace: See you soon!

I turn on the shower, the sound of rushing water providing a soothing backdrop to my thoughts. As I move toward the dresser and closet to retrieve fresh clothes, I come to an abrupt halt, my heart pounding in my chest as I fixate on the window of my bedroom, which is slightly ajar.

Was I that drunk last night that I opened it and don't remember?

A frown forms on my face, a hint of unease starting to wash over me and I shake my head in a failed attempt to calm my nerves.

I move cautiously with measured steps toward the window, the smell of forest rain permeating from it as I stretch out a trembling hand to close and lock the latch. Peering into the dense woods, my eyes strain to catch any signs of movement, my senses on high alert.

It feels as if my body and mind are at war with one another, and it's a long moment before I'm able to tear my eyes from the forest as I turn my attention back to the room.

My gaze sweeps across every corner with renewed suspicion. I quickly grab the steel baseball bat from the closet, gripping it so tight that my knuckles turn white.

My heart races, and I force deep breaths to steady my raging pulse, before methodically searching each room.

I must be going crazy. There's no way I don't look insane right now.

Convinced that the house is clear and all windows and doors are securely locked I make my way back upstairs, the steel baseball bat still held tightly in my grasp. I keep it with me as I step into the comforting warmth of the shower, letting the water wash away my frayed nerves and the lingering unease.

It's not long before I'm standing at the front door, taking one last glance around to ensure everything is in order as I send a message to the group chat with Henry and Candace.

Lara: Heading over, be there in a few.

Chapter 4

Arriving at the office with no complications is a relief I didn't realize I needed until I park and my shoulders slump gratefully.

Clicking the lock button twice on the key fob, I hurry into the building where Candace sits as usual at the reception desk. "Any messages?"

"Nope, but remember Claire was adamant about meeting with you at 5 PM today. You don't have much time."

Shit, I wonder if she'd kill me if I canceled on her.

My thought process must be evident on my face as Candace adds with a grin. "We will never be able to find your body if you skip on her today, Lara"

I sigh loudly and stomp past the desk. "I'll just meet with her from my office."

"Have fun!"

My eyes roll at her cheerful tone and I swing my office door open, setting the pack of samples down on my desk.

Taking a few moments to prep my workstation and set up my webcam from my laptop before joining the video call with Claire. I'm a bit ahead of schedule, but I'm a 'If you aren't five minutes early, you're late' kind of gal.

It doesn't take long for Claire to join the call and her webcam connects. She's at her home office, a full bookshelf behind her on one side, a window on the other. Her blonde hair is tied back in a loose ponytail and the gold in her glasses make her hazel eyes stand out more.

"Lara! Appreciate you taking the time to meet with me today".

As if she didn't strong-arm her way into my calendar with Candace.

"I would never miss an opportunity to meet, especially if work allows."

"I'm happy to hear things have slowed down then. How has your move been?"

Slowed down? She can't be serious.

"It's been great. The locals are nice. Though I'm debating exchanging my high heels for a closet of plaid shirts."

Claire snickers loudly and then quickly composes herself, as if she shouldn't laugh this hard at my clear disdain for lumberjack attire.

"I was wondering how your choice in clothes was going to change. Thankfully it's still summer. I can't imagine you'll enjoy Minnesota winters with five or six inch heels."

I snort. "You are absolutely correct, I've ordered Alaskan snowshoes from Amazon. They'll be here in 3 days. One can never be too careful with how temperamental mother nature might be. Today, it could be summer, and tomorrow it could be ten degrees and snowing."

Claire smirks, restraining herself from another outburst of laughter before the humor drops from her face and I brace myself for the impending pivot to the real portion of the conversation.

"So, tell me about the nightmares, Lara"

I sigh loudly. "There's nothing new to talk about. They're the same as they always have been."

Claire eyes me with a raised brow as she waits strategically. She knows I'm uncomfortable with silence in these meetings.

"It's the normal dream where I'm in that room, and I hear him approach from down the hall. I wake up when he opens the door, and I'm soaked in sweat."

At least this is the easiest nightmare to talk about.

Claire has yet to know the actual depth of my traumas. I resigned myself to the knowledge that all those memories will never get verbalized into existence. That would make them real.

There's a drawn out pause from Claire as she thinks through that information. "How has the move into the new house been? Has anything happened that's made you feel anxious?"

I rub my temples again and suck in a breath, blowing it out my mouth as I prepare to tell her when my door opens.

Saved by the bell.

"Hey Lara, are these the samples? The lab team is here to process them." Henry speaks loudly as he and Candace are standing in the doorway, Candace winks at me slyly.

"Ah, apologies. I have to meet with them about these samples. It's quite important."

Claire is quiet for a moment. She won't argue but we both know she's not happy that I didn't talk about things the way she would prefer. Exposing my scars was never something I did willingly in these sessions. I don't do vulnerability.

"Alright, I'll reach out to Candace and book more time with you next week. Until then, Lara, please make sure you're taking those meds I prescribed for your sleep. They will help until we are able to sort through things."

"Thank you, Claire. Have a great evening."

I hastily end the call and slump back in my seat, shutting my eyes dramatically.

"Is the lab team really here?" I open one eye and wait for their reaction.

"They'll be here soon. Seems like the contractors that we hired to gather air quality samples got here early and they met up with the lab team about 20 minutes ago."

I open my other eye and frown at Henry, "How? I didn't see them when I was at the lake getting my samples."

Henry merely shrugs and waves his hand dismissively, "Not sure, maybe they went to a different area and got samples there instead."

Both Candace and Henry leave toward reception again, and I'm left pondering the missing ribbons and my bedroom window as I walk the samples over to the processing lab.

Chapter 5

Friday passes by quickly, and I settle into a comfortable routine. My day begins with an early morning run, followed by a refreshing shower and breakfast. I go to work, review test results from the other lakes as we wait for the samples I gathered to process, have a quick dinner at the office with Henry and Candace, and then head back home.

My Saturday routine is interrupted by a sudden knock on the door and the sound of the doorbell ringing. I'm jolted out of a daydream and quickly turn off the shower, towel my hair, and put on my robe before scrambling downstairs to answer the door.

A hurried knock sounds out again as I peer through the peephole.

"Lara! I can hear you on the other side of the door, mouthbreather!"

I flick the lock and yank it open.

"Bitch! I do not!"

We both laugh and Tammy throws her arms around my shoulders for a tight hug.

"What are you doing here?"

"You didn't think I'd miss your birthday did you?!"

I groan loudly and squeeze her back.

"Don't remind me. I'm aging. Creams won't fix everything, Tammy."

"That's what botox is for." She declares and wiggles her eyebrows suggestively.

I start to close the door behind her, snickering as she shouts, "Wait, I need to get my suitcase!"

She sprints outside quicker than anyone might expect from a five-foot-five woman with heels on, and I wait patiently as she lugs in two full suitcases, storing them against the wall in my living room.

"Are you moving in?" I choke back laughter as she struggles to wheel them into place.

"I didn't know what people were wearing down here! So... I went the safe route and brought one of every kind of style." She turns to me and grins, her green eyes bright against her fair complexion and brown hair.

"Hope you brought plaid and jeans!" I laugh and turn to the kitchen to pour coffee for both of us as she frowns. I doubt she has lumberjack attire, and she likely doesn't know if I'm serious.

"I don't own anything plaid..." She mumbles as she sits down at the bar chairs along the island.

"We'll have to make do, then" I chuckle and her eyes narrow on me.

"You haven't been responding to my messages." She states, as I jerk my head back and frown, "I haven't received any."

"Ugh, don't tell me the reception out here is that shit."

"I've been getting messages from Claire and my team, but that's it. Nothing else."

"Weird. Well, you didn't miss much. Just be thankful I'm an expert PI and I hunted you down anyways. We're going to the bar for your birthday, or whatever is like a bar here."

"How **did** you find me, anyways?"

Tammy looks over and grins widely at me. "I emailed Candace."

I roll my eyes, "Of course Candace is just giving my address out. Not that I mind you having it, but what if it was someone pretending to be you?"

"No one would do that, you're not, like, the president or something."

I mean, clearly, but damn if she doesn't have to be this brutal about it.

"That's fair" I reply, still feeling uncomfortable.

"So, the bar. Tonight. We have a date with Jack Daniels and Patrón that we won't be missing. I already invited Candace and Henry, and told them to head over once they're done overworking themselves at the office."

Sighing dramatically, I concede and wave her toward the living room. "Okay, make yourself comfortable, I'm going to resume my shower then and get an outfit suitable for the occasion. You can use my shower and we can pick something for you to wear out of all this." I say, gesturing to her two giant suitcases.

"Deal!" She calls out while I walk down the hall to my bedroom.

After showering, I pick out a tight black dress adorned with white lilies around the hip and rib cage before heading into the living room where Tammy sits, fully absorbed in a movie. "Alright, shower is all yours."

"Sweet!" She chimes out cheerfully, snatching her toiletry bag and scurrying into the bedroom. Moments later I hear the squeal of the shower turning on, and I move to the liquor cabinet, pouring myself a shot of whiskey. Tossing my head back, I wince at the burn in my throat, choking down a cough.

Normally, I can handle my liquor more than most, I always assumed it was due to my aggressive appetite absorbing all the alcohol. That said, there's no way I'm going to let Tammy go shot-for-shot with me. That wouldn't be fair to her and I won't risk my friend being hospitalized with alcohol poisoning, nonetheless for it to happen on my birthday.

Two shots later Tammy returns wrapped in a white towel and eyes the glass and whiskey in front of me.

"Anything we need to talk about?"

I shake my head, "No, want one?"

"I'm okay right now. Once I'm dressed, sure."

I nod, walking over to help unload her suitcase.

"Tammy, this is insane" My eyes are wide as I pull out more dresses than I've ever seen in my life. Her sole response is a satisfied grin as I begin to dig around for attire appropriate for the evening.

"I think you have more dresses in here, than I own of clothing entirely." I hold up a tiny piece of fabric that looks like it wouldn't even fit on a teenager and blink at her with pure concern in my face. "Did you have a child I'm not aware of?!"

"It's shapewear, Lara! Sheesh. Have you been under a rock for the past year?!" She snatches the tiny clothing from me, but my jaw drops.

"Don't tell me you squeeze into that and wear it. Actually, don't answer that."

Tammy cackles, tossing it in the suitcase.

"I do. Not all of us are blessed with the body of an ethereal goddess, little miss ma'am." The sass in her voice makes me roll my eyes and shove her playfully.

I grab a little red dress that has gold stitching and hand it over to her, snatching up some red heels as well and tossing them her way. I watch her face light up, and she holds them to her chest.

"These would look great. We might stand out but that's fine." I say, and she squeaks excitedly before hurrying to the bedroom to change.

I decide to stuff her clothes back in the suitcases while I wait. Having removed two items, one would assume it would be easier to zip them shut, but I have to use all of my body weight, and it's still a struggle to close them.

Two and a half hours later we are done getting ready, sitting at the kitchen island making some mixed drinks and listening to music when the doorbell rings.

Tammy jumps up to answer, but my arm automatically shoots out to grab her, and she winces from my death grip on her arm. "Sorry.." I mumble, walking past her to look through the peephole as Candace's voice sounds from the other side. "Lara Ray, if you don't open this door and let us drink with you, I am going to skinny dip in our precious lake as your punishment."

I giggle and unlock the door, opening it to see Henry's eyes wide at her statement.

"Ah, sorry Henry, I should have kept it closed. I'm a poor wing-woman." Both women choke out laughter and Henry shakes his head.

"Come in, shots for everyone!" Tammy shouts over the music, while I close the door behind them.

After a sloppy three-hour pre-game party, Henry, as the official designated driver, delivers us safely to the bar. As we step out of the jeep, the crowd of people smoking outside send a glimmer of excitement down my spine.

This isn't a true club like the big ones in the city, and we are all slightly overdressed, but I doubt anyone truly cares.

We pay our cover fees and step to the darkened room with neon lights, the bass pulsing into our bodies as we slowly weave through the crowd toward the bar. Henry and Candace lead the way to an open spot large enough to fit two people. Tammy and I stay close as they order a round of lemon drops, and Patrón.

As I move to pass cash to the bartender, Tammy snatches it from my hands and stuffs it in my bra roughly. "Oh no, you don't. Miss Independent can let her friends spoil her for one night."

I huff dramatically but concede. I won't argue for now, I will simply pay for everything with a vengeance tomorrow and for the foreseeable future.

"Want to dance?" Candace shouts as she grabs and spins me around to the melody, holding me with one hand and her drink with the other.

"We're still waiting for our tequila!" Tammy squeals as she pulls us both back to the bar and I giggle.

Candace leans over and whispers in my ear, "I think I'm already drunk, can you take both of these for me?" I respond with a nod as the bartender, as if on queue, sets the shots down in front of us, with a slice of lime for each.

Tammy and I stand side-by-side as Candace glances from between us with a knowing look in her eye. I wink at her and down the first shot, chasing it with the lime before throwing back the second with ease.

Tequila is much easier to shoot when you're already somewhat intoxicated.

Pushing both glasses away, the bartender eyes me warily, and I smirk at him, "Can I get water with lemon, please?"

Relief flickers across his face as he pours the water, plops a lemon and small straw in the cup before sliding it over to me and I hand him a bill. From the corner of my eye, I can see that Tammy is watching, but she won't argue the generous tip. We both know people are severely underpaid and a little kindness goes a long way in this country.

"Are you sure, sweetheart?" He asks loudly over the music.

"Absolutely, keep the waters comin'!" I squeal as Candace and Tammy drag me into the middle of the floor. We sway and gyrate to the music as everyone else does.

An indeterminable amount of time goes by, and I'm sure I must be at least decently intoxicated as I open my eyes from our dancing only to realize that Tammy and I are alone amidst the crowd of people.

"Where's Candace?" I ask into her ear as we sway to the music.

She glances around, trying to see past the bodies but it's so cramped neither of us are able to spot her.

"She said she was going to find Henry but, I can't see either of them." Tammy slurs out, and I grab her wrist as my dancing slows to a stop.

Maybe we overdid it a little too much with our pregame.

"Let's get some water and see if we can find her from the bar."

Tugging her along as we move away from the crowd of bodies toward the bartender from earlier, he sees us coming and grins. With a nod he slides two waters in our direction, each with a lemon and straw.

"Have you seen the guy and gal we were with by chance?" I shout over the music to the bartender, and he glances around, then points in the direction of the dance floor.

Following his gaze, I notice Henry and Candace on the other side of the room grinding their hips together in tune to the music and my smile widens.

"Thank you!" I shout over to our newfound beverage serving friend, and he nods before moving to pour drinks for the other patrons.

Tammy and I refill our waters one more time, and ask for two fresh ones for Henry and Candace before making our way to them. They are red-faced and are dripping sweat, gratefully downing both refreshments. Reaching the bar once more, the bartender sets out four waters as Henry orders a round of Patrón and a mixed drink for each of us. He distributes the tequila and holds his non-alcoholic beverage out for a cheers.

"Cheers and a happy 25th birthday to our best friend and coworker. May tonight be a night to remember!"

Tammy and Candace both cheer and shout 'Happy Birthday!' as the three of us toss back our shot of tequila. Candace gags and immediately chomps on her lime as Tammy and I choke down a laugh.

"Did I hear it is a little lady's birthday today?" Tammy's eyes flicker wide with shock as she and I both turn in the direction of the voice. A man in his mid-to-late forties stands behind us a little too close for comfort. His skin looks leathery and wrinkled from overexposure to sun and even in the dark his teeth are yellow and crooked.

"Yep, it's my birthday," I say curtly and Tammy goes to pull me closer to Candace and Henry.

I gasp as the man grips my wrist tightly, almost to the point of pain, "I'd like to buy you a celebratory drink." It was a statement, not a question. He's making a demand.

My heart rattles in my chest. The mixture of my traumas and alcohol making a noxious blend of anxiety and building anger within me.

"Hey!" Tammy's voice sounds out in warning.

"I've got plenty to drink, thanks." I wrench my grip from him and slide closer to the bar. The bartender is already staring at the man, leaning into the bar with his arms splayed out as he watches the interaction.

"Is he bothering you ladies?" His voice carries over the music, and heads along the bar turn toward the man. The creep, clearly flustered and realizing he's been caught, waves a hand dismissively before disappearing into the crowd.

I glance at the bartender with a relieved look, "Thank you for that."

"Not a problem, sweetheart. Men like him never seem to get the hint. Happy Birthday." He winks and continues to help other patrons as I turn around, nursing my drink while Tammy, Candace and Henry chatter idly.

My fingers tremble around my glass as I grip it with both hands. I can't help how rattled I am after that interaction.

Sometimes, it feels as if the universe is playing some kind of trick on me, sending these men in my direction throughout my life as if it is some cruel game.

The lights flash to the music as the hairs on the back of my neck stand up, my stomach flips uneasily and my nerves feel like live wires teetering on the edge of being tripped.

Scanning the crowd, I start to wonder if I've finally overdone it on the booze when my gaze falls upon a figure standing beneath the dim light of the billiards area. My insides twist, my heart pounds heavily in my chest and I know with every fiber in my being that the individual I'm staring at is causing my system this distress rather than the alcohol.

Even from where I stand, he's intimidatingly tall. The corded muscles in his shoulders and arms are well-defined through his dark short-sleeved shirt as he crosses them in front of his chest.

The dim light does nothing to brighten the jet black hair that falls over his forehead loosely, and the dark stubble that lines his sharp jawline. But the most striking feature is his vibrant green eyes that hold a note of familiarity and make him stand out even from this distance.

His intense stare freezes me in place and my heart feels like it could leap out of my chest. There is something about him that screams red flags and my body's fight or flight response could be triggered with one wrong move.

Candace and Tammy each grab an arm which forces me to tear my gaze from the stranger as they tug me toward the bar for another shot.

"What are you so fixated on?" Candace slurs as her glazed over eyes lazily scan the crowd.

My gaze flickers back to the spot where the stranger stood and dread settles like rotten food at the bottom of my stomach when he's no longer there.

"Nothing, just zoned out. I'm going to stick with water for now. I'm pretty drunk" I lie, the guilt of it only adding to the mixture of emotions I'm not ready to process. I've never felt more sober in my life.

As the crowd gets increasingly rowdy, we agree it's time to head home. Candace loops her arm through my left, Tammy hooks hers around my right arm, and we stagger out of the bar together as the two girls giggle, following closely behind Henry as he leads us to the jeep.

My mind repeatedly wanders to that piercing green gaze throughout the ride home. After dropping Candace off, it's not long until Henry pulls into the driveway, waiting for Tammy and I to stumble inside before he drives away, and I quickly lock the door. Tammy staggers toward the living room to the couch, but I grab her arm before she gets too far.

"Showers first but," I chime out, "Wanna crash in my bed? It's a California king." I finish in a singsong voice, pretending the night didn't phase me as she cheers.

At some point I'll process what happened, but that's for another day. Hooking her arm around mine, I lead her unsteadily toward the bedroom, her giggles filling the air as we nearly knock over numerous vases before finally deciding to turn lights on in each room.

Chapter 6

Caspian

From the shadows of the forest, I grind my teeth as she and her friend stumble into the house and the driver disappears down the road. The lights come on one at a time and I drag a hand through my hair, watching the rooms they move to, muffled giggling and chattering echoes into the still forest around me.

The restraint it took to stay out of sight tonight proved more challenging than I originally thought.

I purposefully avoided the pictures in her files for years. I had an idea of what she looked like now based off descriptions, but nothing could have prepared me for how fucking attractive she is.

I knew getting closer without her noticing wasn't going to be easy because she's fucking smart, but I foolishly didn't expect to be this drawn in.

The moment I saw her across the bar in that tiny black dress, with her white-blonde hair reflecting against the flashing lights, my gut twisted, and I knew this was a lost cause. All these damn years I've been watching from afar, keeping her at arms length while champing at the bit for progress, wasted.

All that forced distance for nothing.

Some say 'patience is a virtue' but, it's never been my forte, which is why this amount of restraint is unheard of for me. Considering what I saw tonight, though, I doubt I'll be able to stay away much longer. If the uncontrollable desire to go in there and drag her out is any indication, she doesn't have long.

I surprised myself having held my resolve in leaving her alone. Thankfully, time is up and Lara Ray has run out of it.

Exhaling a ragged breath, her bedroom light comes on, and the plumbing squeals as they take turns showering. I dig my heels into the ground, anchoring my back against the trunk of a tree as their silhouettes pass by the covered window and more giggling sounds out from the house.

I nearly broke my own boundaries watching the pathetic excuse for men surrounding her and her friend dancing. If I hadn't taken the time to follow them to their cars after and beat them within an inch of their lives, I'd be worse for wear.

They didn't see me coming.

Three on one doesn't appear to be good odds to most people, and they certainly thought as much. Releasing that pent-up frustration and seeing the raw fear on their bloody, bruised and broken faces seems to have helped curb my impulsiveness, at least in the interim.

The lights flick off one at a time and the house goes silent. Minutes pass by as if they're an eternity, and I leave the shadow of the forest, slowly approaching the front door to twist the knob. There's momentary give before the movement stops. It's locked.

Good girl.

If there's ever been something Lara's been consistent at, it's locking up every door and window. Likely from the years of stalking and danger drilled into her head with the threat of randomly being taken in the middle of the night by the boogeyman. The copy of her spare key that I know she keeps hidden in the back under the bird bath burns a hole in my pocket as I internally praise her.

A jolt of satisfaction rifles through my body as I consider how well I've trained her, though indirectly.

She became strong, cautious and resilient because of me.

Lara Ray, the bright scientist whose parents were killed all those years ago, is who she is, all because of me.

Chapter 7

Lara

A throbbing pounds inside my skull as I groggily roll onto my side, the light streaming in through the window turning my eyelids pink, and I squeeze them tight. Movement on the bed jerks me upright as my eyes snap open painfully, and they land on Tammy's small form shifting around while still half asleep. Taking a deep breath, I quietly drag myself to my feet and make my way to the kitchen.

I pour a glass of water, and fill a second cup before walking into the bedroom, setting the drinks on the end table and plopping down on the bed next to Tammy, gently shaking her to wake up.

She groans loudly and rubs a hand down her face which already looks a little green. "Ugh, I feel sick." She slowly sits up and clutches her stomach as if that will ease her queasiness.

"Here, have some water. I'll grab a bucket, just in case." I chuckle as my own flips in circles. I can only imagine how worse off Candace and Tammy are.

Rest in peace, liver.

I'm still giggling internally as I head to the kitchen to get the bucket and start breakfast. Popping two hash browns in the toaster oven, I grab the large pail from under the sink, and walk into the bedroom.

Tammy is hunched over, still clutching her stomach, and she gives me a pained look as she sees what I'm carrying.

"The bucket is a good call. I'm gonna hurl."

I set it in front of her and rest my hand on her shoulder, "I'm about to make some breakfast for us, so hurl away and we can reward ourselves." Pacing out of the room, I cast a glance to the bed and see Tammy hunch over the bucket as she empties her stomach of its contents.

I fall into a rhythm while making breakfast as the shower turns on from the bedroom. By the time Tammy comes out, I'm placing some cheese on top of the eggs, hash browns and sausage, and rolling each of our breakfast burritos.

She drags herself into the chair across from me and presses her forehead to the counter. "I love you, but fuck, I never want to drink again."

I can't stop the laughter that chokes out as I slide her plate over, and pour her a cup of coffee. "I can't say I blame you. You drank like a fish last night. You drank more than I did, and that's impressive."

She groans as she takes a big bite of burrito and hums in approval with a full mouth. "Fuck Lara, this is delicious." she mumbles, "I'm not just saying that as hungover Tammy. This is so-", her praise cuts off as she takes another large bite and hums happily as she chews.

I smirk and dive into my own burrito, and we sit in comfortable silence as we finish our breakfast.

"My flight is today at five. I wish I could stay longer but, I was only able to take two days off work." She frowns in disappointment, resting her head in her palm.

I wave my hand dismissively, "Totally understandable, do you need a ride to the airport?"

"No need, I can cab it. You're going to work, yea?" She leans back in her chair and takes another big sip of coffee.

"Yeah. More of the tests should have come through yesterday so, I really need to compare the data to see if there are any variations in the results."

"On a Sunday?" She raises a brow at me and I shrug.

"Candace and Henry work on weekends," I say. When she levels me with a look I continue, "Plus, I'd like to know the results as soon as they're in."

"There's the real reason, you're just as impatient as they are." She says, standing up with a sarcastic huff as she puts her plate and cup into the dishwasher before closing the distance between us with a tight hug. "Happy Birthday again sweetie. If you need anything, you know you can call me, right?"

"Of course, the same goes to you." I squeeze her back before releasing her to pack her suitcases while I get ready for work. Once we're done getting dressed, we meet at the door and both give each other one last hug before going our separate ways.

The remainder of the day passes with a blur at work and I feel like I'm on autopilot as I filter through test results that are nearly exact replicas of one another.

None of this makes any sense.

I sigh loudly and groan, rubbing at my temples.

This has to be some sort of prank.

That should be my new mantra.

My exasperation is interrupted by a knock at the door.

Henry.

Frustration pours out of me as I stomp over and swing the door open, cutting my friend with a glare.

"Come in." My tone earns me a soft chuckle as Henry takes a few steps in and leans back against the wall next to the door.

"I see the results of the tests are coming up empty. Though, I could already deduce that from the sighs and stomping echoing down the hallway"

I stalk to the chair and throw myself dramatically into it.

"Make it make sense! The results are essentially carbon copies but somehow the overall composition, performance of the soil, the micro-organisms, the flora itself.." I stick my hand in the air and count with four fingers to emphasize my point, "It's all indistinguishable from the other lakes on paper but is somehow just.. Superior. There has to be something we're missing."

Henry crosses his arms, one of his hands rubs his short beard along his jawline.

"What if we brought back some of the plants, and transplanted them to monitor performance from there, or in a controlled environment like the lab."

My jaw goes slack as I stare at him. "You're absolutely brilliant, Henry." I sigh deeply in an attempt to cleanse the negativity from my body.

This has to give us something.

Henry cocks his head to the side and grins, "That's why you keep me around and pay me well." He winks and pauses before continuing, "I'll go to Grace Lake and grab a few plants from there tomorrow. I'll text you pictures of the flora I collect so you can aim to grab the same variation."

I nod and Henry is silent for a long moment, we hear Candace cackle from the front reception and share a look.

"Candace and I are finally giving it a shot. I just wanted to say thank you for all your advice and listening to me vent."

I toss him a conspiratorial grin and chuckle, "I knew it would work out. She just had to open herself to seeing someone she works with. I hope you're both happy and stay that way."

He nods and turns to leave, "Oh, before I head out you should know, there were reports of a murder last week, a town over. They're saying it's some serial killer but they can't find his motives and his target selection varies. There's a chance he won't stop through here, but we should be careful."

I nod as his words sink in, settling in my abdomen like a bag of rocks, "I'll be careful. I always have my bear spray on me and almost always have a knife but I'll be extra cautious. Thank you, Henry."

He waves over his head as he leaves me alone with my thoughts. Part of me plans another trip to gather more plant life from the lake, the other considers the possibility of a serial killer in our midst. All while a pair of green eyes flutters around my mind.

Who are you, mystery man.

Chapter 8

Lara

I open my eyes and glance around.

The fireplace of the cabin is lit, but a bitter chill nips at my skin from where I'm seated on the hardwood floor, piecing together a puzzle in the middle of the bedroom. My mom sits inches away, her light brown hair is a stark contrast from my nearly silver locks. Her hazel eyes gaze back at me with encouragement as I compare the last few pieces to a small gap in the center. The image is a picture of a night sky with northern lights over a body of water.

Peaceful.

As I put a piece into place, it snaps together with the others, and I look up triumphantly as a loud knock reverberates through the house. The sound is commanding and intense. I could feel it vibrate into my legs from where I sit on the ground.

I glance at my mom and she frowns, "I'll get that, it's probably your father and he locked himself out. Stay here, okay kiddo?" She leans in to kiss my forehead as the knock comes again. Three louder bangs, somehow sounding more urgent than the last.

As she leaves the room, I slowly move to crack the door open a sliver, barely enough to see the back of her as she answers the person outside.

She retreats a step, turning defensively as someone moves in toward her and her body is tense, her arms raised slightly. From where I am, her face is not just afraid but almost angry as her mouth curls into a snarl. The look is such a stark contrast from what I remember of her, that it's hard to reconcile her to the mother I knew.

She continues to talk angrily to the person before her, but I can't hear what she's saying. My heart drops as the stranger takes a step further through the doorway toward her.

No. No, it can't be.

I can see from his side profile, a vibrant green eye stares furiously at my mother, his face framed with strands of straight jet-black hair, brows pinched together as he shares words with her. She lunges at him, and he grabs her wrists with ease before I tear my eyes away.

Her shriek resounds in the air, "Run!" her voice is shrill as crashes sound throughout the cabin.

Suddenly my limbs move, and I'm sprinting out the backdoor to find my dad, but I know how this ends. My legs carry me to the woodshed and as I place my hand on the door, my gaze falls to the trail of blood at the bottom of the doorway. My arms weak with dread push it inch by inch, revealing my father's unmoving body in the middle of the room. Crimson coating the wood that's fallen to the ground next to him, and his own axe buried in his chest. His eyes face upward, unfocused and unseeing.

Choking down a sob, I retreat a step and trip, scrambling backwards into the snow as I try to get away from the shed. Movement catches my attention from the corner of my eye as jet black hair moves in the window of the cottage.

That gets my legs working again as I shove myself to my feet, and sprint into the frozen forest.

I gasp and sit upright, sweat slicked over my body, hair sticking to my neck and chest as I struggle to catch my breath.

Just another nightmare, Lara. You're safe. You're not that weak little girl anymore.

Logic and emotion war in my mind as it argues that it didn't feel like just another nightmare and I don't think I truly know what safety is. After going to college and leaving the foster system, I spent years and an exorbitant amount of money on self-defense classes. I trained in Krav Maga, I took Kendo and frequented a gun range, got a permit and purchased one to keep in the house, although I usually opt to grab my baseball bat in tense moments of paranoia.

I could never shake the feeling that I was not strong enough yet. I always assumed it was the remaining fear of being eight years old and being helpless to save my parents.

I reach over and sigh in resignation as I open my messages to my conversation with Claire.

Lara: Another nightmare. Different one tonight.

Within a few seconds the message delivers, and I'm about to toss my phone aside when I see her read it.

My screen flickers as I groan loudly at Claire's incoming call, putting my head into one of my hands, the other slides to answer.

"Do you ever sleep?" My voice is hoarse and I grimace.

She ignores my question, knowing it's deflection, "Tell me about it"

I rub one palm against my face, "I would rather not, honestly."

I hear her huff on the other end of the phone, "What dream was it, Lara?"

I suck in a breath and blow it out unsteadily. "It was the night my parents were murdered."

Claire's quiet for a moment so I continue, "I saw a man at the bar on my birthday and he looked familiar. In my dream, he was the one who came to the house."

To her credit, Claire's voice remains even as she probes further, "Are you saying you saw your parent's murderer at the bar or are you saying you saw a man and he became the murderer in your nightmare?"

"I have no idea here, Claire. I'm assuming the latter. There's no way it would be the same guy, right? It's been years. It's probably just my mind playing tricks on me." I hardly sound convincing and clearly don't believe my own statement, but I hope she does.

Claire is quiet for another moment, "Are you taking the medications I prescribed for your sleep?"

Fuck.

"Not last night, I don't like how deep my sleep is when I take them."

"That's the point of them, Lara. You need a full night's rest. When was the last time you slept for a full 8 hours?"

I chuckle quietly, "My birthday, I drank my weight in alcohol and slept like a babe."

"Not a healthy coping mechanism. Take the meds, Lara. You need them."

"Yeah, yeah. I'll take the meds, Mom." I concede with sarcasm, knowing full well that I won't and Claire laughs.

"Thank you. Now, get some rest. We can discuss this more next week."

"Thanks, Claire." I click the end button and look at the time before tossing my phone onto the bed.

Four AM. Perfect time for an early morning run.

After an uneventful but paranoia-filled run, I shower and change into hiking clothes. Grabbing my bag, I hurry out the door and lock up behind me.

The peaceful scenery is filled with the cheerful chirping of birds as I deviate from the narrow path and enter the thick brush. The tranquility of nature washing away the residual anxieties of my dream.

Walking deeper into the forest, I make sure to tie ribbons on the trunks and branches of trees, tugging on them to ensure they don't disappear again. It doesn't take long before I notice the soil turning sandy and pause to gather samples. Following Henry's list of flora and photographs, I find plants that resemble the ones in the images, carefully uprooting them and storing them in my bag. Once I'm satisfied that we have a good sample size for our tests, I trace the trail of ribbons and begin the hike back.

Around the halfway point, I find yet again that the markers I tied on the trees are no longer there. A frustrated huff escapes my throat as I check my compass, surveying my surroundings for any movement. Unease once again sinks into my gut, bringing forth the anxieties from this morning, but I push forward.

The forest thickens and I pause to glance at my compass. It is still showing the correct direction as I scan the unfamiliar area before scaling over a knee-high plant and continuing forward. Every seven steps I glance down to my compass to make sure I haven't suddenly ventured off course.

As I pass a large oak tree, something snaps nearby and my head jerks in the direction of the sound.

Please be a deer.

With the sun high in the sky casting shadows along the dense underbrush, and they dance around as the wind blows through the canopy. My heart pounds in my chest and I shiver as the hairs on the back of my neck stand on end.

On high alert, I take a few more steps toward the tree, gripping my bear spray tightly in my clammy, sweat slicked palm. The forest is quiet now. The birds have stopped chirping happily, crickets are silent and the rest wildlife has either disappeared or holds a bated breath.

The incessant buzzing of the forest has become so absent that the rise and fall of my chest seems to echo in the space surrounding me, with my heartbeat pounding in my ears like a war drum.

A crunch sounds out behind me and I whirl around, my heart beating frantically in my chest. The bear spray slips from my grasp and clatters onto the ground as my gaze falls upon the older man from the bar, his appearance disheveled and worn. His ripped jeans are discolored at the seams, and his dirty black shirt hangs loosely on his frame. His leathery skin bears the marks of numerous scars that I hadn't noticed the other night, all in varying stages of fading. He meets my gaze with a cold, empty stare, and a malevolent grin slowly spreads across his lips.

"You look lost, little lady," his gravelly voice echoes the still air, sending a shiver down my spine. Panic wells up inside me as I realize the bear spray lies on the ground, out of my immediate reach.

Fuck.

Glaring into his dark, emotionless eyes, my pulse quickens. Memories of a scared eight-year-old girl running from a cottage flood my mind and I quickly shut them out. I have no time for wallowing in my past, if I do, I'm dead. Assessing our surroundings, I search for any possible escape routes or anything I could use to beat him.

He's standing a few feet away but with his long legs, he will quickly catch up. My escape hinges on his lack of cardio or my ability to outmaneuver him through the bushes and underbrush. Diving for my bear spray isn't an option with his size, if he gets a hold of me regardless of my training, there's a good chance I'm done for. The bear spray will hit me too at close range, not to mention that I'm downwind from him.

First, I take a cautionary step back as he mirrors the movement forward and sneers, "You made it too easy, coming out here again alone."

Sweat beads down my neck and spine and I suppress a shiver of dread.

I need to buy time.

I need to think.

"So, you were the one following me? Did you remove my markers?"

He ignores my question, looking at me with smug anticipation. "He's going to be real pleased with me when I bring you to him." Leathery man smirks and his crooked, discolored teeth make me cringe.

I frown, angling my foot behind me, "Who is 'He'?"

"No one believed that dumb bitch, but surprise surprise, the prophecy is real. You will be the one to break it because **you**," He points his index finger through the air at me, "You are the key."

What? This guy is certifiable. It would be just my luck to attract this psycho.

"What prophecy? I'm a scientist, not an inanimate object." My voice cracks and I know my efforts to delay won't last much longer.

His grin widens, but he doesn't respond to my question. A faint howl sounds off in the distance which captures his attention, and the distraction is enough of an opening for me.

I drop everything and dart to the right, launching myself between two trees before leaping over a fallen log covered in moss. Curses are thrown behind me, and I can hear the quick thud of his boots against the forest floor as he sprints after me.

I'm not sure how long I'm flying through the woods, going as fast as my legs can carry me, but my chest is burning. I'm a distance runner, not a short circuit sprinter. I've stupidly exerted too much energy but the adrenaline surging through my veins doesn't give me any room to falter.

I can hear him gaining on me, his ragged breaths compete with mine as we thunder through the trees in a twisted game of cat and mouse.

Landing on the ground after a leap over a high log, I chance a quick look behind me and nearly stumble when he's nowhere to be seen there. I take a few more long strides, scanning the empty forest for any sign of him.

Just as I'm about to continue running, an arm suddenly wraps around my waist, pulling me back into a broad chest as if I'm a rag doll, and a large hand clamps over my mouth.

No. This can't be happening.

How did he end up in front of me?

Panic surges through me as I feel a pinch in my neck and a cry escapes my lips, muffled by the hand over it.

As dizziness consumes me in my frantic state and I thrash around, with each movement the world spins out of control as I desperately try to break free. The hand over my mouth loosens and I gasp for air, taking in a deep breath that seems to barely satisfy my starving lungs as my limbs grow heavy and numb.

The stranger supports my body, holding me upright as I slump forward, the forest floor coming into view as my neck can no longer keep the weight of my head up. My mind races as my heart rate slows and soon after the darkness begins to close in at the corners of my vision, everything goes black.

Chapter 9

Darian

Lifting her limp body over my shoulder, I glance around for any sign of the asshole chasing her. He's nowhere to be found which isn't surprising. The moment he noticed me approaching from the side, he disappeared behind a tree.

The drug was a decent concentration, and she should be out for at least an hour. Plenty of time to get her to the safe house and away from prying eyes while I get the information I need.

I want to say I'll start slow and ease her into questioning, but I doubt we have the luxury of time. If one hunter has found her, I'm certain others will.

I need to know what she has that they want, otherwise she's as good as dead.

Adjusting her on my shoulder, I'm not entirely surprised at how light she is. She has considerable muscle for how lean she is, which makes sense since she's a runner, and I'd swear most of her weight comes from her chest and ass. Carrying her takes less than half a thought, and it's not long before we get to the truck as I place her in the passenger seat, her head dips forward as I lean in to buckle her seatbelt.

Her white hair billows into my face as a breeze passes through, and I inhale a deep breath of her scent. Even after running for who knows how long, she smells like a blend of lavender, honey and vanilla. It's so intoxicating that I find myself hesitating, sucking in a final deep breath before prying my body from hers.

Back in the driver's seat, I throw it in drive and take off down the road. Nervously glancing toward the passenger side every few minutes as her head nods with each bump. Her features are completely relaxed and peaceful, but I'd be a fool to think she'll remain this way when she wakes up.

The thought of her becoming frantic and afraid when she comes to, has me white knuckling the steering wheel.

I'm fucking anxious.

For years since I found out she was someone the hunters were after, I've hidden in the shadows and tracked her from a distance. I knew the day would come where we'd meet, but I hoped it wouldn't be like this.

Putting the truck into park, I grimace.

The conditions of us meeting are, unappealing at best.

She's going to lose her damn mind. I'll be lucky to get any information from her at all.

I exit the truck and move to her side, careful not to jostle her too much as I unbuckle the seatbelt, and hoist her over my shoulder, contemplating where to put her as I carry her into the building.

Bedrooms are a definite no-go.

The last thing I want is to give her the wrong idea of what I plan to do to her while she's vulnerable. I'm not a fucking psychopath. The kitchen has too many weapons in case she gets free and decides to stand up for herself. After seeing her run from the hunter in the forest, I wouldn't put it past her to have capabilities for self-defense.

Not that I'm concerned about getting injured, I'd just hate to have to explain my way out of that one.

The living area and spare room, as well as the study are the remaining options. Having decided, I move into the space, using my free hand to snag some rope, then a chair. I set both on the ground, facing the door and gently lower her down my chest to the seat. Her body leans into me as I get her settled, and I feel her inhale deeply against my neck and release a soft sigh.

I freeze.

Tilting my head, I glance at her face through her soft, silky strands of hair. Her eyes are still closed, and she doesn't seem to be aware or awake yet so I take a nervous breath to center myself.

I'll dose her again to keep her out for a few more hours. That will give me time to watch the perimeter and ensure we weren't followed.

My heart pumps steadily in my chest as I pull away, letting the back of the seat support her unconscious body as I tie her hands and legs to the chair. Looking her over, it takes everything in me to stand before exiting the room.

Whatever the hunter from the forest wanted with her, it's nothing good, but if she has any desire to survive I need to get answers.

Chapter 10

Lara

The first thing I notice as I come to is the nausea.

Next is the throbbing in my head as my chin tucks into my chest. As I slowly regain consciousness, I keep my eyes closed to gather my senses. I'm sitting in an upright position and can feel my hair falling forward around my face. Carefully pulling on each limb tells me that my wrists and ankles tied to the chair I'm seated on.

I peel my eyes open slowly, one at a time. They feel crusted closed, as if I've been sleeping for weeks. My tongue is stuck to the roof of my mouth and my lips are cracked. Overall, it feels like I wandered the Sahara desert for days without water.

The room is not made of wood, or brick but instead looks to be built from stone. A soft red carpet covers the floor and the space appears clean but otherwise empty outside of a second seat by the door.

I lean back to ease my stiff muscles and freeze when the chair cracks, the echo breaking through the silence of the room.

Memories flutter by as I count the passing moments by force of habit.

One second.
Two seconds.
Three seconds.
Four...

The door knob turns and sweat beads down my temple and spine as my breath shortens. My anxiety and PTSD are in full effect as the entryway reveals a terrifyingly beautiful man.

A pair of mismatched eyes stare at me from beneath jet black hair tied up away from his face. One eye is bright and a vibrant forest green, the other is devoid of color in a white-blue hue. A long jagged scar runs from his eyebrow to his cheekbone with a smaller one parallel to it along the length of his temple, as if he were mauled by an animal.

His shirt does nothing to hide the layers of defined muscle beneath them as they tense and flex with his movements. The tattoos up his arms and along his neck are covered with various symbols as if written in a different language.

He looks like he could give a champion weightlifter a run for his money with the way his chest tapers down his abdomen to his jeans, which are form fitting enough that I can easily see he doesn't skip leg day.

My cheeks burn as I realize I've been seriously checking out my captor, and my gaze flicks to his. He cocks his head and a tinge of amusement dances across his handsome face as he takes a step forward.

Dragging a chair from the other side of the room and flipping it around so the back faces me, he sits down. Crossing his muscular forearms onto the chair and leaning forward, he eyes me warily.

I peer down to see myself fully restrained, glancing back to him with wide eyes as the gravity of my situation settles into my chest.

Regardless of how attractive he is, I'm completely at his mercy.

My subconscious begins to connect dots irrationally as memories of my past flood through my mind and my breathing picks up.

He studies me for a long moment, clearly taking in the panic that I'm sure is plainly written on my features.

"Tell me your name." His voice sounds muffled like it's underwater as my pulse rages in my ears.

My name? Why the hell does that matter? What kind of sicko is this guy? Is it going to go next to someone else's on a list somewhere of people he murdered?

Each breath becomes more difficult than the last. I clench my eyes shut, and every gasp seems to be deeper as I find myself consumed by another PTSD episode. It is as though I'm drowning above water and unable to catch my breath. My chest feels like it could explode as I struggle to come back to the present.

My breath gets caught in my chest as ice-cold water is poured over my head. My eyes snap open to reality, and my shocked gaze meets that of my captor.

"I haven't touched you, if that's what you're worried about and I'm not going to. I only knocked you out so we can talk." His deep voice is strangely soft as he sets the glass on the floor next to his chair, and sits down.

He kidnaps me, drugs me and ties me to a chair, then thinks it's touching me that's the main issue?

My jaw clenches and I cut him a glare, "Not everything is about you, asshat".

Anger it is then. Better that than fear.

My outburst earns a raised brow from him and amusement paints his handsome features.

"Tell me your name."

He repeats his command from earlier, leaning into the chair to level a stare at me and my cheeks burn.

My heart pounds in my chest, "Lara."

"Lara…?" He grins and parrots my name as more of an open-ended question.

"Yep. Just Lara. But that isn't important. What is important is knowing why the fuck I'm tied to a chair and being attacked by strange men." I shout, "What do you and your little leathery skinned henchman want?"

I should really watch my tone, but I have been known to be hot headed in tense situations. Claire said it's a defense mechanism, but I always figured it was because I'm a bitch deep down.

He's quiet for a moment and his jaw clenches, "That wasn't my henchman. I work alone."

My eyes narrow, but my temper remains as hot as usual. "Right. And I'm supposed to believe that?"

He ignores my question.

"What did he say to you? Did he say what he wanted?"

My brows furrow in confusion.

If he's not with the other man, they may be after the same thing, and by my luck I've been caught up in the middle. But, I have nothing of substance to offer except the crazed maniac's ramblings.

I remain silent, and let him continue to wonder whether I have some kind of information in the hopes that I stay alive long enough to escape.

He sighs, grabbing the empty glass from the floor then walks out of the room without locking it. Moments later he returns with more water and brings it to my lips, tilting it slightly.

"The drug dehydrated the shit out of you. Drink." The authority in his tone, much to my surprise, has the desired effect as my lips part to sip the offered water.

After finishing the glass he looks at his phone with a frown and I watch him move to exit the room, but he pauses, glancing back at me.

"That individual from the forest, he's been killing people across the country for months. Most recently he killed someone just east of here."

Leathery man is the serial killer?

I snap out of my thoughts as he continues, "Consider yourself lucky that I spooked him or you could have been next."

I snort and watch him disappear through the doorway.

Consider myself lucky, while I'm tied to a chair and held hostage.

He is painfully beautiful, but delusional.

I test the ropes around my wrists, they are tied but not nearly as tight as expected. With some time, I could slip them. I lean forward and peer at my restrained ankles, noticing that the legs of the chair are not bolted to the ground.

Men. Always underestimating the acumen of women in what appear to be glaringly hopeless situations.

I twist and turn the ropes around my wrists, one at a time. My first binding comes free after what I estimate has been five minutes of failed attempts. My other restraint unravels much faster with the help of my available hand. Standing cautiously, I pull both ropes down my ankles, tugging them as low as possible, and then tilt the front of the chair, working the bindings lower until they slide free.

A satisfied grin creeps across my face and I hesitantly turn to the door. There are no windows, which means I'll have to take my chance on the entrance he used.

I gently push the door open, alert for any sign of him, but the building remains eerily quiet. Slipping past the doorway, I crouch and tiptoe down the hall, scanning for any movement. The doors on both sides of me are slightly ajar, and there's one closed at the end where I'm assuming my captor disappeared to.

I peer into each room, and notice that one is a bedroom and the other a study. Cautiously scanning and confirming that they're empty, my attention is drawn to the window behind a large wooden desk in the study. I quickly make my way to open it, revealing a thatch roof nearly ten feet below. With a deep breath, I pull myself over the ledge before easing down, dangling from my hands as they scream in protest.

Unable to hold on much longer, I let go. A flutter of fear and adrenaline twists throughout my body, but I manage to land with a crunch. Finally exhaling a steadying breath, I center myself and continue my escape.

Keeping my footsteps soft, I cautiously move over the roof until I slowly approach the lowest point. I hook my arms under, my fingers finding a ledge, and I grip the wooden beam with my fingertips, adjusting with the hope to keep myself suspended.

My hands feel like they're on fire, muscle and skin included but gradually, I ease my body down, putting more of my weight onto the beam until I'm dangling from it. My heart races as I let go, bending my knees to absorb the impact of the fall to solid ground and roll forward.

Finally feeling a sense of freedom, I push myself to a crouch and glance around. The building is surrounded by forest with the sun beginning to set, but the moon lights my way as I sprint into the woods.

Chapter 11

I don't know how long I've been running.

The forest is dark, the only reprieve from it is the crests of moonlight pouring through holes in the dense tree cover, but those are sparse. My vision adjusted slightly when I first escaped but, not enough that I can run at full speed. I tried a few times but tripped and scraped my knees and forearms when breaking my fall. Thus, I've resigned myself to the 'as fast as I can without risking further injury' speed.

I push past the burning in my limbs. The numbness in my fingers and toes from the overnight chill and exhaustion radiates throughout my body. Once the adrenaline of the initial escape wore off, there was nothing more I wanted than to lean against a tree trunk and get some much-needed rest.

There's no time for that yet. Not while I'm being hunted by one psycho killer and some other man as well.

But as I drag myself through the forest I can feel my pace slowing further. My running turned into a brisk walk, and now I'm unsteadily wandering the bush. I have to rest, if only for a few minutes.

I spot a shadowed tree near the outside of a moonlit clearing. The cover of darkness makes it a good place to observe any creatures or people approaching. I wearily pull myself to it and sink down to my knees, easing my body against the trunk.

My breathing and heart rate both slow, and I tilt my head back as my eyelids become heavy. Every blink feels longer than the last.

A dangerously close howl jolts my body alert and I scan around the darkness. There's no sign of any large creatures, and crickets and frogs are still chirping as movement catches my eye from the other side of the clearing.

My gaze slowly drags over to it, and terror freezes me in place as a lone black wolf stalks toward the tree. Its eyes appear to be set on me from where I sit in the shadows and cold sweat licks down my spine.

If that animal is hungry, I am screwed. My only option will be to climb this damn tree.

The creature stops its advance underneath the moonlight, still staring at where I sit under the tree with its bright hazel eyes. We stay like this for a long moment, gazing at one another as its ears perk toward me every now and then, sometimes they twitch left or right. I watch with rapt attention as the wolf cocks its head in an oddly canine manner, before turning to the side and sniffing the air.

Does he smell me? Is he thinking it's dinnertime?

My gut sinks, and I'm sure the anxiety of waiting for my impending doom might actually be the death of me before this animal is.

A few moments later I watch in disbelief as the wolf turns to the right and disappears into the dark forest in the direction it sniffed, leaving me to wonder if it saw me at all or if I was simply imagining things.

I sit still for a while longer, hearing the rustle of leaves from where the animal had disappeared. My eyes strain in the darkness as the black wolf walks back into the clearing, dragging what looks like a decent sized bush toward the tree.

My eyes bulge as I watch this giant creature stop mere feet from me and release the branches from its razor sharp, teeth-filled maw. I'm pretty sure at this point I've forgotten how to breathe. The wolf regards me for a moment before taking a step back, staring attentively as it releases a sudden huff of warm air that forms an ominous cloud around it.

I frown as the giant creature steps forward, and while I'm certain this is my end, I blink as it uses its nose to nudge the branches closer to where I sit. My gaze falls to the bush and my eyes widen seeing it covered in large, juicy looking berries.

There's no way.

"You can't be serious," I mutter under my breath, and the wolf's ears perk forward with a twitch.

The wolf noses the berries closer to me again and takes a healthy step back, turning in a circle twice before it curls into a ball, keeping hazel eyes fixed on me.

I lean forward to grasp a small piece of the bush and pull its branches closer. My sights remain glued to the wolf whose eyes are shut, but its ears are still alert and twitching with every sound.

I pick a berry off the bush and tear my gaze from the creature.

Hopefully these aren't poisonous. Maybe I shouldn't eat it. Would a wolf even know if they're dangerous to humans?

My stomach grumbles loudly, and decide to take the chance, putting my faith in a random wild canine who I'm sure would opt to eat me in a moment of desperation.

I pop the berry into my mouth and chew tentatively. The flavors explode over my tongue and I realize it's just a giant blueberry. I sputter, choking back laughter as I pull more off the bush and scarf them down.

I didn't realize how damn hungry I was.

Once I've cleaned the branches of all the berries, I lean my weight on the tree and look at the wolf, still unsettled that its hazel eyes are fixed on me.

"Um. Thank you, for the berries.." The creature shakes its head in a purely canine manner and I frown, rubbing my hands on my face.

"God. I'm talking to a wolf. I really have lost my mind."

A quiet snort brings my attention back to the animal before me and if I didn't know better, I'd swear it wore an amused expression.

I glance through the canopy to the moon in the middle of the night sky, weighing my options of resting or continuing the journey. I doubt I'd make it far if I tried to go any further.

Now that my hunger is no longer in the forefront of my mind, my body feels like a giant sack of potatoes.

"Think there's any chance that if I fall asleep, you won't eat me?" The wolf's ear twitches and a huff of air is its sole response.

"Right then, and I suppose you wouldn't be willing to wake me up in an hour" I joke with a twinge of sarcasm and settle into the tree.

Chapter 12

I awake to something cold pressing against my cheek.

My eyes snap open, and I'm leaning into soft fur, face to face with my newest canine companion as I scramble back to a sitting position.

When the hell did it come close enough for me to curl into it?

As I shift further away, the cold air sends shivers down my spine. At least I didn't freeze to death.

With a glance, the moon has moved a bit since I fell asleep. I'd assume it's been a couple of hours, max.

I freeze, shifting my gaze to the wolf who is again staring at me with what I could swear is canine amusement.

"You woke me up like I asked."

The wolf remains still and continues to watch me.

"I must be going insane. That has to be it. I hit my head or whatever that man drugged me with clearly has side effects that include hallucinating or talking to wolves."

I stiffly push to my feet, my joints cracking and popping as I stretch my back and arms.

"Well, this has been fun my new furry friend but I must be going before either of those guys show up." I shudder at the thought and glance around.

"You wouldn't happen to know which direction the nearest town is, would you?"

The wolf stares at me.

"Right. I knew that was too good to be true. Definitely hallucinating. I'll just pick a direction then, and hope for the best."

I turn one way and pause with a frown. I twist another way and hesitate there too as I bite my lip with indecision.

Sighing, I choose a path and start the journey across the moonlit clearing, toward where the wolf went for the berries. As I walk, I glance back to see my canine hallucination stand up, shaking its coat before it leaps into the darkness.

I walk for what feels like hours, the sun has barely risen and brightened the forest enough that I managed to find a blueberry bush on my own and ate my fill. A rustle to my left makes me jump as the wolf appears, huffing once before looking at me intently.

I move to take a step forward, and it snorts loudly.

Frowning, I glance to the brush where the wolf came from and tilt my head.

"Do you want me to follow you?" I ask hesitantly.

The wolf turns around and heads in the direction it came.

I don't know why I expected a response. One hundred percent fucking mad.

After walking for a few minutes, the sound of trickling water fills the air and I find myself picking up my pace as we come upon a small freshwater stream. Though I am sure there's plenty of things I'd rather not ingest living within it, I can't go much longer without hydrating.

I kneel, dipping my hands into the running water, lifting it to my mouth and drinking deeply. The wolf moves slightly downstream and takes its fill as well.

I stare at my new companion with a mix of awe and disbelief.

This is one resourceful hallucination, I suppose.

On one hand, I likely would have been crippled with hunger, dehydration or frozen cold by now. On the other hand, I have apparently befriended a wild animal and have repeatedly humanized its actions and mannerisms.

Mad. I have officially gone mad. Perhaps I've died.

Shaking my head, I watch as the wolf jump over the stream, toward a patch of woods.

"I have no idea if you will understand this but, thank you for leading me here." The wolf glances at me, its fur twitching slightly before continuing on.

Despite my reservations and defying all sound logic, I follow it.

Hours go by and the sun grows dimmer beneath the canopy as we continue through the forest. The area seems to buzz with sound as we pass a particularly dense part of the woods. Ducking to avoid a low branch, and pushing through a section of foliage, I raise my head to see a path ahead with buildings just beyond the treeline.

A town. We found civilization. Thank god.

Not that I minded traveling with my new canine friend but, I do have a life to get back to. I'm sure after a full day without any word from me, Henry and Candace have in all likelihood, lost their minds.

The wolf stays behind in the forest while I make my way toward the small community of buildings. I spot a church and some other various properties beyond that. Continuing down the road, I glance at each establishment I pass until my gaze falls upon the sign in front of me.

Maria's Antiques.

The small shop's open sign is flashing, with the P and E burnt out. Something about this store feels like it's tugging deep inside of me. Every fiber of my being is drawn to it, and I have no choice but to go in and take a look around.

Chimes sound as I open the door and step inside. It's quiet and dimly lit with an overwhelming amount of dust in the air as I scan the shop.

A short, heavy set woman with black hair wearing a brown dress steps out from the back room, and she smiles, "Good evening! What can I getcha?"

I try my best to return the gesture through this strange sensation in my body and shake my head, "Just looking for now, thanks so much."

She nods, turning toward the back room again. "Call if you need me otherwise I'll be in here, sweetheart."

I venture down the main aisles, slowly making my way to the front counter, looking at all the trinkets and gadgets. Most of which aren't worth much and appear to be items traded or sold out of desperation or created by people picking up hobbies for making necklaces and bracelets.

As I approach the register, a peculiar buzzing and vibrating sensation courses through my body. My eyes are drawn to a piece of jewelry displayed on the back wall: a delicate gold chain with an oval amulet. At the center of the globe, a stationary moon appears to float surrounded by some type of clear liquid or substance.

Certain that my mind is playing tricks on me, I try to shake off the strange sensation and turn away from the jewelry display. But as I do, a sudden jolt of pain shoots through the center of my body, gripping me between my ribs. I gasp, clutching at my chest, the intensity of the pain leaving me breathless.

What the hell is happening to me?

I rub the area, turning to the counter again and loudly call toward the back room, "How much for this necklace?"

The woman walks out and follows my gaze to the amulet with a nod of her head. "Beautiful piece, been here a while. I don't like to sit on inventory either, so I'll give it to ya for a steal of a deal. Twenty bucks."

I nod and unzip the hidden pocket of my sports bra. "Do you take cards or cash only?"

"Either, sweetheart." The woman pulls the amulet off the wall and starts to wrap it before I hold my arm out.

"No need, I'll wear it now. I'd rather not be carrying anything."

She nods in response and places it on the counter in front of me, ringing up the item on her computer. I tap my card, waiting for the payment screen to show 'Approved' before securing the amulet around my neck and the moment it's in my hands, the vibration radiating through my core stops.

She hands me the receipt and heads toward the back room. "Come back sometime soon!" She shouts before disappearing.

Leaving the shop behind, I continue down the road and tuck my card into my bra. I pull out the bills I stuffed in there before I left the house last and thank myself silently for having the foresight and taking the precautions I did for these 'just-in-case' situations.

Yay for overthinking, I guess.

A gas station comes into view up ahead, and I head directly to it. I need to eat something more substantial than blueberries, a drink and use the washroom. As I walk the aisles I snag a sandwich from the to-go fridge and a bottle of water, then carry them to the counter to pay.

The food is stale and dry, but the drink helps it go down. Once both are polished off, I use the washroom to relieve myself and splash some water on my face. As I gaze in the mirror and take in my appearance, I chuckle at how completely disheveled I look. My fingers comb roughly through my hair to detangle it, splashing water on it lightly to tame the frizz. Using damp paper towels, I clean off my scratched arms and legs until I'm satisfied that people won't think I'm loitering.

Leaving the gas station, I glance down the street and an odd feeling settles in as I realize that I haven't come across a single motel during my walk.

Random tree in the woods, it is.

I release a sigh, acknowledging that I truly must have gone mad since I'm contemplating, and slightly in favor of sleeping in the woods again, hopefully with the company of my new canine friend.

As I step into the tree line, a wave of unease washes over me and sits deep within my core.

Something's not right.

I hesitate.

My instincts sending out red flags and warning signs. I quickly glance to one side, to see nothing but empty forest when suddenly pain blooms across the back of my skull and I succumb to the dark.

Chapter 13

My head pounds and I wince as my eyes peel open slowly.

My heart rate spikes as I recall my last few moments before I presumably lost consciousness. I feel sharp, radiating pain through my chest which tells me that the amulet I got from the antique shop is no longer around my neck.

Shit.

I'm laying flat on a bed that smells as though it hasn't been washed in months. It reeks of body odor, dust and mildew. The room looks like it's part of a run down house, the walls are covered with tacky, yellowing and peeling floral wallpaper.

There's an antique wooden dresser near the door with some clothes, tape and other various items on top, and a nightstand sits opposite the bed. A mirror along the length of the wall allows me to take in my current predicament with unfortunate clarity.

My arms are tightly restrained above my head to the frame of the bed, and each of my legs are secured to their respective corners of the bed by my ankles. I've been stripped of my torn hiking clothes with just my sports bra and underwear left on.

My entire body shudders and tears spring to my eyes as dread sets in. I feel exposed and vulnerable. I pull at my arm restraints, twisting frantically in an attempt to break them, but the thin rope bites deep into my skin.

Hissing from pain and frustration, a bang from another room sends my mind into a frenzy and I start screaming at the top of my lungs. Hurried footsteps sound through the hall and the door swings open. I watch with wide eyes as the Leathery Man grabs a cloth and duct tape from the dresser. He shoves it roughly in my mouth to muffle the sound and then rips two long pieces of duct tape off before he secures them to my face. I'm still thrashing and making as much noise as I can, ignoring the agony in my limbs in a desperate attempt to alert anyone to my presence.

A howl sounds off in the distance and I pray that it's somehow my canine friend. That it's able to get to me out of here. Deep inside I'm aware it's a foolish thought.

My captor seems to ignore the wolf's call as his face twists into a dark smile and his eyes roams the length of my body. I watch with terror seizing my body as he walks over to the dresser, grabbing hold of the amulet I purchased, lifting it between us. The slight movement toward me gives momentary relief and I swallow a whimper as his gaze flickers to me.

"You really must be blessed by the Gods to have found one of the keys so quickly."

I frown at his statement but make no more sound, waiting for him to continue.

Blessed? He's a fucking idiot and a psychopath. Great.

The lines on his skin deepen as he grins maniacally, "Though, now that I have this key, I doubt he no longer has any need for you."

I work alone.

Those words echo through my mind as Leathery man continues.

"He will use this key to find the rest." He pauses, staring at me with a vicious madness in his eyes, "You will be my reward for delivering this key to him, and you can be happy to know that your body will still be used for good. It would be a pity to let such a beautiful work of art go to waste."

He licks his lips and my body instinctively pulls at my bindings as he sets the amulet back down on the dresser with reverence. The movement of the artifact radiating pain throughout my body, but the terror gripping my mind is all I can focus on.

He glances over my body once, before his gaze flicks to my bleeding wrists, and he grins widely, "Please, keep doing that. I want you coated in your own blood and begging me to stop by the time I'm done."

He removes a condom from his pocket and tears it open with his disgustingly yellow teeth.

My eyes widen as he takes off his belt, and slides his pants down eagerly. Tugging on the waistband of his boxers, his erection springs free and fists his cock twice as he takes in my restraints, and he throbs repeatedly in his hand. As if his own body can't contain itself from what it is about to do to me.

The look on his face is one that sends cold notes of dread down my spine. There's no way I'm going to be able to stop this. He starts fitting the condom over the head of his swollen dick and I turn away, looking at the wall as he steps closer to tower above my body.

My muffled cries sound through the air as he rips one side of my underwear off and slides the remnants down my other leg. I'm hyper aware of the cold air against my newly exposed skin and I squeeze my thighs together tightly, pulling more on my restraints.

Breathing raggedly through his mouth, I desperately force my mind anywhere but here, and I can't tell if I'm imagining another howl that sounds closer than the last as I hold onto any ounce of hope that I'll make it out of this.

I twist and turn frantically as the bed dips, and he settles himself between my legs. He presses his weight onto me, holding my body against the bed to keep my thrashing down as he lines himself up to the entrance of my vagina. I'm begging and pleading into the makeshift gag, but they come out as muted sounds that he ignores.

Bucking my hips in a desperate attempt to delay the inevitable, he wraps one arm around my waist to hold me still, and uses his other hand to position his cock in place.

In one long, rough thrust he forces his dick inside me, groaning as he slides deeper until his balls are flush with my ass. The movement yanks the restraints around my ankles, the ropes dig in, and I feel blood trickle down my skin.

A whimper escapes my throat at the pain, and he squeezes my body tightly against him as if impaling me wasn't already enough.

"Don't move now," he growls and his dick throbs as if threatening to come, "We don't want the fun over too quick for the first time, do we?"

I squirm, the screams from my throat still muffled.

I'll do anything to stop this.

"Fuck." He grunts out, holding me in place even tighter as his forearm presses against my throat, cutting off my air supply as tears escape my eyes.

His breathing evens out, though his dick still feels like it's going to explode at any second as he withdraws out of me. I foolishly hope for a glimmer of a moment that he is done.

He must see it on my face as he palms my breast, hunger evident on his face.

"You almost feel too good." he groans, as if already anticipating being inside me again, "You'll learn to like it." his gravelly voice kills whatever hope I had as the head of his cock nudges my entrance.

I thrash once more, desperate to stop what's to come as he pushes his bulbous head into me in one long stroke.

But this time he doesn't stop. There's no reprieve from the feeling of him pushing inside of me or the pain. He thrusts into me with relentlessness as if he's a starved, rabid animal, and I'm his first meal. It's as if a demon has taken over his body, aimed to fuck me whether I want it or not before being banished to oblivion.

"You're going to make me come," he grunts urgently, "This tight fucking body is going to make me come."

My mind retreats into itself further with each long stroke and while I'm aware of my body being defiled, my conscious escapes to that of my newest canine friend, Candace and Henry, their happiness, and Tammy.

While my mind compartmentalizes and disassociates the best it can, I hear his breathing become more ragged, the disgusting smell cascading over me with increased tempo. My body is limp, and my eyes are squeezed shut while tears stream down my cheeks.

I just want it to stop. Even if I die now, I just want it to stop.

I'm vaguely cognizant of the excruciating pain around my ankles as his thrusts become increasingly urgent and forceful. His weight shifting with each movement causing more blood to seep onto the bed as he slams into me.

"I think I'll keep you for a while." He grunts between pants of exertion. "You will stay here and I'll fuck this tight pussy over and over, any time I want to."

He gets another two rough, deep thrusts in, "Fuck I'm close," He grunts, clearly torn between dragging it out and finding his release when a sudden crash sounds out from across the house.

He pulls out abruptly and stumbles to the door of the room with his cock still hanging out.

Watching through puffy eyes and blurred vision, my assailant yanks the door open and takes a step back. A guttural, vicious growl shoots relief through my body and I whimper into the cloth as a fresh wave of tears stream down my face.

A dark blur leaps across the room and my assailant's screams end abruptly with a gargle as crimson liquid sprays onto the walls, mirror and furniture.

I'm vaguely aware of my wrist restraints going slack as the silhouette of a man comes into my blurred vision again. On instinct, I start to flail and punch with my newly freed limbs, ignoring the pain in my wrists as my hits connect.

My hands are tugged over my head, and the duct tape is ripped off my face in one movement before the cloth is pulled from my mouth.

I'm still thrashing and sobbing when an unfamiliar voice speaks.

"Stop."

The command freezes me in place and I blink rapidly to clear the tears away.

"It's alright. I'm not going to hurt you, but I need to free your legs."

I nod, still unable to see my rescuer clearly as he moves to my ankles to cuts the restraints. I hear him mutter a curse as he extracts the thin ropes that have burrowed deep into my flesh. My limbs feel numb, dulled, only registering the pressure of him removing them.

My vision slowly clears, and I turn my head to look in the reflection of the mirror, and in the center of the room the body of my assailant now lies in unrecognizable pieces. There's blood coating the entirety of the floor, the wall, bed and dresser. My canine friend stands next to the bed, its dark fur covered in crimson, while eyeing the man in front of me as he rises to his feet.

The man before me has thick, jet black hair that is buzzed short around his neck and gets longer at the crown of his head in what I know to be a fade haircut. It's mussed and hangs an inch or so over his forehead, and he has piercing green eyes that look dark and shadowed as he gazes at me.

My heart skips a beat as I recognize that it's the man from the bar on my birthday. The one who was standing across the room near the pool tables.

He glances around quickly, his jaw flexing as he sets his sights on the wooden cabinet as he walks to the dresser. His eyes flick to the amulet, but continues to open each drawer and promptly close them.

Releasing a frustrated sigh, he reaches his arms over his head, tugging his own shirt off and holding it out toward me. I stare at the piece of clothing and then blink at him, before taking it gingerly from his hands.

"Can I help you?" he asks, the muscle in his jaw feathering as I nod.

He angles forward, sliding his bare arm under the small of my back until his forearm braces most of my upper body, and he lifts me -being surprisingly gentle- into a sitting position.

From this close distance, I get a good glimpse of his broad, muscular body and sun kissed skin. He reminds me of a beefed up Olympic swimmer. Under different circumstances I might have been able to appreciate him physically but all I feel right now is numb and nauseous.

"All I have is my shirt, there's nothing else to wear and I'm not sure what he did with the clothes you were wearing before."

I nod weakly, and he helps me pull the shirt over my head. It's much too big for me, and smells like a light woodsy cologne, it's a welcome change to the dust and odor of the bed.

Hugging myself tightly and shifting to let my legs dangle off the bed, I see him pick up the amulet. He glances at me before leaning in to clasp it around my neck. With our faces mere inches apart, I can see the question in his eyes, but I'm too exhausted to talk.

"Can you stand or walk?" His voice is quiet and soft, a stark contrast to his commanding tone earlier.

I suck in a breath and make an attempt to rise to my feet, pain radiates from my ankles and my muscles shake as I put more weight on them.

Within seconds my legs give out and I fall sideways. He quickly wraps his arm around my waist, cursing under his breath while my canine friend whimpers from the doorway.

I feel his other arm hook under my knees, and within seconds I'm off the ground. Cradling me to his chest, he carefully carries me out of the room, down the hall, and he kicks the front door open, before sets me onto a wooden stump outside.

"Stay here. I'm going to take care of the house and then we can go get you cleaned up."

A statement, not a question. He's lucky I'm too exhausted to argue.

The wolf walks over and sits against my legs, settling the weight of its heavy head onto my thighs causing me to stiffen at the contact.

I look down to see its hazel eyes staring back at me and I instinctively reach out to pet its head.

The motion is soothing for both of us, I think.

"I've decided to name you Dana." I mutter to the wolf, and she raises her eyes to meet my gaze, tilting her face to the side.

"Pretty sure you're a she, considering the lack of hardware, and after everything, you deserve to have a name."

Dana rests her head on my thighs once more and exhales a soft canine sigh. I hear crackling and the door opens to the house as smoke rises out of the broken windows, dark plumes float into the night sky.

The similarities to what happened to my parents are too striking to ignore now. Particularly since I dreamt of this man being the one who stood in the doorway with my mother the night both she and my father were murdered.

"You.." My voice is no more than a pained whisper.

He glances at me and raises a brow.

"It was you that killed them, wasn't it?" I asked quietly.

"You're going to have to be more specific, I've killed a lot of people in my life."

My eyes grow wide at the nonchalant admission, and though I'm exhausted, I can't help but confront him now that I am faced with dots that I'd be a fool not to connect with his recent actions. It's not like I have anything to lose at this point by doing so.

He could have killed me in that bed when I was restrained. He could still do it now.

I swallow painfully, "You're the reason I was placed into witness protection, you're the stalker aren't you? My parents and I were staying in a cottage. Seventeen years ago-" My throat tightens as a tear streams down my cheek.

There's a long pause and I use his shirt to clear my face as he eyes me, the muscle in his jaw working.

"I'm not your stalker, Lara. I'm the detective that was assigned to your case and put you into witness protection to start with." His voice is soft as he digs to his back pocket.

The... Detective?

There's no way.

That was nearly 20 years ago... He was a detective back then?

My eyes widen into saucers as he shows me his badge and ID from his wallet as if to prove his point.

"We need to get you cleaned up, we'll talk more at my place." He says with quiet indifference.

"No." I shake my head.

He raises a brow, "No?"

"We go to my place. I need clothes, I need comfort. We talk, but in my home, not yours," I pause for a moment and throwing caution to the wind decide to add, "Also, just in case you're lying, please don't kill me."

He chuckles as he walks over, picking me up with minimal effort again as his voice reverberates within his chest. "If I had a reason or desire to kill you, Lara, you'd have been dead a while ago."

He glances at me as he emphasizes 'a while ago' with dry amusement.

"That's reassuring." I mumble sarcastically and fall quiet as he carries me down a path to a truck parked on the side of the road.

He opens the door to the passenger seat and sets me in gently.

I watch as he looks at and speaks to Dana, "You can ride in the back or run there, up to you. Just, don't ruin the seats." She huffs and hops into the backseat.

"She understood you?" My eyes are saucers as his lips twitch and closes the door.

I've gone mad. That is the only explanation. I'm officially one hundred percent certifiable. I can never tell Claire any of this, or I will be permanently admitted. They will lock me up in a straight jacket, in a room with padded walls and throw away the key.

The driver's side door opens and the truck shifts as he settles into his seat as the engine turns over. It rumbles to life as he pulls onto the road. I blink slowly as exhaustion creeps up, and I find myself soon lulled to sleep by the sway of the truck.

Chapter 14

I rouse as the engine cuts off, before the driver's side door opens and shuts. Blinking the sleep away, relief washes over me as I notice that we are parked in front of my house.

I don't have the time nor the energy to ask how he knows where my house is.

The passenger door opens, and next thing I know, I'm cradled against his bare chest once more. Dana leaps down from the back seat and follows us to the entryway. "Oh, I don't have the-" A jingle of keys cuts me off as he unlocks it.

"I found the spare." I blink at him as my front door swings open and Dana walks in as if she owns the place, sniffing around and investigating each room. "Which way is your shower?" He asks, and I point down the hall toward the bedroom.

Carrying me into the washroom, he slides the shower door open before setting me down gingerly near valve that turns on the water.

He's mere inches from me as he searches my face, "I'll grab some clothes from the other room for you. Are you able to stand and shower on your own?"

"I'll be fine." My cheeks flush as I nod, my gaze flicks to the floor.

He's quiet for a moment, "Alright, I'll be in the other room with the wolf. Call if you need me." he says, stepping back out of the shower.

"Dana" I whisper.

"Hmm?" I see him pause and turn toward me.

"I named her Dana."

"Dana it is then." He laughs softly before exiting the room.

Twisting the knob on the shower, I wait for the temperature to climb enough for me to step under the steady stream. Normally I'd have it set to some ungodly level of heat, but these wounds most likely wouldn't agree with it, so lukewarm water it is.

I stand there for a moment and suck in a breath. I shift my weight onto my injured ankles and a whimper crawls up my throat as pain radiates from my Achilles tendons and up my calves.

Biting the inside of my cheek, I pull off Mystery Man's shirt, tear off my sports bra and stagger under the falling water.

The minimal heat sears pain into my wrists and ankles as it cascades over me and tears begin to fall down my cheeks, mixing with the gentle water sluicing off my skin as the unreal events of the past few days replay through my mind.

My legs quiver, the strain aching in my ankles and a pained cry catches in my chest as I lean on the wall for support. I cover my face with my hands and slide down to the floor.

I feel broken.

The door to the bathroom opens slightly and hear the clack of nails against the tile, accompanied by a whimper as Dana looks in at me. She seems to hesitate before pawing the entrance to the shower in a clear request to come in. Pain radiates from my wrists as they bear my weight while I crawl over to roll it open. Dana walks in and sits under the water with me, blood that had dried onto her fur now rinsing down the drain in a stream of crimson.

I ignore it and wrap my arms around her neck, sobbing into her fur.

"Thank you." It's all I manage to choke out in a whisper through the tears, and she nuzzles her face into the crook of my neck. We stay like that for what must be ten minutes or so before I decide that a proper shower and rinse for us both is needed. I pull back and stroke the fur on her head, "Let's clean off and get some answers, huh?"

Dana's ears twitch and I stand carefully, wincing through the pain that lances within my limbs. Using one of the adjustable heads, I rinse her fur off first considering the vast amount of blood that coats it. Once she's rinsed, I hobble gingerly out of the shower to the cabinet and grab an organic oatmeal body wash I brought with me in case I found any stray dogs or cats.

I was a magnet for them in California. By the time I lived there for two months I had already found homes for multiple.

It doesn't take long to finish shampooing and rinsing her. Once fully clean, she pauses and glances at me. The hesitation and assessing look causes me to frown at her in confusion.

"What-" My question is cut off as Dana shakes all the water out of her fur. I squeak in surprise and then break out in laughter.

She huffs and moves to stand at the other end of the shower while I wash and rinse myself.

Turning the faucet off, I take cautious steps to the towel rack and wrap myself, then glance at Dana. "I'll give you an entire steak if you go into the other room and shake water onto our Mystery Man out there."

Dana snorts with what could only be amusement and slips out of the room quickly, water still dripping from her thick fur.

I wait in anticipation and silence for a long moment before I hear him cursing loudly at Dana, and her nails clacking quickly as she hurries back in the bathroom to what she can presume is safety.

She zips into the room and I grab a secondary towel to start drying her fur more to avoid the stink of wet dog later on. Mystery Man stomps in the bathroom with a huff and I have to concentrate all my effort on not showing amusement.

"The wolf is going outside."

Dana growls and bares her teeth at him, hackles raised.

"I don't think she wants to. Why are you trying to throw her out anyways?" I ask, feigning innocence.

"It just got water everywhere. I'm nearly certain it was on purpose." He crosses his arms and frowns at her as if she knows every word he's saying and will suddenly speak to argue his statements.

I bite the inside of my cheek so hard that I draw blood in a desperate effort not to laugh.

"She's a wolf, Mystery Man. I doubt it was on purpose. You know how dogs are after baths, they get the zoomies, roll around and shake a lot. Can't really blame her, can we?" I continue to feign innocence as thoroughly as I can until Dana looks at me and huffs with a twinkle in her eyes that tells me she's enjoying this as much as I am.

My commentary is completely ignored as he raises his brow in pure amusement and barks a laugh. "Mystery Man?" He chokes out and bursts into laughter again while I'm left blinking at him.

He smiles and laughs, what a surprise.

"Well it's not like you told me your name." I say, heat rising to my cheeks while rolling my eyes for added dramatic emphasis.

"Caspian-" He chokes out in a failed attempt at suppressing a laugh, his green eyes bright with amusement, "My name-, my name is Caspian." He composes himself with a deep breath before he continues. "I've been called many things in my life, but Mystery Man. That's one for the books."

"Well, Caspian. I think we have plenty to talk about, so I'll meet you in the other room after I change." I motion for him to leave, and he tips his head before backing out of the bathroom.

Dana clacks after him to the doorway pausing to cast a glance at me.

"You sleep with me in my room, you're not going outside," I tell her, "and we will talk while I get you your well earned steak. Shake if you want it raw, huff if you want it cooked."

I say the options as a joke, but Dana's eyes twinkle, and she huffs loudly before leaving the room.

I blink, taken aback.

Did she truly choose cooked steak or am I humanizing an animal once again? God, this is yet another thing I can never tell Claire.

Treading carefully on shaky legs, pain radiating with each step, I reach in the closet, grabbing a soft pair of pajamas and pull them on before venturing to the kitchen.

As I peer into the living area, Caspian is sitting on the couch watching Gladiator and Dana is laying on the love seat near the front window.

I suppress a snort at the sight and open the fridge, rifling through the meat drawer.

"Are you hungry?" I call out, leaning back to look at Caspian in the living room.

His eyes widen and he turns his head, "You are going to make me food? We haven't even talked about-"

"Don't." I hold my palm toward him, "I plan to make the food prior to you telling me so there's no rash decisions."

He laughs under his breath, the slight smile on his face sending butterflies through my chest as he concedes, "Sure, I could eat. I can make it though, you're still injured."

I shake my head. "Cooking is therapeutic, and therapeutic is what I need after tonight."

He nods once in response and leaves me to it.

I methodically prepare two steaks, potatoes and asparagus. It takes me longer than normal due to my injuries, but finally I get everything cooked. I portion Caspian's food and mine, with a third plate holding the larger of the two steaks on it.

I put one on the ground, "I'm true to my word, Dana. Here ya go."

As she trots over, Caspian's brows are pinched in confusion, "What word?"

"That, is for me to know and for you to hopefully never find out." I wink at Dana as she saunters to her plate.

She huffs and digs into her steak with renewed enthusiasm.

Caspian sits across the island from me and looks at our plates, his brows still furrowed.

"Oh, drinks. How rude of me. What would you like? I have water, OJ -pretty sure he was guilty by the way-, and I have soda."

Yay for humor as a deflective coping mechanism.

I turn to see Caspian staring at me with a raised eyebrow and an amused smirk, "I'll take water, thank you."

I nod, grabbing a glass, filling it with filtered water and some ice, before sliding it over to him. I snag a soda for myself, cracking it open and setting it next to my plate which has half a steak on it now.

I blink and point to the meat, "You didn't have to-"

"Sit. Eat. We have plenty to talk about and the night isn't getting any younger."

I nod, doing as he says and dig in. The serious note to his voice brings reality crashing back and the weight of everything sits heavy on my mind as I slowly lift forkfuls of food into my mouth.

At least soon I might get some answers.

Chapter 15

Once all three plates are cleaned, we settle into the living room. I sit on the love seat, Dana sits on the floor against my legs, eyeing Caspian on the couch.

My heart flutters in my chest as he clicks the remote to turn the TV off and leans forward onto his knees.

"Where do we start? With the killing of my parents or with what happened the past few days?" The confidence in my voice completely feigned.

Caspian eyes me with an intensity that makes me want to squirm. "I think we should start with the basics. Tell me about yourself, what you have been doing that led you here up to the man from the house and what he said to you." His voice is steady and the level of calm in it unsettles me.

I set aside my reservations about his questions on the premise that it's been years since I left witness protection and started working. I suppose during that time I may not have had any updates to my file if I wasn't deemed in danger or at risk.

I rub my temples and sigh deeply. "I'm sure most of this is in a file somewhere, but I will humor you. My name is Lara Ray, I am a scientist studying the surrounding lakes for various reasons. I work for the government with a team of individuals to do so. Individuals, who are probably freaking out by now. Shit, I don't know where my phone is."

Caspian shakes his head, I take the meaning as 'Worry about messaging them later'.

I continue, "Right. Anyways, I first saw the man from the house on my birthday at the bar, the same night I saw you, actually.

Then I saw him at the lake when I was gathering samples, that was before I fled from some guy with two different colored eyes who also wanted to know what had been said to me. The man Dana killed didn't say much that made any sense. He mentioned a prophecy, he kept referring to his boss and mentioned some woman being right about something." Caspian's eyebrows pinch together slightly, but he lets me continue.

I pause and clear my throat in an effort to do my best Leathery Man impression, "The guy was like 'You really must be blessed by the Gods to have found one of the keys so quickly.' Whatever that means." I roll my eyes and lean forward, wrapping my hands around Dana's neck for comfort.

Caspian's eyes flicker between Dana and me as he tilts his head, rubbing his beard as he thinks.

"And how did you come across the amulet?"

"When I ran from the guy with heterochromia, I ended up in some town and saw this antique shop... It was as if I had a literal need or was being pulled to go in. That's when I saw the necklace and…" I trail off and rub the same spot where the pain radiated when I tried to turn away from the amulet.

"And what, Lara?" Caspian barks and startles me out of the memory. I don't miss the tension in his jaw as I continue.

"And... I couldn't leave the store without it, as in, I physically couldn't. I tried to turn and walk away after seeing it, and felt excruciating pain here." I rub the spot along my diaphragm with a frown.

My eyes flicker to meet his gaze before speaking again, "What is the significance, Caspian? What is the amulet and why did that asshole want it?"

He's silent for a while as I watch him contemplate the information. My eyelids begin to weigh heavier the longer I wait and my mind wanders as I give him time.

After what feels like an eternity, I sigh heavily before looking up, only to find he's staring at me, with uncertainty clear on his face. "Are you going to tell me what's going on?"

"I can tell you what I know, but I don't know everything. I also can't control whether you will believe what I do tell you."

Stop stalling, asshole.

"Just tell me, Caspian." My tone is more curt than intended, but I don't apologize for it.

He pinches the bridge of his nose and sucks in a deep breath, "You are aware of other realms and magic, yes?"

Holy fuck.

I nod in response.

"Wonderful. That saves us plenty of time in this explanation. To make a very long story, short. Twenty five years ago, powers beyond our understanding bound magic on earth and sealed any and all from entering and leaving. Those who were here already like I was, have remained on earth in whatever form they were in when magic was bound. It appears there is a way to break that binding to magic so that we may return to our realm and my brother has discovered that you are at the heart of it."

I stare at him for a moment and narrow my eyes.

"Your brother?" My voice cracks.

Caspian nods, "You said you met someone with two different colored eyes, yes? Likely one green and one white. That would be my older brother, Darian."

I blink at him. All of a sudden their physical similarities make sense. Both muscular, easily a foot taller than me, jet black hair, sun kissed skin. But I distinctly remember Darian had tattoos visible, so between that and a few minor characteristics...

Holy shit they're not human.

This is a lot of revelations, and somehow I feel like this is just the beginning.

As I align physical attributes, it dawns on me that both men look to be in their thirties and something doesn't add up when I begin to consider that Caspian had been assigned to my case seventeen years ago. "You said that you were stuck on earth when magic was bound twenty five years ago, how old are you?"

His eyes flash and meet mine, "Two hundred and forty-seven."

My jaw goes slack but Caspian continues, "This all being said, if my brother has hired one person to hunt you down in his efforts to retrieve the keys, there will be more."

I swallow audibly and nod at his words, though the meaning of them has yet to sink in.

"And my parents?" My voice is quiet and small, and I keep my eyes low to the ground.

"They were being tracked for years, receiving threatening letters and pictures of you," his voice cuts off and my eyes flicker up to his as his jaw clenches, but he continues. "My brother killed them in his search for the key to restoring his magic."

Anger and guilt crash over me in a wave as I sit silently for a long moment, but I do what I do best and bottle it down, "Well, I think that's enough life altering revelations for one day." Standing and carefully walking over to the linen closet, pulling out a blanket and handing it to him. "You're not angry or upset?" he asks, assessing my reaction as I consider his question.

Bold of him to assume I'm not angry.

I hold his gaze as I answer, "I spent the majority of my life being scared. When I wasn't scared, I was angry. Since being on my own, where I no longer fear for my life, my anger is always below the surface. I've been angry for so long, for more reasons than I can count."

I shake my head, "Knowing the **reason** my parents were killed is what makes me angry. It doesn't make me angry at you but your brother and whatever drives him to restore his magic."

His expression becomes hard and unreadable, so I leave him with that as my emotions threaten to overwhelm me. I use the walk to the bedroom to clear my mind, grabbing one of my pillows, before I return to the living room, and hold it out to him.

"So, what happens from here?" I ask quietly as he puts it on one end of the couch.

"Well, my brother will be sending more hunters. So for now, the plan is to keep you alive. Secondary to that is to find the other keys before he does."

I nod lightly, "Right. Don't die and find the other pain inducing amulets. Great. I'm going to sleep now." I rub my face and walk away, waving dismissively, "Help yourself to coffee and the fridge in the morning, Mystery Man." I smirk at his quiet chuckle as I tread gingerly to the bedroom with Dana in tow.

~

I open my bleary eyes to see my foster dad standing in front of me. His beer gut hangs over his sweatpants as he looks at me with his beady gaze, a vicious hatred in his eyes as he snarls and reaches for my arm.

I gasp as he squeezes my bicep painfully, and his lips curl into a malicious smile at my reaction as his other hand wraps around my throat tightly, cutting off precious oxygen and blood supply.

"You're useless. Worthless. You're nothing. You're lucky we get paid to keep you alive or you'd be dead by now."

He releases me suddenly and turns away. Walking to the other side of the room, he takes off his belt, gripping it tightly in his hand.

He swallows another swig of whiskey, putting the bottle down on the dresser before he sneers at me. "Turn around."

I hesitate and tears stream from my eyes, "No." I say with a trembling voice, fear and anxiety gripping my chest.

Anger flashes across his features as he stomps angrily to me. "No?" Spit sprays from his mouth as he shouts, "You think you can defy me? You're only making this worse for yourself. You know what happens to little girls who disobey."

Throwing my arms between us, as if they could provide me with any sort of protection from him. "No, please! Please, don't!" I beg, and he smiles widely before he grips my arm, twisting me around roughly. The sounds of the back of my shirt tearing resonates through the room and a sob escapes my throat.

I hear the air whoosh and the metal buckle clank before I feel the pain. I whimper as the first one connects. There is more coming, so I bite my cheek to stay quiet.

If I make any noise, he gets angrier and the angrier he is, the worse his attacks are. He whips the belt along my back repeatedly, the clasp splitting my soft skin with every harsh strike.

Another lashing comes. I squirm, whimpering as pain lances down my spine.

"Quiet!" He bellows from behind me. I know his next swing will do more damage than the last.

Another strike comes.

And another.

And another.

I endure five more strikes before the agony becomes unbearable.

Inhaling a deep lungful of air, I scream as the final hit connects and pain sears across my spine.

I'm still screaming as I'm shaken awake.

Dana is standing by the door growling as Caspian hovers over me and I gasp desperately for air. He reaches around to my back to try to help me sit up, and I bat his arms away like they'll burn me, the pain still fresh in my mind.

"Lara, it was just a nightmare. It's okay. Fuck. You're okay."

I look past him to the room around us frantically. My gaze locks with Caspian's, his face merely inches from mine as I try to collect my bearings. I move to rub my palms to my eyes, inhaling sharply as the movement stretches the wounds on my wrists.

"Who was it?"

I freeze.

His question and the edge to his voice makes my cheeks burn with embarrassment. That's twice he's seen me in my most vulnerable states.

Releasing the breath I had been holding, I answer without thinking, "My foster parent. Or, rather, one of them."

I'm not sure why I decided to respond honestly to his question. Normally I avoid talking about what happened at the foster houses. Nobody wants to listen to someone else's trauma. We're all dealing with our own demons.

I glance up at Caspian's unreadable expression before he leaves the room and I blink.

I suppose that was enough of an explanation for him.

Dana jumps onto the bed, settling against me, and I run a hand over her fur, "Sorry about that, Dana. If you want to sleep in the other room, I wouldn't take it personally, you know."

She gives me a side eye and huffs in response before leaning more heavily into me.

Does this make her qualified as an emotional support animal?

Can wolves even be ESA's?

To my surprise Caspian returns with a glass of water, crossing his arms as I drink gratefully.

"So what did your foster parent do to you in this dream?"

I choke slightly on my last sip and cough while he takes the empty cup from me and puts it on the side table. I'm silent for a long moment and inhale deeply, preparing myself to verbalize a piece of my history no one knows.

"This one's name was Frank. Frank didn't like my existence. He used varying methods of showing me how little my life was worth, but his preferred method was to use his belt as a whip. Particularly, he enjoyed when the metal pieces tore skin. That always got the best reaction."

Claire would kill me if she knew the secrets I haven't told her in years, I'm telling to some random century old person.

Caspian's face remains unreadable, his jaw clenching and pulsating is enough to tell me he doesn't particularly enjoy the thought of that method of torture.

Same here, Mystery man.

The room is quiet for a while as I reflect on that memory and as I stare down at my wrists, my mind wanders.

"How did you and Dana find me, when... Leathery man had me?" Caspian's lip twitches at the name, but his face remains serious as he thinks for a moment.

"Dumb luck, really. When I got wind that my brother had you, I headed to the nearest town and waited to see if you'd pop up. By the time I rounded the area you were being held, the wolf was flagging down my truck and I followed the direction he was sprinting."

My suspicion at his 'dumb luck' is interrupted by a small revelation in his words and I pause, "He?" I ask nervously.

"He," Caspian affirms with a nod.

My hands gesture between my legs, "How do you know he's a he, if he has no manly bits?"

Caspian's lips curl up in a poor attempt to smother a smirk. "Scent is what mostly gives it away. He is also not a wolf, so the 'manly' bits as you so kindly called them aren't there in that form which is on-brand for those who can shift. Our kind has no need for them since we have our normal forms."

Wait. "You can smell that he's a 'he'!?" I squeak, my jaw goes slack and my eyes bulge out of my head, turning to look at the creature laying against me, and then back to Caspian.

What the fuck else can he smell?!

Caspian barks a laugh and Dana, or Dan or whoever, jumps off the bed and cowers in dejection. "To be fair, he is a wolf right now, but whenever magic is returned he will have another form that is much more human in appearance, with very manly parts."

I groan and glare at the canine hiding behind Caspian, "You saw me naked! Now I have to rename you, Dana is not going to work. Dan. Your name is Dan."

Dan huffs again and Caspian sighs, "Well now that that is settled. Time to sleep, it's way too early to be awake."

I take a deep breath and look at Caspian, "Any clue where my cell is?"

His face is guarded as he nods before leaving the room and Dan whimpers sadly from where he stands.

"Get on the bed you big furry oaf. Once magic is back, though, the bed is off limits."

Dan's tail wags as he curls up alongside me and I shake my head as Caspian returns with my phone in hand. "How did you get ahold of it?" I ask, taking it from him.

Caspian winks, "I've mastered the ability to recover lost items over the years, it seems."

I look at the screen and groan loudly at the 76 missed messages, 40 missed phone calls and 15 missed video calls. I unlock it and start damage control, first sending something to Claire.

Lara: Another nightmare. Different one this time, we'll talk about it in a few days. Need to sleep for now.

The message is instantly read, and I see her type back.

Claire: Glad to know you're alive! Candace and Henry both reached out. We will talk soon about the nightmare.

My next message goes to the group chat.

Lara: Hey you guys, everything's fine. Crazy few days. I'll catch you up later. Just know I'm alive and ok.

Candace is instantly typing.

Candace: That's totally what a serial killer would say to throw off time of death. Say something only Lara would know or else I'm calling the police!

I roll my eyes and sigh, though she's not wrong. I'd totally assume the same.

Caspian leans back against the wall with his hands in his pockets, watching with amusement as I flip the camera on and my side table light, I hold out my phone and press record.

"Candace, I appreciate the concern but it's really me, not a serial killer with my phone pretending to be me." As I finish my sentence, Caspian laughs quietly from the theatrics of it.

I click send and shoot him a look. "It's a valid concern, I would worry too if someone went MIA for days and suddenly sent a 'Hey guys, I'm alive' text. That kind of text screams 'I'm not really alive, just throwing you off my killer's trail'."

He laughs harder, my phone chimes and I glance down.

Candace: Thank god you're okay. Who was laughing in the background of the video?

Candace: Lara, is there someone there with you?

Candace: Oh my god, it's the serial killer.

Candace: LARA BLINK TWICE IF YOU NEED HELP.

Lara: It's a long story but no, not a serial killer.

I suppose he did admit that he has killed many people.

I snort and look up at Caspian. My cheeks flush when I find his eyes on me and I opt to let him in on the inside joke.

"They heard your laugh in the video right at the end and asked if the serial killer was there with me. I said you weren't, but I suppose in essence you are, given what you said about having killed many people."

Caspian's lips twitch before his gaze falls to my wrists and his face hardens, becoming once again frustratingly unreadable. "They don't have to worry about him anymore. The wolf solved that problem."

I nod and open my phone again.

Candace: Okay, I believe you, for now. Get some sleep, we can catch up later.

I close those messages and wince as I open Tammy's conversation.

Lara: Hey girl, sorry the past few days I've been MIA. Lost my phone and then wandered in the wilderness. Everything is good now though. Love ya.

The messages deliver but aren't instantly read. It's super early on the west coast. She's probably asleep.

I rub my palms to my eyes and sigh, ignoring the pain in my wrists. "Thank goodness that's done."

"Yep, now I can really kill you and no one will suspect me" My head jerks toward him as a grin creeps across his face.

I narrow my eyes at him and glare at him through slits. "No one would have suspected you, anyways, Mystery Man."

"Even better." The mischievous look he gives me makes me roll my eyes sarcastically.

Caspian pushes himself off the wall, walking toward the bed

and my heart thuds loudly in my chest. He reaches to the side table and grabs the glass from earlier before heading out of the room with a dismissive wave and flicking the light off.

"Get some sleep, Lara."

Grumbling as I roll over, I wrap an arm around Dan's neck and burying my face in his fur with a deep contented sigh.

Chapter 16

My eyes open and a yawn creeps out as the sun filters in through the curtains. I stretch my arms until they make contact with soft fur and I look over to see Dan laying next to me, though his ears have twitched and perked so I know he's at least awake.

I kick off the blankets and slide to the edge of the bed, cracking my neck and spine before getting up. The events of the past few days whirl through my mind as I grab my phone from the side table.

Candace: So. Are you gonna spill the tea?

Henry: Why would she do that on purpose?

Candace: Not literally, you buffoon!

Henry: Oh, I googled it.

Lara: 'Henry the Boomer' has a good ring to it. Chat later, gonna get ready and get in soon.

I snort at their antics and stand while tying my hair up into a messy bun. The ache around my ankles and wrists has slightly lessened after a full night's rest. They're not the most severe injuries I've had in my life. The scars that mar the skin on my back are proof that I've endured worse.

Not many people have gotten close enough to me to understand the extent of those traumas. Tammy looked at my back one time when we were changing and didn't ask questions.

She still hasn't, actually.

Caspian may be the first to know the truth of how I got them. Yet another thing I will never tell Claire.

Thankfully, enough time has passed that those scars are no longer raised, red and angry. The past years have since faded them into pink and white lines. The worst part is that some of them were still healing when he'd take the belt to my back causing the process to start all over. Those are the ones that are the least appealing to look at now.

It's just skin and flesh, though. I'm sure if you put my bones under X-Ray you'd find the imaging littered with old breaks and fractures. I had given up counting the injuries by the time I had stayed with two foster homes within my first year, considering not all abuse is visible to the untrained eye. Through the duration of being in the system, some of the mothers would simply pretend I wasn't there, starving me while they fed their own families. I'd have to eat the dog or cat food when they weren't looking or eat from the garbage just to survive.

That form of torture wasn't my favorite, but it also was nowhere near the worst I'd endured.

The worst was the psycho I stayed with four years into the system. I was twelve and his wife was always high on some kind of drugs. He would bring his friends over, and they'd take turns with her, making me watch. It was only a couple nights of forced observation before they did the same to me. Though, -thankfully or not-, I was never given any of the drugs, but they were brutal enough that whilst defiling my body for their own dark, selfish needs, I'd have broken bones from the aggression they expended.

Lost in my thoughts, I slowly make my way to the kitchen, absently following the smell of coffee. As I round the corner my gaze falls upon Caspian who is still shirtless, sitting at the counter with his hair disheveled as it hangs over his forehead.

I flush as he looks up from his coffee with hooded eyes and the corner of his lips quirk, "Someone slept well?"

I snort and grab a mug from the cupboard, lazily pouring some coffee and yawning again.

"Like a baby. At least, the second time around."

"Good. That means we can get right to work then." Caspian takes another sip of his coffee and my brows furrow in confusion.

"Well, I do have a day job that I still need to work on and since my samples are no longer viable after being held hostage and going missing for two days, I'll have to collect more."

He raises a brow at me, "Are you implying I do not have a day job?"

"I'm not implying anything, I'm simply stating I still have mine to do. What does a century old serial killer's killer do for a day job, anyways?"

"I'm a detective, so I investigate things." He says it in such a matter-of-fact way that I snort.

Of course. It's fitting actually.

"Right, I should've known that's what detectives do in the day-to-day," I say coolly as Caspian laughs under his breath.

Dan walks to the front door and whimpers.

"Oh shoot, you probably have to go outside, huh?" I assume based on normal dog behavior as I hurry over to open the door for him. I stand there a moment, unsure if he'll come back or if I should wait for him.

"He will probably hunt for his breakfast. Come finish your coffee." Caspian's voice is thick as I turn my head and see him staring at my back with a hardened gaze, his jaw flexing before his eyes avert to his coffee.

"Was that all from him?" Caspian's voice has a lethal edge as he takes a sip.

Cold sweat slicks down my spine and I nod, at a loss of what else to say. I grab a breakfast bar from the cupboard and toss it over to him before snagging one for myself.

"I have to head in to work, so I have no time to make breakfast. Make yourself at home, as you now know, the spare key stays hidden under the empty bird bath out back. Just make sure you replace it if you need to leave to get more clothes or to do… whatever it is detectives do every day.”

I leave without glancing at Caspian, but I can feel his gaze burning into my back as I walk to the bedroom to get dressed and do my hair.

I put on a pair of dress pants that cover my ankles, a long sleeve blouse, with a blazer on top before grabbing my purse and heading to the door to put my heels on. Glancing to the empty front room, my chest falls.

Why the hell am I disappointed? I shouldn't want him to stay here.

Even my own thoughts aren't convincing enough.

Grabbing my keys and phone with a frustrated sigh, I step out of the house and lock up.

Pulling into my reserved spot fills my veins with relief as a sense of normalcy returns. My heels click with each step toward Candace's desk and the moment I see her, her eyes light up and widen with shock.

She promptly hangs up the phone and scurries over to me, throwing herself into my arms while squealing.

“Don't you ever scare us like that!” She chides and squeezes me tighter.

“Sorry Candace, wasn't intentional, by any means.”

She sighs dramatically, and I feel her head nod against my shoulder.

Footsteps near to the hall before I hear Henry's voice, “About time you showed up. We thought we may need to pack up or send a rescue team out.”

I wince at the mental image of a rescue team discovering me in the state I was in when Caspian and Dan found me.

My voice comes out slightly strangled as I respond, "Yeah, that forest is no joke."

"Did you get the samples still or did you have to eat them for sustenance?" His tone is light as if he's joking, but there's a seriousness to it that can't be avoided.

"I actually lost my pack early on, so I'll have to go get more samples… Wild blueberries were snacked on instead" I winked at him and release Candace to give him a quick hug.

"I'll head out tomorrow and get more samples. Today, I'll catch up on some analytics on some of the initial data from the samples you took."

Henry nods and moves to the side as I pass him to go to my office.

"Lara, Claire made an appointment for next week on Monday. I gave her five PM again. Can we go for dinner again after?"

"Sure thing, Candace," I shout as I push the door to my office open and throw myself into work.

The day passes quickly, and it's five in the afternoon before I know it. A knock at my door sounds and Candace's voice calls out my name softly. I frown because this is unlike her, normally she walks right in.

"Come in."

My door opens and reveals Candace standing awkwardly next to a fully clothed Caspian and my jaw goes slack.

Fuck. He's even taller than I remember.

"What are you doing here?" I wince at the edge in my voice but keep myself composed.

"Sorry Lara, I tried to say you were busy but he insisted." Candace fidgets nervously as she looks between myself and Caspian.

Holding his right hand up, which has a bag of takeout held in it, he laughs and raises a brow. "You're telling me that you've eaten lunch and/or dinner already today and you don't want Chinese take-out? Shame." The playful edge to his voice and the temptation of my favorite food is undeniable.

I'm such a sucker.

Caspian turns to leave and I curse myself internally, "Wait!" I shout reluctantly and his lips twitch as he glances at me with pure amusement.

I sigh and wave him in. Candace has turned pale and looks like she's seen a ghost.

"There's enough for your friends, I just need to grab the other bag from the truck."

I chuckle and look at Candace, "Go grab Henry, we can eat in here." She nods and scurries off.

Oh, to be a fly on the wall for what she's going to tell him.

Caspian returns shortly after with the second bag of takeout, setting the boxes on my desk as Candace drags a shocked Henry in the room and everyone piles food onto their plates.

I snag some lo mein and sweet and sour shrimp, popping one of them into my mouth. The flavor combinations and grease coat my tongue and I groan softly.

"This is the best Chinese takeout I've had to date," I mumble, popping another shrimp into my mouth as Caspian chuckles quietly and Candace hums her approval of the lo mein.

"Where is this from?" Henry swirls some noodles, slurping them up loudly before he leans back chewing with a satisfied smirk.

"There's a woman about 45 minutes south, she moved here a few years back with her husband and they make the food in their house for a select few people. It takes a while to get into her good graces, but it's worth it."

I watch Candace with a grin of pure amusement as she tries to use her chopsticks to pick up an onion off her plate repeatedly and fails. She sighs out of frustration, snatching her fork up and stabbing it, before angrily shoving it in her mouth.

My eyes move to Henry who is glancing between Caspian and me with a hesitancy in his demeanor. "So, you're the individual who was laughing at the end of the video last night, I'm assuming?"

My jaw drops and Candace gasps, all eyes turn to Henry and then to Caspian who coolly sets his plate down and leans back. He folds his ankle over his knee and braces his arm along the top of the chair Henry's sitting in. Emanating cocky relaxation.

"I am," Caspian's bored voice echoes in the room as he picks a piece of lint off his leg, and my entire body flushes at what that insinuates. I look at him, finding his gaze on me already, but his face is unreadable.

He looks at Henry, "You and Candace are her good friends, yes?" They both nod before he speaks again, "What has Lara told you about the past few days?"

Is he probing to see whether I told them things I shouldn't?

My heart races as I glance to them before my eyes land on Caspian. He slightly shakes his head and I stay quiet.

"Just that she got lost in the woods. I'm guessing you were the one to find her?" Henry quickly putting puzzle pieces together has always been his strength. His problem-solving skills are unparalleled. It was one of the reasons I recruited him for this project. I needed someone who thinks outside the box and can challenge my process.

"I was. I am sure you're aware that there's a serial killer on the loose. I was searching for him in the woods when I found her." I chew the inside of my lip nervously at how much information he is openly divulging considering the fact that Caspian burned said individual's body in an abandoned house.

"I knew it had something to do with the serial killer. See, babe. I was right." Candace gasps and looks at Henry who grins triumphantly as Caspian continues.

"It seems he has his sights set on our friend Lara, here. So you'll be seeing me around every now and again while I do my job to keep her safe and catch the bad guy. That's alright with you two, I assume?" Candace and Henry both gape at him.

He glances over at me and winks. My cheeks burn and the corner of his lips twitch up in response which only makes me flush more. He slowly gets up to toss his plate into the garbage bin and sits back down.

He has no plans to leave anytime soon I suppose.

Candace and Henry bicker about serial killers and documentaries they've seen as they pack up the leftovers and Candace goes to hand the bag to Caspian but he shakes his head.

"You guys keep the rest. I can get more any time."

Excitement radiates off Candace as she grabs Henry's hand and nearly drags him out of the room. "Nice meeting you! Talk to you later, bye Lara!" She calls out from the hallway and I suppress a laugh.

I start to move from one cupboard to another, grabbing equipment for my trip to the lake tomorrow to gather samples. The tension in the air thickens with every minute that passes until it's nearly palpable.

Caspian watches my methodical movements but says nothing as I place the last container into the bag. I whirl to face him and hoist the heavy pack to my shoulder.

"I, uh, I'm going to head home now." I say awkwardly, cringing at myself. My cheeks burn again as he smirks, like he can somehow tell that my brain and body are at war with each other.

He nods once before standing and moves to hold the door open for me. I curse internally and compose myself as I walk past his towering form.

My heels click down the hallway, echoing through the building and as I wave goodbye to Candace, she smiles widely as she glances between us.

I shake my head, mostly in exasperation as we move to the parking lot.

These people are going to be the death of me.

Chapter 17

Caspian

This woman is a god-damn enigma.

She's strong, smart, incredibly kind but in the same breath, infuriating and stubborn in ways I'm unable to understand. The fact that she is the key to everything wrenches my insides apart, and I can't make heads or tails of it. Her insistence on going to work after what she endured alone was shocking to say the least.

My knuckles turn white as I grip the steering wheel tightly, fighting the urge to speed up, attempting to keep a good distance behind Lara's car.

Staying at the house last night was a mistake. I shouldn't have shown up at her work nor should I have brought food with me for her and her coworkers.

I just couldn't stand to let her out of my sight for too long after finding her in that rundown shack tied to that fucking bed. The moment I walked out of her house this morning everything felt wrong.

It's making me insane.

It's the same fucking feeling I have driving on this vacant road as I follow her.

I got halfway home this morning before realizing I couldn't stay away tonight. Seeing the raw terror in her eyes when she woke up, hearing about Frank fucking Mores and witnessing first-hand the scars he gave her made my blood boil. It didn't take long for me to have one of my men pick him up.

He thinks he likes torture?

I'm happy to oblige.

If he thinks a belt buckle is a creative form of inflicting pain, he's severely out of his element. I will bring him within an inch of his life and have him begging for death's embrace by the time I'm through with him.

That's if the old asshole's heart doesn't give out on him first.

I didn't put her in there for asshats like Frank to try to break her. I put her in foster care to keep her away from my fucking brother. It was the only way to get her out of his reach.

I might not be able to undo the trauma she endured at the hands of cocksuckers like Frank who have napoleon complexes, but I sure as hell can make them regret their life's choices.

I might not be able to do much to change the course of things bound to happen, but revenge?

Revenge I can do.

The rational part of me argues that I shouldn't give a shit about what happened to her in the past. She's alive right now and that's all that matters for the future. I should stop vying to bring a smile to her face and simply do what I came here to do.

The less sensible piece of me doesn't give a single flying fuck about logic or rationalization. If it means never seeing that fucking terror on her face again...

The steering wheel groans, and I release my grip slightly.

I knew having Frank taken from his house to be brought to one of my estates was stepping out of line from the original plan, but I'll be damned if he continues to breathe freely.

Hell, I'm already damned.

It's not like anyone can or will stop me from bringing him to some sick and twisted sense of justice. I won't let him die until his eyes show the same terror I saw within Lara's last night.

Until then, he will beg, wish and pray, only to be denied

death.

My sole regret through this entire week is that Cain didn't suffer more for what he did to her before the wolf killed him.

I consider the future and the irrational voice inside my head wins over as impulsiveness becomes my strongest trait.

It's a gamble, things could go well or horribly wrong.

That voice is the same one that drove me to go to Cain's hide-out knowing he had Lara captive. Something inside me refused to sit back idly while she was within reach.

Thank fuck I did. I'll be damned if anything stops me from being involved now.

My phone buzzes in my pocket and I glance down to see a text from Ian and return my eyes to the tail lights ahead of me.

My jaw clenches as I consider what's to come. As the prophecy digs its claws in I know I'll have a choice to make, and as the fork in the road nears I find I am at odds with myself.

Growing conflict lives inside of my veins as I spend more time with Lara and that is a terrifying reality.

Chapter 18

Lara

I watch Caspian's headlights in my rearview mirror the entire drive home.

Relax, Lara. He's making sure you're not going to die.

He's not interested in a broken woman like you, forget it.

I take a cleansing breath as I pull in the driveway then blow it out, steeling myself as I get out of the car and walk over to the front door.

I put the key in and twist it, but there's no resistance.

It's unlocked.

I hold the knob and turn my head slightly to Caspian's truck, my eyes wide with panic.

He must have some idea of what's going on from the look on my face as he hurries over, because he gently moves me behind him and pulls out his gun. "Stay here."

I nod.

Like there was any chance of me going in there right now.

Caspian disappears into the house, leaving me in the dark and I wait with bated breath.

Any second now, he will come back. He'll be okay. I must have forgotten to lock it.

Minutes go by, and I'm about to walk in when an arm loops around my neck in a tight choke hold.

Instinct has my arms reach up to my attacker's forearm initially. Within a moment's notice my self-defense training takes over. I slide my leg behind my assailant and throw my arm out to the side. Putting all my weight into the chest of the aggressor, we both fall backwards, landing with a grunt.

As we hit the ground the grip on me releases and I roll off, instantly pushing to my feet to face my attacker.

He must be six foot tall, more muscular than Henry but nowhere near as much as Caspian or his brother. In the dark his hair looks black and his eyes are shadowed. I see him reach into his belt, and he grabs a knife, taking a step toward me.

"Who are you?" I ask loudly, hoping that Caspian can hear.

"Does it matter?" He growls, and I catch a glimpse of his teeth as I stare at his shadowed face.

Caspian's voice sounds out into the stillness of night, as shock and something else flashes across his features, "No. You're right, it doesn't matter." he says, his voice cold and hard.

The man opens his mouth and I yelp at the loud bang that sounds out as the man falls to his knees. He looks down at the blood seeping from his chest before he glances at me. His gaze lingers on Caspian for a long moment, and he crumples face-first to the ground.

I stare at him, my eyes fixate on the pool of blood and I don't realize I'm shaking until Caspian's hands cup my face, turning me away from the body.

"You did well. You're safe now. Come, little one." His voice is as gentle as his touch. He positions his body between me and the man on the ground as he ushers me inside the house.

"You're alright." He repeats as he guides me to the living room couch. He grasps my cold hands, still trembling from leftover adrenaline and pulls them to his mouth, brushing his lips against my knuckles as he blows warm breath over them.

"You're safe, Lara." My name snaps me out of my daze and my eyes lock onto his. I retract my hands, wrapping my arms around myself and blowing out a shaky breath with a nod.

Caspian lingers for a moment, glancing around before leaning in to wrap me in his blanket as a shudder wracks its way through my body.

Concern paints his features as he searches my face for a second with his large hands on my shoulders and I shiver involuntarily but not because of the cold.

My breath gets caught in my lungs as he leans in, wrapping his arms around me tightly. My heart is pounding in my chest so loud, I'm certain he can feel and hear it.

"Breath, Lara." His voice reverberates throughout my body and electric butterflies flutter from head to toe as I exhale shakily. The heat radiating off him seeps through the blanket and clothes.

I tremble again.

"Inhale." He commands in a soft tone and I suck in a deep breath as his hold tightens.

"Good. Now exhale." Another shudder comes over me as I blow out my breath.

Caspian pulls back to look at me with a hard expression. "I'm going to deal with the body. I won't be far. The house is clear, but I'm going to keep a knife with you though, alright?"

My anxiety is piqued at the thought of him leaving, but I nod.

Placing the handle of a blade in my hands, he covers them with the blanket before disappearing out the front.

Moments after he walks out, the door pushes open and my momentary panic is quickly washed away when familiar dark fur stalks through the front room.

Dan sniffs around and his ears twitch every which way before he settles himself against my knees comfortably. We sit there in the quiet for a while and my eyelids get increasingly heavy. I set the knife under the couch cushion and lay down with the blanket still wrapped around myself, burying my head into the pillow. I blink again, but this time my eyes remain closed.

As the front door opens I'm instantly alert, sitting up to see Caspian walk in with his hair mussed and framing his face. He turns his head to look at me, glancing at the pillow where I'm laying and his lips twitch at the corners before he continues to the kitchen.

"Did you get some rest?" He asks softly.

I nod.

"Good. We need to get a new lock system for your house and some cameras set up. We can get it all done tomorrow."

I pause because I know what he's going to say, but I say it anyways, "I need to get samples from the lake tomorrow."

He raises his eyebrow, "Not by yourself. Absolutely not."

"I can take Dan." A weak effort, but I figured I'd try.

"Still not enough."

I huff in protest, but after this unfortunately eventful week, I know he's right.

"I can get Henry to install the cameras, if you do the locks in the morning. Then we can go to the lake together?"

Caspian pauses for a moment and searches my face, "Fine."

"Thank you."

He freezes and studies me, the seriousness in his voice sending a jolt of trepidation down my spine, "Thank me if you make it out of this alive."

The next morning, I'm making eggs for breakfast when there's a knock on the door. Caspian answers it without a shirt and Henry's eyes nearly bulge out of his head. His shocked gaze meets mine as I fight back a grin.

If he finds shirtless Caspian attractive I'd have to be a doorknob not to, I suppose.

Dishing eggs onto two plates, I slide one over to Caspian as the two men spend the next two hours setting up an elaborate security system.

To get inside, you have to use biometrics. Any movement in the house will trigger a notification to an app on both mine and Caspian's phone with a snapshot image, with the ability to watch the video footage live.

The cameras around the house leaves a blind spot in the bathroom, so there is some sort of privacy, but it has an audio device that records when it catches voices. There's a gun now hidden underneath the sink and behind the toilet in case of emergencies.

There's a gun above the fridge, one under the mattress in the bedroom and another beneath the coffee table in the living room.

I think there's more firepower in my house than in most towns.

Once the security system is set up, Caspian, Dan and I hike down the trail, making the journey to the lake.

We get to the familiar part of the path where it narrows, and we veer off, venturing our way through the dense bush, following our compass for directions and marking trees with ribbons every thirty feet.

My footing is careful as I deliberately step in areas that will disturb the plant life as little as possible.

I feel eyes on me and my gaze meets Caspian's.

"You're really passionate about this stuff, huh?"

I laugh quietly and nod, "Yeah, this *stuff* is how we survive. If we can't take care of the earth, its ecosystems, plant life, wildlife… I'm not sure we deserve our place in the food chain if we can't respect the world around us."

We fall into quiet steps after that until I notice the ground starts to become sandy again.

Pulling my bag off my shoulder and setting it down, I carefully extract and pack up the matching flora and foliage as last time.

Once satisfied with the variation, I move to place the straps of the heavy cargo on my shoulder but Caspian snatches it from my hand and lifts it over his own instead.

My eyes narrow at him, "You better not be taking it because you think I'm weak."

"Never. For a human, you're surprisingly strong. I just have immortal strength, therefore, I take it."

I roll my eyes and fight a smirk, "Yeah, yeah. Multi-century old Mystery Man with immortal strength. Got it."

He laughs, the sound sends heat swirling through my body, and we hike back the way we came.

I notice my ribbons remain undisturbed and with every marker we pass, relief drowns out the tension in my limbs. I find myself walking with renewed certainty as we get onto the narrow pathway that leads to the house.

If Caspian notices, he says nothing. I check the app on my phone and Dan runs ahead to scout the woods for anyone who might surprise us as we get back.

The cameras around the house show no movement, and with no notifications, I'm feeling good, but there's an edge of tension in the air I can't quite place.

"I'll need to bring the samples to the lab right away. Are you staying here or…?"

My voice trails off, and I feel unsure how to continue the fairly basic question. It seems silly, but there's a particular vulnerability to asking someone to come with you somewhere, regardless if it's for safety or more selfish desires.

Selfish desires? I'm delusional.

Caspian glances around the forest before his green eyes land on me for a moment. "I'll come with you, we can take my truck."

I nod and tamp down the excitement building in my chest.

Stupid girl.

We make it to the house where Dan is waiting for us by the door but instead of going inside, we go straight to Caspian's truck. As soon as he opens my door, Dan hops in and plops into the back seat, and it's not long before we take off.

The drive to the lab feels shorter than usual, we unload and walk into the building together. As we near Candace's desk, she squeals and grips the wood so hard her knuckles turn white.

"Is that a wolf?" she shrieks, pointing at Dan.

I blink and glance down, realizing that he was with us still. He shakes and gives a huff as if the attention makes him uncomfortable. I snort a laugh and pat his head as if he was a true canine.

"Yeah I guess I made two new friends in the woods, a Mystery Man and a wolf."

Candace's face pales and I can't help but release a genuine laugh that springs tears to my eyes.

Her features soften as she glances between me and Caspian. Her cheeks flush bright pink and I follow her gaze to see him staring at me with one of his eyebrows raised and his lip tilted up making my own face burn.

Smooth, Lara.

We walk to my office and Dan hops onto my chair, looking around while I methodically pull out the samples and organize them alongside their sisters from the other lake that Henry brought back.

Our phones chime in unison and my eyes snap to Caspian's as we both look at the cameras through our app.

A car pulls up to the front of the house with its headlights off. A moment goes by and palpable tension is rolling off Caspian. I shift closer to stand next to him while we both watch from different camera angles.

The familiar beautiful man is dressed in a black hoodie and jeans, he gets out of the car and walks over to the front door, pausing to inspect the remnants of the giant pool of blood that has seeped into the ground.

He takes a quick look in the windows, and then he glances up, his mismatched eyes flash in the limited light beneath his hood. The man gives a theatrical wave to the camera as he quickly walks back to the car and speeds off.

A growl sounds off, but it's not coming from Dan, I look up at Caspian and his face is contorted into rage as he stares at the empty space where the car was.

"Was that who I think that was?" There's a long pause, the cords in his neck flex along with the muscle in his jaw as he clenches his teeth.

A sharp inhale gets caught in my chest. "That was my brother, Darian. Evil incarnate in the flesh."

Dan growls and I don't need to ask how bad news his brother is.

All I can wonder is why the evil incarnate didn't kill me when he had me in his grasp that night.

I finish the samples in a daze and put everything away while Caspian types furiously on his phone. A knock at the door sounds, and he points his gun at a shocked Henry in the doorway.

Henry's hands jerk up with his palms forward and his face pales, "Woah, I just wanted to see if you wanted to get dinner."

Dan growls and Henry somehow blanches even more, "That's… a really big dog."

I laugh but it comes out sounding strangled, thankfully Caspian composes himself much quicker, and he holsters his weapon.

"Sorry, we're just jumpy. We're going to have to pass on dinner tonight. We will grab something on the way home."

Henry nods as color seeps back into his skin, and he waves to us as he steps away.

I blow out a breath I hadn't known I'd been holding and lean weakly against the desk.

"Are you okay?" Caspian's voice is flat and indifferent.

I nod.

He pauses to study me before he speaks again, his voice back to normal. "Let's go get some grub and get to my place so we can make a game plan and sleep."

I nod again and grab my purse. I reach for the door, but before I can open it, Caspian's hand shoots past my shoulder from behind me and holds it closed.

The air gets caught in my lungs as I turn to find my face a mere inch from his and his breath skates over my skin. Heat swirls in my body and my heart pounds frantically in my chest at his proximity.

"He will not get to you, Lara. Not while you're with me." he says with a certain cockiness that makes my insides twist in an unfamiliar way.

My eyes lift from his mouth to hold his gaze and I nod lightly.

Caspian leans back, removing his hand from the door so that I can open it. It's a long moment before my nerves calm enough and the three of us file out of my office.

We drive for fifteen minutes until we reach a small pub with music playing. Caspian glances in the back at Dan, "Can you stay put for an hour or so while we get food?"

Dan huffs and his ears twitch backwards.

"I'll get a steak to go, and some fries."

They perk forward.

"Medium rare?" His voice is dripping with amusement and Dan's ears twitch but stay pointed in front of him. He laughs under his breath and exits the vehicle.

"I'll get a second steak for you." I mutter quietly to Dan, and he leans forward to nuzzle my arm with his ears still perked.

My passenger door opens, and I whirl to see Caspian grinning at me as if he knows I promised our canine friend a second serving.

I flush and step out of the truck, following Caspian inside.

We're seated at a quiet table toward the back of the building. As we sit down I note that it's close to an exit and another set of doors to the kitchen.

Good choice, Mystery man. Real smart.

A waitress comes to the table with two waters and menus, setting one of each in front of us. "Good evening, what can I get you started with?" She leans in toward him, her leg pressed against his thigh where he sits.

White-hot jealousy ravages through me and I have to fiddle with my straw to calm myself. I look up at Caspian as I plop it into my glass.

He glances at me and back to her. "We'll each get a steak, medium rare, mashed potatoes on the side, bearnaise sauce and truffle aioli on the side. A side of onion rings as well. We'll get two steaks to go, medium rare."

The waitress blinks at him and hurriedly writes down the order. "Anything else to drink?"

"Water is fine for me." I interject.

Caspian mumbles the same, and she scurries off toward the kitchen.

"Do people do that often to you?" He raises a brow, waiting for me to clarify. "Do they-" My face burns with embarrassment and I think twice about my question. "Nevermind, I don't know what I'm saying."

He laughs and leans back in his chair, stretching out his legs. His knee brushes my leg and my body jolts, but he doesn't pull it away.

It's still firmly pressed against my leg as the waitress returns with our onion rings, two plates and sets of silverware, she gives us a brief smile and disappears into the kitchen again.

I glance around the pub, my nerves rattling as I search for any indication someone is looking for us. I try and fail to locate any mismatched eyes in the room. Everyone seems to be drinking and eating happily, in their own worlds without any care.

"My brother won't look for us here. What he did today was likely nothing more than a scare tactic. He knows we can find the amulets and he knows you are his only way to do that. I doubt he even knows what they look like."

What did he say to you in the forest?

Did he say what he wanted?

Darian's voice echoes inside of my mind.

I look at him and lean back in my seat, tilting my head to study him.

His jawline has stubble on it, and he has a few loose strands of black hair that are long enough to touch his cheeks. I shift in place and my leg rubs slightly against his, I watch as he freezes and a light flush creeps up his own neck.

Good to know he's not entirely unaffected. At least I'm not alone in that aspect then.

"I really would rather not discuss anything to do with your brother or men who want to do abhorrent things to me right now, Caspian."

Emotion flickers across his face and he nods, "You're right. What do you want to talk about, then?"

"You."

Caspian's eyes flash for a moment as he chuckles, dragging a hand through his hair, "Me? Or the Netflix show about the guy who's a stalker?"

I level him with a deadpan look, "Funny."

Caspian tuts with a laugh, "So serious. What would you like to know about me?"

"Anything. Tell me about where you grew up. What you enjoyed. What you miss most. What you'll do once you return."

His eyes drop to the table, and he's contemplative for a moment. "I grew up in somewhat of an extravagant lifestyle. My father was a very important person to our people. Everyone loved him and my mother until the day they died. My favorite place growing up was the lake just outside of the city. It had a beautiful waterfall and the lake was so clear you could see every creature and plant in it."

He goes quiet, with a distant look to his eyes as if suddenly transported to that far away place. Even the waitress bringing out the remainder of our food isn't enough to snap him out of his trance.

"Do you think it's still as beautiful as you remember?" I keep my voice quiet, but his eyes snap to mine, and his sad features relax.

"I hope so." He says softly, his gaze dropping to the plates in front of us. With a deep breath he tilts his head to the food, "Dig in before it gets cold. Dan would kill us if we wasted a good steak."

I snort and cut into my steak, dipping it in aioli and plopping it in my mouth with a groan.

"Aioli. Aioli changes everything." I mumble as I cut another bite, adding more aioli before shoveling it in my mouth.

A faint smile creeps across Caspian's face as I savor the taste, shaking my head. "I can't go back to regular steak after this. You know this right? I'm going to have to learn how to make this at home."

We finish our meal as the waitress brings out two containers with a steak in each, and we head to the truck. The moment I get in, Dan's sniffing echoes through the cab as Caspian and I share a look before opening both containers and putting them on the seat.

"Don't make a mess, mutt" Caspian warns as Dan growls. His response is short-lived as he takes a bite of the steak and his tail wags, if it wasn't part of his spine, I'd be worried it could fly off.

Chapter 19

We drive for fifteen minutes and the route is winding with turns and twists. We gradually venture deeper into the woods until we've pulled off a paved road onto gravel. The pathway ends, and we cruise along a well-worn path big enough for the truck to fit through.

We continue down the road for a minute in silence, tree branches and leaves lightly slapping against the side of the truck.

I pull out my phone and quickly open up my music app, turning on 'John Denver — Take Me Home, Country Roads' and bite the inside of my cheek hard as I suppress a smile.

"You're kidding me." Caspian mumbles. Dan snorts from the back as we pull up to the house, and I turn off the music. Comedic effect reached, there was no need to drag the joke out.

We unload from the truck as Caspian opens the front door for us, "No dogs on the bed." he raises a brow as Dan huffs, padding over to the living room before he disappears into the hallway.

I take a few steps forward and look around as Caspian turns to me, motioning for me to follow him.

We walk down the hall to the end, there's an open door which leads to what I assume is a master bedroom by the look of the gigantic bed in the center. Caspian turns the knob of the door closest to us and extends his arm in a gesture for me to go inside. I take a step in and glance around, my jaw fully slack in varying levels of awe.

The room is warm and cozy inside, the walls are a light shade of tan and the bed is dark burgundy with a deep brown frame. There's a tall wardrobe that matches the color of the bed and a full length mirror alongside the dresser.

There's a closed door across from the bed and I eye it warily before glancing at Caspian who is staring at me with guarded emotions.

"The door leads to a personal bathroom. I'd never put you in a room where you would be connected to another room like that. I'd sooner have you sleep in my own bedroom and I'd sleep on the couch before I'd put you in that position." his voice is level, but his eyes are bright as he speaks.

My face burns at the mention of his bed and I nod, hugging myself to soothe the butterflies roaring throughout my body.

I set my purse down on the dresser then turn to face Caspian, "Thank you."

He nods as he walks to the doorway, "There's towels in the bathroom, I grabbed some clothes to bring with us, they're in the bag by the shower. Get some rest tonight."

My gaze lingers on the closed door after he leaves, and I move to the bathroom, my jaw drops as I look around.

The room is intricate stone tile, the floors are warm and the countertop is marble with bright lights illuminating the entire area from the backlit mirror. The shower has two heads, one stationary waterfall and one a manual. There's toiletries placed around the room, a new toothbrush and toothpaste next to the sink. He seriously thought of everything someone could need.

What a darling host, Mystery Man is.

Twisting the handle to turn on the shower, soon the chaos of life fades away with the cascading water. My skin is pruned and wrinkly by the time I get out, wrapping myself in a towel, I walk to the bag and sift through the clothes.

There's a tank top, a sweater, sweats, jeans and a blouse. I roll my eyes at Caspian's selection.

Men. No appreciation for variation.

I think back to Tammy and her two suitcases she hauled into my front room for one night of dancing and snort quietly before using my towel to dry my hair. I begin to brush my teeth when I realize I haven't heard back from Tammy still.

A frown creeps across my face, unease sinking deep in my gut.

I spit my toothpaste out, rinse my brush and wipe off my mouth before hurrying into the bedroom to grab my phone.

I'm only three steps toward the bed when I freeze, seeing Caspian standing on the other side of the room with Dan curled on the bed.

As the cool air caresses my skin, I instinctively cover myself with my hands to try to preserve some semblance of modesty.

Caspian's eyes quickly avert, Dan simply stares at me unblinking.

Pervert. Remind me to punch him when he's no longer a dog.

I whip back to the bathroom and grab my towel to wrap myself before returning to the main room, my heart thundering in my chest.

"To what do I owe this pleasure?" My voice cracks and I swallow loudly.

"We. I. Well, I wanted to see if you had everything you needed and Dan should sleep in here. My home is secure but just in case.." Caspian's eyes burn into my soul while he speaks, his voice thick as he trails off.

I nod, "I have nearly everything I can think of. Any chance we can grab more of my clothes from the house? Pajamas, bras and underwear, maybe?"

Caspian blinks and then laughs while scratching his head, "I knew I was forgetting something. We can go tomorrow when it's daylight out. Dan will run ahead of us once we get onto the last road there. Stick close to me while we get what you need, and we'll bring it back here."

Walking to the side table to grab my phone, I nod in agreement and unlock it to look at Tammy's conversation.

No new messages. I frown.

"What is it?" I look up at Caspian, his head is cocked to the side as he studies me.

"When we returned to my house after everything happened, I had an absurd number of missed messages and calls. I responded to Tammy but haven't heard back from her. She hasn't even read my messages which is unlike her." I frown as I look at him before continuing, "It's not uncommon for her to go a few hours without responding because of the time difference along the west coast from here but, to go days? My gut is telling me something isn't right, Caspian."

He crosses his arms over his chest, reaches up and rubs his thumb along his jawline.

"So we'll look for her then." He says while nodding slightly.

A wave of shock and relief washes over me and I gape at him, "You'd help me?"

He gives me a hint of a smile, "She's important to you, so it goes without questioning that I would help. She seems like a fierce friend."

My chest swells with relief as I nod.

"Alright, I'll need you to send me her address, some pictures of her, and send me screenshots of the messages between you two so I can see when she stopped responding."

I open my phone and start sending everything to Caspian, his cell chimes, and he chuckles as he flips through the pictures and screenshots.

He makes his way to the door, glancing back at me, "If you wake up before me, help yourself to anything in the kitchen. Once we eat, we can head over to the house."

I nod as he exits the room and I open my phone to my group chat.

Lara: I'm not going to be in tomorrow. Need to handle some stuff so don't freak out when I'm not in.

The message sends and instantly shows read.

Candace: Use condoms!

I roll my eyes and snort.

Lara: You're sick and twisted. He's a cop and working.

Henry: I'm in the wrong line of employment, if that's part of the job.

Candace: Excuse me?

Henry: I don't mean with other people, babe. Clearly I'd only be a detective for you.

I roll my eyes and laugh, setting my phone on the side table before placing the towel in the bathroom and walk to the bed, crawling under the blankets and shivering at the chill.

Dan shifts closer and warmth seeps from his body as my eyes shut and exhaustion claims me.

Chapter 20

The sound of screaming jolts me from my sleep as a pair of large hands grip my shoulders, shaking me.

My instincts and training automatically kick in, and I knock the arms off, they reach me again, grabbing me by my biceps and I act. Within the blink of an eye, I'm rolling to the side and off the bed with blankets in tow, landing with a grunt.

I quickly free myself of the tangled covers as my attacker grabs me around the shoulders in an attempt to render my arms useless. I dodge under his reach, gasping one of the limbs and twist it behind his back, kicking out his knees, and he drops to the ground with a thud.

I shove his body down until he's laying on his stomach with his hand angled painfully along his spine.

I'm panting and straddling my assailant, my body weight and one hand on his twisted arm between my thighs, my other holding onto his non-contorted arm in case he decides to move it.

My heart rate starts to calm and the blood roaring in my ears quiets down as I catch my breath.

Dan walks up to me, nudging me with his cold nose.

Oh, now he shows up. Where was Dan when I was being attacked?

I look back to my shirtless assailant and realize he has shorter jet black hair and is solely wearing sweatpants.

Oh god.

I release his hands to cover my mouth, shifting my weight onto one leg instead of straddling Caspian fully, I stare at the back of his head in pure horror.

"Oh my god. I'm so sorry, Caspian. I had no idea it was you." His arm twists into a normal position and I look at Dan, "Why didn't you stop me?!"

Dan whimpers and his ears lay back flat.

Caspian's body vibrates with a deep chuckle that shoots heat into my core as he shifts in place to turn over beneath me, leaning backwards onto his arms.

"Well at the very least, I know you can handle yourself with self-defense in hand-to-hand combat."

My face burns and I cover my head with my hands again. "What the hell just happened? Why was there screaming when you woke me up?"

Caspian glances at Dan and then back to me and his eyes narrow, "You were the one screaming, Lara."

My jaw goes slack and my hands drop, resting on Caspian's deliciously defined abdomen, "What?" My voice comes out more breathy than intended as I try to keep my mind off of how he feels below me.

His brows pinch together and he tilts his head, "You don't remember?"

I shake my head in response, "No. I was sleeping and heard screaming when I was being woken up. I felt your hands on my shoulders as I woke up, and I just acted." I explain.

He nods in understanding, and there's a long pause as I replay the events in my mind. Glancing at Caspian, I notice his intense gaze fixed on my face while I remain seated on top of him.

What...?

Even in the dark, I can discern heat in his eyes as they darken, sending nervous butterflies throughout my body.

I blink at him, feeling my chest tighten as the realization hits me.

The blanket that was once wrapped around me is nowhere to be seen, and I'm naked, still partially sitting on top of a shirtless Caspian.

Oh my god.

My entire body flushes with a heady mix of embarrassment and desire as I move to push myself off of him with one hand.

Before I can go anywhere he grasps my arm and yanks on it, pulling me further onto his chest and the air gets caught in my lungs.

His free hand firmly grips the back of my neck, tangling in my hair as he holds me tightly against his body. The warmth of his breath caresses my skin, sending shivers of anticipation and heat down my spine.

"Tell me to stop." Caspian whispers against my lips, the need in his voice makes the butterflies within me flutter frantically.

I know my body wants this, and in many ways I do too.

Yet I say nothing.

I've never been given the option to choose, and now that the moment occurs where I am, I'm frozen in indecision.

When I don't respond to him, he groans and his lips crash against mine.

His mouth is soft, but he kisses me as though I'm his salvation as his lips move against mine. He leans back toward the floor, drawing me further into his hard chest. His arm hooks around my waist as he grinds into me.

The hard length of him squeezes against my clit against his sweats, the friction sends jolts of pleasure within my body and I inhale sharply. Caspian quickly deepens the kiss, his tongue dancing against mine as my head swirls.

Every movement he makes is deliberate, as if he knows exactly what to do as he squeezes my hips tighter.

I grind into him as pressure builds in my body. It's as if he can sense my pleasure and within seconds Caspian has flipped us.

The hand that was around my waist has made its way to my breast as he breaks our kiss to lean down and take my nipple into his mouth.

He sucks hard.

My body bucks against his, and a husky moan escapes my throat.

"I'm going to make you feel so fucking good."

The need in his voice makes me whimper as he kisses his way from one breast to the other.

His hand makes its way between my legs, and he groans when he feels how soaked I am.

"Fuck, Lara." Caspian slips a finger in, and my hips buck.

The way he's looking at me, watching my response to his body nearly does me in. His emerald eyes darken as his thumb starts slow circles around my clit making my toes curl and my back arch into him.

"Caspian," I pant, digging my nails into his arm at my side.

I'd forego all pride to get on my knees and beg him to keep going at this point. Another moan escapes my throat as he slides a second finger in and starts to pump his hand while working my clit.

"You look so fucking beautiful like this" he groans.

Taking my breast in his mouth again, he bites down on my nipple and I gasp as he slides a third finger in.

I can feel my orgasm building, pleasure mixed with the pain of his bites nearly overwhelms my system as he thrusts his fingers inside of me.

I'm panting through my increasingly frantic moans with the waves of pleasure that threaten to crash over me, but suddenly he pulls his hand out, leaving me empty as he draws back.

His eyes are hooded as he grabs a couple pillows from the bed and places them under my hips before pulling my legs over his shoulders.

"I-, I've never..." I bite the inside of my lip and our eyes meet.

He raises a brow.

"You're telling me you've never been worshipped before?" His voice is deep with heat, but he asks as if the idea of it is incredulous.

I nod.

There's not a single word I can muster right now seeing his head between my thighs.

He chuckles darkly, the warm air feathering over my bare center and I fight the urge to clench my legs together.

"Well, allow me to have the honor of being the first."

My eyes are wide as he leans in with unwavering eye contact, and I'm about to protest when he squeezes my thighs with his large hands.

"When you come for me for the first time I want to taste it. I want you to come in my mouth and I want to tongue fuck you into oblivion."

My thighs clench at his filthy words, but he holds them still as he grins at my reaction and my clit throbs. He leans in, casting his warm breath over my wet pussy, and he licks once up the length of my soaked center before swirling his tongue around my clit.

"Caspian, my god." I gasp and my hips buck against his tight grip on my thighs.

He works my body expertly, and soon my orgasm crests. As he slides his fingers in and sucks at my clit, I moan loudly with desperation.

I'm so fucking close.

"That's right. Right now, I'm your God. Now clench that tight, filthy pussy around my fingers and let me feel you come."

His words undo me as he works my body with precision, and my eyes squeeze shut.

My orgasm rocks through my body as he rhythmically thrusts against me and I ride out each wave of pleasure.

I'm panting my eyes snap to his as he pulls his fingers out and puts them into his mouth, sucking my arousal off before leaning in between my legs and using his tongue to get every last remnant of my orgasm.

It's as if I'm a four-course meal, and he's quite literally cleaned the plate. Having no prior experience with this kind of intimacy, I have no clue if this is typical.

Can it really be that enjoyable for him?

Once sated, he crawls over my limp body, kissing me deeply before pausing to rest his forehead against mine.

"You should get some sleep. We have a busy day ahead of us." He breathes and extends a hand to help me up.

My head is foggy from the afterglow of my orgasm, and I still can't believe that happened. I hardly know him, and truth be told, I don't know that I really trust him, but somehow I was okay with what we just did.

My cheeks flush as the mental image of his head between my legs comes into my mind.

Alright, I was more than okay with it.

Still, I know that something doesn't seem quite right between us. He holds too many secrets close to his chest for me to trust him, and I have this nagging paranoia that keeps telling me to wait for the other shoe to drop.

I accept his help to stand up and nod in answer to his question, keeping to my thoughts.

"I'll be in the other room, just call out if you need me." He leans over and his lips brush against my temple before he goes to leave.

"Caspian."

He turns to look at me, "Yes?"

"That will never happen again," Relief fills me when my voice holds steady.

He chuckles darkly and my thighs clench, "We'll see about that."

I glance around the room and see Dan come sauntering back in. His canine eyes narrow on Caspian leaving. I can't help but feel appreciative that he gave us privacy, though I doubt he could escape the sounds I made with his canine hearing.

My cheeks flush as I replay what happened, and I crawl into bed.

I'm going to sleep like a rock.

My eyes open to soft light seeping through the windows and the smell of coffee, eggs, and...

Bacon.

My eyes fully snap open, and I shoot out of bed while my stomach growls angrily.

How long did I sleep for?

I walk quickly to the bathroom and pull on the jeans and blouse, snatching my phone from the side table. No word from Tammy, 2 messages from Candace and Henry's chat, nothing from Claire. Sighing, I send something to Tammy first.

Lara: Hey girl, haven't heard from you. Are you doing alright?

I watch the message deliver and my chest tightens with anxiety before opening the group chat.

Candace: Don't forget about your appointment with Claire on Monday, Lara!

Henry: Yeah, and we're going for dinner after too. I'll water the plants today, they'll be good throughout the weekend.

Lara: Thanks guys. I'll text you later, don't get into any trouble while I'm out. Notify me if there's any emergencies or anything out of the normal happens.

Candace reads the messages and starts typing.

Candace: Okie Dokie Artichokie! Enjoy your time off and don't forget the condoms!

My cheeks flush as I remember the night before. Granted, we didn't get to the point of needing protection, but if we had...

God bless female contraception and IUD's.

I'm thankful I had the foresight when I was younger to research ways to avoid unwanted pregnancies. I had never had a boyfriend throughout my teenage years into adulthood.

I hadn't felt or known physical attraction, really, until I met Caspian and unfortunately, as much as I dislike admitting it, Darian.

I still knew back then that men are animals and take whatever they want when opportunity arises. I did enjoy drinking more than I should so it was logical to have a form of birth control that couldn't be forgotten and lasts a long time.

A ten year implanted form of contraception seemed like the best decision in the moment and current me couldn't be happier for it. Even still, I am determined to ensure Caspian and I don't do anything like that again.

Following the overwhelming scent to the kitchen, I find Caspian standing over the counter. The room is large, it has white and gray marble countertop, pristine white cupboards, a stainless steel fridge, stove and oven.

Three plates are set next to one another on the counter, now with eggs, bacon and toast on each. I suppress a giggle at the notion that we're feeding a wolf as we would a person as I plop down on one of the seats.

Caspian places the egg pan into the sink and moves to the cupboard to fill a glass with orange juice before sliding it across the counter to me.

I take a few sips as he passes a plate and silverware over to me, before walking to the coffee machine to pour some into a mug.

My brain falters as he hands me the full mug and for once stops working altogether as our eyes meet. I realize after a long moment that he had actually said something to me and I blink to try to bring myself back to reality.

"I am, so, sorry. Can you repeat that?"

Caspian's lips twitch, and he laughs under his breath lightly, "Cream or milk? Sugar?"

My cheeks heat as I nod, breaking eye contact to avoid zoning out again, "Cream and sugar please. Thank you."

He turns to open the fridge, placing the cream on the counter before reaching to grasp the sugar. I can't help but appreciate the corded muscles along his back and arms that ripple with his movement.

Get with the program, Lara. It's never happening again.

… A girl can look though, right?

He places the cream and sugar in front of me and I realize he had been holding them up for me to take from him.

"Fuck, I'm so sorry. I've never zoned out this much in my life." I mumble, snatching both from him as he chuckles knowingly before returning to his food.

Dan comes sauntering toward his plate as we all dig in. I watch his dark tail wag as he sniffs the food before taking a mouthful and chomping down.

"I messaged Tammy again today." I mumble after swallowing the last bite of eggs.

Caspian stiffens but continues to chew a piece of toast as he looks at me.

"She still hasn't read anything I've sent her. This is really out of character. I checked all social media too and she's been radio silent. Also very unlike her considering she's a social media manager."

Caspian nods and checks his phone, then slides it into his pocket.

"I reached out to a few contacts last night and 2 of the 4 have gotten back to me. From what I know so far, Tammy took PTO last second, and said she had a family emergency. That was the evening you met… what was it you called him?"

"Leathery Man."

"Right. Leathery Man, the day you met him in the woods."

"Right, the night your brother drugged me."

Caspian continues, "Tammy's PTO is still ongoing for another two and a half weeks. Apparently, she had quite a bit saved up. My other contact pulled her bank and credit card records. It seems she flew into town the day she took PTO."

My eyes widen and I squeal, "She's here!?"

"So it would seem." Caspian's demeanor remains unchanging, but there's tension he's holding in his neck and arms, which likely means I'm not getting all the information.

"So what are your other contacts looking into?" My voice wavers and is quiet, I almost don't want to know.

"One is pulling video footage from the airport and surrounding buildings but we're running into some red tape. The other is looking at hotel and motel records near the airport since her credit cards don't have any charges beyond plane flights."

Unease makes my stomach flip at the thought that she might be in trouble, and have been for days. It must be clear on my face because Caspian is staring at me with a hard look when he speaks again.

"If she's anything like you, she will be strong enough to make it through this. Assuming the worst and that my brother has her, he won't kill her. He needs her alive to get to you. He won't be able to convince you to come to him if she's dead."

My chest tightens and I nod, staring at the countertop as his words sink in. I can only hope his brother shows her the same decency he did for me that night.

He may have drugged me, but he didn't do anything else. In fact, he seemed adamant that he wouldn't.

We will find you and bring you back safely, Tammy. I promise.

Chapter 21

As we pull into my driveway, I glance around to see if I can spot Dan or anyone in the woods but the foliage is so dense that I focus my attention on the house.

It's dark inside and there are no windows or doors broken, we didn't get any notifications of anyone coming around after Caspian's brother. It's safe to say that it's empty, but you can never be too careful.

Caspian enters first, I close and lock up behind us, before following him through the rooms. He pauses at each door, gun held ready as he checks every space small enough for someone to hide within, under or behind. After a few minutes, Caspian determines everything is clear, and we go to my room to pack my clothes. I walk to the closet and pull out my suitcase, and another duffle bag.

First, I pack an assortment of comfortable clothes, pajamas and underwear, then move onto casual wear and two dresses, one pair of business attire pants and a blouse. The duffle bag is perhaps a bit too full, but I'd rather have what I need.

Once I'm in the living area, Caspian shoulders the duffle bag, I lock up behind us and Dan meets us by the truck before we make our way back to Caspian's house.

The drive to Caspian's is different during the day. The worn down road has beautiful oak and birch trees, and a small river on one side, barely visible through the thick underbrush filled with wildlife. As we drive down the path, we see deer eating, rabbits darting from one bush to another and birds fluttering around the canopy.

"You sure you're not like a disney prince or something?" I ask, smirking as I turn to glance at Caspian.

"Yeah, I'm sure." The way his expression hardens keeps me from making any further Disney jokes, but I store away the information for later. There's something about Caspian's past that seems to haunt him and I plan to find out what that is.

The truck pulls out beyond the forest line and I gape at the house. It's huge. It's like a mini mansion.

It's modern looking. It's painted white with lots of windows that reflect a mirror image of the surrounding area. The roof has solar panels on it, and it appears to have a three-car garage.

"The windows are bulletproof. There's cameras everywhere excluding the bathrooms. There's a pool in the backyard but it's only usable during the warmer months and there's a hot tub as well."

I'm fully slack jawed now, and he chuckles before putting the truck in park.

As we walk up to the house, I hear Caspian's phone chime from the security system, but mine doesn't. He glances over and must see the unspoken question on my face, "I have the same security system in each room and outside, so the same notifications."

Oh god, there's a camera in the bedroom.

My eyes widen as I look at him.

"So last night-" I start to ask but Caspian cuts me off.

"Was on camera, yes." He nods once, his emerald eyes searching my face.

"Was it…" I can't finish my question.

Thankfully, Caspian has no such hesitations, "Recorded?"

I nod.

He cocks his head to the side and eyes me, "Did you want it to be?"

I rear back and I blink at him, his question catching me off guard.

Do I wish it was recorded?

What would I do if it was?

Would I want to watch it?
Would I care if he did?

Caspian chuckles as if he can read my influx of questionable thoughts, and I shake my head as I trail behind him to the door.

Following him inside, he turns to me after taking off his shoes. "Let's get a small pack of stuff, just enough for a night or two and we'll drive to a town nearby where Tammy could be staying and see if we can pick up a trail."

I nod, heading to the bedroom with my suitcase while Caspian hauls my duffle bag along behind me. I do just that and pack light, carrying my bag into the main living area, setting it down on the coffee table in the center and I wait.

Caspian comes in a little while later with a bag of his own. He strides across the room to where I stand, the movement so deliberate that my heart pounds in my chest as he maintains eye contact while stalking toward me.

As he stands before me, my pulse flutters and I swallow thickly. Memories of his lips against mine come to the forefront of my mind as I clear my throat and Caspian gives me a knowing smirk.

He leans down to wrap his fingers around the strap of my bag, pulling it alongside his own with a slight chuckle before turning and waving for me to follow him.

"Ass," I mumble as I walk, and he barks a laugh.

We drive to a small town not far from the airport. It has a low population of people, but there's a little low-key motel and a couple rental properties that are far away from prying eyes. Pulling in to the parking lot, we get out with our bags in hand and go to the front desk to check in.

I scan the surrounding area and buildings, the windows, the vehicles nearby and anyone coming or going. I'm partially keeping an eye out for Tammy, and the other part of me is watching for Darian.

We let a reluctant Dan out of the truck when we pulled off the main road so that he could survey the nearby woods. There's no way we'd be able to stay in a motel with a wolf without being noticed.

Caspian's movement catches my eye as he turns to me with the key in hand with a nod, then heads in the direction of our room we've rented. As we enter, he checks the bathroom and closet, and the mirrors before he turns off the lights to look for any hidden cameras.

Once satisfied, he stores the bags inside the dresser on the lowest shelf, placing a bedsheet overtop of them. He holsters his gun and shoves his hands in his pockets before glancing at me.

"Are you up for exploring the town a little and grabbing a late lunch?"

I nod enthusiastically. The thought of food alone makes my mouth water.

We hop into the truck and drive to a small diner about 3 minutes away. The place is packed with locals and there's a buzz of excited chatter humming through the dining area.

Taking a seat at one of the last available tables, the waitress pops up alongside us with a cheerful smile. Caspian gets a beer, I get a Moscow Mule, and we order some fries and onion rings for the table.

Caspian leans back in his seat as the waitress walks away to put in our order. "We're getting drunk on this road trip?" I ask jokingly as I glance at a group of guys across the room, they've erupted with cheers and are high-fiving each other.

Caspian follows my gaze with a genuine smile, "A lot has happened recently, can't stay uptight the entire time. We deserve some fun every now and again."

I laugh and my eyes slide to him, "You're starting to sound like Tammy."

I watch his face flash with something unreadable just as the waitress pauses by our table, she drops our drinks off and looks between the two of us, "Anything else you want to order or is it just the rings and fries?"

"I'll take a burger, please. Medium rare with a side salad and house dressing." I say with a smile, she pulls out her notepad and starts writing down the order.

"And you, sir?"

"I'll take the same, just the burger though." The waitress nods, "That'll be right up."

We both watch her walk away before Caspian's gaze falls on to me. "Tell me about her."

My eyes drop to the table as I gather my thoughts back to my missing friend. I'm silent for a long while, recounting some of our greatest moments.

"Tammy is a fierce friend. Loyal, caring. She's unapologetically honest, and she would do anything for those she loves. She works too hard and plays even harder. We met in California when I was still in university and I had taken a trip to study the wildfires and the effect on the local ecosystem."

I mindlessly rub the still-healing wounds on my wrists as I continue.

"I went to a small grocery shop and dropped my card on the ground. She picked it up, and I'm not sure what she saw when she looked at me, but she asked if I was from the area or visiting, and we hit it off from there. Over the years I learned that she clawed her way into her corporate position. She wasn't a foster kid or an orphan, but she didn't have an easy upbringing by any means. Her mom was addicted to opioids and her dad to gambling."

"When I started working with the government, I moved temporarily to California to continue my work and we continued to bond. When I moved to Florida to research environmental catastrophes and cancer reporting from local water sources, that was the first test of our friendship. You see, when you don't live near one another it can really affect your relationship with them. Unsurprisingly, Tammy and I were close friends regardless of the distance between us."

"Even while being such a workaholic, she saved her PTO to visit for every holiday and birthday knowing that I didn't have a family. Christmas, Halloween, Thanksgiving, Easter. Any and all holidays, she was there."

I fall silent while I think through old memories. Caspian clears his throat, his emotions guarded and unreadable.

"She seems like the kind of friend you deserve. We will find her. If she is as you say, I'm sure she's found a way to make the best of her situation while she waits for us to find her."

I nod my head but stay silent, afraid to speak more as emotion clogs my throat.

Our waitress comes back with our food in tow, placing the fries and rings on the table and my salad. "Your burgers will be out in a few minutes. Enjoy!" She chimes and hurries off to her other patrons.

I take a deep sip of my drink, then grab a fry and pop it into my mouth. It's silent for a few minutes and I stand up without saying a word, walking over to the bar.

The bartender leans to me and raises an eyebrow, "What might I get you, miss?"

"Two shots of tequila, please."

His eyebrows shoot up, and he glances at the clock, then back at me.

Clearly he's not aware that it's five o'clock somewhere.

He nods and holds his hand out, "I.D. Please."

I slide my ID to him, then some cash, and he passes me two glasses.

Walking back to the table, I place one and slice of lime in front of Caspian, holding my shot up between us to cheers, "To friendship, loyalty, and fierce friends"

A ghost of a smile flickers on Caspian's face, and he knocks his glass against mine before we both toss the alcohol back, chasing it with the lime.

I make a face and Caspian barks a laugh.

"Can't have balls of steel every time, unfortunately." I plop the lime into the empty shot glass and take a long sip of my mixed drink.

"You were pounding them back on your birthday."

My heart stutters in my chest.

How long was he watching me?

Waving my hand dismissively, I take another fry, "I was already drunk" I say before popping the fry in my mouth.

"Ah" Sarcasm drips from his voice as he smirks.

I stand abruptly and walk back to the bar, handing a hundred dollar bill to the bartender.

"Four shots of Tequila" his eyebrows shoot up to his hairline, and he blinks at me before glancing at the clock nervously and back, then nods.

As the bartender steps away to get the shots, I turn and my gaze automatically falls to Caspian talking to the waitress. She laughs and flips her hair over her shoulder as a pang of jealousy hits my gut like a hot knife as he smiles and his eyes rove down her body.

He's not yours, idiot. He can talk to who ever he wants.

My mind shoves those thoughts away, regardless if I enjoy the mental image of ripping her hair out.

She walks away, and I notice the sway of her hips more exaggerated than it was earlier when she was taking our orders.

That's it. She's going to be a bald bitch before today ends if she isn't careful.

The bartender warily hands me a small tray with four shots of tequila and an equal number of limes before going to grab the change from the register.

"Thanks, keep it." My voice comes out level and curt.

He blinks with shock, "Are you sure? That's more than the actual shots."

I laugh dryly and wave before taking the tray, "Yeah, I'm sure."

If I end up ripping that waitress's hair out, he won't be thanking me later.

I bring the tray to our table and Caspian's eyes grow wide with amusement.

I eye him with suspicion, "What is it?"

"I ordered more drinks too," He says with a chuckle.

"Oh, we're getting drunk, drunk then." I say dryly and start arranging the shots in between us but Caspian halts my hands.

He stands up and moves to the seat beside me, then sits down and leans back, putting an ankle over his knee and his arm on the top of my chair.

He grins with a mischievous twinkle in his eyes that sends heat straight to between my thighs and I clench them automatically in my seat.

"Alright, now I'm ready to go shot for shot." He says with a wink.

We both take a shot, chasing it with a lime and I grind my teeth to avoid making a face but fail miserably as I shiver.

"I thought you could handle liquor." Caspian says sarcastically, his lips twitch upward as he watches my reaction with amusement.

"Not my fault their tequila is bottom of the barrel" I mumble and take another sip of my mixed drink, finishing the last of it.

Caspian lets out a laugh with a broad smile that reaches his luminous green eyes.

In an effort to recover from embarrassment, I playfully push at his chest and grab another shot, placing one before him and the empty ones near the edge of the table.

As if summoned by the empty glasses, the waitress walks up with the drinks that Caspian ordered, setting them in front of us and taking the empty ones.

"Would you like anything else?" She doesn't direct her question at nor including me and my face flushes with anger.

Chill, Lara.

"Do you want anything else?" His voice completely blanks my mind, and I'm flushing for all different reasons now as our eyes lock.

"Maybe a round of water for both of us, please, with lemon," I tell the waitress with my head slightly turned to her, but my gaze hasn't left Caspian's.

"And for you, sir? Anything else for you?" Her voice is sickly sweet, and I peel my gaze from Caspian to look at her as she bats her eyes at him.

I wonder if he'll be willing to bail me out of jail when I'm done with her.

"I'm good for now."

My entire body freezes.

For now?

She nods with a smile as her eyes flick to mine. With a smug look she whirls and hurries to the next table while I'm stuck breathless at his choice of words and deliberate actions.

Am I overthinking or reading too much into this?

"So." My voice cracks and I wince, before clearing my throat.

"So." His tone is fully amused now, and I know if I look at him, I will fold. I decide to do the logical thing any woman would do, and focus on getting our tequila and limes in order.

"Take another shot and then we talk about how long you were stalking me before your brother captured me." I take a moment to glance at him, and he's grinning almost too much, "Creeper." I mutter and his smile grows wider.

I quickly grab a glass and toss it back, and chug the mixed cocktail that the waitress brought out. Caspian downs his shot and takes a long sip of his own drink.

"Do you want me to carry you out of here?" He asks with a hint of amusement and I flush at the mental image.

"I can handle my liquor, as you well know. Now explain." He grimaces and downs the rest of his drink to avoid the question and my suspicion rises, "So the bar, you knew who I was, clearly."

He nods, "Yes, and I knew of the man that was after you. That night I followed him to the parking lot and he waited for you but left when he saw me waiting by the exit. I followed you home and staked out overnight in case he decided to make a move while you were both out of it."

Holy fuck. So that's how he knew where I lived?

My jaw goes slack, and I gape at him for a moment before I recollect myself.

"Well, I suppose I should be thanking you, then."

"Later." He says with a wink and my entire body feels like it's suddenly on fire.

God. How am I supposed to sleep in the same room as this man tonight and avoid doing anything?

It takes conscious effort to focus on the conversation, as I file away the information.

A thought dawns on me and the heat in my body suddenly runs cold. My question is no more than a whisper, "Do you think that he gave Tammy's information to your brother after that night?"

Caspian's face hardens as he glances down to the table, nodding slightly as he speaks.

"It is more than likely he did, that's why I'm running with the assumption that my brother has her somewhere and is waiting to use her as bait."

My veins turn to ice, buzz forgotten.

"She'll be alive, Lara."

I lift my gaze to meet his, "Alive is not the same as being healthy or thriving." I whisper, knowing full well the difference.

The waitress brings out the burgers and places them in front of us and hesitates for a moment. "Another round of drinks, please." She flicks her gaze from Caspian to me and I hold her stare, "And another round of tequila."

She nods and walks to the bar, I glance at Caspian who is assessing me with a raised brow.

"For good measure," I say with an affirming nod.

He chuckles and we dig in to our lunch.

Chapter 22

We finish the last of our meal with idle chatter, and as we are about to leave, I sway. Feeling more than a slight buzz, Caspian's hand moves to my elbow automatically, steadying me.

I toss him a grateful smile, "Thanks."

He nods, moving around to the aisle to walk out with me as the waitress approaches us to say goodbye. As she passes, I notice her shake Caspian's hand, and she slides a piece of paper into it.

Jealousy rears its ugly head again, this time accompanied by anger and fueled by Jose Cuervo, almost makes me act out on the spot.

Oh, I'm going to jail. Good thing orange suits me.

Caspian pauses, he grabs my arm to stop me from walking away, and lifts the piece of paper up between him and the waitress.

She blanches and glances nervously to each of us.

"This doesn't look like a receipt." He frowns innocently and unfolds it.

Son of a bitch knows exactly what it is.

I snort as Caspian chokes down laughter, and the waitress's face flashes to me with anger etched on it.

He pretends to struggle to read it, and shows it to me, then back to her.

I bite the inside of my cheek to keep from bursting out laughing. "Ah, I'm sorry I don't understand binary that well. Never did well with computers. What is this supposed to be?"

Laughter bubbles up in me and I can't hold it down anymore. My chest heaves and tears spring to my eyes with pained restraint.

Caspian's face is pure mischievous amusement, while the waitress is glaring at me as if I just kicked her child.

She scoffs, stomping away like an angry toddler while I fight to control my laughter. A few patrons who observed the scene are also chuckling before they go back to their meals.

Caspian's head tilts, and he stares at me for a long moment, as if debating whether he should say something.

He probably shouldn't.

"Orange would look good on you but you're not going to jail any time soon."

I freeze and my entire body feels like it's made of molten lava.

Oh god, I said that out loud.

He smirks at me, "You did."

"I'm never drinking with you again."

While Caspian is somehow sober enough to drive, we opt to explore the area on foot to walk off the alcohol more efficiently and take in the town.

There aren't many people around, a car passes by every few minutes but other than that the streets are empty. The first building we approach is a bank, across from it is a medical office. We pass by a dental practice, a law firm and as we get closer to the gas station, and I glance to Caspian, "I need a washroom."

His lips twitch, and he inclines his head toward the building, "Let's stop off there."

I nod and hurry in to break the seal.

Before leaving, I snag two candy bars and pay for them, then walk outside to where Caspian is waiting, tossing him a bar, "Don't say I never did anything for ya."

He grins and unwraps the bar, taking a big bite as we continue down the road. I do the same with my own and chew slowly as we walk alongside a property that has trees shielding it from prying eyes.

My chest feels tight and I freeze in place.

"What is it?" Caspian's voice is guarded and quiet.

I take a few more steps and I can feel the pull inside my body, my free hand instinctively goes to hover over the spot.

Glancing at Caspian, I can see the question in his eyes and I nod.

We both turn to look at the property and head toward the house. As we step closer, the pull gets stronger until I'm fighting to breathe. There's a car parked in the driveway as we walk up the porch and knock lightly.

After a long pause we hear footsteps nearing, and an older woman pulls the door just enough for her face to peer through as she eyes us warily.

"What do ya want?" She spits out from the cracked opening.

She is missing teeth and what few remain are crooked. Her skin is sagging, wrinkled and loose. She's covered in moles and her frizzy, dull gray hair reaches her shoulders where it splits at the ends.

Caspian's face is hard, and he doesn't miss a beat as he stares at her, "I'm a detective with the local sheriff's office and this is my partner. We're investigating a serial killer around these parts. Can we come in and ask you a few questions?"

Oh, he's smooth.

Her eyes narrow, and she looks like she's about to protest but Caspian interrupts whatever attempt she had on her lips, "It will only take a few minutes."

She sucks her teeth and opens the door to let us in and the scent of ammonia wafts over me like a tidal wave. There's at least 14 cats that we can see running around, and they have used nearly every surface as their litter box.

I wrinkle my nose as the smell invades my senses.

Glancing at Caspian, his eyes are fixed on me as I feel the pull deepen, bringing me back to the present and I look around. Pain radiates when I angle to the left, turning to the right, the tugging sensation increases, so I point in that direction subtly to Caspian who nods.

The woman looks around her house, then at Caspian, and lands on me. "What do ya want to ask me?" she asks impatiently.

"Ah, actually, do you have a washroom I can use?" I ask, as if I didn't already just use the washroom.

She narrows her eyes but nods, "This way."

I scurry after her as she leads me down the hallway I indicated earlier to Caspian. The pull has grown so great I can hardly stand, and it gets stronger with each step.

She points to a flimsy door and grunts before heading back the way she came.

She walks out of sight and I turn until the pain lessens. The pull is coming from behind a closed door across from the bathroom. Taking a steadying breath, I glance down the hall to make sure it's empty and move to carefully turn the knob.

Thankful that the hinges are quiet, I ease the door open slightly and peek inside.

The room is empty.

It looks like a main bedroom, but one that hasn't been used in a while. There's clothes scattered around the floor. Pants, shirts, socks. My gaze falls to the belt hanging off the bed and memories flutter across my mind making me swallow audibly.

I take a step toward the pull. It's coming from the bed.

Slowly walking to the side of the bed, I bend down, getting to my knees and leaning to the floor, I look under the frame along the wall for an amulet.

Balls of fur and dust coat the ground. There's a disturbance of the thick layer of grime in a long line as if someone had pulled something out from underneath the bed.

Towards the wall I catch a glimpse of a round object, partially obscured by dirt or grime. It appears to be bronze, but I can feel with every fiber of my being that it's the amulet.

I reach out, grasping the light metal with my fingertips and slide it to my palm before backing out to sit on my knees. As I wipe the pendant with my shirt, I notice the clear fluid surrounding an intricately carved dual-faced head at the center, each face staring in opposite directions. I peel my eyes away from it, tucking it securely into my shirt with a relieved sigh.

The floor beneath me creaks as I push to my feet and I hear a sharp, muffled gasp from the closet. My head snaps in the direction of the sound and I move slowly to the doors, every memory I have of avoiding people with cruel intentions flickers into my mind.

I keep my voice calm and level, but it comes out no more than a whisper, "I'm going to open the door. I'm not here to hurt you, please stay quiet and take deep breaths."

Gently tugging the handles to the side, it groans loudly, and I hear a whimper, along with a muffled cry.

Two pairs of brown eyes stare at me with a level of terror I'm all too familiar with as they hide amongst the rows of hanging garments. My heart sinks in my chest at their tattered clothing that does nothing to hide the bones jutting out from their filthy, bruised skin.

I grit my teeth but keep my emotions masked in an attempt to soften my features to be as open and welcoming as possible. The two girls look no older than seven. One is maybe half that age.

The eldest child is desperately trying to muffle the younger girl's cries, her hand pressed firmly against the little one's mouth as tears streak through the layers of dirt on her face.

"My name is Lara," I say softly. Both children look at me and then glance to the door with wide eyes.

They're petrified.

I meet the gaze of the youngest, "No one will hurt you while I'm here. I used to be like you." Shifting my attention to the older girl, "Do you want me to help?" The younger child glances up to the older one, and after a moment of hesitation, the eldest nods in agreement.

"Okay, we need to get to my friend in the front room. I want you to stay behind me, no matter what. I won't let them take you back. They'd have to get through me to get to you, okay?"

I hope you're ready, Caspian.

I hold the hand of the older child, the youngest tucked into her protectively. Part of me wonders if the older one is doing this solely to get the younger one out of here.

If only we'd had that luxury.

My chest tightens and resolve coats my veins as I walk confidently down the with both girls in tow. As we round the corner, Caspian is facing us and his eyes widen as he glances between me and the children.

Whatever he sees from the three of us must be enough for him to know I won't leave them here.

The woman turns around and her face contorts in a mixture of surprise and rage as she sees the girls beside me. She reaches her arm toward them, but Caspian has quickly positioned himself between us.

"They are our foster kids! You can't just take them!" She shouts, as she steps to the side and Caspian matches her movement.

He glares at her, "By the looks of it, they're extremely underfed and I'd be willing to bet that after a proper bath, those bruises would look much, much worse." his voice is cold, vicious and lethal, sending a chill down my spine.

"Tim! Tim! They're taking the children!" She shouts franti-cally, and loud steps resound through the house and the youngest, now trembling where she stands, begins to cry.

"Lara. Take the girls outside." His calm, commanding tone grabs my attention amidst the chaos.

I nod and escort the children out, ignoring the woman shout-ing behind us. With each step, their pace increases until they're both running, and I'm having to jog alongside them to keep up.

The moment we get out the door, the two hug each other while sobbing.

Shouting ensues and I wrap my forearms protectively around them as they cry harder. Caspian steps out of the house with his phone against his ear, his knuckles covered in blood as he speaks to someone.

I can't hear him over the crying and sniffling of the children, so I just tighten my grip on them. The eldest has her arm wrapped around my thigh and has buried her face in my leg as silent tears fall while she holds the youngest's head into her chest as she wails.

"I called a friend, he's about 10 minutes away. He'll pick us up until we can figure out what to do next."

I nod with relief and rub both girls' backs soothingly, his eyes track the movement and soften.

"Did you find what you were looking for?" he asks, tearing his eyes from the girls to meet my gaze.

"I wouldn't have been able to leave without it," I say to him softly.

"Or without them." He responds, and I fall silent.

We hear shouting inside the house and things slamming, mak-ing both girls flinch at every noise.

I bend down to be level with them and hold them to me, whis-pering quietly, "Let's walk a bit further away to get away from the noise okay?"

Both girls nod and quiet down as we slowly walk a few paces from the house, Caspian trails silently behind us with quick glances back to make sure we aren't being followed.

As we get to the road, I lean down to look at both girls, "So you know my name is Lara, this is Caspian. What are your names?"

Caspian gives an awkward wave to the children as they look at him.

"I'm May, she's Rose." The older girl, May, says with a sniffle. Rose glances at me and nods.

"Well, May and Rose. I'm so sorry for what you two have gone through. We're going to get you somewhere safe though, okay?"

May nods but squeezes my hand tightly. Rose lets go of May, moving in front of Caspian and looks up at him, "Thank you." She says with a hoarse voice and throws her arms around his legs in a hug.

Caspian's head jerks back ever so slightly as he looks at me with wide eyes and I suppress a laugh.

It only takes a few more minutes before a black SUV pulls up as Rose holds Caspian's hand as I grip tightly to May's.

Caspian nods at the driver before opening the rear passenger door to let May, Rose and I hop into the back as Caspian seats himself in the front. The driver is a lean, broad shouldered man with dirty blonde hair, he gives us a warm smile as we settle in.

"Lara, May, Rose… this is Lionel. Lionel, meet Lara and our newest friends May and Rose." He points to us as he finishes the introduction and I return a small smile. May squeezes my hand as she and Rose give a meek hello.

"I have a contact nearby, she and her husband work special cases like this. We'll head there first." Caspian keys in an address to the GPS and the SUV starts to move.

It doesn't take long before we turn off of the main road, and I can't help but notice Rose and May visibly tense which makes my chest tighten.

Thankfully, the large white house we pull up to is welcoming with enormous windows, flowers of various colors in front of a wide porch with four rocking chairs.

A large oak tree shades over part of the grass and along the side behind the fence, horses are grazing and drinking water. Both girls look at the giant creatures with awe, and I find myself smiling at their reactions.

Lionel puts the car in park, and we filter out as we follow closely behind Caspian. Each girl takes one of my hands as he skips steps up the porch to ring the doorbell.

A few moments later, the door opens revealing a typical southern bell looking woman gazing at us with bright blue eyes that crinkle at the sides from too much laughter. Her luscious blond hair curled past her shoulders over her yellow blouse, neatly tucked into her faded blue jeans.

"Welcome, welcome! Any friends of Caspian's are friends of ours!" She looks at the girls and I with a warmth I'd imagine every mother should have.

It sends a pang of sadness into my chest that I'd never known someone like this, but I'm thankful May and Rose will.

"Well you gals look like you could use a warm bath and some food, huh?" She turns to me and for the first time I see the note of worry in her eyes, "I'll show you to the washroom if you'll get them cleaned up? I'll bring some new clothes for them before you're done."

I nod and look at the girls with a soft smile, "Let's go wash that dust and grime off you." Their tiny hands squeeze mine, and we follow Caspian's friend down the hall as he and Lionel converse quietly.

After a shower, both girls' bruises are stark contrast against their fair skin, but their eyes are bright with hope.

What a wonder fresh clothes and washing up will do.

I rub my thumb over the amulet in my pocket as the girls get dressed. I decided to be moral support as they get themselves ready to give them a sense of independence.

May still helps Rose get dressed, but I have a feeling both of them prefer that for a semblance of normalcy.

"We're ready." May's quiet voice sings out, and I glance up to them from where I sit on the floor.

"You both look lovely. Are you hungry?" I ask as I push to my feet, reaching my hands out for them as they nod before we walk back to the living area.

Caspian, Lionel, southern bell and her husband are in the living room as we emerge from the hallway.

Everyone falls quiet, and I can see four sets of eyes widen as they assess how bad the bruising is on both children.

Avoiding making the girls feel awkward, I adopt the same lighthearted tone I used to have whenever convincing everyone, including myself, that things were fine.

At some point in my life this tone and voice was ingrained in me because of how frequently I utilized it. Teachers, adults at school and other kids fell for it without a second thought.

I was afraid of the consequences if anyone found out what was happening with me. Best to hide it rather than face the result of my actions.

"Everyone, this is Rose," I hold Rose's hand up, and she waves shyly with her free hand. "And this is May." I hold May's hand up, and she waves with her other hand too.

"Nice to meet you, Rose and May. I'm Stacey and this is my husband Dylan. I made some roast and mashed potatoes if you're hungry?"

Both girls nod eagerly as Stacey stands up, "Well come with me to the kitchen and let's dig in! We have chocolate cake for dessert too!"

Rose's eyes widen in surprise, her excitement evident in the way her gaze darts between May and Stacey. May's jaw drops slightly, mirroring the astonishment on her younger siblings face.

They turn their attention back to me, and hesitate before taking a step to follow Stacey.

Relief floods through me, and I know there's an ocean sized pool of emotions I'll have to process when this is done.

Sitting on one of the couches, I nod toward the kitchen with a warm smile, "Go on, I'll be right here."

Dylan, Lionel, Caspian and I watch the trio disappear into another room and I let out a breath before putting my head in my hands.

"You alright, Lara?" I don't look up, but I nod into my palms.

"What an experience that was after the brunch we had." Caspian's tone sounds light as he tries to deflect the subject.

"Caspian, what happened to those girls? They look like someone used them as a punching bag." Dylan's tone darkens as he speaks, and I swallow before glancing up at them.

Caspian is staring at me as Dylan waits for an answer, but it's Lionel that responds.

"I think we all know what was happening to them. I, for one, am happy we got them out of that fucking place when we did."

Caspian nods and finds his voice, "Those pieces of shit were just cashing in on state funds by fostering kids." He looks at Dylan and leans back, pausing for a moment. "Will they be able to stay with you for a while? I think they're a long term case but I'll leave it up to you two, of course."

Dylan's eyes flick to the direction of the kitchen, then back to Caspian and I put my head into my hands again. "Yeah, we will keep them for quite a few years I think, and if or when they do move on, it would be to a good family that we approve of."

I shut my eyes tightly and bite the inside of my cheek as tears fall silently into my hands.

"Wonderful. Thank you both for doing this." There's a pause before he speaks again, "Do you mind giving us a moment?" His voice is quiet, and it sounds like he's standing now.

I hear shuffling and a door clicks shut. Lionel and Dylan's hushed voices murmur in from another room as footsteps stop just in front of where I sit.

"Lara." Caspian's voice is close, and I know he's in front of me, "Lara, look at me." His hands wrap gently around my wrists as he pries them away from my face, cautious to not put too much pressure on my still healing wounds.

I gaze at him with a sad smile, taking in his relaxed features as he looks at me with a softness I've never seen before.

"They're safe because of you. They'll never know that kind of treatment again. You know that, right?" He says softly, with all the confidence in the world that these two girls will be okay.

I find myself clinging to that desperate hope as I try to get my bearings. Nodding, I wipe the tears from my cheeks, and he gives me a genuine smile that nearly makes my heart stop.

"Good. Let's go see our newest friends and see how they're settling in, yeah?" He says, lacing his hand in mind as he leads me through the doors to the kitchen.

As we enter the room, Rose is digging into a piece of cake, smearing chocolate icing across her cheek as she stuffs the spoon in her mouth. May is taking huge gulps from a cup of milk, with half a slice of cake in front of her.

Stacey turns to us and clasps her hands together with a bright smile that is genuine. "Well! If it isn't our friends Caspian and Lara! Did you come for cake too?"

Caspian chuckles and shakes his head, "Sorry Stacey, watching my figure."

I snort and the image of him nearly unhinging his jaw like a snake while shoving a burger down his throat flickers through my mind.

His eyes flash to mine, narrowing as if he knows what I'm thinking.

Stacey looks at me next, and I wave my hands across my body, shaking my head. "No thank you, I'm still full from my lunch."

Caspian laughs quietly, "We were just hoping to see them before we leave, actually. We should be getting back." he says, squeezing my hand gently before releasing it.

Rose and May stop what they're doing and jump off their seats. I crouch down as they sprint the few small steps, and hug me tightly.

I whisper softly, wrapping an arm around each of them, "You will be so happy here. Stacey and Dylan are good people. They will have my number and if you ever want to talk, just call me alright? If you guys want me to come visit, just tell me and I will be here."

I pull my head back to look at them as they nod and though there are tears in their eyes, none fall.

That alone sends relief through my body, reassuring me that I'm making the right choice as both girls walk to Caspian, hugging him from either side and my chest swells. He ruffles their hair, and they make angry noises before scurrying back to sit and finish their cake.

Lionel and Dylan come in from the other side of the room and with amusement on their faces as they watch the girls dig in.

"Well, shall we get going?" Lionel turns to us and we both nod. Though it's only been a few hours, exhaustion has set deep into my bones and I can't wait to relax in the motel after a long, hot shower.

The drive back to the motel is quick, and we're soon stepping in the door to the room. I yawn as I tear open the drawer and grab some pajamas from my bag, hurry into the washroom and shower.

Once clean, I wrap my hair in a towel and pull on my pajamas. As I walk out, Caspian moves past me to take his own shower and I plop onto one of the beds with a satisfied sigh.

My eyelids get heavier as I blink, and finally they stay closed. It feels like mere seconds later the shower turns off and Caspian's footsteps echo through the room before the bed dips and my eyes snap open.

"What are you doing?" My voice is thick with exhaustion, but it still manages to sound like a squeak.

"Dan isn't here and you're going to have nightmares whether you admit it or not. This is better than people calling the police if you start screaming. This way, I can wake you up before you get to that point. Now get some rest."

His voice is so matter-of-fact, and damn him, but I'm too tired to argue so I grumble and turn over. He laughs quietly under his breath as he flicks the light off on the side table, before settling into bed.

I slowly rouse from sleep and my limbs feel heavy as I lay on my stomach. I'm sprawled with the sheets twisting around my legs, a thick blanket on top me and Dan is flattened against my back.

Bare skin touching my legs and the warm breath feathering over my hair snags my attention the events of last night replay in my mind.

My heart stutters as I realize that Caspian is half laying on me, his legs intertwined with mine.

My entire body flushes with heat, and my mind goes completely blank.

Do I move? Do I wait until he wakes up? What if he's already awake?

My pulse thunders as I shift slightly, hoping that I can slip from the bed without being noticed.

My hopes are smothered as Caspian's muscular arm around my waist tightens, and he drags me closer into him, bringing my back flush to his front.

My body tenses at the movement and there's a long moment before I feel it.

The length of him throbs against my back and my breath gets caught in my lungs. It pulsates again and my heart hammers within my chest, threatening to crawl out my throat.

It wouldn't take much for me to roll on top of him and...

Nope, not going there.

"Breathe, Lara." Caspian's sleep laden voice is deeper than usual, and I feel my pussy clench.

Blowing out a breath I hear him chuckle behind me, "Ass." My voice cracks and I wince.

"Mmm. Yours is nice." he mumbles, and I decide to haul myself out of bed before my traitorous body makes any decisions for me.

My legs get caught in the sheets as I struggle to clamber out of bed, which only prompts a hearty laugh from Caspian. I finally push to my feet, twisting to look at him with exasperation.

His half lidded eyes peek at me from where his face still rests against the pillows, as if he was hardly bothered by me launching from the bed.

He's smirking and I shoot him a glare, "I'm sleeping in-"

Caspian cuts me off abruptly, "My bed tonight, or whatever bed I sleep in, you will too."

"What? Why do I not get my own bed?" My voice squeaks.

"You didn't have a nightmare last night. I don't even think you dreamed."

I blink at him, "I was exhausted, clearly." I manage to say coolly, placing my hands on my hips.

His eyes track the movement as he rolls to the side, leaning on one arm.

From this angle, the corded muscles of his abdomen are on display, tensing as he moves.

"You also are in a strange place after helping two little girls out of situations no doubt similar to what you went through. You should have had a nightmare last night, Lara. You and I both know it."

I do, doesn't mean I'll admit it.

I huff and move to the washroom, clenching my thighs as the wetness between them threatens to expose me.

Traitorous fucking pussy.

By the time I come out, Caspian's pulling his shoes on, glancing at me with a knowing smirk. I glare daggers at him and stalk to my bag, grabbing my clothes out and setting them on the bed.

Two can play at this game.

Facing him as I tear off my pajamas, his eyes widen as our gaze locks, and I don't miss the heat in his expression. I turn away, making a point to pull my pants on slowly, bending at the hip to pick them up, stretching with emphasis and I hear him choke a cough.

Fighting a smile, I put my pajamas into the bag and set the

bag next to Caspian's. "So, where to, now?"

Caspian's quiet for a moment, then pulls out his phone and scrolls around on what I'm guessing is a map. "Tammy's cell is still pinging from the coast. So it's safe to assume it hasn't left, but that leaves us with one option, and that's to search nearby towns here and then lastly, to search the city she lives on the coast." he says, pointing on his phone at two different places before continuing, "I think we could go here, next" His finger lands on a town on the screen that doesn't look to be far from us, "And we can search in somewhat of a circle until we round back to where we started unless we get a hit from her cards or phone."

I take a deep breath, "Okay. Let's go find her."

Chapter 23

We drive to the next town which is somewhat livelier.

There is a clear hustle and bustle through the streets with people stopping to chat with one another. It's not long until we turn off the main road into the driveway of a rental property.

Pulling the bag over my shoulder, I follow Caspian in the house. He inputs a PIN into his phone, a beep sounds out, and he pushes the door open, peering around before he turns to me, inclining his head toward the hallway, "Alright, put your stuff into the bedroom and let's go explore."

Driving through the streets, I keep a lookout for Tammy's green eyes and prominent facial features. After a while with no sight of her, we drive circles around the miniature city before slowly make our way into what would be considered 'downtown'.

Traffic congestion is heavy, and it's a struggle just to find a place to park. There seems to be some sort of event happening that has local police cruisers blocking off streets with their lights on. There are tents set up along either side of the road and people walking from one vendor to another.

"A farmer's market." I breathe with excitement as we finally pull into an empty spot before walking through the streets at a slow pace on foot, scanning the crowd.

Caspian's fingers gently wrap around my elbow, "Let's grab something from one of these vendors and we can watch while we get breakfast."

My eyes widen as I turn to him, "Like a stakeout!" My voice is a whispered squeak.

Caspian blinks twice and barks a laugh, "I guess that's one word for it."

I rub my hands together with excitement as we pass by a handful of tents before settling on one, we order a couple breakfast burritos with drinks and find a table to sit at.

Caspian sits facing me so that we can scan the incoming crowd behind each other without looking suspicious.

An hour goes by and I've gotten antsy, fidgeting in place, only pausing when Caspian shoots me a look.

Note to self, stakeouts have zero mental stimulation.

We had finished eating a while ago, there's no sign of Tammy anywhere and I heave a defeated sigh. "This isn't working," I say irritably and rub my temples.

"We haven't spent long here but if it makes you feel better we can walk to burn some of this anxious energy you have."

I shoot him a glare but push to my feet, and he laughs under his breath.

Ass.

My hands fidget with the empty drink. It slips and falls to the ground with a clatter and I huff, angrily cursing as I bend to pick it up which makes Caspian laugh harder.

It's not anxiety, it's anticipation. Yup. That is it. Screw you, Mystery Man.

Caspian tosses me a knowing smirk and I huff before wandering down the busy street away from him. My frustrations soon forgotten as I spot a vendor selling shirts with custom images on them. I browse through a few of them, snickering some of the clever phrases that I know Caspian would wholly roll his eyes at if I was wearing them right now.

The 'I'm with grumpy' shirt has an image of the dwarf from Snow White and the Seven Dwarfs.

I wonder how much they'd charge to put Caspian's face on it.

I laugh quietly to myself as I leave the vendor behind to continue down the road, and I glance back to see Caspian trailing not far away.

We venture into a few more tents, one has custom pictures with intricate frames that look hand made. The next creates custom dog harnesses and collars. The one after that sells homemade jams and spice blends for BBQs.

Eventually the vendors are all local farmers who are selling ripe and in-season produce, with a colorful spread of fruits and vegetables across their tables. There's only a handful of tents down the pathway, but I abruptly stop as I see curled brown hair standing at a handcrafted jewelry vendor at the end of the street. The woman's height looks similar, and build, the curl of her hair is not exactly right nor is her choice of clothing, but I still sprint toward the tent.

"Lara!" Caspian hisses at me as I take off. I dodge and side step people as I near the woman.

She turns as I'm only a few feet away and her brown eyes look at me with shock. "Oh, excuse me miss, I didn't see you there!" Her voice has a southern accent to it.

I nod, murmuring an apology as I catch my breath, my heart dropping into my stomach as she walks past me.

Caspian places his hand goes to my shoulder as if to comfort me, but my disappointment is overwhelming. Blowing out a breath, I turn to leave but hesitate at the tug in my body and I glance to Caspian with wide eyes.

His brows pinch together, and I frantically glance around before my sights fall to the vendor in front of me.

Caspian's voice is hushed as he leans in, "What is it, Lara?"

Suspicion fires through my body and I look around us. Everyone is enveloped in their own bubbles, paying no mind to us and the person working in the vendor is giving more attention to her phone.

This almost seems too coincidental.

My hand goes to my body where the tug feels tight, and I look Caspian in the eyes with caution before murmuring, "I almost can't believe it but there's an amulet here."

His head jerks back as I point to the jewelry in front of us and we both turn to scan through the items for sale. There's a variation of earrings in the displays, some bracelets and anklets on another that I briefly skim over.

"There." Caspian eagerly points to a set of hanging necklaces.

Each one has similar features to the amulets we have, just in different variations and I frown. "How do we know if there's one or multiple?"

Caspian's eyes flick from me to the vendor employee and then light up, "Excuse me, can we see those necklaces there?" He asks, while pointing to the amulets.

She looks up quickly like she was caught doing something she shouldn't and rushes, "Yes, of course. One moment."

She pulls them off the wall and sets them on the counter in a line and Caspian smirks, "Let's see which one looks best."

I raise a brow but nod as Caspian tilts his head away from the counter, "Step over here, for better lighting." I could almost roll my eyes at how not subtle he was and suppress a snort. As I take a step to the side and away from the vendor, pain lances through my body and I wince.

Caspian lifts one and hands it to me, tilting his head as if studying how it looks on me, but he's simply staring at my eyes for any indication that something has changed.

I shake my head almost imperceptibly.

One down, four to go.

"Hmmm. Let's see this one." He puts one away, and grabs the next. I shake my head again, the pain still radiating in my abdomen is making my legs quiver.

Three left.

"Not quite right, let's try this one." He hands me another, and I shake my head again.

Two left.

"Ah, maybe this one," he suggests, handing me an amulet adorned with a captivating depiction of waves in its center. The image seamlessly blends into the liquid trapped within the pendant. My body sags with relief, and I nod eagerly but instead of handing it to me, he pulls it back. Instantly, a surge of pain courses through me, causing my knees to weaken.

Despite my visible discomfort, Caspian remains indifferent.

I'm about to release a whimper when he grabs the final one, "Actually, maybe this one?" I shake my head as it's placed next to my neck.

"We'll take this one." Caspian holds the true amulet up for the employee to scan, the movement threatening to send my knees buckling beneath me until finally he holds it in my direction and a shudder of relief crashes over me.

Breathing hard, as if I just ran a marathon with sweat beading down my temple, I step away as Caspian pays for it. My eyes scan the crowd and land on a tree in the distance where I spot a hooded figure.

For a moment, I'm nearly positive mismatched eyes stare back at me from beneath the dark hood, but within the blink of an eye, the person has disappeared completely.

I must be going crazy.

We get back to the truck and Caspian's cell chimes. He checks the screen, his jaw clenching as he unlocks it in a hurry. Cursing at whatever he sees before dialing a number.

"Check the warehouse. I don't care if you just checked in. Check the warehouse!"

My heart beats loud in my ears and I flinch at his shouts, keeping my eyes directed out the window.

And here I thought I had a temper.

"Good. I want you to call in extra support, double the guard on rotation." He hangs up and sucks in a deep breath, composing himself and I take my chances to look at him just as he glances at me with a wince.

I can't help but feel like I was just witness to a conversation or event I shouldn't have.

"Sorry about that." He grits through his teeth.

"Did something happen at your warehouse?"

Real subtle, Lara.

"Just a report of a possible robbery for an important item I've got stored before it goes for sale."

"I didn't know you were in that business." I try to remain casual, but there's something in the back of my mind telling me to keep my guard up.

"There's much you don't know about me." The indifference in his tone is off-putting, and I'm silent as he shifts the truck into gear.

Isn't that the truth.

Chapter 24

It's an hour drive before we get into a small town just northeast of the last. Desperate to relieve some of the awkwardness and tension as we seem to be nearing our destination, I try to stir up conversation.

"Where to now?" The journey is so silent that my voice is incredibly loud in comparison.

"There's another market here." His response is curt and leaves more questions, but I can tell he isn't in the mood to field any of them. Whatever happened at his warehouse has left him in an incredibly sour mood.

Caspian is already such a hot and cold individual, but this is complete stonewalling. We venture further into the small community of buildings, and my mind wanders to Dan and my chest aches with loneliness.

I wonder if Dan knows where we've gone or if he thinks we're still back in that town where we saved May and Rose. We pull over a few streets down from the little market set up in a small park. It's hardly half the size of the last, and I wonder how long we'll stay here looking for Tammy.

Caspian shuts off the ignition abruptly, even going so far as to slam the truck door causing me to flinch.

His actions and behavior are proving that I am a fly circling a spider's web. One wrong move and I could be its next meal.

We head toward the market and I leisurely stroll from one vendor to another, searching for Tammy in the small crowd of people as I meander through.

I can feel tension rolling off of Caspian as he checks his phone repeatedly by the last vendor tent and I approach him cautiously, "No sign of her here."

He raises his head with a cocked eyebrow in confusion, and I clarify, "No sign of Tammy."

Understanding flashes through his features, "Unfortunate. I was hoping we'd find something or catch her scent."

My stomach drops and I glance around, suddenly feeling out of place and paranoid, but there's no sign that we're being watched and nothing appears to be wrong, so I brush it off.

"We'll head to the rental, then head to the next town in the morning."

My head jerks back, "I need to work tomorrow."

"No, this is more important. If we don't find her soon, you never know what might happen to her." Caspian says plainly as he gives me a hard look.

My insides twist as I think of Tammy being held captive for this long and blow out a reluctant breath, "Okay, let's go, then."

We get back to the rental as the sun goes down, the cover of trees giving the illusion of it being darker. As we pull up, Caspian throws it into park and sprints to the building.

My eyes track him to the house as my gaze falls on the wide open door and my heart thrashes in my chest. Caspian disappears inside and I quickly lock the truck. My body feels like a stone in the seat as I wait, glancing around at the treeline for any indication that I need to run. After a long couple minutes, Caspian appears and I click the unlock button as he stalks to the truck, swinging my door open.

"Let's go. The sooner we go to sleep, the sooner we can get the fuck out of here. Nothing will happen while I'm with you."

His words are confident, but there is not a single thing about them that gives me any reassurance. Deciding not to pick this battle, I nod and step out of the truck, following him into the house as he bolts the door closed.

There's stuff thrown everywhere, our bags were rummaged through, but it doesn't look like anything was stolen.

"What do you think they were looking for?"

Caspian's jaw clenches as his gaze flickers to the keys around my neck, but he doesn't answer. Considering how much pain I feel simply turning away from the amulets, I can only imagine how excruciating it would be to have them stolen.

Part of me wonders if I would go numb if I got far enough away or if I'd just pass out from the pain. I shiver at the thought of ever testing that theory.

Caspian must see me shudder and places his large hand on my shoulder, "It's alright, Lara. I don't think the thieves knew what they were looking for. As long as it stays that way, I don't think we have much to worry about."

I'm quiet for a moment before the realization dawns on me, "Do you think the report you got about the warehouse earlier was a precursor to the rental being broken into?"

Something flashes across Caspian's face, but before I can get a read on it, it's gone.

"I don't know," His tone has flattened, and he gestures toward the bedroom, "Shall we?"

Butterflies flutter throughout my body, but they're not the same light and airy ones I felt the first few nights spent with Caspian.

These feel like an omen.

I move to the bedroom, searching for a pair of pajamas and promptly shower. Taking as little time as possible, I adopt the same thought process as he did earlier. The sooner I get to sleep, the faster I can get out of bed, and we can continue looking for Tammy.

I quickly pull on my pajamas, returning to the room as Caspian passes by to shower, saying nothing before he closes the door behind him.

I hear the faucet squeal as the water turns on and my exhaustion from the day settles in. Before he finishes, I'm already fast asleep.

If there's one good thing about sleeping in a bed with Caspian, it's that I don't have nightmares. Or any dreams for that matter.

I fall and stay asleep until one of us wakes up. Once again our limbs are intertwined when I open my eyes, and it's a conscious effort to avoid my body's traitorous desires.

I have to constantly remind myself that simply because Caspian's attractive, doesn't make him a good partner, regardless how attentive he was with his mouth and hand.

Dragging myself out of bed, I go to the washroom to change and put my dirty clothes into my bag. As I'm putting my pajamas away, I see a small folded piece of paper in one of the pockets where I keep my socks.

I frown and glance to the lock on bathroom door, making sure it's turned before unfolding the paper.

Beware the duplicitous nature of your traveling companion. You are not safe.

A warning is the best they could do?

I snort at the notion of someone thinking that I assumed I was safe.

I haven't felt safe a day in my life.

To say he's duplicitous though, implies it is common knowledge to someone else of his deceitful behavior.

Either this individual is trying to warn me or make me trust Caspian less.

Admittedly, I already hardly trust him.

His actions and behavior recently has shown that he's a loose cannon with a one-track mind, and unfortunately it seems less like Tammy is the focus and more so that it's on finding the amulets before his brother does.

A loud knock at the door jolts me from my thoughts, making me jump, and I nearly drop the tiny piece of paper.

"Lara, we gotta go." Caspian's voice is cold and my pulse stutters.

I toss the paper into the toilet and flush it, "Be right out." A wave of relief crashes over me when my voice holds steady, and I watch the paper disappear.

Time to go into this with fresh and open eyes.

We drive three hours to the next town on the list.

It is a small community of people who live pretty far off the beaten path. Their cars are old and worn, and they mostly travel using horses or bikes. We stick out like a sore thumb as we drive through, dust flying behind us as we cruise toward the small cluster of buildings and farming lots.

As we drive past a property, I feel the almost imperceptible tug, followed by a crash of pain that slams into my body and I gasp while shouting to stop, smacking my hand on the window.

Caspian slams on the brakes and the truck fishtails to the side. I fumble to unlock the door in my frantic state. My blood pumping into my ears, the roaring sound of it drowning out his shouts behind me.

As I throw myself out of the truck my knees buckle, giving out beneath me, and I crumple to the ground.

I turn toward the tug and suck in gasps of the dusty air until I cough. The relief from going in the right direction gives my body the strength it needs to carry me as I push myself to my feet. Movement in my peripherals tells me Caspian's made an appearance at my side, and I glance to see shock etched onto his face.

"Is it another amulet?" I really look at him, and though he's asking, he doesn't seem surprised.

He simply looks as if he wants to confirm what he already suspects which furthers the nagging suspicion in the back of my mind that something is off.

It's obvious that my reaction could only be indicative of an amulet nearby, but I let my paranoia and psychoanalysis go.

Realizing that I haven't answered his question as his brows furrow, I nod. "Yes, sorry, that was intense in comparison to the last ones. Must have something to do with us nearly driving past it."

My explanation seems to placate him as he glances at the house with a sigh, "Well, let's go get it then." he says, stepping toward the building and I follow close behind.

We approach the property using the front pathway. It's a large wooden house, painted blue with a white porch that wraps around it.

There's a stable beyond it and another building that reminds me of my father's wood cutting shed at the cottage.

Images flutter through my mind and I flinch.

Caspian must have seen my reaction as he suddenly asks, "You alright? Are we going in the right direction?"

I nod and point toward the wood shed, "The tug is coming from there, but I'm concerned about snooping on someone's private property." I indicate to the horses visible in the stable, and the bikes tied up on the side, "Someone is clearly home."

Caspian glances around in assessment and nods, "Right. I'll go to the shed and look around. You stay here and distract them in case they come out or notice me."

Unease settles in my body, but I nod once as Caspian takes off.

He crouches along the wall of the building, moving until he disappears out of sight and I fiddle in place, facing the direction of the tug as I wait anxiously. I hear some clattering in the house and my limbs tremble with adrenaline.

Time seems to crawl by, and after what feels like an eternity, the tug changes. It grows stronger slightly, and then it's moving. I breathe a sigh of relief as Caspian comes into view along the side of the house and hurries toward me.

"Here." He hands me the amulet in a rush, and relief fills my veins. I catch a glimpse of the intricate depiction of an owl inside as I tuck it away in my pocket, feeling a sense of both relief and apprehension.

"We need to leave, now," he says urgently, and I raise an eyebrow.

"Why?" I ask, confusion and dread whirling in my gut as Caspian remains silent with a guarded expression.

My eyes instinctively scan his body, alarm bells going off as I notice the spatters of blood on his clothes.

"Why are you covered in blood?" I whisper.

"We need to get to the truck." Caspian response, his tone is indifferent again and devoid of any emotion.

Frustration boils within me, and I refuse to let him brush off my question. "Caspian, answer me!" I hiss.

Suddenly, his demeanor changes, and his face contorts with anger. He whirls around to me, his emerald eyes blazing. "I had to kill someone to get the amulet," he confesses through clenched teeth. "Now we need to go."

My mind goes blank as Caspian's words sinks in, and the clattering sound echoing from the house snaps me back to reality. Within seconds we're in the truck, the engine roaring to life as we speed away. My fingers instinctively find the newest amulet, and I grasp it tightly before adding it to the collection hanging around my neck.

As we race through the countryside, I can't shake off the unsettling feeling that whoever gave me the warning is either proving to be right, or has driven a deeper wedge between Caspian and I.

I also can't help but notice how the initial purpose of our journey, the search for Tammy, seems to have been overshadowed by obtaining the amulets.

The questions linger in my mind, but I hesitate to bring them up as Caspian's grip on the wheel tightens. His driving grows more erratic by the moment, and it's clear that something has changed between us since that day at the market.

It's an uncomfortable two-hour drive from the latest amulet to my place.

Familiar road names start to appear and a wave of relief washes over me. My shoulders gradually relax as my thoughts wander to Candace and Henry, to Tammy wherever she is, to Dan.

I wonder if my life will ever be normal again after this.

Bold of me to assume that there will be an 'after this'.

Reaching the familiar driveway of my property instantly lifts my spirits. I eagerly unlock the door, and we make our way inside, flicking the lights on as we go. As I grasp the doorknob to my bedroom, a sudden jolt of surprise and anger runs through me when Caspian tries to push past.

I hold my ground, blocking his path with a firm hand against his chest. "Nope! Not tonight. I sleep in my own bed, alone, with no one else."

His face remains expressionless as he stares at me, the cold, detached look sends nervous sweat down my spine as I bar him from my room.

He could easily overpower me and do it anyways, yet for some surprising reason, he's allowed this.

Sucking in a deep breath as if it were courage itself, I twist him around by his shoulders and firmly push him away from the bedroom. "You get the couch tonight. I need to be alone. I swear to god, Caspian, if I don't have my own bed to myself tonight, the world will serve as witness to my wrath."

I catch the sound of his scoff echoing down the hallway as he retreats.

Step into my bedroom, firmly shutting the door behind me and locking it, I take a moment to collect myself. I'm sure that won't hold if he really wants to get in but, at least it'll buy me some time if he tries to come in unannounced.

What could have changed in such a short amount of time that could have made him act this way?

It's like he's a different person altogether.

Part of me wonders if it had to do with the warehouse incident, but the nagging voice in my head screams at me that the amulets have more to do with it than anything.

That's not even beginning to mention the lack of effort to find Tammy.

Mentally and physically exhausted, I collapse on the bed after tossing my bag to the floor with a deep sigh of relief. As I inhale, the comforting scent of a fresh forest rain invades my senses and I suck in deeply. My muscles begin to relax, as if they're melting into the bed, releasing the tension from the past few days.

Remembering that I still need to shower, I groan before dragging myself from the bed.

I spend extra time showering, soaking up the heat and comfort of the familiarity of my own home. As the water sluices off my body, I glance down to my wrists, inspecting the scabs that have started to peel off, revealing bright red and pink shiny skin underneath.

Just another set of scars to add to the list.

My mind strays to Rose and May. I find myself wondering how they are settling in with Stacey and Dylan. Images of their smiling cake covered faces pop into my head and my chest feels light knowing that if any good came from this, it was getting those two girls out of there.

Trepidation still weighs heavy on me when I consider how or why Caspian was able to get caretakers for the girls as quickly as he did. Clinging to the hope that he is just having a bad week, I set my concerns aside knowing that I can reach out to Rose and May sometime soon to check in on them.

Caspian is such a complex individual that it is frustrating. On one hand he is profoundly observant and quick to act, understanding and nonjudgmental.

On the other, he is cold, callous, calculated and indifferent. I find myself forgiving the negatives to see more of the warmer side of him like getting a hit of some drug. I have to constantly reign my body in to align with my mind knowing that I cannot fully trust him.

I'm not fool enough to believe that I could change him, but I find that he almost seems like he's in conflict with himself on some fundamental level.

In the small moments outside of our search for Tammy, I find his presence calming and enjoyable. The second we begin our hunt, it's as if a switch flips, and he's put walls up and takes on an entirely different demeanor.

I turn the faucet off, snagging a towel to dry myself, lost in my thoughts.

Memories of Dan in the shower when I assumed he was not a 'he' flick through my mind, and I laugh quietly under my breath as I wrap myself in a towel. Grabbing a set of pajamas from the dresser, I dry my hair off and flop dramatically into bed.

My mind continues to process the events of the past few weeks as I lay in bed for hours, unable to stop myself from over-thinking. Slowly, as a fresh wave of forest rain scent washes over me, I succumb to sleep.

Chapter 25

I startle awake to a large hand firmly but gently covering my mouth.

A deep voice whispers into my ear from where I lay, warm breath cascading over my skin making me shiver, "Quiet, I don't want to have to drug you this time. I want this to be your choice but you have to come with me."

My vision adjusts to the dark as I turn my head, coming face to face with Darian's mismatched gaze as he stares at me intensely, his features illuminated by the moonlight peering through my open window.

That doesn't sound like much of a choice at all.

My heart pounds frantically in my chest, nearly stopping as he leans down to my ear again, "I'm going to remove my hand from your mouth, but please do not scream. It won't do you or your missing friend any good."

My eyes narrow at him. Is he threatening me and Tammy or is he saying that exposing him right now will have ramifications?

Darian's calloused hand slowly releases my mouth and I wet my lips before whispering, "Tell me where Tammy is. Where are you keeping her?"

Darian jerks back as if struck and anger flashes across his face, "I haven't done anything other than track where my brother is keeping her. She's in a warehouse on the coast being held captive." his whispers are nearly inaudible but his gaze flicks to the door.

My jaw drops as the realization hits me and I blink at him, "The threat to the warehouse?"

Darian nods slightly, his voice soft as he answers, "Was me, yes."

My heart skips a beat, "And the note?" I ask, searching his face as he nods once.

My head is swirling as he leans closer, eyeing the locked door. His words are hushed but urgent, "We don't have much time, Lara. My brother's intentions for you are not what you think. You are gathering the keys while he holds your friend hostage. You understand what this means when you've found all the keys, yes?"

Images of Tammy being killed alone in a warehouse pop into my head and I look at Darian with a renewed sense of panic.

"And what happens if I leave? Won't he just kill her then?"

"You are the key to him finding the other keys, he won't kill her because you have leverage. We need to leave now though, otherwise he will simply drag you to where he suspects the other keys are, and your friend will die."

I weigh the options present and though everything Caspian's said has led me to believe Darian is the villain, I can't help but feel like he's been painted as such by the true wolf in sheep's clothing.

"Before I go with you, I need you to tell me the truth," Darian nods once so I continue, "17 years ago my parents were killed in a cottage. My father was killed in a wood cutting shed, my mother inside the house and both were burned to the ground. Tell me why you murdered them."

Darian's lips thin as his jaw clenches and pulsates, his mismatched gaze searches my mine for a long moment.

His eyes drop, "Those were not your real parents, Lara. They were not good people, and they had terrible things planned for you and many others. I will explain everything, just, **please**, we need to leave."

He says the last few words, his eyes flick to mine and my entire being gets sucked in. Instinct tells me to accept his explanation as minimal as it is. We don't exactly have the luxury of time and I give him a nod.

Fuck. I hope this is the right call.

He pushes to his feet and my eyes track the movement, accepting the hand he's offering to help me out of bed. He's even taller than I remember, towering over me by more than a foot and I swallow audibly.

Taking one step toward the closet, Darian gently stops me with his hand on my arm and my brows pinch together as I look at him.

He leans in to whisper, and I shiver as his lips brush against my ear. "I have some of your clothes at my place, so we can leave now. Val is waiting for us at the house."

Ignoring that he's already stolen my clothes, I tilt my head and whisper, "Val?"

Darian hands me my running shoes, and as I slide them on, he replies almost inaudibly, a smirk dancing across his handsome face, "The wolf."

Dan is really named Val?

My mind is swirling yet again, overwhelmed with more information than it knows how to handle, and I rub my temples to soothe my aching brain.

Darian chuckles softly as he slings my bag over his shoulder, and just as I reach for my cell on the side table, his hand intercepts mine, halting me abruptly. "Don't. I have a new phone for you at the house, this one has either a copied sim card or your original with a tracker on it, so if you bring it, he will just send people after you and directly to our door."

I feel the blood drain from my face as I gape at him but quickly recover. My hand reaches up to touch the amulets along my neck before silently following Darian out the window.

Chapter 26

Shutting the window behind us, we venture into the dense forest.
The darkness is all encompassing, with occasional glimmers of moonlight penetrating the canopy, casting eerie shadows on the forest floor.

Navigating through the undergrowth, I find myself stumbling not once, but twice, as my feet trip over roots. My ankle twists on uneven ground and I sway, teetering too far to the side as Darian's large hand curls around mine. He tugs me toward him and I manage to keep my balance, but to my surprise he doesn't let go as he leads the way me through a smoother path free of fallen logs and roots.

How does he know where we're going?

It's not long before we come across a narrow pathway much too small for vehicles, but looks to be an ATV road or some kind of maintenance path. Tucked off to the side of this secluded trail in the distance, my gaze fixates on a sleek, gray and black motorcycle that stands like a sentinel, with its dark hues blending seamlessly with the surrounding shadows.

Oh my god, I'm going to die.

I hear Darian's chuckle and can't help but glance at him, finding his eyes already fixated on my reaction.

Heat rises to my cheeks, "I've never been on one of these before." I admit, nervous butterflies making my stomach do flips.

He responds, his tone laced with playful encouragement, "There's a first time for everything, Lara."

My cheeks burn hotter.

We reach the motorcycle and Darian passes me helmet, holding it in my direction. "Put this on," he instructs, "It might be a little big, but it'll protect your skull in case of an accident."

I blink at him, a hint of excitement mixing with my nervousness, and I quickly slip my head inside the helmet, eliciting a chuckle from Darian. His handsome features turn focused as he secures the strap under my chin before he gracefully climbs onto the bike, gesturing for me to take a seat behind him.

My heart gallops in my chest and I move closer, throwing my leg over the top, straddling the seat but giving a full inch of space between us as I grip the sides of his jacket.

My uncertainty with every aspect of this is on clear display as he laughs quietly before taking hold of my hands, tugging them across his waist securely.

Heat once again rushes to my cheeks, intensifying the blush that was already painted on them as he squeezes my hands against his abdomen.

Thank god I have a helmet on.

"Move forward a bit more, so you're pressed against me. Once we start moving, I don't want you sliding off the back," Darian instructs, tapping my right knee to emphasize his point.

Heat courses through my entire body, turning my limbs into molten lava. I obediently shift forward, aligning our thighs and pressing myself closer to him, but his hands grip the back of my knees, pulling me flush against him until I'm more so straddling him rather than the seat. My grasp around his waist tightens as I lean into his shirt, freezing as the familiar scent of forest rain envelops my senses. I realize in that moment, it emanates from him, and my mind races to make sense of it.

"Hold on tight," he says, his voice barely audible over the roar of the engine as it comes to life beneath us. Within seconds, we're off, speeding down the path with an exhilarating rush.

The first minute of the ride is intense as the wind whips against my skin and the sensation of being so exposed takes some getting used to. It's not long before I'm embracing the adrenaline rush, and the ride becomes a thrill, each passing moment filled with excitement and freedom.

We merge onto the main road, and Darian accelerates, propelling us forward with exhilarating speed. The scenery blurs as we zoom down the open road, and contagious laughter escapes my lips as he skillfully maneuvers the bike, effortlessly weaving from one side of the empty highway to the other.

I can never give Henry shit for reckless driving, ever again.

After some time, Darian veers onto a well hidden path, cleverly disguised to resemble a frequented deer crossing.

"Where are we?" I shout over the rumble of the engine as we navigate through the overgrown path.

"On the other side of the lake you've been researching," Darian replies, his voice tinged with a mischievous tone. If I could see his face, I'm confident there would be a smirk accompanying his statement. I can't help but fight back a grin of my own, even with my helmet on.

We make a wide turn into a clearing and my jaw drops in awe.

The house before us is grand yet modest, exuding the charm of a cottage but on a much larger scale than any I've encountered. It could easily accommodate seven people with ample space to spare.

Perched just a stone's throw away from the lake, the house is merely 20 feet from the crashing waves and a picturesque sandy beach reflecting the moonlight and brightening the whole area.

"This is stunning," I breathe, my eyes drinking in the incredible scenery around us.

"Thank you. I built it myself," he says with a touch of pride, guiding the bike into a garage connected to the house and switching off the engine.

"You built all of this yourself?" I can't hide the disbelief in my voice, which prompts Darian to burst into laughter.

"Yes, believe it or not. I'm quite the carpenter without magic. This was a fulfilling project that kept me busy for a while," he explains as he helps me dismount the bike, a hint of satisfaction evident in his tone.

The memories of Caspian's words about Darian's obsession with magic flood my mind. "So, this is what you did when your magic was bound from Earth twenty-five years ago?" I inquire, trying to piece together the timeline.

Darian's expression softens, and he gently corrects me, "No, Lara. This is what I started over 150 years ago when my brother was banished, and because we share the same bloodline, I was as well." he says with a sad smile.

My eyes widen into saucers, "Banished?" I ask, my voice comes out as a squeak and I wince internally.

Well this just got more complicated.

I remove the helmet, my gaze fixed on Darian's back as he unlocks the garage door with a combination of his fingerprint and a randomized code from his phone.

"Banished," he confirms, his voice laced with bitterness. "Seems like my brother conveniently forgot to mention that minor detail."

I let out a weary sigh and rub my temples. "Of course he did," I say, my voice thick with sarcasm.

I can't help but wonder what else he conveniently omitted.

Darian's gaze softens as he turns toward me, "I understand your apprehension, Lara. I really do. All I ask is for a chance to show you who I truly am. I'll do my best to fill in the gaps and provide the missing pieces of the puzzle. Hopefully, with time, you'll come to see that I'm not the person my brother may have portrayed me to be."

I meet Darian's gaze, "He painted you as quite the villain, Darian."

Darian's expression changes, and he pauses for a moment before responding, "I don't doubt that I'm somebody's villain. There are things I'm not proud of, actions that have caused pain to others. But it's important to remember that every story has two sides, Lara."

Darian's words echo in my mind as I follow him through the open door and down a short hallway. Entering the main living area connected to the kitchen, I take in the cozy ambiance of the space as Darian gently places my bag in what appears to be a spare bedroom before disappearing beyond the doorway.

The room is adorned with simple yet comfortable furnishings, creating a welcoming atmosphere amidst the unfamiliar environment.

There are no visible gaps or flaws in the construction of it, a testament to the attention to detail that Darian put into its design. Modern lighting fixtures illuminate each room, casting a warm and inviting glow.

Moving into the kitchen, he's combined practicality with contemporary style, and it's evident that no expense was spared in outfitting this space, with top-of-the-line appliances.

From the well-crafted construction to the modern amenities, every aspect of this house exudes a sense of quality and comfort. It's clear that he put great care in creating a home that offers both sanctuary and modern convenience.

I sink into a chair in the kitchen, feeling exhaustion weigh heavily on my mind as I close my eyes, rubbing them with the palms of my hands. My attention is caught by the faint sound of nails clattering against the floor and my eyes snap open as Dan -Val- hurries into the room.

Relief nearly overwhelms me, and I throw myself toward him, wrapping my arms tightly around his thick, fur-covered neck.

I whisper softly, my words muffled against his warm coat, "I've been worried about you."

Darian's voice breaks through my reverie, dripping with amusement. "You think you were worried? Val has been driving me absolutely insane. I was tempted to take him to the pound just to get a moment's peace." he says with a grin.

Val huffs and shakes his fur in a purely canine manner before settling against me as he and Darian share a look, as if they have some form of silent communication.

Confusion swirls in my mind and I cock my head to the side, "Wait, so you two have a history together..." I state, trailing off to prompt Darian to fill in the blanks.

Val's ears twitch, and Darian heaves a sigh, as if resigned to explaining the situation. "I suppose since I'm the only one capable of verbalizing it, I'll do the honors," Darian says, a touch of feigned annoyance lace his words. "Val is like a brother to me, despite the absence of a blood relation. We've known one another for nearly two centuries," Darian explains, "During one of his visits to me magic was bound here, and he happened to be in his wolf form at the time. He's remained this way ever since."

As the puzzle pieces click into place, I blink at him. "So, when I escaped..."

Darian interrupts, completing my thought. "When you ran from the safehouse, I sent Val to help guide you."

My gaze narrows, suspicion tugging at my thoughts. "You sent Val after me but not the man that..." I trail off, the words hanging in the air.

Val's ears pin back and he growls.

Darian shakes his head, "I haven't sent anyone other than Val," he says, his voice thick with remorse, "My intention was solely to ensure your well-being, to protect you from starving or dying in the forest. I didn't know where you were headed or where your path would lead."

"I understand why you might think the hunters were my doing, especially considering Caspian's accusations. I wasn't lying when I said I work alone," Darian winces, "I suppose I did lie. Val is the only exception to that."

His honesty is refreshing, and if I'm honest with myself, it's hard not to trust him already. It doesn't help that I'm confident I can rely on Val, and if Val trusts Darian, he's in my good graces.

But this means that much of what I've been told by Caspian is a lie, including that Darian sent the Leathery Man after me.

And if he didn't send him...

A mixture of emotions wells up within me, I let out a strangled laugh as memories of the leathery man and the dangers I've faced since that day in the forest flood my mind.

Val leans his weight onto me more, and I cling to him tightly.

"I should never have run from you." I say, my voice thick with regret as Val whimpers softly.

Darian levels me with an assessing gaze, and for a moment I almost can see the knowledge of centuries on his face before he responds, "You had no idea what my brother was doing. Ther's no way you could have known I wasn't there to hurt you."

I let out a wry laugh. "Well, being drugged and tied to a chair certainly doesn't scream 'this is for your protection', I suppose."

Darian winces, "No, it wasn't my finest moment." he admits, scratching the back of his head.

There's a long moment of silence as I contemplate the events after meeting Darian, "Caspian's explanation of that night was filled with inconsistencies. In hindsight, I shouldn't have accepted it at face value," I confess, my voice laced with a mix of regret and frustration. "I remember hearing Val's howls in the distance while I was bound to the bed. That tiny shrivel of hope was what kept me going... even as he..." I pause, my words catching in my throat as it tightens with emotion.

Darian, to his credit, remains attentive as I struggle to find the words.

"When Val attacked him and Caspian freed me from the bed, I didn't immediately question how I was found, I simply assumed that Val had somehow led Caspian to me. But now that I think about it, it does seem like more than a mere coincidence that Caspian happened to be in the vicinity, doesn't it?" I nervously meet Darian's gaze, somehow hoping that my suspicions aren't true.

Darian remains silent for a long moment, his jaw tense as he grinds his teeth. I search his face, my gaze dropping to his mouth as he finally responds, "I won't jump to conclusions, assume the worst and accuse my brother of premeditating what happened to you during your captivity," he says, his words deliberate as he continues, "But considering that the man who held you captive was working for him, it's highly likely that Caspian was aware of your location at the very least."

I nod, my gaze fixed on the floor as I absentmindedly stroke Val's furry head. We sit in silence for a long moment, and I'm grateful for having the time to process it.

"So..." My voice is hesitant as I struggle to find the right words. Being forward and blunt isn't typically my style, but this situation calls for it considering how much disinformation I've been given.

"So," Darian echoes, a trace of amusement in his voice.

"You don't want magic back?" I ask, genuinely curious whether Caspian was lying or not.

Darian's smirk deepens before he responds. "Oh, I want it back more than anything." My heart drops, until he continues, "But what I don't want is for my brother to regain his abilities."

My jaw drops in astonishment. "You would sacrifice your own magic, and essentially your freedom, just to keep him bound?"

Darian nods resolutely. "Yes."

Is he truly that bad?

I suppose after his recent behavior, I could fathom how Caspian could be that terrible, but there were times he was kind, caring and perceptive. It makes no sense.

"Why?" I ask, cringing at my accusatory tone.

"My brother has committed countless terrible acts in his life, Lara. Some of the most unforgivable things. He was banished for his insatiable quest for power, his relentless pursuit of becoming a god," Darian explains, "He was banished by the Gods for his misdeeds."

The Gods? I truly have gone insane.

I remain silent as Darian's hands flex repeatedly at his sides, a clear sign of the memories and traumas that still haunt him.

"What did he do?" I ask softly, my voice barely audible but his jaw clamps shut, clearly not ready to delve that deep into his past.

I suppose I'm not the only one unable to talk about my traumas.

Silence lingers between us, and I decide to do us both a favor, shifting gears to steer the conversation away from the darker revelations. "So, you mentioned that my parents weren't really my parents,"

Darian's eyes snap to mine and relief flickers across his face at the subject change.

"That's correct. I don't have all the details, but from what I know, your biological parents were missing, and you were born during the time when magic was bound. Your adoptive parents, the ones you knew as your parents, were actually from our realm, not Earth. They practiced blood magic and performed rituals that involved sacrificing lives to temporarily nourish their own magical abilities. I believe my brother suspected you were to play a role in the restoration of magic but was unable to move forward with it until recently."

My jaw drops, "So when you came to the cottage that day..."

Darian nods, finishing my sentence for me, "I knew they were planning to make a sacrifice that night."

I exhale heavily, shaking my head. "This is all so overwhelming, Darian."

His expression softens, "I know, Lara. It's a lot to take in, and I'm sorry for burdening you with all of it at once. But you deserve to know the truth."

Darian's jaw tenses as our eyes lock, and I don't miss the remorse in them. If he's lying about any of this, he deserves an award, "For what it's worth, and it may not be worth much, but I am truly sorry for every part I have played in your suffering. It was never my intention, and I cannot undo the past, but I can promise to do everything in my power to make things right."

I pinch my lips together and nod, feeling the weight of his words setting in. We remain silent for a moment, before his voice breaks through the quiet. "I'll show you to your room," he says gently. "Val can sleep with you if you'd prefer. If you need me, I'm just across the hall."

I raise a brow at him. "So I'm not a prisoner?" I ask, half joking but the humor in my question falls flat.

Darian looks at me earnestly. "Do you wish to leave?" he asks, his tone genuinely curious.

The thought of venturing out on my own, exposed and vulnerable until Caspian inevitably tracks me down sends a shiver along my spine.

I shake my head.

He's got me there.

"No, I don't." I reply.

And it's true. The last thing I want is to be caught up by more hunters or stuck in Caspian's endless list of lies. I've gotten more information from Darian tonight than I got from Caspian in the days we were together.

"In the morning, we can discuss further plans on how to free your friend and consider whether it's necessary to locate the rest of the amulets," he offers, as if I have as much say in how we approach what comes next as he does.

Wait...

I jerk back, not bothering to mask my surprise, "So you are aware they're amulets?"

Darian's voice deepens, coming out as a low growl, "I became aware when my brother nearly had you on your knees with one at the farmer's market," his tone laced with anger.

So that was him under the tree.

I feel less insane now...

Slightly.

I grimace, "You saw that?" I ask, a healthy dose of embarrassment washes over me.

Darian's response is firm. "I believe anyone with a functioning pair of eyes could see the pain you were enduring," he states plainly.

Which means Caspian also knew and did it regardless.

A shudder runs through me, and Val lifts his head, gazing at me with concerned eyes as Darian rises from his seat, moving toward the hallway that leads to the bedrooms.

"Come on," he says gently, gesturing for me to follow. "Let's get some rest tonight and tackle our problems tomorrow."

I give a nod, grateful for the respite as Val and I trail behind him to our respective rooms.

Chapter 27

A heavy weight presses down on my body, and panic threatens to take hold, but a soft whimper draws my attention.

My eyes snap open, only to be met with Val's hazel gaze locked onto mine. He gently lifts himself off my body and settles alongside me on the bed.

Inhaling deeply to calm my nerves, I rub my hand on his cheek to his ear. "Is it safe to assume I was having a nightmare?"

His ears twitch, and he responds with a quiet huff.

"Thank you, for everything," I say gently, and he nuzzles my shoulder, releasing a snort.

A giggle bubbles out of me, and I smile at him, appreciating the moment of lightheartedness.

"You know," I drawl, "this may be a bit taboo of me to say, but as much as I know I shouldn't ever look forward to magic return-ing because of Caspian, I can't help but anticipate a day when we can actually have a conversation, you and I."

Val gives me a full snort before he flops into my lap, rolling onto his back, his legs flailing in the air and I laugh even harder at his antics. "Am I to assume this means you want a belly rub?" I tease, knowing exactly what he's after.

He wiggles on his back, tail wagging furiously.

Amidst the laughter, a knock sounds at the door, and my heart stutters, but I manage to call out, "Come in!" through my giggles.

Darian's impressive form steps into the room and dark blue jeans. As he enters, his black t-shirt barely covers the muscles of his tattooed arms, and they strain against his sleeves as they cross over his chest. The veins in his forearms are on full display, and as he leans on the door frame, locking his legs in front of him, I can't help but appreciate the dark blue jeans that hug him perfectly.

For a moment, the mental image of him hulking out, turning green and everything triggers another wave of laughter and I find myself unable to stop as I rub Val's belly.

Darian's lips twitch, clearly amused Val embracing his canine mannerisms.

After a few long moments, I finally manage to collect myself and the laughter subsides as Darian clears his throat, his baritone voice still somehow gentle.

It's the concern in his face that brings me crashing back to reality, "My brother has noticed your absence and has sent teams of hunters to find you," Darian says, and I shift my gaze between him and Val as they share a look.

Do they have some kind of secret language or something?

I clasp my hands together in my lap in an effort to calm the nervous energy filling my body, "So what do we do?" I ask.

Darian's brows furrow as he rubs his jaw thoughtfully. "We have a few options," he begins, his tone serious. "Option one: We tell my brother that we will find the remaining amulets, but he must release your friend unharmed. Option two: We don't tell him anything and we search for the remaining amulets ourselves."

My head jerks back in confusion, the weight of Darian's words sinking in. "We're going to continue hunting for the amulets?" My voice filled with surprise.

Darian's neck muscles visibly tense. "Yes," he confirms, his voice resolute. "We are going to break the binding on magic ourselves."

I gape at him, my eyes widening in disbelief.

He said last night that he doesn't want magic back?

Was he lying?

Suspicion coats my body, and I start to wonder if I made the wrong decision in coming here.

His eyes burn into mine, doing nothing to calm my heart rate, "If we don't find them," he explains, speaking as if he has considered all possible options and outcomes, "Caspian will never stop hunting you. Your life, the lives of your friends and everyone you hold dear, will be caught in the crossfire. Not to mention civilian casualties."

Glancing over at Val, his face looks somber as his gaze rests on the bed and my chest falls in resignation. With a last ditch effort, I voice the lingering question in my mind.

"But what about the 'Gods'? Won't they be displeased if we break the binding? Aren't they going to smite us or something?"

As I gesture in the air with my fingers, emphasizing the word 'Gods,' and Darian shoots me a look.

The seriousness in his voice gives me pause, "Regardless of your beliefs, they exist, and I'd recommend against mocking them."

I can't help but roll my eyes. "Well, forgive me if I don't feel particularly grateful to the divine beings who banished their own 'Darth Sidious' to wreak havoc in my world."

Darian chuckles at my Star Wars reference, and I shoot him a deadpan look before considering our choices and their potential consequences.

An extended silence stretches between us and eventually, I let out a resigned sigh.

"I suppose we have no choice but to inform him that we intend to search for the remaining keys."

Darian raises an eyebrow. "Oh?"

"If we choose not to inform him, he might act impulsively, potentially endangering Tammy and others I care about. If we tell him we're to find the remaining keys, he might call off the hunters, under the belief that he's getting what he wants. The worst-case scenario of informing him is that we will still be pursued."

Darian nods thoughtfully and pushes off the wall, making his way toward the bed. As he reaches me, he retrieves his phone from his pocket and dials a number before handing me the device.

"Just press send when you're ready," he instructs, "I've blocked the number. Try to keep the call brief. Even though it's blocked, they can still trace it, but it will slow them down. They'll need to obtain the call data from the carrier, which takes at least 24 hours."

I nod and take a few deep breaths to steady myself before pressing the dial button. The phone rings once, and I hear his voice on the other end, filled with irritation.

"What do you want?" he snaps.

I keep my gaze fixed on Darian, who stands tall above me, his eyes flashing with anger.

"Caspian," I say, my voice steady.

"Lara? Where are you? Are you hurt?" His tone sounds concerned, but I can see through it.

I roll my eyes at his words, unimpressed by his act.

How did I ever fall for it?

Stupid girl.

Centering myself, I keep my voice flat. "Stop, Caspian. I know everything," I say, sucking in a deep breath before continuing. "I'm going to search for the remaining amulets on my own. In exchange for finding them, I want Tammy released."

Silence hangs in the air, and I double-check the phone to ensure I'm still connected.

"Caspian," I repeat, prompting him to respond.

"You know nothing." His voice drips with lethal calmness, sending shivers down my spine.

Ignoring him, I reiterate my demands firmly, "Release her unharmed, and I'll find the remaining amulets for you."

"It's my brother, isn't it?" His chuckle resonates through the phone, followed by a deep sigh that seems almost relieved. "Of course it is. I should have known."

Tense silence hangs between us before Caspian resumes speaking, his tone hard, "Bring me the amulets, and I will release her. She will remain unharmed, for now. Delay in finding them, and I can't guarantee she'll be in one piece," he counters, his threat hanging heavy in the air.

I feel a surge of anger bubbling up within me, but I manage to maintain my composure as I grit out through clenched teeth, "Hurt her, Caspian, and it will be the last thing you do."

Caspian responds with a mocking laugh, "Oh, come now, little one. Did the kitten finally grow some claws?"

I remain silent, refusing to engage further with his taunts as he lays out the next steps, "I'll send my brother the general locations of where we know the amulets are located. Bring them all to me, and I promise she will be released."

"Unharmed," I interject firmly.

"Unharmed," he parrots, his annoyance evident in his voice. I can almost picture him rolling his eyes on the other end of the line.

Hanging up the phone, relief and anxiety wash over me as I blow out a shaky breath. Darian takes his cell from me, placing it into his pocket before grasping my hands with his, and only then do I realize they're trembling.

I meet his gaze, "You do not need to fear him, Lara," he says in a gentle tone, his thumbs rubbing the back of my hands in a soothing manner.

I furrow my brows, "And why is that?"

He winks and gives my hands a reassuring squeeze. "There are scarier things that go bump in the night," he says, a ghost of a smile on his face as he walks out of the room.

I blink in surprise before glancing at Val, "Does he always act so cool and mysterious?"

Val lets out a huff of air, nudging my hand once, and trots after Darian and I realize that there's still so much I've yet to learn about the three of them.

After taking a refreshing shower, I open the closet to find it filled with a variety of clothes. The dresser drawers are neatly organized with underwear, pajamas, socks, and bras. My cheeks flush with a mix of embarrassment and gratitude as I imagine Darian gathering all these items while I was away.

How the hell did he get in and out of the house without tripping the alarm?

Slipping into a pair of comfortable shorts and a tank top before heading to the kitchen, I find Darian already busy serving up a delicious spread of waffles and fruit onto several plates. He adds a dollop of whipped cream to each one and generously drizzles maple syrup over Val's plate before placing it on the ground. Val's tail wags excitedly, and I can't help but grin at his enthusiasm.

Darian glances at me and lets out a chuckle. "Waffles are his favorite. But add maple syrup, and it's..." he says, placing his hands in the air as if to emphasize his point.

I raise an eyebrow, "And here I thought it was the whipped cream that sent him over the moon," I remark, my voice filled with amusement.

Darian laughs loudly, his smile genuine and my heart nearly stops in my chest at the sight, "Unfortunately, pup cups are not his preferred treat," he says, sliding a cup of coffee and a tray of creamers and sugar my way.

I sit at the table and eagerly take a bite of the waffle. It's so good that I can't help but groan in delight, placing my head against the back of my hands in sheer bliss.

It's fluffy, crunchy, and sweet but not overpowering.

Fuck, this is good.

Darian chuckles at my reaction, and I raise my head to meet his gaze.

"Is it safe to assume the waffles meet your standards, too?" He asks, his mismatched eyes bright with amusement.

I reply with a nod as Darian's phone chimes on the table. I watch as he briefly checks the message and his expression grows serious.

Sensing the sudden tension in the air, I speak softly, "Time to go?"

He nods, "We leave in 30."

"I'll go get dressed then. Any idea where we're going?" I ask, mentally preparing to gather my things.

Darian rubs his jaw thoughtfully, "It looks like we're heading to the coast."

A wave of apprehensive excitement crashes over me, knowing we're going to be closer to Tammy. We quickly pack our carry-ons while Darian arranges a flight. He's been on the phone intermittently since we received the location, and although I can't hear his conversations, he seems to be incredibly focused on setting up our trip.

Following him to the garage with my bag in tow, he pulls back a large tarp off of a sleek black truck, placing our carry-ons behind the seat as Val settles in beside them.

"We were able to arrange for Val to come with us on the plane?" I ask, curious why he'd be coming with us if he is unable to fly.

Darian mouth curves into a grin, "Yes, we're taking my private jet. It'll be just the three of us. We'll head to the executive airport nearby, and it'll be a direct flight."

I gape at him.

A private jet? Who is this guy?

His eyes sparkle with amusement at my reaction, "Have you ever been on a private jet before?"

I shake my head in response, a mixture of guilt and excitement conflict within me as I quietly justify the use of a private jet, and we make our way to the airport.

Chapter 28

We leave the truck in a quiet satellite lot just outside the airport, before entering the main doors of the building to check in. After passing through security, we navigate past the bustling corridor lined with small fine dining restaurants, and various lounges on the way to our designated gate.

I stop abruptly, feeling the familiar tug and I freeze.

In an airport of all places?!

Darian takes a few more steps ahead before he realizes that I've stopped and turns to look at me, his brows furrowing in concern. Val moves to stand by my side protectively, his gaze fixed on my hand resting on my abdomen.

I slowly turn to my left and let out a gasp as a sharp pain shoots through my body and Darian quickly comes to my side glancing around briefly.

"Here, it's probably this way." He says, his hand firmly gripping my elbow to provide support as he guides me in the other direction and gradually the pain subsides, transforming into a strong, persistent tug.

We arrive in front of a Tiffany & co., and Darian places our carry-ons outside while I stand in the doorway, sucking in a deep breath.

I go move, but Darian places his hand between us, stopping me in my tracks.

"I'll search for it. You stay here, alright?"

I blink at him. "Stay here?" I ask, confused why he wouldn't want me to confirm he's got the right amulet in a store filled with necklaces.

He nods confidently. "I know what they look like. I'll find and bring it to you instead of..." He trails off but we both know exactly what he was referring to.

Still. What's the catch?

I eye him warily and tracking his movements as he enters the store, walking through the aisles with purpose. Eventually, his attention settles on a case and an employee approaches him, gesturing to the selection beneath him. Darian stretches his arm out, pointing to one of the displays to the side and without uttering another word he hands over his card.

"One amulet, coming right up." he says with a grin, the bag in his outstretched hand, and as I take it, a wave of relief washes over me.

Reaching into the bag, I carefully retrieve the dainty piece of jewelry and hold it in my hands, examining the intricate details of a beautifully carved bow in its center, adorned with delicate arrows that float with the liquid encased in the pendant.

There's no way this is so easy. There was hardly any discomfort.

What did Caspian gain from having me find the amulets?

Tearing my gaze from the jewelry, I glance at Darian, still in awe. "I... thank you," I whisper and emotions tighten my throat.

Darian nods, a soft expression on his face, and gestures toward the gate.

We make our way onto the tarmac, where the sleek jet is already awaiting our arrival. Stairs extend from the aircraft to the ground where a figure who exudes an air of authority stands at the base of the steps.

"Terry," he says with a nod that Terry reciprocates, taking out bags and motioning for us to ascend the stairs.

The plane is spacious and my jaw remains slack as I do a full 360. Two sets of plush chairs on each side provide ample seating with what looks to be a queen-sized bed in the middle large enough to accommodate multiple people. Adjacent to it, a mini bar catches my attention, with a private washroom further down the aisle.

Holy fuck this is cool.

I hear an amused chuckle and turn toward the source, finding Darian looking at me with a smile on his face. Once again, the sight of it sends my heart into overdrive as I find myself glancing to his mouth, unable to keep my focus on his eyes.

It should be illegal to have a smile this attractive.

"I should have recorded your reaction. That was priceless," he says with a grin.

I suppress a smile, and give him a forced glare before striding over to claim a seat as Val walks past me, heading straight for the bed area and promptly curling up on it as if he's done this a million times.

The flight attendant approaches us with a warm smile. "Good morning, Mr. Cathorn. It's good to see you again. And a pleasure to meet you, Ms. Ray," she greets us. "Is there anything I can assist you with before we depart?"

Cathorn?

I file that information away to process and look up later.

Darian glances to me momentarily, and I shake my head. The last thing I need to do is drink with him. I already can't keep my eyes to myself.

My avoidance is short lived as he turns his attention back to the flight attendant, "Two glasses of pinot, please, Heather," he says politely, and surprisingly professional.

I groan internally. There's no way I'll turn down a good glass of pinot.

She nods, looking between us with a smile, "Of course, Mr. Cathorn. I'll bring them right away." She walks over to the mini bar, preparing the glasses and my head snaps in Darian's direction.

"It's early morning! Is it a habit to be drinking before noon?" I whisper, as if I hadn't taken multiple tequila shots less than a week ago with Caspian at a similarly ridiculous time.

That was then, and this is now.

Darian snorts, waving a hand dismissively. "Come on, Lara. Live a little. Life is too short to worry about time constraints on things like the consumption of alcohol."

That's rich coming from someone centuries old.

Soon after Heather returns, placing them on the table in front of us. "Here you go," she says with a smile. "Enjoy your flight."

I can't hide the grin on my face as I pick up the glass of pinot and take a sip, "Damn, that's smooth." I whisper, eagerly swallowing another small sip.

The flight attendant comes back into view as she proceeds to the middle of the room, providing us with a safety demonstration, highlighting the emergency exits, and reminding us to fasten our seatbelts.

As she leaves, I notice Darian's demeanor change as his impressive form relaxes into his seat, and he takes a long, drawn out sip of his wine, tossing me a knowing wink when he catches me staring at his mouth.

My heart skips a beat, and my cheeks warm.

I'm in so much trouble.

The pilot's voice crackles through the audio system, but his words are garbled and difficult to comprehend. I give up trying to decipher the message and instead turn my attention to the window as we taxi toward the runway.

The plane's engines grow louder, and my stomach flutters in response. It's a familiar sensation that always accompanies takeoff.

Gripping the arms of my chair, My eyes squeeze shut as I take a deep breath, feeling the engines roar as we mark our final turn to the runway.

I startle at a sudden intrusion into my personal space, and my eyes snap wide open to find Darian leaning over me. His hands rest on either side of my body, his face mere inches away from mine. His mismatched gaze captures my attention completely as I forget how to breathe.

A surge of warmth spreads through me like wildfire amidst an ocean of tinder, igniting a deep fire within my core. It's as if he's sucked the air from the plane itself as his proximity overwhelms me and my cheeks flush deeply.

No one has ever affected me like this in my life, and it's equally infuriating as it is concerning.

His large hands brush against the sides of my hips, their slow movement sending shivers down my spine and my heart pounds in my throat. With a deliberate and measured pace, his fingertips gradually make their way into my lap, intensifying the electric tension between us.

What is he...?

A rush of heat engulfs my entire body, making it feel as though I'm being consumed by the scorching intensity of the sun as I squeeze my thighs together. In the midst of this overwhelming sensation, I hear a subtle click that pulls my attention downward.

To my surprise, Darian has securely fastened my seatbelt in my lap and I blink down at the metal clasp before lifting my gaze to his.

The aircraft surges forward as a faint smirk graces his lips, amusement dancing in his mismatched eyes as he settles back into his seat as if nothing out of the ordinary just occurred.

The heat in my cheeks burns hotter, and I'm momentarily lost for words, both bewildered and flustered by his actions.

Stupid girl.

As we reach cruising altitude, after Darian and I have stretched our legs, he sets up a movie on one of the large wall-mounted TVs. Time seems to fly as the film progresses, and before I know it, the end credits start rolling marking the halfway point of our flight.

Deciding this is a good opportunity to stretch my legs and move around a bit, I push to my feet to alleviate some of the stiffness that has settled in my muscles.

Not wanting to trouble Heather for drinks any further, I opt to retrieve the pinot myself, glancing at Darian, a mischievous smile.

"Wine?" I ask, raising an eyebrow.

He nods, extending his glass toward me and I playfully swipe it from his grasp before moving to the mini bar, a slight sway in my step. Like a sixth sense, I feel Darian following close behind as I open the bottle of wine, pouring its contents into our awaiting cups.

We stand there for a moment and I lean back against the bar, taking a long, leisurely sip and curiosity fueled by the wine emboldens me.

"So, do you have any family living in the realm you're from?"

Darian's gaze falls to the floor, his expression turning distant.

My heart drops as I'm certain my first question to get to know him ultimately ruined the lighthearted mood.

There's a heaviness in the cabin and his voice carries a hint of sorrow as he speaks, "I have no blood relatives," he begins, "Caspian killed our parents and nearly took my life as well. The only family I have left are my closest friends, the ones I consider my true brothers. That said, with the magic being bound, outside of Val, I don't know what's come of them in recent years."

I swallow hard. "Caspian... he killed your..." I whisper softly, trailing off as I struggle to comprehend the scars he bears, both visible and not.

Darian's features harden as he no doubt recalls the memories. "Yes," he says, "Caspian is responsible for the loss of our parents, my eye, and these scars. I should have died that day."

A long moment of silence passes between us before I decide to change the subject to what I hope is a slightly better memory for him, "These brothers of yours," I say, meeting his gaze. "Tell me about them."

Darian's silence lingers for a brief moment, but soon, a small smile graces his handsome features, lighting up his eyes as he recalls fond memories.

"Each of them are fierce, loyal, and determined to be royal pains in my ass." he says with a grin.

"I met Cade when I was still young," Darian begins, "And then Kieran and Zayne entered our lives a few years later. We formed a bond that was unbreakable at that point. Then, when I was thirty-five, we found Gray. And eventually, Valerian became a part of our family as well. From that point on, we were inseparable."

Val's full name is Valerian?

He swirls his wine in the glass as he continues, "I've always felt a deep sense of responsibility for them," Darian admits quietly, "And in a way, I've felt like I failed them by being away for so long. I don't know if they'll understand why no one has returned, where I went, or if I even had a way to get back to them and our people. All I can hope for is that they watch out for each other and keep one another safe."

"Kieran," Darian begins, a soft smile gracing his lips. "He was the peacekeeper among us. Whenever conflicts arose, he was the one who would resolve our disputes. He had the remarkable ability to see beyond our differences and find common ground. Kieran was the glue that kept us together,"

"Cade, on the other hand, was not the most personable individual. He had a certain enigmatic quality that set him apart. He was often misunderstood, known to initiate conflicts simply because others couldn't fully grasp his perspective or intentions."

Darian laughs quietly, "Gray... he was a force to be reckoned with. Unhinged might be an understatement in describing him. I remember a time when one of the acolytes took something that belonged to Kieran, Gray stabbed him in the eye, all while laughing, and then tried to trade the eye back to its original owner in exchange for what was taken. When the acolyte refused, Gray tossed the eye into the waters where the seers practiced their premonitions, and then asked the individual if he could see a future where the eye grows back."

I blink at Darian, catching the subtle twitch of his lips as he reminisces, "Zayne... he was the epitome of strategy and precision. A mastermind in his own right. If I ever needed someone to plan a war or execute a flawless assassination, Zayne was the one I could rely on without a shred of doubt. His ability to calculate every move, anticipate every outcome, and adapt to any situation was truly remarkable."

A deeply ingrained sadness flickers across Darian's features as if the memories of his brothers alone transport him back to those cherished moments, that forever remain out of reach.

It makes my entire soul ache.

"How old were you when your brother was banished from the realm?" I ask softly.

He holds my gaze for a long moment, as if unsure how I'll react, "I was fifty. It's been almost two hundred years since I was separated from my realm."

He finishes his drink before collecting both our glasses, placing them carefully in a holder within a nearby cupboard, and I can't help but imagine the pain that would accompany being torn away from cherished friends like Candace, Henry, and Tammy.

Suddenly, the aircraft unexpectedly jolts with turbulence and my balance is thrown off. I stumble forward, losing my own footing as I fall face-first into Darian's chest.

Instinctively, he places his arm gently around the small of my back, steadying me as I lean against him. The contact between us sends a surge of warmth coursing through my body, reigniting the undeniable sensation in my core.

It's just the wine.

I quickly try to recover and mask my reaction, using both hands to push off of Darian's abdomen, my fingers inadvertently tracing the contours of his well-defined muscles along his stomach, while my heart hammers erratically in my chest.

Despite my attempt to create distance, his hand remains firmly planted on the small of my back, keeping me pressed against him, intensifying the heat that engulfs my insides.

The wave of desire courses through me, and my thighs squeeze together, struggling to maintain my composure and remain upright.

"I-I should go sit down." I breathe as the jet continues to hit turbulence and I find myself bracing against Darian's solid frame once more.

"Mmm. Probably a good idea." he responds, his voice thick with desire that entirely mirrors my own, sending shivers down my spine.

I inhale deeply as I retreat a step, attempting to regain my composure, before unsteadily moving back to my seat.

You made it in one piece, Lara. Good job.

My emotions, however, are far from being in one piece.

A shudder runs through me as I recall the last time I felt desire and intimacy with someone, as guilt laden memories of that night swirl in my mind. A cold dread settles in the pit of my stomach, reminding me of the consequences that came with such vulnerability.

Don't make the same mistake twice, Lara.

Chapter 29

As we start our descent, the environment below turns from a pale sand color to a swirl of green reaching into mountain ranges. In the distance, the ocean paints the horizon a deep blue, and it's nearly impossible to know where it ends.

We remain seated as the jet gets lower in altitude, my ears popping every few minutes as we approach another executive airport, and soon gracefully land on the tarmac.

A large SUV waits for us a few feet away from the stairs of the jet, and Darian places our carry-ons in the back.

"Hope your flight was satisfactory. Have a wonderful day, Mr.Cathorn." Heather turns to me and smiles, "You have a wonderful day as well, Ms. Ray." She gives me a warm look before climbing the steps onto the jet as we continue to the SUV with Val in tow.

It's not long before we're cruising through the crowded city, only stopping to grab some takeout, and soon I find that the street names look familiar. My heart skips a beat when I realize we're near Tammy's apartment complex.

"What are we doing here?" My nerves are on full display in my voice as it cracks awkwardly.

"We're staying across from your friend's apartment. According to my brother, one of the amulets is supposedly there."

My eyes widen, and I look up at the high rise building with shock.

"How did she have one and I wasn't aware of it?"

Darian shrugs, "Not sure, maybe she acquired it after you had been around and she just never brought it near you." he offers, the uncertainty of his explanation genuine.

Having parked in the enormous underground garage, I mindlessly follow him and Val to the elevators. The apartment has so many floors that my ears pop again as we ascend and my chest tightens. As the doors open I can feel the same sensation that I had felt at the airport. It seems with each amulet I acquire, the more intense the pull and pain is when we come across another.

The feeling is so overwhelming that as we exit the elevator, I can't move any further. My body is visibly trembling with effort to stay upright as I brace my weight against the wall.

"Fuck." Darian's brows furrow with concern, and he twists to Val, "I'm going to bring the carry-ons inside, stay here with her and we'll go straight to the other apartment to look for it."

Val huffs and props himself against my leg for added support as we wait for Darian to return. He is gone for a few minutes that passes as an eternity, but once he comes back into view, his face is serious with thought.

"Put your arms around my neck," he instructs.

I blink at him, "Excuse me?"

"I'm going to carry you. It's a long walk and you can hardly stand."

I shoot him a glare and as I shift my weight on my legs, they buckle, and I nearly collapse.

Darian catches my arm and scoffs, "Gods, you are stubborn, aren't you?"

I snort, "You have no idea."

Darian scoops my legs up, cradling me in his arms and carries me down the hallway to Tammy's apartment.

The pull is strong and my lips thin as he sets me on my feet to unlock the door using a pin pad with one arm still hooked around me.

"How did you get into her apartment?" I ask as Darian laughs with a certain slyness that makes my eyes narrow.

"How do you think I got into your house?" he retorts with pure amusement and I roll my eyes.

"How **did** you get into my house?" I ask, levelling him with a look.

"Lets just say, I am well versed in electronics" He says with a grin.

I shake my head as he opens the door and Tammy's familiar scents drift from the apartment. My humor quickly turns as I fight the tears threatening to fall, and I inhale a ragged breath as I give in to them, collapsing into Darian's arms.

He says nothing, but holds me tight to his chest as the tears fall, driven by the overwhelming scents of her expensive perfumes and incenses used that still linger in the air.

After a few minutes, I manage to extract myself from his arms before taking a single step deeper into the apartment, but his hand abruptly stops my movements, "I can look around for it again, if you'll wait here?"

I nod, "It'll be faster if I can at least pinpoint the direction of the room it's in."

He assesses me for a moment and reluctantly gives me a quick nod. I shift to the hallway on the right and pain shoots from my abdomen to my toes, so I turn to the left hallway and the tug intensifies.

Taking a few assisted steps toward the kitchen, but the direction of the pull stays centered, indicating the amulet is further down. Darian's fingers gently wrap around my arm as he brushes past me, disappearing out of sight as he checks the rooms ahead. It's a long moment before he reappears with a grin on his face.

He holds a necklace up and the tug lessens as he places the amulet in my hand. This one has a beautifully detailed peacock depicted in the center, its vibrant feathers spreading majestically as shimmering liquid surrounds it.

"This seems too good to be true that we've come across two within a day." My voice is thick with concern as Darian nods.

"Caspian must have known where both of these were since he specifically said to use the executive airport and stop by Tamara's apartment. I'd wager that he just had no way of knowing for sure nor pinpointing the exact locations. It's unsurprising that he would have had this all mapped out from the start."

I clasp the amulet on my neck alongside the others and sigh with nervous relief before we make our way to the place we will be staying.

Darian opens the door, letting Val go in first to sniff around.

The apartment is enormous, surrounded with floor to ceiling windows that have motorized blackout curtains covering them. There's a long couch along the wall, with a large, mounted flat screen TV across from it. The kitchen and front room are attached in an open concept, with an island in the center. The appliances are all stainless steel, but the fridge has a large touchscreen on it that displays the date and temperature inside.

Okay, let's face it, Lara. You desperately need some upgrades at home.

Darian snickers as my eyes scale the room and as he presses a button on the wall next to me. With a click, the area starts to gradually brighten and my gaze snaps to the windows where the curtains are raising from the floor all the way to the ceiling.

The gasp gets caught in my lungs as my eyes adjust to the light and I quickly close the distance to the window.

God. This is...

"Incredible."

The windows boast the display of mountain ranges and forest that descend into neighborhoods of houses which gradually become more compact. The dense communities stretch as far as the eye can see, until finally in the distance, these suburban homes turn into the concrete towers of downtown. The view is littered with various high rise complexes that reach the sky, some nearly the same height as the building we're in.

I glance at Darian, and he's staring out the window with a somber expression. I can't help but wonder what goes through his mind in moments like this.

Does he think about how far down the path of darkness his brother has fallen?

Does he think about his brothers and wonder if they're alive?

Does he wonder if he will ever be able to see them again?

The silence eats at my nerves and I find myself itching to fill it with anything.

"So what do we do now?"

Smooth, Lara.

Darian's lips twitch and his mismatched gaze meets mine, "Now we wait for new coordinates."

I nod, "Great, and what do we do in the meantime?"

Darian cocks his head and his grin turns mischievous, "I have a few ideas."

My cheeks burn.

He dips his chin slightly, "Mind out of the gutter, Ray."

I blink at him.

"I don't know what you're talking about." I huff in a failed attempt to hide my flustered state, snatching my carry-on and wheeling it down the hallway.

Ass.

I only make it a few steps before I realize I have no idea where I'm going or which door is mine. The first room on the left appears to be an office by the large desk inside and the shelf built within the wall, filled with books and plants.

Taking a few more steps, the next room on the other side of the hall has a giant king-sized bed, a walk-in closet and a large TV hung on the wall.

Okay, so that must be the main bedroom.

There's one remaining room I make my way to and as I get into the doorway my jaw drops at the king-sized bed, large walk in closet and bathroom that appears to be shared with the other bedroom.

The room's outer walls are entirely windows, covered in the same motorized blackout curtains, with a door off to the side.

A click behind me sounds out as the curtains begin to rise, pouring light into the room. Glancing over my shoulder, Darian leans against the door frame. His features are soft, relaxed even and my eyes linger on him for a long moment before I move to the windows.

The door leads to a railed off patio that hooks around the length of the bedroom, with a generous sized hot tub on the end. A couch along the windows faces the city below, with a long table in front of it.

"You can sleep in here if you want, I'll take the other room. We will have to share the bathroom if that's alright with you."

My eyes flick to his, "You don't want the master?"

He tosses me a genuine smile that sends my heart fluttering in my chest, "I'm good with the other one, it's right across from the study and I can do some work from there while we wait for Caspian's next set of coordinates."

I glance once more around the room and then to Darian, as he waves dismissively and leaves before dragging my carry-on to the walk-in closet. Putting away my meager selection of clothes, I toss myself into the enormous fluffy bed with a deep sigh.

I must have fallen asleep because I jerk upright to movement on the bed, relieved when it's just Val looking at me with both ears perked.

"Are you coming in here to nap too, or did you intend to wake me up?"

Val huffs and looks toward the door.

"Ah, my furry alarm clock." I tease and push to my feet, stretching my limbs fully before moving down the hall, leaving Val as he curls up to sleep.

He just wanted the bed for himself, I bet.

Halfway down the hall, I glance around out of force of habit and my body stills as I pass Darian's room.

He's standing in the center with a pristine white towel hugging his waist. A fresh set of clothes spread on top of the bed in front of him. His black hair falls around his shoulders, still dripping water and on full display are his detailed tattoos spread across his sun kissed skin like a living canvas.

There's a life-like, iridescent, black-scaled dragon with eyes the color of molten gold along his right shoulder blade. Its wings are spread but curled as if halting in mid-air, with white and red fire jutting from its mouth toward his spine. Opposite to the dragon is a silver raven with bright violet eyes that looks as though it's in flight and about to collide with the flames of the dragon. Along his spine, below the two creatures who appear to be locked into battle, there's a tattoo that looks identical to Val, staring directly at me with his light hazel eyes and dark fur. The resemblance is uncanny.

Beneath the mystical looking creatures, is a swirl of ice, water, earth and shadows, begins to encircle the three as if creating a deadly tornado of elements threatening to envelop them.

The canvas slowly turns and the incredibly detailed artwork I'm admiring is gone, replaced by impressively corded muscles along his abdomen and his broad chest. More tattoos trace from his neck down his shoulders and arms. They aren't depictions of any battles or creatures but almost look to be a ribbon-like design with some kind of symbols tattooed within them. These markings trace down his chest and abdomen to the deep inclined V around his hips. My attention catches on the two protruding veins that clearly display before disappearing beyond the towel.

A deep chuckle snaps me back to reality and my thighs instinctively clench together as desire pools in my core.

"Oh my god." I breathe and slap my hand over my mouth, but it's too late and my eyes regretfully flick to his.

Darian tosses me a knowing grin, "Not a god. Just very, very blessed by them." he says with a wink and my cheeks burn.

"I'll be in the other room." I mumble out, and I'm positive that I've turned as red as a tomato as I hurry into the living room.

Traitorous body.

It's a few minutes later when Darian comes in, fully clothed. "I assume you wouldn't mind going out for dinner and snag a few drinks? The shower is all yours now."

His smirk hasn't left his face, and I'm nearly positive I could die of embarrassment here and now.

Why the fuck does he have to be so hot?

Not trusting words, I nod once and hurry off to the master bedroom to grab clothes. I opt to wear a simple black halter dress with a light cardigan and hop into the shower.

By the time I'm finished getting ready and entering the living room, I'm no longer red, but my body hasn't calmed down any. I have to keep my focus on breathing through the nervous butterflies that flutter around inside me as he takes in my appearance.

There's a look in his eyes that makes my entire body hum with excitement and I find myself craving it like a woman starved.

"Lead the way?" I give him a smile and that seems to snap him back to reality, and we head out of the apartment.

Darian brings us to a restaurant in the heart of downtown that sits atop a newly built high rise, with the outdoor view of the mountains and the rest of the city.

We walk in, bypassing the front desk check in -to my confusion- and the hostess turns bright pink as she stammers, "Mr. Cathorn! Lovely to see you tonight, weren't expecting you in but we will send a waiter to your table right away."

I curiously watch the interaction between them. The hostess appears flustered, but Darian isn't being intimidating or rude, he's merely smiling at her kindly, "Not a problem, Sarah. We'll get settled and enjoy the view while we wait."

She nods and gives a slight bow, "Yes y-, Sir."

Darian glances back at me with a smile that threatens to stop my heart where it sits in my chest as he extends his hand out. I slide my fingers into his palm, a static shock zaps our skin momentarily and jolt slightly, laughing as he leads me through the restaurant.

"So, is this a place you frequent often?" I probe, determined to learn more about Darian's outwardly mortal but luxurious life.

"You could say that." He smirks but stays focused on guiding me through the restaurant.

He glances back at me and I shoot him a glare, making him laugh a little harder as he holds a door open that leads to the outside patio seating.

"I own the building, including the restaurant within it and I employ everyone who works here." He says softly near my ear as we make our way past tables.

That's when I notice the waiters and waitresses pause to give him smiles or waves as we pass them.

My jaw goes slack, but I manage to keep myself from completely gaping.

"You own all of this and the jet?" I whisper to him incredulously as we get to a portion of the patio that has a single table surrounded by beautiful planters with vines encasing it to give it privacy, the opening displays a full view of the city below. There are soft lights weaved through the vines to give added ambiance and there's a small propane fire in the center of the table.

"Stunning." I breathe.

As the sun sets over the horizon and shadows encase the city, the lights of the buildings and streets get brighter, which only adds to the appeal of the sight. This feels like a dream.

I glance at Darian, and he's staring at me with an unreadable expression on his face.

"Stunning." He affirms quietly and my cheeks burn again.

He gestures to the table and my heart hammers in my chest when I realize my hand is still held in his. Releasing it with a smile before seating myself, eyes widening as he pushes my chair in gently for me.

Is he always this much of a gentleman or is this all a ploy?

Suspicion plagues my mind as the minimally kind gestures from Caspian threaten to ruin the moment.

Darian sits and must see the conflict on my face, "Would you rather go somewhere else to eat? I didn't mean to make you uncomfortable coming here, but the view is incredible and the chef's are extremely talented."

Considering him for a moment I laugh softly and drop my eyes to the table, "I'm not uncomfortable here. It's just... the events up until today have simply made me question motives more than I ever have before. I don't mean to offend you at all."

I glance at Darian and his jaw clenches, but he nods, "I can promise you, the intent with tonight is just to have a beautiful view while eating good food." There's a slight twinkle in his eye as he adds, "Though, you'll just have to judge the latter for yourself, I suppose."

I chuckle and a waitress approaches our table with a genuine smile, placing a menu in front of each of us.

"Good evening, Mr. Cathorn! How are you both doing tonight?"

Darian smiles softly, tearing his gaze from me to the waitress.

"Hello Ilana, great to see you again. We are doing well, just flew in today so we are excited for a good meal and drinks. How is your husband doing since his surgery?"

Her face lights up as he mentions her husband, the tightness in my chest lessens.

"His recovery is going slow but well. He is doing physical therapy twice a week and needs additional testing monthly for the next 6 months before they reassess his progress. Thank you for asking."

Darian eyes her for a moment and then nods once. "Let him know we're thinking of him and if either of you need anything..."

She seems to pause for a moment and glance between us before holding out her pad of paper and pen, "You said you wanted good food and drinks? Pick your poison!" Her genuinely cheerful tone rings out.

Darian glances at me and then to the waitress, "I'll take the usual for myself. Get a glass of it for Lara as well, and whatever else she would like."

I blink at him and bite my lip, "I'll take whatever tequila you have, please."

The waitress glances at Darian, and he nods once prompting her to note something down before tilting her head back up, "Any idea what you'd like to start with?"

"Calamari for the table for sure. Does John still make those egg rolls off the menu?"

Ilana giggles, "Does he? He makes them nearly every day. We are voting to add them to the menu this week with how often they're requested."

Darian laughs and nods his head, "Well, we can't **not** have them then, as long as he's up to making us some."

She notes it down and tilts her head, "Sounds great. I'll get these in and be back shortly."

Within a few minutes, Ilana brings us each a glass of whiskey and a couple shots of tequila. She places them between us respectively and hurries off to the kitchen.

My eyes find Darian's and I lift my shot into the air, "Should we 'cheers' to something?"

Darian is thoughtful for a moment and raises his glass to mine, "To the hope for a better future than the past we leave behind."

I smile and bump our glasses together lightly before tossing the liquor back, surprise rifles through me when it goes down smooth.

"Oh, this stuff is dangerous, and I'm assuming it's incredibly top shelf."

Darian laughs, "Another cheers, your turn this time."

I'm quiet for a moment as I hold the second shot up, "To the version of ourselves we became... and the version of ourselves we've yet to become."

Darian gives me a slight incline of his head as he lifts his glass to mine before we down the tequila.

Plopping the glasses to the table, it's quiet for a moment when I finally speak, "Alright big man, hit me with some little known facts." My voice comes out with more heat than expected, and I internally wince.

Darian chokes on his whiskey and barks a laugh, "Fine. But only if you do the same."

It's a conscious effort to stop staring at his mouth, "Fine."

I'm quiet for a moment while my mind battles with questions to ask.

"So you have brothers still in the realm you were banished from, but what about sisters or extended family? Were you not romantically interested in anyone before your banishment?"

Real, real smooth Lara.

His eyes flick to mine and I take a soothing sip of whiskey in an effort to mask the burning in my cheeks.

"No, I no longer have any blood relatives outside of Caspian and my life was complicated when I was growing up. I didn't have time to pay attention to anyone for any romantic interest when I was learning about my powers and how to fight with and without them. So to answer your questions, no to both."

I nod and take another sip of my whiskey, avoiding his burning gaze as my fingers fiddle with the tablecloth.

"Why did you decide to pursue studying the lake?" He asks leaning back in his chair.

I pause for a moment to think through his question. "I don't know if I have a good answer to that, or at least one that doesn't sound like a cop out." I smirk at him and add, "When I first graduated, I took random jobs to try to build on the research I had been compiling about global warming and environmental impacts humans are having on important ecosystems. It seems the more I researched, the less people wanted to listen to my theories, so I decided to take a different approach."

"If I could find ways to improve our agriculture or heal the land of the toxins or wastes dumped into them, perhaps we could leave this world better than how we found it. When I was offered to research the phenomenon at the lake, it just seemed like it was the only right option. It just felt like that's where I needed to be."

Darian's face holds some type of emotion that I can't put my finger on, and he nods thoughtfully.

Ilana approaches with four more shots, and places two in front of each of us. A waiter comes up behind her with a tray of egg rolls and calamari, setting them on the table along with two fresh glasses of water.

Darian smiles warmly, nodding to them as he tosses a piece of calamari into his mouth, "Delicious as usual. Thank you so much."

Ilana beams, "Would you like anything else?"

"I'll take a steak, medium rare with potatoes and asparagus."

Ilana nods and turns to me.

"I'll have the same but with a side of caesar please, and if you have truffle aioli, I'll die happy if you can add that."

Ilana giggles, "Our truffle aioli is the best! You'll love it and I'll have them put extra on for you."

I hold my hands to my chest with appreciation, "You're the best, thank you so much."

She smiles widely at both of us before heading to the kitchen as I hold up another shot for a 'Cheers'.

Darian raises a brow and his lips twitch as he mirrors the action.

"To a wonderful dinner, with not-so-terrible company and damn good tequila."

Darian barks a laugh, and we take our shot before digging into the appetizers.

"Alright next little known fact." He swallows a bite of his egg roll, "What would you like to know?"

I think for a moment and grin, "What was the earliest time you remember invading my personal or private space?"

Darian's eyes widen, and then winces as he thinks back.

"I sort of broke into your house when you went to the lake once. That was when I first started monitoring you at a much closer proximity instead of from afar." He says as he pulls his hand behind his head, scratching the back of his neck awkwardly.

I burst out laughing. "My window?! That was you?"

He smirks, "Yeah, I didn't realize I left it open."

"God, I thought I was going crazy. I walked through the entire house with a bat after seeing the window open."

He winces again, "Sorry. I knew you were being hunted but didn't fully understand why, so I needed to learn more about you."

I laugh again, "You could have simply asked. You know, like a normal person. Maybe a dinner, a drink or two. Hell, even a coffee together would have given you enough information."

"The people after you are not normal. They also don't typically go after normal people, so forgive me for being overly cautious."

I consider his words for a moment and nod, "You're forgiven, but only because these egg rolls are divine." My voice is laced with amusement, and he chokes out a laugh.

"Your turn, Ray" He smirks and sips his whiskey between bites of calamari.

"What do you want to know?" I parrot his earlier question and he grins.

"What is your happiest memory?"

I fall quiet, pursing my lips as I filter through memories.

"When I graduated from university and earned my Ph.D., I met Tammy while doing research and over the course of a month she seemed to learn everything she could about me. She never asked about my past or why I didn't talk about things, just kept herself open if I wanted to talk about things I'd gone through, which I never did."

"The first year of meeting her, she had found out when my birthday was and the morning of, surprised me with flowers, cake, presents, some ice cream and a really corny comedy movie. Not only was that one of the few happy memories I've had, I remember at the time not understanding what I was feeling because happiness was foreign to me. So considering it's the first time I ever felt happy, and it's one of the few times I had been in such a state, I'd say that would be my happiest memory."

Quiet falls over us and my stomach sinks as I worry that I've ruined the mood. Chancing a glance at Darian, he nods once in silent acknowledgement, then raises his remaining shot into the air and I mimic the movement as he speaks.

"To the future and making more happy memories."

Bumping my glass against his, I blow out a breath, "Cheers."

The liquid goes down smooth and Ilana brings out our steaks. Darian snags her attention as she turns to leave, "Ilana, once we're done here, we're going to head downstairs, but before we leave this evening, could we grab two more steaks, medium rare to go?"

Ilana laughs, "You can have whatever you'd like! Just text me about ten minutes before you're leaving and we'll have them brought down to you."

Darian gives her a genuine smile, "Thank you."

She heads to the other tables, and he takes another sip of his whiskey before starting on his filet. "What else would you like to ask me?"

Placing a forkful of aioli covered steak into my mouth, I groan, leaning my forehead against the back of my hands. My gaze slides to Darian and my thighs clench at the heated look in his eyes.

Traitorous pussy.

Desperate to get the attention off of my visceral reaction to the man in front of me, I change the subject.

"So, how did you get into my house by the lake without being detected? Caspian had set up that security system with Henry and had the app installed on his phone."

Darian chuckles darkly, "It's not hard to bypass security systems. One of the first things I learned as years went by on Earth was electronics and computers. The system he set up at your place was a really poor iteration of a security system I created and have marketed for years."

My jaw drops.

What the fuck.

"So you-" I say and Darian cuts me off to explain.

"Looped the feed for each camera and adjusted which loops were playing depending on where you both were once you got back. I had the loop playing in your room the entire time I was in there. It recorded you sleeping while I was hiding and once I was about to wake you up, I repeated the loop of you sleeping while we discussed your escape."

Darian's face is painted with a healthy mixture of mischievousness and smug satisfaction, making me huff and roll my eyes dramatically.

Such an ego on this one.

"Your turn to ask something you'd like to know about me, Mr. Cathorn," I say playfully.

A dark look returns to Darian's eyes as he takes a final bite of his steak, chewing thoughtfully.

I swallow as he rubs his thumb along his bottom lip, tracking the movement as he wipes his hand off on his napkin before tossing it to the table and leaning back.

"When was the last time you've been with someone?"

My eyes flash to his in surprise and then to the table.

"Are we talking sex, or all intimacy?" I ask, my heart pounding frantically.

"Sex." He states, the look in his eye unreadable as he tilts his head.

I swallow audibly. "Voluntarily?" I say, trying to force a tone of humor, but the joke dies on my lips.

Darian is silent as I shift my gaze between the table and him, blinking while trying not to sound utterly pathetic. "I've never uh, willingly, had sex with anyone."

My throat tightens, and I shove my final piece of aioli covered steak into my mouth, chewing slowly. Darian's assessing gaze feels like I'm an ant under a magnifying glass with the sun pointed at me.

I swallow my food and lean back, "Well, this was a delicious meal. Your chef's really outdid themselves, and the view truly is breathtaking."

"Indeed." The look he's giving me makes me want to squirm in my seat, but I manage to fight the urge.

Ilana returns, sliding us each a fresh glass of whiskey and Darian makes his way to my chair, holding his free hand out, "Come on Ray, the night is still young."

My body warms as my hand slides into his, and I sway as I push to my feet. Darian tightens his grip on mine as he guides me through the tables of the restaurant, and we soon find ourselves at the main floor of the building.

Instead of leaving out the front doors, we head the other direction to a large wooden entrance with arching curtains and security detail. There's loud bass reverberating through the door that makes my body shiver and tingle.

As we approach the beefcake guards who are absolute mammoth of men. They must be just over 6 feet, but Darian still stands taller than them by at least an inch or two.

Both guards nod at Darian and me as they step aside.

I shouldn't be surprised. This is his building, after all, and he is their boss.

We pass through the oversized entrance, and it feels like we're walking in a crowded nightclub that had landscaping throughout.

The inside is huge, there are trees everywhere and luminescent moss covers much of the bark on each trunk, extending to the branches giving the giant room a lunar glow.

Multiple bars can be seen from the entrance.

Two of them look to be thick tree roots that have grown into the mold and shape of a typical bar counter with intricate carvings etched within them with symbols similar to those tattooed onto Darian's skin. There's a wide tree in the middle of the room that stands taller than the others with a spiralling staircase that leads to the DJ area.

Without a speaker in sight, it almost sounds as though the music is coming from the trees themselves as the DJ spins his tracks.

There's people dancing throughout the trees, some are huddled into groups and talking with one another, others are sitting at wood tables, leaning back onto comfortable benches as they sip their drinks.

As we make our way through the room, heads turn in our direction and nearly everyone waves, raises their glass or nods at Darian with a genuine smile on their face.

He greets them all similarly to Ilana.

He knows every story, discusses families, their concerns and regards them with equal amounts of interest as he converses with them.

He is genuinely loved by these people and a pang of loneliness resounds through me as we continue to move to the back of the room past the oversized DJ tree.

Darian's hand squeezes mine, and I realize we've been like this the whole time.

No wonder I got a curious look from a couple of people. I'm holding the owner's hand, after all.

Laughing softly to myself, I trail behind Darian while taking sips of my whiskey. Slowly we approach another room and nerves twirl through me from head to toe and back again.

"What does this place remind you of so far?" He asks over the music.

I blink at him, "Well the lake I'm researching, for the most part. Just, if the lake and this nightclub had a baby. A loud baby with good taste in music."

Darian laughs before pushing the set of doors open in front of us and a gasp escapes my throat.

A giant waterfall flows out from a rocky structure on the other side of the room, with countless trees surrounding the small body of water at the base, the luminescent moss coating nearly everything in sight.

It looks entirely undisturbed by the public here.

"This is wonderful."

He nods, gesturing to the room. "I built Haven to preserve this and keep it from prying eyes. It took me 50 years when I was banished but I wouldn't change it for anything. The club has become a safe haven for those stuck here, hence the name and while the club has grown to be quite a popular attraction, this is the true beauty of it."

It feels like I've been shown a little slice of heaven. A place where peace and calm seem to emanate and sink deep into your bones.

Darian leads us closer to the water and watches me as I step forward to stand beside him.

"Was there many of you left here when magic was bound?" Glancing at him as I ask, I can see his face fall.

"There was, though our numbers have decreased greatly with my brother sending hunters after those who remain."

I frown, "Why would your brother send hunters after people from his own realm?"

Darian's face hardens, "Because it feeds him the miniscule amounts of magic that he so craves in order to find his way back."

A shudder runs through me as I consider all those who have lost their lives to him, and how I could have easily been one of them.

I wonder how far he would go?

"And what happens when there's no more people from your realm for him to hunt down?"

There's a long moment of silence before Darian finally speaks, "Then he would move onto killing humans with even less prejudice than he already has."

The look on his face as he stares at me tells me just how bad that could be, and I shudder again.

"You know, there were times where I didn't think Caspian was all that bad. He was almost what one might call considerate, at least, he appeared to be."

Darian nods and takes a deep breath, "I don't doubt that. My brother wasn't always this way." He says softly.

I kneel down to the edge of the water and drag my hand from one side to the other gently while he continues.

"My brother and I were close when we were young. His powers didn't manifest until he was much older than the other kids our age and his were so much different than what we've ever known. He was picked on quite a bit for it, on top of being a second born son. I believe that left him vulnerable to influence and as he reached adolescence, he became more withdrawn."

"He was constantly leaving the city to live in a cabin near the mountains. He stopped coming to magic classes and I noticed his attitude becoming less like the brother I grew up with. My parents tried to arrange a marriage for him one day and that was when all hell broke loose."

"He ran away and was missing for over two years. The search parties we sent after him never returned until we got word that he was staying in a series of tunnels near the mountains and that he was practicing blood magic which is strickly forbidden."

Darian's fists squeeze together and the muscles in his neck flex with tension.

"Blood magic is strictly prohibited for good reason. Anyone practicing is put on trial to maintain balance for magic wielders and those not as strong in their powers. I set out with a few of my brothers to search for Caspian and when we found him, he was completely changed in body and mind. He was no longer a young man searching for himself and unsure. He knew what he wanted, he was grown and he was ready to die for it."

"When we found him, he nearly killed Cade by the time the rest of us intervened. He tried to drain him of his blood for more magic and that was the first time my brother and I fought."

Darian's voice is low with simmering rage, "I vowed to kill him if he ever came back to the city. In the end I couldn't kill my own brother and that led to the rest of the tragic events we know of today. He may not be entirely evil, but we don't know the true depths of his motives and after everything, I don't know that I care enough to find out."

I think back to the moments where Caspian seemed to be genuine and my heart twists within my chest.

I can't help but wonder if Darian considers this banishment to be his own form of punishment for not stopping his brother sooner.

"Perhaps we will never know," I say quietly and Darian downs the rest of his whiskey before turning to me.

"Come, let's get another drink."

He takes a step to the door before sliding his hand into mine, tugging me along gently.

As we near the DJ within the tree, I become increasingly aware of the people around looking at Darian with an odd sense of fondness as we weave through the crowd that seems to have doubled since we entered.

I glance around at the patrons, all painfully human in appearance.

"How many are…?" I pause, unable to properly word my question.

Darian scans the room, "Right now? Mostly everyone is from my realm, only a handful of humans. Most of those in here are regulars minus a few." He glances at me, "This is one of the last remaining places they can go without worrying about being hunted."

I down the rest of my whiskey and nod.

"I suppose that's why they look at you like you're their lord and savior." I tease and he chuckles softly.

We approach the bar and a man with shaved black hair smiles widely, "Well look what the cat dragged in!"

Darian grins as the man walks around the bar to embrace him, "It's been months! Where the hell have you been, D? Dolly's been a terror while you've been gone."

I watch him grimace deeply, "Sorry Lor, duty called."

Lor gives a dry laugh with a shrug, "If that's the case, I suppose you had it worse than we did," He turns to look me over, "I suppose you didn't have it too bad if this is what you brought back."

My cheeks burn as he takes my hand, bringing my knuckles to brush against his lips lightly.

"Her name is Lara and she's off limits, Lor."

My head snaps to Darian, blinking at his words.

Where in the world do men find the audacity?

Lor releases my hand and brings his own to his chest with feigned outrage, "I would never dare to overstep my bounds, my liege." His emphasis on his last two words tickles me.

I chuckle to myself and both men glance at me before Lor walks behind the bar again.

"What can I do for you tonight, then?" Lor's voice is dripping with amusement as he looks between us.

If I have more tequila, I may die.

Darian glances at me and smirks, "Water please, and four shots of tequila."

My heart plummets as Lor tosses him a lopsided grin, "Aye aye, Captain!"

Chapter 30

Darian leads me to a seat at the bar overlooking the gyrating crowd down below as he passes water to me.

This place has a club-like atmosphere, yet it exudes an undeniable sense of comfort. The feeling of security is palpable, putting everyone at ease, as evident by their cheerful faces and the intimate displays everywhere I look.

In fact, intimacy appears to reach every corner of the place.

My sight falls to a group of men dancing with one woman.

Their hands roving up and down her body as they sway rhythmically with the music, almost in a trance. One is kissing her deeply, two are cupping her breasts and taking them into their mouths while another kneels before her.

My cheeks burn as he lifts one of her legs over his shoulder, burying his face under her short dress that's hiked up to her hips.

I can't tear my gaze from her as her deeply hooded eyes roll to the back of her head, any sounds she may make drowned out by the man kissing her and the bass pumping through the area.

No one seems to mind the public display. Most are lost in their own bubble of intimacy or enjoyment merely feet away.

Darian chuckles beside me as he gives me a knowing smirk and I avert my eyes quickly to down my water in a few deep gulps.

Returning my gaze to the masses below, I hesitantly ask, "Is this normal?"

Darian's head nods in my peripheral.

"It is. It's actually more normal to see this back home than to see people be monogamous and jealous of their partners being intimate with others, though it does happen." I feel his gaze on me as I continue to watch the crowd, "Conception is a problem for our people and thus reproduction is looked at with reverence, not shame. If any of these individuals bear a child to term it may be years before they do so. We'd suspected for millennia that our magic makes us unable to reproduce, but there are those who believe that to be nothing more than conspiracy."

"It was a miracle that my parents even conceived my brother and I so close together."

He falls quiet and I look at him.

His face is shadowed, eyes glazed over, and I have no doubt he's recalling memories of days long past. Without giving it a second thought, I reach my hand between us and weave my fingers through his.

I bite the inside of my lip as his eyes snap to our intertwined hands before I speak, choosing my words carefully.

"This may not mean much, because I'm well aware that I did not know them but… If I were them, I'd have been proud of what you've done given your circumstances."

My assurance must have hit its mark as I see him blink twice with momentary shock before his jaw clenches, and his grip on me tightens slightly.

We stay like that for a moment before Lor clears his throat behind us and our hands fall apart as we turn toward the bar. Lor grins as he slides two shots in front of me, then two for Darian, accompanied by a plate of limes.

"Enjoy!" He chimes in a singsong voice as he goes to assist others waiting for drinks.

Darian chuckles and grabs a shot in each hand, turning to me. My eyes widen as I realize he's about to do a double and a nervous laugh bubbles up as I mirror him.

Goodbye, liver.

"Here's to restoring magic and stopping my brother before he makes anyone else suffer."

I beam and clank my first shot glass against his, "And to do so, together. Cheers." I finish, knocking the second shots together, tossing them back as the warmth pools in my stomach.

A short while later, Darian and I are both accepting another water from Lor as his smile falls, quickly turning into something darker as he looks at Darian before hurrying to the other side of the bar.

I hear heels clicking and my eyes scan nearby faces that fill with tension as they get closer.

Even the music seems to quiet down.

A feminine scoff sounds out from over my shoulder, "Funny for you to finally drag yourself back here and I find you drinking with some whore."

Anger flushes over me and I bite the inside of my lip hard enough to taste blood.

Darian tosses his newest refill of whiskey back and turns slightly to look at the woman. His face is relaxed but as he grips his glass, his knuckles are white, and he repeatedly flexes his fingers around it.

"Some of us have bigger roles to play in life, Dolly."

Ah, so this is the so-called 'Terror'.

"If I didn't know better, your 'role' consisted of bringing back a stray instead of dealing with your brother." Her heels click to my side, and it's my turn to throw back the remainder of my drink.

"Careful, Dolly," Darian growls with vicious lethality and the corded muscles in his forearms are pulsating as his hands squeeze into fists.

I follow his gaze and glance at Dolly who is staring at him with amusement in her bright blue eyes. She looks to be in her thirties, with bleach blonde hair and blood-red lipstick with an expertly well done smoky eye. Her silk red dress hangs off her shoulders from tiny straps, and she stands a few inches taller than me with her six-inch heels.

As I look at her, something chews at my gut and the mask of amusement I can see melts into disgust and hatred.

I blink and look at the crowd, the tension in the air around us is palpable as people watch the interaction.

My gaze flicks back to Dolly, her amusement is still painted over her features, but my mind can somehow see the expression beneath it as if plain as day.

What a terrible poker face.

My insides burn with anger as she reaches for my bicep, she painfully grips it, tugging me toward her and off the chair.

"Dolly, let h-"

Before Darian can continue, my rage bubbles over, and I've twisted her arm in a spin to place myself behind her. Releasing a pained yelp as I yank her arm into an uncomfortable position along her spine, thrusting her chest forward into the bar.

"Release me! Release me this instant!" She screams, stomping her heels on the ground.

It's like the events leading up to tonight have activated the fight in my fight or flight response, but I don't have time to evaluate the 'why' behind it as Darian chuckles darkly.

I tighten my grip on her, pushing her further into the bar.

"Darian, call your whore off!"

Grasping the back of her dress, I pull her from the bar as if I'm going to release her, and she relaxes slightly as she straightens.

Instead, I yank her off balance, and she stumbles with a shout. As she attempts to steady herself, I kick the inside of her knees, forcing her ankles to bend awkwardly at the movement as her knees connect to the ground with a crack.

My free hand yanks her hair back, and she gasps, her eyes wide.

My cheek rests against hers as my gaze locks with Darian's, "Touch me again, and you will no longer have hands. Call me a stray or a whore again, and you will no longer have a tongue to speak. I'm done being walked over by assholes like you."

Darian's lips twitch as he stares at me, but the proud amusement seems to fall from his face when he looks at her again.

"Dolly, I want to make something abundantly clear." He says, picking a piece of lint from his jeans and flicking it toward her, "You are no longer welcome here in this building nor any other building I own. Should you appear on our doorstep without invitation you will be killed."

She gasps and her eyes bulge, "You can't do that! I work here! He will kill me!"

Darkness flashes across his features and his voice remains lethally calm, "Then my brother and I finally have something in common. Now leave, your employment has come to an end."

Releasing her with a shove, Lor hands me a generous pour of whiskey as I return to my seat. Dolly scoffs behind me, her heels clicking into the distance as she shouts at people to move out of her way.

"That was impressive, Ray." Darian's voice tickles my ear from where he stands beside me.

"She needed to be brought down a notch," I hear Lor chuckle in front of us, from where he leans over the bar, "Or five," I add with a shrug.

Lor grins, "I don't think I've ever seen a more satisfying sight before in my life. Which is saying much, since…" he gestures around him in a broad way and I laugh.

Downing the whiskey in front of me, I chase it with water as the fuzzy feeling of intoxicated begins to spread through my body.

Darian doesn't seem to notice as he leans closer to my ear, "Come, let's go back to the apartment. Val is probably dying of hunger by now."

My skin flushes up my neck all the way to my cheeks, "Don't we have to text Ilana to tell her we're leaving soon?" I raise an eyebrow at him.

He grins at me, "Already did before Dolly showed up."

Chapter 31

With steaks in tow, we open the doors to see Val waiting impatiently near the kitchen. Darian adds the premium cuts of meat to the rest of our leftovers onto his plate and chuckles when Val dives in with enthusiasm.

With the alcohol fully in control now I spy a bottle of whiskey on a bar table and beam before turning to Darian, "Have you hit your second wind yet or are you down for the count?"

His eyebrow raises, and he glances from me to the table I'm walking toward with a laugh, "Second wind? I'm still sober. Hit me, barkeep."

I snicker quietly before pointing a finger at him, "Careful what you wish for. The last person I was tempted to hit was on their knees tonight."

Heat flashes across Darian's face before he chuckles softly, "If that is me by the end of this night, I'll die a happy man."

My body flushes and it takes conscious effort to focus on pouring the whiskey without spilling and then place the decanter down, sliding one of the full glasses to Darian.

Okay, drunk Lara is coming out to play. Everybody, watch out.

Darian barks a laugh.

I cover my mouth loosely with a hand, "Oh shit, I said that out loud didn't I?"

"You absolutely, most definitely, did." He chokes out between bouts of laughter.

"Whoops," I say dismissively before downing half the glass of whiskey.

Darian empties his, and moves closer to refill it, "So where did you learn to do what you did at the club?" He asks while filling his cup, then turns to top mine off.

Filters at this point, have nearly disappeared for me, melted away with the tequila and whiskey we've been drinking.

I answer truthfully, without a second thought.

"When I went into university, I was an anxious mess being around frat houses and I was terrified of being taken advantage of or hurt, so I did the only thing I could think of. I threw myself into classes that focus on self defense and fighting. It didn't help my anxiety much, but it kept my mind busy when I wasn't doing school work so I suppose it was good for something."

Darian is staring at me with furrowed brows and I blink, realizing that I've said too much.

"Sorry. No filter with the whole alcohol consumption thing." I mumble, but he holds his hand up.

"Don't apologize. I actually prefer this brutal and raw honesty. It's refreshing."

I blink at him and nod lightly, then smirk as I hold up my glass in a comedic 'Cheers', "To brutal, and raw honesty, whether you like it or not."

He barks a laugh and bumps his drink to mine, "I can 'Cheers' to that."

We both take a sip as my thoughts wander to the events earlier in the night, "So what was Dolly's deal anyways?"

Darian grimaces, "She has been involved in the club for the last hundred years or so. She was being hunted by Caspian along with her brother prior to that. When we first met, her brother had just died, but I was able to give her protection and full access to my safehouses, properties and guards. Over time it seems as though she's come to dislike humans and the lack of magic here. She blames humans because there's no one else to blame other than the Gods and she wouldn't risk angering them like that."

I huff loudly, "Oh she felt more than dislike. It was plain as day, the disgust and hatred she felt while she was in front of us."

He raises an eyebrow, "What do you mean?"

"I mean it was easy to tell. Behind that amusement, she was absolutely enraged. She was disgusted. I just can't tell if it was at me or you or everything."

Darian hums in agreement as we both finish our drinks and there's a long pause of silence between us. My mind wanders to showering but then settles on the Jacuzzi outside on the patio and my entire face lights up, "You wanna go swimming, Mr. Cathorn?!"

Darian's mismatched eyes darken as heat flares through them, "That shouldn't even be a question, Ray."

My name on his lips sends tingles down my spine and I grin mischievously.

"Last one there is a rotten egg and has to make breakfast tomorrow!"

Before I get half the sentence out, I've broken into a sprint toward the master bedroom, Darian's laugh and quick footsteps follow behind me.

I scramble to press the button for the curtains to rise, then jog past the bed where Val is peeking at me with one eye before resuming his 'sleep'.

Opening the door to the patio, I check the dial on the side of the Jacuzzi, turning the jets on before tearing my cardigan off. Tugging my dress over my head, I drop them both to the floor and take two steps into the water.

My body tingles with the feeling of being watched, and I turn slowly to see Darian staring at me. His expression is hard, jaw feathering as his eyes narrow before they flick to mine.

My face falls in embarrassment and I stare at the ground between us, "If they're too disturbing, I can put my clothes back-"

"Stop." Darian interrupts me with a growl.

My head snaps back up to look at him, "Stop what?"

He walks closer, peeling his shirt off and tossing it next to my dress, "Don't you fucking dare cover them."

"Do they not disturb you?" Disbelief coats my voice as I feign a teasing tone.

He shakes his head and I scoff.

"Do not lie to me, Darian. You don't need to minimize their severity; I am painfully aware of what they look like. These scars may be a part of who I am, and I'm still learning to live with them but that doesn't mean you have to."

He's quiet as he studies me, and once again, I'm like an ant under a magnifying glass as he does. The look on his face is not one of sympathy but anger and something else I can't place.

I feel as though I'm on the verge of squirming or fidgeting as he speaks again.

"Who was it?" He has a certain calm about him as he steps closer, but I'm unable to find my voice to answer and my gaze drops.

Telling him would mean I've now spoken into existence the truth of my traumas not once but twice.

Verbalizing one of my many abuser's names to Caspian was a possible misstep but, Darian gives me a sense of peace and calm that I've never experienced before.

I find myself more trusting of him, which has only been reinforced seeing how he interacts with those around him.

Can I truly be on the verge of telling both brothers the name of the man who did this to me?

"Lara." He steps closer as he says my name.

I'm still gazing at the spot between us, but with his proximity, I'm simply staring directly into his broad, ink covered chest.

"Lara, I need you to tell me who the fuck did this to you," He reaches up, threading his fingers through the hair at the nape of my neck. His thumbs trail my jawline sending shivers down my spine as he uses them to tilt my head back until my eyes meet his darkened, mismatched gaze that hold the promise of violence, "Give me a name, Lara."

My heart hammers in my chest at the gentle yet authoritative tone to his voice, "Frank." I breathe as his eyes drill holes into me.

"Frank," He parrots, "And Frank is alive?"

I blink once, trying to quickly calculate what I assume was his age and how many years it's been since I was in his custody.

I resign myself to the unknown of whether he is alive or not, and I nod again, "I would assume so."

Darian leans in more, our lips less than an inch apart, "Who was he?"

A shiver trembles through me as his breath skates over my face. The distance between us sends my body into overdrive as he lightly rubs his thumbs against my skin.

At this point I'm uncertain if he's doing it to soothe my mind from the topic of conversation or even aware of it, but the contact is all consuming.

My body ignites and the butterflies swirling in my stomach seem out of control as I struggle to remain focused on his question.

"One of my foster parents." I whisper.

He steps closer toward me and on instinct, I back further into the pool as he continues his advance until we're both waist deep in water.

"I'll fucking kill him." Darian growls and crushes his lips to mine.

One of his hands glides down my neck, and over my breast to my waist, using it to help keep me steady as we retreat further into the Jacuzzi until my back bumps against the side.

His kiss is all consuming, and I find myself fervently returning each sweep of his tongue, every desperate motion as if he were the answer to everything.

He grinds his hips against mine, squeezing my waist with one hand as if the contact isn't enough. He presses himself deeper into me, and I gasp at the pressure as his erection strains against his soaked jeans.

His half lidded eyes darken as he chuckles and repeats the action, taking advantage of my open mouth to deepen the kiss with an intensity unlike any I've felt before.

This is more than just lust.

The passion and desire between us feels like an awakening.

It's as though my entire being could shatter into a million pieces with one wrong move but at the same time, I've never been this whole.

He lifts my leg around his waist, grinding himself against my clit and my mind quiets. My moan into his mouth breaks the little resolve he had.

Our lips part, and I'm breathless as his green and white eyes search mine in an unspoken question.

Do I want this?

I nod, finding confidence I didn't know existed as my body acts on instinct in a desperate need for more of him.

My hands rush to unbuckle his belt and zipper, my fingers graze him through his soaked pants as I tug to free him from them, and he groans.

His clothes and underwear drop below the water my jaw goes slack at the sheer size of him. His cock is impressively thick with veins protruding from it.

It's intimidatingly long.

I'd wager that it's nearly the length of my forearm if I were to compare the two.

I'm torn from my musing as it throbs, and I audibly swallow, watching it bob up and down in the bubbling water with each pulsate.

How the hell is that supposed to fit inside me?

Darian tilts his head as he towers over me, a knowing smirk on his face as my eyes meet his.

"Do you want this, Ray?" His baritone voice is thick, and I nod as my entire body shivers in anticipation.

Darian steps in close and the tip of his cock presses against my stomach as it pulsates.

"Use your words. I need to hear you say it."

The all consuming desire to feel him moving inside me could devour every aspect of my being as my pussy clenches.

My eyes snap to him and I breathe, "I want this, Darian. I want you."

There's a deep rumble in his chest, "Thank fuck." he murmurs.

He rips my wet underwear off with ease, and lifts me with his hands under my thighs as his lips find mine again.

Hunger and desperation a living, breathing thing inside of me as my legs instinctively wrap around his hips, my arms encircle his neck.

His cock throbs against my bare skin and I press in to it automatically, aching for more as he gives me exactly what I need, grinding the length of his erection against my pussy.

A husky moan escapes my lips as the pressure hits my clit.

"Fuck." Darian's last fiber of restraint snaps as he pulls his hips back and his dick angles perfectly against my entrance. He searches my face as he presses the tip in, and a pained moan escapes my lips as I struggle to adjust to the size of him.

His kisses are soft as he slides deeper, and I wince as his girth stretches me far beyond anything I've felt before. His cock massages my walls with every movement and throb as he eases himself inch by inch.

He pauses, looking at me with half hooded gaze as he withdraws an inch before pushing deeper the second time. The burn of accommodating his size makes my eyes water as I breathe through it.

"You feel so fucking good." He groans as he slides out and deeper again.

As my pussy stretches to take more after each slow thrust, the size of him sends electric jolts of pain into my lower body to mix with the pleasure.

The whimper I've suppressed finally escapes, and he stills, searching my face for any indication to stop, but I need movement otherwise it will be a whole other form of torture.

Shivering with anticipation, I roll my hips into his, reveling in how he feels buried deep inside of me. Taking the open invitation, he grips my waist tight as he thrusts all the way in, and a heated cry escapes my throat.

He withdraws to the tip in one long movement, and drives back in fully, pressing my hips onto him as if he can't get close enough.

I've never felt so fucking complete before.

The sensation of Darian losing himself in me is like nothing I have ever experienced as he crushes his lips against mine.

Darian finds a rhythm, the friction of his long strokes as I roll my hips builds pressure in my body. The thick, angry veins feeding his cock rub against my clit with every long, forceful thrust and as my orgasm builds, my nails dig into the skin of his shoulders and back.

"That's it. Chase it, Lara." Darian's voice rumbles, and I'm dangerously close as he drives in hard and his hand pinches my aching nipple.

"Oh fuck." My orgasm crashes over me, and I'm moaning his name as he keeps his pace steady.

As the waves of intense pleasure recede, and I release my nails from his skin and see the bite mark I inflicted at some point. Knowing that I drew blood as my orgasm overwhelmed my senses makes me flush even more.

Darian's pace picks up slightly, and he puts his forehead to mine, our panting breaths casting over one another. His hand slips between us and rubs my painfully sensitive, swollen clit while his thrusts become more unforgiving.

I can tell he's still restraining himself as he drives into me, "Stop being gentle, Darian."

His gaze snaps from my lips to my eyes for a mere moment before he wraps one arm around my waist, using the leverage to thrust so hard and deep that I'm concerned he might actually rearrange my guts.

"You take me so fucking well." His baritone voice sends my nerves haywire as he pistons in and out with brutal force.

All concern falls by the wayside as his other hand continues to expertly roll circles around my clit and I quickly find myself chasing another orgasm.

"You're going to come all over me while I fill you with every last fucking drop," He growls and my entire body shivers, "Come, Lara."

His words are the end of me and stars coat my vision as an intense orgasm rocks through my exhausted body.

My toes curl, and my pussy clenches as my nails scrape his skin again. He drives hard into me as his cock throbs, his own release cresting over him as he thrusts one, two more times before stopping, kissing me deeply in long lazy movements.

He withdraws himself but keeps my body pulled tight to his as we stay like that for a long moment, exploring each other's mouths in the afterglow of our orgasms.

After a short while our kiss breaks off, and he leans his forehead against mine.

"No one is allowed to hurt you and get away with it. Not now, not in the future. I will kill anyone who tries. Do you understand?"

The ferocity in his eyes is genuine as his gaze searches mine, and regardless if the future is unknown, though my life is being thrown into an abyss of uncertainty I can't help but feel like at this moment I am truly safe.

Is this what it is like to love someone? To be loved?

I nod, the tears in my eyes running down my face unbidden as I squeeze them shut.

"As long as breath fills my lungs," He says quietly, pressing a kiss to my forehead, "I will keep you safe."

My chest squeezes as he shifts my weight, pulling my back flush to his front, his arms encircling my shoulders tightly as he relaxes with me in his lap.

Leaning my head back against him, the hum of the jets and the rise and fall of his chest with each breath brings a newfound sense of peace, and he gently traces lines over my skin.

My eyes slowly become heavier, and it feels as though I'm melting into him as comfort and security seep within my bones.

For the first time in my life, I find myself at complete ease, and it's because I'm wrapped in the arms of a man who has killed countless people including those I once called my parents.

I'm painfully aware that tonight, I've given an intimate and irreplaceable piece of my heart to this man, but I find myself with no reservations, no regrets, no suspicions.

It's entirely possible that a part of me has always hoped I could trust him, and now I just trust he will not break it.

Perhaps that is part of the beauty of human nature and falling for someone.

I suddenly feel cold and a shiver wracks through my body and as he cradles me to his chest. My arms instinctively wrap around his neck and I lean my head into him, breathing in his familiar scent as the water trickles off my skin.

His body rumbles with a deep chuckle, and in the corner of my eye, I watch the shared bathroom come into view before he sets me down on the long counter. My skin goosebumps against the cold surface and I suppress a gasp as Darian methodically grabs fresh towels and starts the shower.

Once satisfied with the temperature, he cradles me and moves until we're submerged beneath the steady fall of water before easing me down to my shaky legs.

I watch with rapt attention as he lathers soap over my body, and shampoo into my hair.

By the time we're both clean, I'm so exhausted that I could fall asleep while standing as we dry off, and it's not long before he sweeps me off my feet to carry me into the bedroom.

I'm vaguely aware as he lays me down, pulling the thick, plush blankets over me before the bed shifts with movement and my mind goes blissfully quiet.

Chapter 32

Caspian

"We received word last night on her location. We have units tracking her movements and positioning for engagement."

Pinching the bridge of my nose, I blow out a breath.

This was a development I didn't see coming, but if opportunity arises I'd be a fool not to take advantage if she is vulnerable and out of place. It's surprising that she remained in such an obvious location so easily observed and lacking thorough security.

Still, it may be in my best interest to let her continue, unaware that I'm watching every movement. Her time is running out.

"Remain on standby. We observe for now, report back routine and habits. I want every detail. Where she shits, pisses, eats and sleeps. I want a full report on all of it."

"Yes sir," Lionel says as the call disconnects.

I sigh deeply and relax in my chair as the door opens, revealing a sneering Blair. She was stuck here in this realm when magic was bound all those years ago and is the one who foresaw Lara's part in the reinstatement of it. I wish I could say she's bitter and impatient because the time spent unable to shift into her serpent but, unfortunately she's always been like this.

Blair has less reason than I have to want magic restored. She has no family, no friends, no position, no title. She has one singular purpose, but she will stop at nothing if it gets us back home.

'By any means necessary' should be her motto.

It's something we've argued at length about.

She leans against the frame with a shoulder and crosses her lanky arms. Her lips curl into a snarl as she glares at me, and my blood pressure instantly rises.

"What is it now, Blair?" I snap.

"I'm becoming impatient, Caspian. She's taking too long to gather the amulets."

I stare into her empty, almost-black eyes and feign boredom, "The amulets are being recovered at an appropriate speed. We will have all of them before the next full moon."

Blair scoffs and shakes her head, her black hair swishing from one side to the other.

"She has found half of them. At this rate it will be months before magic is restored and we undo your banishment."

My jaw clenches. I despise this conversation with my entire being. The requirements for breaking my banishment is one thing, reinstating magic is a whole other topic I wish to avoid but every time Blair opens her fucking mouth, it's all that I can think about.

"It has been two weeks that she's been gathering them. They will be recovered in due time."

Blair's eyes narrow on me, her doubt evident in her gaze. "Are you sure you're willing to do what is needed, Caspian? You've been different lately, and Samira--" Her voice trails off, but I know her well enough to sense the underlying concern beneath her restrained tone.

"Enough!" I snap, my voice laced with an edge of fury. "It will be done. Now get out."

She huffs in frustration and whirls to leave, slamming the door behind her, and I'm left alone with my thoughts.

This intricate web of good versus evil is going to make me come undone. The question is, will Lara unravel with it?

Chapter 33

Lara

The brightness flooding into the room turns the back of my eyelids a tinge of pink, and I slowly crack them open, seeing Val's dark fur in front of me.

My stomach is queasy from the alcohol, gurgling loudly beneath the covers as a heavy arm dangles around my waist and I hear a chuckle behind me.

Darian's muffled voice is rough with sleep, "I lost the deal of making breakfast but couldn't bring myself to get out of bed, so forgive me, but I ordered food."

I laugh quietly and try to sit up, but find myself trapped beneath the mess of blankets and the weight of both Darian and Val.

My bladder feels like it's going to explode.

"I don't wish to disturb either of you, but I urgently need to use the washroom and can't get up."

Darian chuckles, flinging the blankets off before getting up, and I roll my eyes as Val huffs but remains where he is.

As I start to walk to the other room, Darian's phone chimes and I glance at him. His jaw flexes as he looks at the screen and I know it's not a notification of the food being delivered. "It's another location, isn't it?"

His eyes flick to mine, and he gives a subtle nod, "It is, but it's not exactly close. We'll eat breakfast and then we need to pick up some supplies before leaving. Val, you'll be coming with us." Val's head perks up, and he glances at Darian with concerned eyes.

"Where is it?" I ask hesitantly.

"It's far into a conservation area about one hundred and forty miles away. It's in the middle of nowhere near the mountains." Darian's voice doesn't convey any concern, but the tension in the air is enough to make my skin prickle.

Val's ears being pinned back doesn't help either.

I take a deep breath and head into the washroom, "Well, one problem at a time. Let's eat first before my stomach decides to eat my other organs."

I enter the kitchen to the smell of breakfast and sigh with relief.

"Is that bacon? Please for the love of God tell me that's bacon."

Darian laughs and slides a plate with eggs, sausage links and toast to me. He starts loading it with bacon and my eyes become saucers.

In his hands is a giant container of heaven and I determine right then and there that I must be dead.

"Darian," I breathe, and he looks at me with concern, "Pinch me, please."

He laughs, pinching my forearm hard causing me to yelp.

"This isn't heaven? I'm either dead or this is the best day of my life." He chokes on air as he laughs, and I sigh dramatically before shoving a slice of bacon into my mouth with a groan.

"This was exactly what my hangover needed," I say, patting my stomach as I lean back.

Both Darian and Val have the same satisfied smiles on their faces as I'm certain I do as I stalk over to the couch and plop down.

"So what will we need for this trip?" I decide to broach the topic and Darian rubs his jaw at the counter before answering.

"Water, plenty of it and food. A tent and a couple bedrolls, blanket and some other odds and ends. Rations and water will be the most important. Val can hunt for us as long as we have fires but water will be the most crucial to have a steady supply of, particularly for you since you're human. Val and I can go longer without water and be okay."

I nod and chew my lip, "So how close can we get by vehicle?"

Darian pulls out his phone and swipes around on a map, "We can get within 60 miles of it, the rest of the distance will be on foot. We'll need to plan for a four day round trip at the very least."

I nod, pulling myself to my feet and groan as my head throbs, "I'll see what I have for hiking gear that we packed, but we may need to make a stop."

He nods as he puts his plate into the dishwasher, "I didn't pack anything for hiking so, we'll definitely need to make a stop… or seven."

I chuckle and make my way back to my room, Val's nails gently tap the floor as he trails close behind, leaping onto the bed and observing me as I organize the contents of my carry-on.

I sort through the clothing, ensuring I have essentials such as underwear, socks, running shoes, athletic shorts, joggers, a tank top, a long-sleeve shirt, and a lightweight jacket.

By all counts, considering the duration of the trip, I'll need at least two more outfits for warmer weather to be comfortable.

The last thing we want is to endure damp clothing while hiking and sleeping, as it can quickly lead to illness and given the unpredictable climate of the mountains, it's essential to be well-equipped for most scenarios.

I grab a duffel bag from the closet and shove my clothes in it, my new phone is turned off and fully charged as I tuck it into one of the pockets along with the charger.

Hoisting the bag over my shoulder, Val and I head to the living area where Darian is waiting.

"All I need is an extra set or two of clothes," I say as we approach.

Darian grins and nods, "I need the same, we'll also need some non-perishable food and water so we'll stop off at the nearest outlet mall first, then we'll go to the grocery store on the way out."

He walks over to me, brushing a lock of hair from my face and tucking it behind my ear, "We'll follow your lead once we start to get close unless it's clear where it's located, then just let me bring it to you."

I meet his gaze and offer a subtle nod, feeling a gentle tenderness radiating from his eyes that tugs at my heart.

With my duffel bag in hand, he effortlessly slings it over his shoulder and strides toward the door, holding it open for Val and me, "Let's get this key." He says with a wink as we walk past him.

We arrive, and a sense of unease washes over me at the sight of the overwhelmingly crowded parking lot.

It shouldn't come as a surprise that an outlet mall in California would be this packed on a Saturday, yet I foolishly wished we'd be some of the few here. It's not that I despise crowds, but recent events have left me feeling cautious and wary of people.

As we finally secure a parking spot near the entrance, my gaze shifts from Val to Darian, "What are we going to do with Val?" I ask.

Val huffs and puts his head down dramatically as Darian chuckles, "Like any good dog, he's gonna stay here with the vehicle on while we go shopping."

Val growls but doesn't lift his head up, and I can't hold back the laugh that escapes my throat. His ear flickers, but he remains motionless.

"Maybe we can grab you a giant pretzel or something from the food court." His eyes lock onto mine the moment the word 'pretzel' leaves my lips and I burst into another laugh. He lets out a huff playfully, and shuts his eyes once more.

Darian and I step into the mall teeming with families and kids of various ages accompanied by their friends. All eyes seem to gravitate toward him with curiosity, given his towering stature that surpasses that of most men around us.

As we navigate the crowds, finding the nearest athletic wear store, a young lady in the store's uniform approaches us when we step inside. Her smile holds a hint of apprehension but appears kind, "Is there anything I can help you two with today?"

"Ladies and mens athletic shirts, and shorts please." Darian adopts a strictly business tone, and I bite the inside of my cheek to stifle a laugh.

"Right this way."

She leads us at a brisk pace, navigating through the aisles until she finally stops, gesturing toward the men's athletic clothing section with one arm. Then, she extends her other hand to point out the women's athleticwear on the opposite side of the aisle.

"This side is the men's section, and here is the women's section," she explains. "Feel free to let me know if you need any further assistance."

With a smile, she heads back in the direction we came from. We both find gear for two days, one for a particularly warm day and one for a day that is cooler as we hike further up the mountain.

As we stand in line, three women ahead of us catch my attention with their repeated glances and hushed conversations. Over time, the whispers grow louder, reaching a point where I can actually hear them.

The brunette leans toward her companions, "Did you notice his eyes?"

"Yeah, and his scar! He's so freaking hot." The blonde responds.

"You should ask for his number!" The other brunette chimes in.

"Oh my god, no!" The blonde hisses back.

"Think that's his girlfriend with him?" The first woman asks. The blonde glances over and responds with a scoff, "Doubt it. Who dyes their hair white?"

I pretend I don't hear them and turn my head to gaze at clothes off to the side in an attempt to tune them out as they continue their tirade.

"Look at her ankles and wrists, she's got red scars on them." One of them says.

In my peripheral vision two girls turn slightly, trying poorly to be inconspicuous.

The blond gasps, "Oh my god. I bet it's because she's into freaky stuff."

"What makes those kinds of marks?" One of the brunettes asks.

"It's called bondage or something, I think." The other brunette says.

"Maybe she is a whore or prostitute and one of her clients was into something crazy." The blonde adds.

After a brief moment of silence, the line inches forward, causing a slight shuffle among the people. Eventually, the blonde breaks the blissful peace of quiet, "My money is on him being her personal trainer or friend and she's a prostitute or something." They all giggle.

I'm too sober to deal with this.

"You should go ask for his number, Hailey." The brunette says as the other nods.

The blonde, Hailey, gasps dramatically, "Oh my god but what if that's his girlfriend? That'll be totally embarrassing for me!"

The second brunette glances over and then back at Hailey, "Look at them, they're totally platonic. If they were together they'd be holding hands like a real couple."

I'm caught off guard as Darian reaches over to tuck a stray lock of my hair behind my ear, causing my eyes to snap to his. He passes his clothes to me and leans in.

"I actually forgot something, can you hold onto these while I grab it?"

As the calming scent of forest rain envelops my senses, I nod, tucking his clothes alongside mine as he disappears into the aisles off to the side.

The women in front of me watch as he walks away and collectively sigh, continuing their banter about him.

"I wonder what his name is," Hailey says wistfully.

"I bet it's something strong, like Jeremy." Brunette two offers thoughtfully, and it nearly takes all my effort to suppress a laugh.

"Why don't you go ask him?" Brunette one suggests and nudges the blonde.

Hailey tilts her head, "He's not here now, and I'm not chasing him. He should be the one to chase me."

Lord almighty, forgive me for uttering these words but if they represent the future of human intelligence, I might as well abandon all my research endeavors. Willingly.

As the line inches forward once more, the women fall silent as Darian reappears clutching a pair of shoes, and a set of form-fitting women's shorts with a matching sports bra.

I raise an eyebrow and smirk with amusement as he approaches our spot in line.

"I understand the shoes, but are you taking up wearing women's clothing?" I'm fighting a laugh as I point to both articles of clothing and continue, "No offense but, I don't know if either of those will fit you."

Darian chuckles, taking all the items from my hands with a shake of his head.

My brows pinch together in confusion, "Care to explain then?"

He cocks his head and grins, "I saw them earlier and wanted to see you in them. I forgot to grab them on the way out."

As I blink at him, his grin widens into a full smile, and I realize he has dimples.

Dimples.

How did I not notice them before?

I'm so fucked.

Darian steps into me, and with his free hand, tips my chin. I inhale sharply as he leans in, and kisses me once softly.

It's then I feel his tongue subtly against my lips in a silent request to open for him and I eagerly oblige, meeting the passion in his kiss with my own.

After a long intimate moment our kiss breaks off, and his forehead leans against mine. "I wanted to do that at the apartment, but if I had, I don't think we'd have left."

My cheeks burn and he smirks before pressing a tender kiss against my brow. It takes a full minute to recollect myself, but once I do the women in front of me are glowering to one another and silent.

Did he do that on purpose?

The line shuffles forward, and the women ahead of us make their way to the register to purchase their items. As they leave, they steal a final lingering glance in our direction before grabbing their bags and exiting the store.

I join Darian at the register and begrudgingly concede as he insists on paying for all our items, despite my protests.

With our main reason for coming to the mall achieved, we take a slight detour to the food court.

My gaze lands on the enticing Chinese takeout joint, and I glance over at Darian who wears an amused grin, "Why don't you go ahead and order that? I'll take care of getting the pretzel for Val. If we return with anything else, I'm afraid he might bite my finger off."

I laugh and nod, "Whoever is done first grabs a table!"

Darian chuckles, heading to the other side of the food court while I get in line. Unsure of what to get, and whether Val will want any, I get a surplus of varieties and two large waters in to-go cups.

Heading across the seating area, I find an empty table nearby where Darian stands in line. I sit, place the spread of food down, and take a sip of water while I wait.

Darian's line hasn't shifted at all, so I turn on my phone to check my messages.

Candace: Hey! WE MISS YOU! Nothing special to report. We're running tests still, but there's diddly squat coming of the results outside of the flora we removed and monitored here. The one from the lake nearby is wilted slightly, the others are unchanged.

Henry: We are going to transplant from the lakes and see if the ones from the further locations grow stronger. Stay tuned!

Candace: Oh yeah, Claire called, and she was really pissed you missed your session. I told her you took a vacation, and she was ecstatic that you were taking time for yourself. She's having me call her once you're in the office to schedule a follow-up.

I grimace and text back.

Lara: Interesting news, good thinking on transplanting them. Make sure to take detailed notes and photos of your surroundings before and after. Don't forget to test the soil composition ahead of time and after one through five weeks.

Lara: Also, thanks for the heads-up about Claire.

Lara: Think she'll fall for it if I tell her I'm taking a permanent vacation?

The message displays as read instantly and Candace starts typing.

Candace: I think she would be concerned and would not fall for it at all. We all know you better than that, Lara.

Henry: LOL

Candace: When are you coming back?

I chew my lip while I think.

Lara: Perhaps a week, could be two. I'll let you know once I have a better idea.

Candace: Alright hun, miss you! Stay safe!

I power my phone off, turning my attention to where Darian was in line.

Irritation wells up within me when I see the same group of women from the store earlier behind him, giggling with each other.

My eyes remain fixed on the scene unfolding before me as Hailey steps forward and places her hand on Darian's arm. He tilts his head, angling his gaze over his shoulder, his striking white eye meeting hers, and his eyebrow arching inquisitively.

I watch her as she engages in conversation with him, and he responds with a dry, dismissive laugh, before shaking his head.

A mixture of jealousy and anger surges through me as I witness her head tilting, and her fingers trace down his arm.

My emotions subside as he firmly grabs her hand and squeezes until she yelps before he discards it to the side. I catch a glimpse of his enraged expression as he utters something to her, then turns away to place the order for Val's pretzel.

Hailey turns to her friends crying, and they rush to hug her in a supportive manner, rubbing her hand soothingly as they whisper to one another.

Well, that was unexpected.

Darian steps aside to wait for Val's pretzel, as the three girls turn away, seemingly abandoning the desire for pretzels. I find myself in their path as they make their way to the opposite side of the food court.

The brunette notices me first, whispering something to the others as they all shift their gaze to me. Hailey stomps up to the table and looks down at me.

"Your boyfriend is an asshole and a psycho! You should leave him, you deserve better than that."

I blink and cock my head in confusion, "What?"

Boyfriend? I deserve better?!

She sighs dramatically and flips her dry, blonde hair over her shoulder, "You heard me. He hit on me in line for pretzels. We saw you guys at the athleticwear store. I figured you should know that he hit on me, but I said no."

I can't help but laugh, and her eyes narrow at me.

"What are you laughing about!?" She nearly yells.

As she shouts, Darian comes up behind her with the pretzel in one hand and briefly halts before any of them know he's there.

"I'm laughing because everything you said is a lie." I pause and grin at her, "How's your hand, by the way? You may want to ice that."

Her face turns bright red as she opens and closes her mouth like a fish out of water.

Darian speaks up from behind the women, and all three of them jump in surprise, "Cat got your tongue all of a sudden? You didn't have any problem earlier when you told me to," He puts his free hand on his chin thoughtfully, "How did you put it? Oh yes. You said I should, and I quote, 'Leave that white-haired whore'."

His eyes shimmer with a blend of amusement and anger, made evident by the subtle ripple of muscle along his jawline beneath the stubble of his beard.

I laugh again, "Oh interesting!" I attempt my best impersonation of Hailey's squeaky voice as I quote her, "She told me, 'He hit on me in line for pretzels'. Which is strange because I could have sworn I saw her get painfully rejected... unless I'm mistaken?"

Darian chuckles darkly as he walks around them to sit next to me, "Painfully is a colorfully accurate word for it, yes."

As he puts the pretzel on the table the women are still standing there awkwardly, and he glances up at them.

"Are you going to leave or do you need another reminder why you're literal specks of dust in this world in comparison to the woman next to me?"

My eyes widen at his comment, but I blink and busy myself using my chopsticks to scoop some noodles and shrimp onto Darian's plate, then my own. Hailey huffs dramatically and stomps away, the two brunettes following closely behind her.

"I thought they'd never leave." I mumble as I dip the shrimp in sweet and sour sauce, popping it into my mouth with a groan.

Darian chuckles and scoops some fried rice onto my plate before doing the same to his own.

"If they didn't, they'd definitely leave after you almost orgasm over fucking Chinese takeout."

I nearly choke on shrimp and cut a glare at him, "If I didn't know better, one would think you're jealous of my food."

The heated look in his eyes tells me I'll regret that comment later, and my cheeks flush as I scoop some lo mein into my mouth in an attempt to mask the effect he's having on me.

Traitorous body.

As we make our way toward the car with leftovers in hand, I notice Val in the passenger seat, his ears alert and attentive as he watches us approach.

"I wonder how far away we were when he knew we were coming." I say.

"I'd wager he knew once we were 5 feet out the mall doors." His voice drips with amusement as he opens the passenger door for me then moves to organize our clothes into the duffel bags.

I pull the pretzel out and Val's tail whips excitedly against the seats as I hand it over to him. His giant maw devours it in four bites, and I laugh loudly.

"Did you have to inhale it? You're going to give yourself indigestion!"

Val lets out a huff, sniffing the Chinese food from the front seat and another laugh escapes my lips as I unpack our leftovers, placing them on the floor between us for Val to indulge.

Darian gets into the driver's seat, glancing at Val's sloppy eating, and chuckles, "I knew he would be excited about it, but didn't realize he'd be this... enthusiastic." He gives Val a pointed look, "Clean up your mess after, yea?"

Val huffs in agreement and returns to his noodles.

Chapter 34

We arrive at the grocery store where Val and I remain in the car. As soon as Darian closes his door, I instinctively lock the SUV and Val's eye flick to mine.

"Force of habit, sorry." I mumble, shifting in my stead as Val nudges my arm affectionately before resting his head on my lap, and we remain that way for a long moment.

It's hard to imagine how the world will change when magic is available again, as I watch a woman nearby load a case of bottled water in her car.

It makes me wonder if those who were stuck here will know immediately, or if they'll one day realize they can channel their power or shift finally and never know why.

I glance down and Val's eyes are closed while I rub along his snout, stopping at the top of his head.

"Have you thought about what it'll be like once you're able to shift back?" I ask, and his eyes snap open in surprise, eliciting a laugh from me at his reaction. "Sorry, I didn't mean to startle you. I'm just curious, though. Have you considered it?"

His ears perk forward, and his chin tilts down in response.

I nod and continue, "I've considered it too. Part of me has wondered what your other form looks like. The other part of me wonders whether or not it'll finally hit me that I've had a man sleeping in my bed for months."

Val huffs in amusement and his fur twitches.

"Are you nervous to be able to shift into your human form?" His ears pin back.

"So you're excited about it?" I ask and his ears perk forward.

My god, I can have a full yes or no conversation with him.

"Oh this is fun," I laugh and continue, "Do you think Darian is looking forward to having magic back?" His ears twitch and his gaze drops to the ground.

"Ah, is it bittersweet?" Val's chin dips again and his ears perk forward.

"Do you have family back in your realm?" His ears pin back.

"Were you lonely here at all, being in this form?" Val's ears first perk forward, then back and forward again.

"Hmmm. Do you mean that you were lonely at times?" His ears perk forward and tail wags.

"You weren't lonely with Darian?" I guess and his ears stay facing forward.

What else can I ask him that he can answer yes or no questions to?

There's one unknown that has been eating at me for a while and I muster the confidence to inquire about it.

"Did you lead Caspian to me that night at the house?" His ears pin back and my gut twists.

I should have known it wasn't dumb luck.

"I see." I sigh and glance out the window.

The SUV rocks slightly, and suddenly Val's large body is halfway between the front seats, and each of his paws are positioned on either side of my legs, with his nose nearly touching mine.

He huffs once, blowing my hair backward, and he nudges my cheek with his wet nose. His head rests gently on my shoulder, pressing his weight down onto me. It feels strangely comforting, and I instinctively wrap my arms around his thick, furry neck.

Eventually, Val retracts his head and redirects his attention to the parking lot. His fur bristles and he stands tall, completely shielding me from view.

To any onlooker, it would appear as if a wolf is occupying the seat, and I'm concealed from view entirely.

His giant body vibrates with a low growl, we both jump in surprise as a knock sounds on the door to the left where Darian stands with a mixture of concern and confusion on his face.

I press the button to unlock the vehicle, and Darian opens the door to place the bags in the back as Val hovers over me, still obscuring my body from view protectively.

Darian hops into the driver's seat, eyeing Val cautiously before scanning the lot in front of us. "How long has he been like this?"

I frown, "He began just around thirty seconds before you knocked." Darian curses, swiftly jumping into the seat and shifting the SUV into drive.

What the hell?

"What's going on?" I ask, keeping my voice calm.

Darian pulls onto the main road, and as he expertly navigates through traffic, he glances repeatedly in the rearview and side mirrors every few seconds.

"He must have scented or heard hunters nearby and was blocking them from seeing you." Darian's voice is level as he weaves the SUV in and out of traffic before pulling onto a frontage road along the highway, and he presses the gas to the floor.

Once he's seemingly convinced we're not being followed, he keeps his speed steady as Val moves to the backseat again.

After approximately an hour and a half, we arrive at the secluded hiking trail that meanders through the woods, accessible only via obscure side roads.

Veering off the main route, we drive into an open field before finding a suitable spot to park the vehicle. We then unload our supplies, packing the food and water into our duffel bags.

Darian grabs both, pulling one over each shoulder and I blink at him, "I can take one if you want."

He chuckles and shakes his head, "These aren't heavy, I won't tire carrying them."

I blink and concede with a nod.

We set down the path and I note the sun's position, recognizing that it's almost two in the afternoon. Aware that dusk is fast approaching, I quicken my pace, and Darian effortlessly keeps up while Val dashes ahead, scouting the path for potential hazards.

It's not long before I'm thankful he's carrying both packs. Running is one thing, but hiking uphill is a whole other ballgame.

My thighs already burn.

The quiet between us gradually gnaws at me, and I surrender to the urge to fill the silence.

"So what's the first thing you'll do once magic is back?"

"I've never really given it thought. It may depend on the circumstances of its return and what is happening in the moment. It's hard to say for certain."

I offer a nod before moving to my next question, "What do you miss most about your realm?"

He's quiet for a moment, and when he answers I can hear the longing in his voice, "I miss my brothers the most," I tilt my head, and he adds with a grin "We were closer than I think family might ever be and though we weren't blood related, we still grew up together. Part of me wonders if they're still alive after these years of banishment. If I return-" I narrow my eyes at him, and he chuckles before correcting himself, "When I return, I'll find my brothers and we will right all the wrongs against us and our people."

He goes quiet as the forest seems to tighten around the path, reducing the sunlight peeking through the canopy above us.

"I'm certain they're alive, and you will return to them. I promise." I say softly.

"What will you research once magic is restored?" Darian asks, and I cast a confused look at him.

"What do you mean?"

He chuckles, "Well you're currently researching an area that is simply an echo of my realm, and you can see the results of that today."

Though I knew magic was one of many possibilities, hearing Darian reaffirm that his realm plays a part in my endless search for answers brings a sense of failure to my mind.

"I suppose I could return to monitoring global warming but that was like banging my head against a wall. I suppose it's hard for me to say for certain as well."

My gut twists as I imagine the future, hopelessly researching climate change and Darian returning to his realm.

It's a mental image I'm dangerously close to not accepting after spending time with him.

That future looks bleak, colorless, boring, and stagnant.

Darian remains silent, and I foolishly wonder whether he's lost in the same train of thought as we continue along the path until the forest grows darker with the sunset.

We come to a stop as the thick undergrowth recedes, providing enough space for us to pitch our tent.

"We'll set up camp here." Darian says softly and gently puts our bags against a tree.

I crouch down and start to dig the tent and bedrolls out. In a matter of minutes, our shelter is set up, and the beds are spread out inside but a feeling I can't quite place still weighs heavy in my chest.

It's as though something squeezes my still-beating heart, threatening to turn it to dust.

Darian hauls over a fallen tree for us to sit on, and retrieves a couple of water bottles from our bags, passing one to me as I settle beside him.

Taking a few sips, my mind wanders but continues to fall back to the thought that someday soon, my life will return to how it was before this hunt for keys.

I can't put into words how much my entire being detests that thought, but I shove the feeling deep down.

Darian breaks the tense silence, "We put in five hours today. Tomorrow we'll follow the path for another six, and then we'll head north off the path until nightfall. If we keep our pace we will reach our destination by then, if we have any delays, we will have to get the amulet in the morning and then head back."

I nod absentmindedly and take a sip of water.

My mind and emotions are entangled in conflict, so much that I don't trust myself with idle conversation.

"I'll be back, going to use the washroom." I murmur, striding into the forest while keeping on the top of the tent in sight.

I locate a secluded spot concealed by foliage and attend to my needs before retracing my steps. My heart sinks when Darian is nowhere in sight, prompting me to settle against the sturdy trunk of a tree and release a deep sigh.

I am exceptional at a few skills in life.

Processing my emotions has never been one of them.

I've often chosen to bottle them up and push them aside, relying on distractions until the pressure becomes too intense. In the past, I had research to immerse myself in, work to occupy my mind, and friends to share a drink with.

Here in this forest, however, where it's just Darian, Val and I, on a journey that brings me one step closer to losing that feeling of security and completeness. The weight on my very being becomes unbearable.

The tears gather in my eyes and I squeeze them shut, attempting to contain the emotions that tighten my throat. Taking a deep, shaky breath, I exhale slowly and survey my surroundings.

I can't let myself break.

Spotting a branch in the distance, I fixate on it and stride over to the tree, feeling the restless energy within me needing an outlet. I jump, grasping onto the branch, allowing myself to dangle from it.

As the rough bark bites into my skin, my muscles tremble as I lift my body so that my chin reaches the top of the branch. I focus on the pain with every repetition, my muscles tiring with each one.

Time becomes a blur as I continue, pushing myself beyond the limits of exhaustion.

My chest heaves, my muscles tremble and tears stream down my face, but I do not stop.

My palms become slick with a mixture of blood and sweat, they burn as I squeeze with numb fingers as they threaten to give way, desperate to remain suspended and my body quivers with exertion, but I do not stop.

It's only when a whimper pierces through the haze surrounding me, snapping me out of my intense focus that makes me pause and I release my grip on the branch, landing on unsteady feet.

The forest has fallen completely dark, and despite the shade of his fur, I can make out the faint outline of Val nearby.

Overwhelmed by my emotions, I sink to my knees, my hands squeeze painfully into tight fists against the ground. Tears stream down my face unbidden.

"I can't do this anymore, Val." I whisper, my voice cracks as Val presses the top of his head to my collarbone and the sob I had been desperately suppressing finally escapes, breaking through the dam of my emotions.

Is this what it is to love? To feel pain simply at the thought of them no longer being present?

The floodgates open, and I surrender to the overwhelming wave of emotion. Wrapping my heavy, exhausted arms around Val's large body, I bury my face into his fur and shudder.

I can't keep doing this.

Why the fuck have I been fighting for so long?

What have I been fighting for?

For a life that has never chosen me?

One filled with pain and loss?

For a past that aimed to destroy me in every way?

For a future that I don't belong in?

The tears continue to flow freely, absorbed into Val's fur.

When magic returns, I will become no one again.

I will be Lara Ray. The scientist who clawed her way out of her past and evolved only to be irrelevant to the future of a species that sought to break her at every step.

In a way, they succeeded.

I am broken.

I am shattered into a million pieces, only being held together by glue that has finally come undone.

I will lose people I've grown to care about deeply, and nothing will be able to stop that.

Val pulls back, his eyes filled with sad understanding, and he hesitates for a moment, before rubbing his cheek against mine.

If I'm going to make it through this I must stop relying on them.

A little voice in my head quietly reminds me, there's a good chance I will not make it through this anyways.

Maybe that's for the best.

I know the moment they're gone, I will shatter completely.

Hell, I'm already crumbling while they're still by my side.

No. If I'm to make it out of this, I will find a way to do so as the woman who made it through hell and back.

Gathering my strength and determination, my resolve sets in, letting out a shaky breath as I release Val and wipe my cheeks before rising to my feet.

"I'm sorry you had to see that, Val. I'll be alright. I have been up until now, and I will continue to be long after you're both back home." My voice quivers once more, and I wince, quickly clearing my throat to regain composure.

I glance down at my palms, noticing the blood still trailing from them at a slow pace.

We return to the tent and where Darian's seated on the log with his head slightly tilted. His dark black hair hangs loose, accentuating his eyes that stand out even more against the shadows of the forest.

His gaze tracks my approach and his eyes shift briefly to my hands before returning to my face, which I'm certain still shows signs of puffiness and tears.

His brows pinch together as he watches me take a seat on the log, my hand weakly reaching out for the bottle, but Darian is -even now- a step ahead. He grasps the water and effortlessly twists off the cap, pouring a small amount of liquid over my palms.

I clench my jaw as a sting spreads through my hands.

I move to take the bottle, but he pulls it away, keeping it out of my reach.

"I can do it." I grit out.

I see his hair shift in the limited light of the forest as he nods, "I know full well you can."

"Then let me." I retort.

"No."

His response is so curt that I look at him with shock, but his jaw is clenched and his face unreadable.

My throat tightens.

I'm mentally desperate to mend the crack in the floodgates, but the fractures have multiplied, spreading like a web of impending destruction and I know deep down that it's only a matter of time before it completely crumbles.

Darian rinses my palms gently, and disappears into the tent for a moment, returning with an ointment and some bandages. His ministrations are quick but effective, and before I know it, both my palms are wrapped and no longer dripping blood.

"So, do you want to tell me what this was about?" He asks softly.

I withdraw my trembling hands from his and shake my head lightly, "You've already done enough for me and you won't always be here. So no, I don't want to talk about it."

His frown deepens, but he doesn't press any further, nor does he stop me as I push to my feet and walk to the tent to sleep.

As I lay awake, staring at the shadows above me, Darian's distant murmuring carries in the silence of the night, accompanied by a soft huff from Val.

The choir of crickets chirping fills the air, becoming more deafening as the minutes drag on until eventually, sleep takes me under.

I wake slowly, my eyes struggling to adjust to the darkness as I glance to Darian's undisturbed side of the tent.

A sense of unease settles in my gut at finding the space around me empty. The silence is deafening, not even the faintest sound reaching my ears outside of the increasingly frantic rhythm of my own heartbeat.

Something's not right.

I gather my strength and push to my feet, swaying on uncooperative legs as my muscles protest the sudden movement, but it's the adrenaline coursing through my veins driving me forward.

Approaching the tent flap with caution, the sound of the zipper fills the air with each notch as it echoes through the oppressive stillness around me. After what seems like an eternity of unease, I manage to create a small opening, and carefully peer outside. The log where Darian and I had spent time together sits vacant, and Val is nowhere to be seen.

With the tent flap lifted, I cautiously sneak out, remaining crouched as I assess my surroundings in the minimal light offered through the tree cover. A sensation in the pit of my stomach is urging me to run, but I don't move.

I struggle to pinpoint where this panicked feeling is coming from.

Am I dreaming?

Giving myself an aggressively firm pinch, wincing at the pain, a shudder runs through my body and I cautiously make my way to the nearest tree, pressing my back against it for support. With my heart pounding, I focus on controlling my breath, taking slow and steady inhales as I strain to listen for any signs of danger.

Where are Darian and Val?

A sudden snap of a twig sounds out to my right, and I fight the urge to turn quickly. Instead, sliding my gaze in that direction to catch a glimpse of movement and two figures in the distance.

Another snap, this time further behind the figure, draws my attention, and I make out the silhouette of a third man heading in the direction of the tent. Recognizing the potential threats, I quickly shift into a crouch behind some low-hanging branches, cautious not to snag on any.

I watch intently as the first man points toward the tent and does a series of hand signals to the others. My heart thunders as he glances behind him to where the third man follows closely.

Dread and panic surge through my body, but I fight to maintain composure.

The men form a tight circle around the tent, while my eyes catch the movement of a fourth and fifth figure sneaking in from a slightly greater distance.

With a sinking feeling, I realize that it's only a matter of time before they discover the tent empty and my mind races, searching for a plan to hide.

I need to get out of here.

Slowly glancing behind me with my heart pounding in my chest, I back away into the darkness with careful steps, avoiding any twigs or roots which could betray my position. As I increase the distance between myself and the men, I hear the sound of the tent zipper being ripped open, followed by the loud voices of the intruders.

As my attention is distracted from the path, I inadvertently place my weight on a root that gives way with a resounding crack. The noise triggers shouting in the distance, and without looking back I sprint deeper into the dark forest.

The thunderous sound of footsteps reverberates behind me, echoing my frantic heartbeat. Although they haven't gained ground, my body is reaching its limits and desperation floods my thoughts as I search the surrounding darkness for any possible hiding spots or means of escape, but find none.

Running remains my sole option, and I surge forward with every ounce of lingering strength, knowing that I can't sustain this pace indefinitely.

I gulp in a deep breath, desperately trying to stay composed amidst the chaos. The branches lash against my already sore arms, leaving what I'm sure are scratches and blood trailing down them. My pajamas, torn and muddied, hang in tatters around my legs, while each step sends shooting pain through my bare, bruised feet, pierced by the occasional sharp twig.

I'm so focused on my frenzied escape, that I fail to notice approaching footsteps until it's too late and an arm coils around my waist, yanking me off balance. A scream claws out my throat as I crash to the ground and my assailant tumbles with me.

The force of the impact steals the air from my lungs, leaving me gasping and coughing in a struggle to regain my breath. As I desperately try to inhale, the weight of my attacker pins me down, further reducing my ability to breathe.

Before I can recover, I cry out as my arms are wrenched behind my back, contorting my body in an unnatural position. My face is mercilessly pressed to the unforgiving ground, dirt and debris digging into my skin as I fight for air.

I feel someone's face near the back of my head as my attacker snarls through his slightly ragged breaths, "Thought you could escape from us, bitch?"

I can't answer because I'm still struggling to breathe.

"Oi, Ryan! Did you get 'er?" I hear a voice in the distance.

"I caught the dumb bitch, alright." Ryan spits on the ground next to my head.

"Let's get her back to the truck. The others won't have kept those two busy long enough for us to dawdle here."

My self-defense training flashes to the forefront of my mind and my trainer's voice rings into my ears.

Don't let them take you to a second location, Lara.

Fight as hard as you can. Kick, scream, thrash.

Do what you have to do, to remain where you are as long as you can because the odds of being found once you're moved are slim to none.

Better off dead before you're moved than to be kept alive wherever they take you.

My body bucks against the one restraining me and I unleash a piercing shriek for help, my shrill voice echoing through the surrounding darkness. Agony radiates in my side as a foot ruthlessly strikes my body causing me to double over in coughs and wheezes.

But in the midst of the pain, I refuse to be silenced. With cruel precision, my assailant binds my arms tightly behind my back, cinching ropes around my limbs with such force that I cry out again.

"Shut her up!" One of the men screams at Ryan who is frantically pulling me off the ground.

One of the others has caught up, and he scoffs, "I'll fucking shut the whore up myself."

My head snaps to the side as someone's fist collides with my face, and sudden pain radiates from my jaw through my neck. With the taste of copper in my mouth, I see red and thrash against my restraints.

"I'll fucking kill you." I snarl, but my threats do nothing more than make the men in front of me laugh loudly, and the sound echoes into the dark of the forest.

The remaining men have caught up, and I find myself surrounded by all five, their faces shadowed and painted black, and their clothes are dark and form-fitting.

In the dim light, I can discern their physical differences. The one who initially apprehended me has a toned physique, his companions however, display the opposite.

"What do you want?" I ask loudly, wincing through the pain in my jaw, and Ryan chuckles.

"We just want money. Hope you understand it's nothing personal, dove."

I roll my eyes. "Who hired you?"

One of the other men replies with an amused huff, "Someone with a lot more money than you."

With a forceful grip on my arm, Ryan yanks me upright, disregarding my protests as I shout at him, "The fuck do you think you're doing?! Let me go!"

My defiance fuels my struggle, but it merely invites retaliation. A searing pain radiates from the side of my head as I crumple and collide with the ground, my face meeting the earth once more.

"The fuck, Bryce?" Ryan's voice holds a tone of annoyance.

As I struggle to clear my blurred vision with fatigued blinking, I lift my head from the ground slightly.

"Someone needed to shut her the..." Something catches their attention as Bryce's voice cuts off abruptly.

"Shit. I think it's the wolf. Vern, Bryce, go check the surrounding area." The men pause long enough for me to hear a vicious growl resonating through the forest, sending shivers down my spine.

Summoning every ounce of strength I have to push myself off the ground, my knees tremble as I struggle to regain my bearings, and a sharp snap pierces the stillness of the night.

My gaze instinctively darts toward the source, and there, bathed in a luminous shaft of moonlight filtering through the dense canopy, stands the towering silhouette of a figure, cloaked in darkness.

Darian.

A surge of relief washes over me as I recognize the second figure beside him, and my heart skips a beat. Their presence is a stark contrast to the darkness that surrounding them.

Val, standing with his head low and menacing. His fur bristling with an air of fury as a low, vicious growl sends shivers down my spine.

The air catches in my lungs as a gust of wind sweeps through the forest, the flickering light momentarily revealing their blood-stained visages.

Darian cocks his head as he takes in my appearance and his handsome features are fierce as he turns his attention to the men, "I'll only ask you this once. Which one of you fucking hit her?"

Two of the men point to Ryan and Bryce, the third holding his palms up. All five of them look ready to shit themselves.

One of the men runs, but Val lunges and within seconds he's on the man's back. The sound of flesh tearing and a gargled shriek cuts through the silent forest before it abruptly goes quiet.

Ryan and Bryce tug at my restrained body, their desperate attempts to remove me from the scene evident in their frantic movements as the other two men approach Darian, intending to buy time for Ryan and Bryce to make their escape.

I can only watch helplessly as the two men jump to action, each of them throwing their fists at Darian. Within a moment he's snapped the first man's neck, with a hand fisted into the second man's hair, smashing his head against a tree repeatedly until his skull crunches.

My eyes widen with shock when Darian releases the fistful of hair and the man's body crumple to the ground.

It happened so fast, had I blinked, I would have missed it.

"Shit." Ryan breathes as Darian turns his attention to him and Bryce. The bushes to my left rustle as Val emerges, his coat still dripping with fresh blood.

"Val," Darian growls and points at Bryce, "Don't kill that one yet." He states before lunging at Ryan.

Val circles Bryce to keep him busy, but my eyes are glued to the two men before me.

In a blur of movement, Darian evades Ryan's attacks with precision as he blocks incoming punches, countering with powerful strikes that find their mark on Ryan's face.

The fight's already over when Darian expertly deflects a punch aimed at his abdomen, his final move twists Ryan's arm into an unnatural angle before a sickening crunch sounds out.

Ryan shrieks, gasping from the pain.

Darian doesn't even look winded.

I watch my original assailant fall to his knees, screaming loudly as his arm dangles limp at his side with bone protruding from it, and his blood drips to the ground.

"Please, I was only doing a job." Ryan begs, his good arm held up in surrender.

I see Darian's white teeth flash into a furious smile, "Wrong line of work, I'm afraid," He snaps Ryan's neck with a crack that makes me flinch, continuing as his body falls lifelessly to the ground, "It doesn't appear to have a very long life expectancy."

I blink while I watch him move toward Bryce and a fresh wave of anger rushes through my veins, "Wait." I say.

Darian freezes instantly and glances in my direction.

"Untie me." I wiggle my arms for emphasis, and Darian moves closer to undo my bindings. As the ropes fall away, he reaches into his coat and retrieves a long dagger, extending it toward me.

I gape at him, "You had this the whole time and instead chose to fight with your hands?"

He shrugs, "I was angry. This was more satisfying."

I shake my head, but deep down part of me understands.

Gripping the dagger tightly, I push to my feet to stand in front of Bryce.

"Kneel." The authority in his voice mixed with everything that just happened sends an unnecessary -and highly inappropriate- amount of heat through my body.

Without hesitation, Darian kicks out Bryce's knees, forcing him to land on the ground with a grunt.

I twirl the dagger in my bandaged hand and flip it back and forth from handle to blade as guilt and anger war in me as Bryce glares at me with pure malice.

I've never killed anyone before.

It doesn't mean I haven't wanted to.

My eyes lock with Darian's fierce gaze. The support and burning emotion I find within them reassures my decision, and I give a single nod.

Almost completely in sync, Darian tilts Bryce's head backward, exposing his neck and in one swift movement, I drag the sharp metal deep into his flesh until it slices through the cartilage of his throat.

He makes desperate gurgling noises, but my gaze remains locked onto Darian's as Bryce collapses to the forest floor.

I really should be more bothered about what I just did, but I feel nothing but relief.

Yet another thing I can never tell Claire.

My attention turns to Darian as he nonchalantly steps over Bryce's fallen body, positioning himself in front of me. His head tilts slightly to the side and excitement brims within his mismatched eyes as they reflect the minimal light available in the forest.

"That was the hottest thing I've ever seen in my life." he says, searching my face.

I jerk my head back, "You're sick."

His dark chuckle sends heat through my body.

This is so wrong. I'm getting turned on when there are five dead bodies around us.

And here I called him the sick one.

My gaze slides over to the corpses littering the forest floor and bile rises in my throat. My stomach apparently not as iron-laden now that my rage has subsided.

Darian's voice breaks my train of thought, "We should clean up and head back to camp."

He's also surveying the corpses around us as he speaks before his gaze lands on me, "There's a small body of water near the camp, we should use it to clean up first," His eyes trail down the length of my body, then Val's before he looks himself over. "Not that I mind blood but I have a feeling you don't want to sleep like this."

Now that the adrenaline has worn off my body is heavy and simply nodding takes a conscious effort, but I manage one.

At this point, I'd be fine to sleep in anything.

Waking up, though? That's when I'd regret it.

He gestures toward Val and I feel his gentle touch on the small of my back, guiding me to turn and follow in that direction.

After what feels like an hour the dense brush begins to thin, revealing a small clearing with a deep stream flowing downhill. Val confidently approaches the water, positioning himself near the point where it plunges further down. Without hesitation, he dives in, submerging his entire body, causing the water to turn a dark shade, even in the moonlight.

I walk over as he resurfaces, moving his soaked body to the edge to shake the excess water out of his fur.

Disregarding any concern for modesty, I strip my tattered clothing off and wade into the frigid water. The chill causing my teeth to chatter uncontrollably as the water rises to my navel. I take a few steps further until the water reaches my shoulders before I submerge my head fully vigorously scrubbing my face and scalp, disregarding the discomfort in my jaw.

Once satisfied that I've cleansed all traces of blood and dirt, I pull myself out of the water into the night air.

The cold penetrates my already frozen skin and my limbs tremble uncontrollably. With immense effort, I move where I had left my torn and bloodied clothes, realizing I'll have nothing clean to wear.

Fuck, why did we come here first?

Debating the idea of walking back to camp nude and risking illness as I get closer to the heap on the ground, I'm surprised to see that there's a blanket and fresh clothes on top of a stump next to my sullied pajamas.

If my teeth weren't chattering, I'd have thanked Darian.

I struggle but manage to pull the clothing on and sit on the stump, wrapping the blanket around my body before looking to the others.

Val is sitting near the edge of the water watching Darian who is waist-deep, finally taking the time to clean himself off. With the moonlight illuminating his back, the creatures inked onto his skin look alive, like they could leap off of him and take actual flight. The lifelike wolf stares back at me as Val gazes at Darian, and I can't help but wonder if the other depictions on his shoulders hold any significant meaning or if he simply has a fondness for ravens and dragons.

My thoughts are interrupted as he disappears beneath the surface, causing dark red swirls to rise to the top and my eyes track the trail of color as it rushes downstream. Moments later he emerges, standing as the water cascades off his head and shoulders.

As Darian stalks away from the stream our eyes meet, and I find myself once again trapped within his mismatched gaze. My cheeks flush as he bends to grab his own fresh clothes and I know I should give him privacy to put them on, but I'm unable to avert my eyes for the life of me.

Even without his tattoos, his body is a piece of art.

Like a beautifully crafted sculpture you'd find in an expensive museum, with hard lines and intimate details. It's the kind of beauty that you'd stand before, staring at the 'Do not touch the art' sign, and struggle not to reach out to, just to see how it feels beneath your palm.

The only difference is that I know all too well what he feels like, and damn if it isn't the closest thing to a heaven that I was convinced doesn't exist.

It's like once my eyes meet his, everything in my being gets sucked in, as if he can see every tarnish, stain and vulnerability of my soul.

Never in my life did I expect to have a connection that runs this deep. This goes beyond physical attraction and defies all rational thought.

I foolishly assumed distancing myself emotionally from him could grant me some semblance of independence in the face of what's to come, but there's something about being by his side that gives me strength.

Once Darian's fully clothed, Val takes the lead toward the camp, and I force my heavy and stiff limbs into motion, determined to follow him.

Chapter 35

As we reach our campsite, a sense of gratitude washes over me at the sight of our mostly untouched tent. The would-be kidnappers hadn't taken the opportunity to destroy anything in their pursuit, and for that, I am thankful.

With weariness taking hold, there is nothing left to do but crawl into our beds and I pull the blankets tightly around my frozen body with a contented sigh.

As the stillness settles around us, my teeth chatter in my head as my limbs tingle and burn at the blood flowing back into them. Darian shifts slightly and another blanket is layered on top of me failing to thaw the icy grip that had taken hold.

My teeth continue to chatter.

Without a word, a rush of chilled air permeates the space as the blankets are lifted, and I feel Darian shift behind me. The delicious heat from his body radiates against my back as his arm encircles my waist and gently tugs me flush to him.

Silently, I surrender to the comfort of his touch, instinctively wriggling closer, melting into him with a deep sigh of content before my mind begins to wander to the events of the night.

"Thank you for finding me." I murmur.

A brief silence hangs in the air, and I wonder if Darian has drifted off, but just as I begin to question his chest vibrates against my back.

"I will always find you, Lara. Even if you cannot see me, I will never be far." He murmurs softly, "I've lived hundreds of years, and met hundreds of thousands of people in this lifetime, many of whom I will never see again. There is not a single one of them that would have made me feel an ounce of terror if their lives were at risk as yours was tonight."

My heart beats like a war drum within my chest as he continues, "I would gladly put all of them to the sword myself if it meant keeping you by my side and that is not something to take lightly, Lara. I experienced true fear today for the first time in centuries, and it was because my misstep could have cost your life."

His arms flex around my body as his grip tightens, and his head leans in closer until his lips graze my ear, "I will never make such a mistake again."

My chest swells at his admission, hope a living breathing thing in my veins as I press myself further into him. With warmth in my body and soul, I let sleep take over in the safety of his arms.

Chapter 36

I awaken as the darkness surrounding us begins to transition gently to the soft hues of morning.

My face is nestled against Darian's chest, reveling the warmth and comfort of his embrace as his arms are wrapped tightly around me.

Peace.

This is what being at peace feels like.

Recalling his words from last night my stomach twists and turns with nervously happy energy.

I tighten my grip around his torso and I release a small sigh. His arms respond to my movements, drawing me closer into his hold. The world outside this tent may be awakening, but in this moment, time seems to stand still.

"Good morning." His voice breaks the silence, and I'm surprised at its clarity and lack of drowsiness.

That's when it dawns on me that he must have been awake long before me but hadn't thought to pull away or get up.

The notion sends butterflies throughout my body.

"Morning." I whisper back, my voice hushed as I attempt to mask the wince at the pain in my jaw.

Darian must have noticed as his gentle touch feathers against the tender area of my face before he delicately tucks my hair behind my ear.

I close my eyes briefly, the sensation is so intimate and foreign from any prior experience in my life that I savor every second.

"I'm so sorry they hurt you." He says quietly, searching my face.

My heart thunders in my chest, caught between awe and disbelief at the contrast of his tender touch and the chilling reality of the violence he's capable of.

As his thumb gently traces a path on my cheek, I can't help but recall the image of his hands, once stained with the blood of those who sought to harm me. It's hard to reconcile the fierce protector to the gentle soul before me.

Yet, it's precisely this duality that draws me closer to him. It's a reminder that perception can be deceiving.

"It couldn't be helped." I say, reflecting on the statements made by my attackers, "They spoke as though they purposefully distracted you to get to me. I'm just thankful you found me as quickly as you did."

Darian falls silent, and I angle my head to get a clearer view of his face. The muscle in his jaw flexes with tension, and his lips press into a thin line as he gazes thoughtfully at the side of the tent.

It's the guilt on his face that puts me into motion.

Sitting up slightly, I place my hand on his chest, "Hey," I whisper, reaching further to squeeze his shoulder, "Don't you dare blame yourself, Darian. It's the fault of whoever hired those assholes, not yours."

He inclines his head though his face is still shadowed, "I won't allow something like that to happen again. I meant what I said last night, Lara. I will never be far from you, from this moment on. Even when you cannot see me, I will be close by."

I lock eyes with him and my heart thrashes in my chest. My pride struggles against the vulnerability building within, but, God help me, I can't stop myself, "And what about when all this is over and magic is returned?"

Darian's features soften, and it's as if he has finally connected the missing pieces of a puzzle, "We will figure out a way forward once magic is returned. Together."

My heart flutters in my chest and hope floods through me as I cling to the possibility that maybe, just maybe, I won't lose my two companions once this ordeal comes to an end.

Stupid girl.

Darian's strong arms tug me closer, and he brushes his lips against my temple, "It's still early but if we leave in the next hour, we can be well on our way back by nightfall."

It's a conscious effort to leave the bed as I release a soft sigh, untangling myself from his arms.

After hiking for hours, time passes in a blur as the sun peeks through the canopy above.

A dull pain in my lungs and stomach brings me to a stop as I pause to catch my breath, removing the lid of my water bottle to take a deep sip as a trickle escapes the seal, running down my chin.

I wipe at it with the back of my hand, wincing at the pain in my jaw as Darian steps closer.

"This is the second rest break in the past hour. Are you feeling sick?"

Darian's mismatched eyes burn into mine as I screw the lid of the bottle back on.

I shake my head, "I'm fine. Just fatigued."

He levels me with an assessing gaze, scanning my body as if it will tell him my ailments like he's some kind of x-ray machine and frowns.

"Come sit for a few minutes then, we have time." he says, gesturing to a fallen tree we passed only a few seconds ago.

The notion is more than tempting as I turn and pain lances through my body, originating in my abdomen.

Within seconds, Darian is at my side searching my face.

I didn't realize I had even made a sound.

"What is it?" he asks, concern painted across his handsome features as his eyes drop to my hand covering my stomach.

Our gazes lock, and I don't need to speak it out loud as his face becomes determined.

"Shit. Can you point us in the right direction?" he asks, and I nod, jutting my index finger toward the forest where we were headed.

My limbs grow increasingly heavier, as if gravity itself drags them to the ground as we draw nearer to the amulet. Each breath comes in more strained than the last as my lungs can't seem to fill enough.

We finally pause, granting me another chance to rest as my knees tremble beneath my weight and threaten to give way. We can hardly make it more than a few feet before our next pause, and it feels like it will be an eternity by the time we get the amulet.

Within an instant Darian is by my side, his arm wrapping around my shoulder and with one motion he cradles me in his arms as he moves toward our destination.

We continue at a brisk pace, and while Darian shows no signs of fatigue, my grasp on his arm tightens into a vice-like grip with each step as we approach the location.

A small, weathered log cabin covered in moss and creeping vines comes into view and Darian moves toward without instruction. Though the roof seems intact, various plant life sprouts from its surface, camouflaging it with the forest surroundings. Peering through the open entryway as the sole entrance, Darian gingerly sets me on the ground.

He says nothing as he glances between Val and me before venturing inside, disappearing beyond view and the minutes stretch on in silence.

My heart slowly beats faster with his absence, and I'm about to call out as he emerges from the entryway grasping the amulet in the palm of his hand.

The rusted chain falls to the ground, discarded, and I gently lift the piece from his grasp. The globe is covered in dirt and moss, but contained inside is a single delicate rose floating gracefully amongst a small pool of liquid, shimmering against the faint light.

Exhaling a breath, my shoulders sag as I unclasp the chain from around my neck, adding the rose amulet to the necklace before clasping it back on and tucking it safely into my shirt.

Darian glances up at the canopy above, "We should be able to hike a few hours back before dark."

Agreeing with a nod, my limbs still shaky but no longer weighed down by lead as we retrace our steps through the dense terrain.

Chapter 37

As the forest darkens, we find a suitable location to pitch the tent while I gather tinder and firewood to ward off the evening chill.

I flick the lighter in the center repeatedly until it ignites. The wood darkens, the flame growing and elongating to reach the top. The larger slabs begin to catch, sending a steady stream of smoke into the air.

Shifting my weight to settle in cross-legged, my gaze is fixated on the amber glow of the fire as Darian takes a seat beside me.

I'm acutely aware of how close we are as he takes a piece of jerky before passing the bag to me. Our arms and fingers brush against each other, the contact sending butterflies through my body as I grasp the bag, and my heart frantically thrums loudly in my chest.

"Lara?" Darian's baritone voice is soft, and I blink before glancing at him.

Meeting his gaze was a mistake.

I can feel the blood rush to my cheeks as our eyes lock. His dimples are on display with his smile, bathed in the warm, flickering glow of the fire.

He looks incredibly attractive, almost painfully so.

"Hmm?" My barely audible voice cracks.

He chuckles with a knowing grin, "Breathe, Lara."

I blink at him and inhale deeply, suddenly feeling light-headed.

Great, add this to the long list of things to talk to Claire about.

My cheeks burn for multiple reasons as I turn my head back to the fire, focusing on my lungs filling as I slowly chew some jerky.

In my peripherals, Darian sets the chips to the ground and extends his hand with his palm upturned. Assuming he wants more jerky, I reach my arm across my chest to pass the bag to him.

His hand wraps around my wrist instead of taking the jerky and my head snaps toward him.

Our eyes meet and my pulse hikes up. I inhale sharply as he tugs me from where I sit into his lap and his free arm quickly snake around my waist.

He presses me flush to his chest and rolls until I'm on my back. His body towering over mine as his silky black strands fall forward, obscuring his eyes from the light of the fire.

It's truly unfair how undeniably beautiful he is.

I never stood a chance at resisting this.

Yet again, I find myself in uncharted territory as my connection to Darian becomes all consuming.

It's as if I've spent my life underwater, and he is my first breath of air.

Darian's gaze is dark and heated and as his eyes fall to my lips, electric energy hangs in the air between us.

The delicious weight of his body sends my pulse racing, and my arms find their way around his neck. I tangle my hands into locks of soft hair, tugging his head back roughly which earns me a deep rumble from his chest in response, sending shivers down to my core.

Wrapping my legs around his hips he leans his full weight between my thighs.

The pressure against my clit sends jolts of pleasure into my body, and I'm desperate for more. I squeeze my thighs around his hips eagerly as he crushes his lips against mine.

He kisses me fiercely, as if he's hungered for this his entire life as his tongue drags across in a silent request for me to open to him.

I return everything he gives with fervent passion. My bones, my muscles, my soul feels as if it's on fire. My moans are swallowed into his mouth as he rhythmically grinds his length against me.

The weight he bears onto me with each movement sends my own desire off like an uncontrollable wildfire threatening to devour everything in its path.

His dick throbs with his next grind against me and I nearly come undone.

He withdraws his mouth, trailing searing hot kisses and bites down my jaw, my neck, then my collarbone.

My entire being is alight at this point, and I'm not sure how much longer I can handle this as I shamelessly grind against him, chasing the sensations roaring through my body.

His arm wraps around my waist, squeezing me tightly to him with every thrust and roll of my hips. Waves of pleasure threaten to overwhelm me as my breathing quickens, and my back arches into him.

We haven't even taken our clothes off yet.

"Darian, I'm so close." My lust-filled voice echoes in the air, and he stills. The hunger in his face along causes me to squirm in protest.

With a soft laugh he lifts my shirt, discarding it to the ground before doing the same with his own.

He effortlessly pushes to his feet, clutching me tightly against him with my legs still locked around his waist, reveling at the feel of his muscles as he carries me into the tent.

The way he handles me with ease is enough to make my knees tremble.

I observe with half-lidded eyes as he sets me gently on the makeshift bed with a heated smirk that sends my pulse raging once more. His gaze travels over my body as I lay beneath him, breathing heavy and flushed, as if appraising me from head to toe.

He hooks his hands under my knees, unraveling my legs from him, and I'm about to protest, but my mouth snaps shut when he leans forward, trailing his fingers down my sides, leaving goosebumps in their wake.

His fingers slide beneath my pants and underwear, tugging them off and setting them aside.

The crisp night air touches my bare skin and I watch with rapt attention as Darian removes his own. As he frees himself from his boxers, my mouth drops open of its own accord earning another dark chuckle from him.

I saw how large he is once before, but I don't think I'll ever get used to it. The man wasn't lying when he said he was blessed by the Gods.

He positions himself between my legs, his hands rest just above my knees before slowly trailing up to my soaking wet pussy, and a husky groan comes from his throat.

He glides his fingers along the entrance before hovering over my clit.

He leans forward, bracing one arm around the back of my neck, "You're fucking soaked," His forehead tilts against mine, as his baritone voice gains an authoritative edge. "You will not come unless I tell you to. You're going to hold it as long as you can. If you think you're going to come, you tell me. Understood?"

I nod eagerly as his thumb finally connects with my already sensitive clit. The gentle circles he rubs around it make me whimper with desperation.

I struggle to ward off the pleasure as he pushes his finger in, his thumb continuing to circle my swollen clit.

His second finger slides in, and I wince as he stretches me, the muscles in my legs twitching in response to his ministrations.

"Darian, please." I beg and my nails dig into his bicep and shoulder as pressure builds in my body and my orgasm nears.

"Not yet."

My orgasm is simmering beneath the surface as I try desperately to ward off the pleasure. Every circle his thumb makes brings me closer to the teetering edge and my body squirms in the conflict between obedience and physical desires.

"Darian, I can't take this. I'm so close."

"Not yet. Fucking hold it."

He withdraws, and I'm nearly certain I've drawn blood by digging my nails into his skin.

I instinctively attempt to tug him closer by pressing my heels against his thighs, but he holds fast, leaning in to trail kisses along my chest and neck as he tuts in disapproval.

His lips burns hot against my skin as he takes my nipple into his mouth, sucking hard before kissing his way to the other.

I'm panting, and looking at him from half lidded eyes as he leans back, reveling in the way my body respond to him with satisfaction.

Certain that I'm no longer on the edge, he places his hand between my legs, sliding three fingers inside of me, and circles my clit once more.

Pleasure washes over me and my eyes to roll back as I grind against his hand.

His voice is thick, "Ah fuck, Lara."

His restraint snaps and excited anticipation floods my veins as he withdraws his fingers from me.

Our eyes meet as he brings them to his lips and sucks them one at a time.

With one finger remaining, he positions it in front of my mouth. Heat flashes across his face as I suck from knuckle to tip, before releasing it with a 'pop' sound which only heightens the tension between us.

"Do you see what you do to me?" Darian says before shifting over me, his body weight pushing me into the blankets further, and I feel the smooth tip of his cock against my soaking-wet entrance as he leans his forehead to mine.

"Everything about you is fucking perfect."

As he pushes into me, his gentle kisses trail down my neck as my body struggles to accommodate his size.

I release a whimper at the mixture of pleasure and pain, and he tenses, searching my eyes for any indication to stop.

The pain should deter me but all I feel is desperation for more.

I need his body, his strength, his being with everything I am.

Fuck the pain.

I squeeze my heels into the back of his thighs in a silent demand.

My mouth drops open as he pushes in further, a deep groan rumbles from his chest as my walls tighten and massage him with every move.

A heated moan escapes my lips as his pelvic bone meets mine, and he pauses, searching my face.

There's nothing quite like the feeling of him being buried inside of me, staring at me as if I'm the answer to everything as he throbs. I squirm against him, my efforts in vain between his weight and how deep he is.

Darian leans in, nipping my neck as he withdraws to the tip before burying himself deep inside me again in one long, excruciatingly sensual stroke.

"I could spend the rest of my life inside of you and it would never be enough." He crushes his lips to mine, his rhythm deep and strong. His pace is slow but precise with each drive into me, as if dragging this out as long as possible, with every movement rubbing my aching clit begging for release.

This is more than just being fucked or having sex.

Each deliberate movement is filled with emotion I can't quite describe.

Devotion, adoration, connection, obsession.

All of the above and everything in between.

My body feels overwhelmingly full and my orgasm quickly returns with a vengeance. Each powerful motion hits at the perfect angle, and my toes curl involuntarily as pleasure radiates from my core, all the way down my legs as I desperately avoid my climax.

One at a time, his large hands slide from my shoulders and along my arms to intertwine our fingers as he tugs our limbs overhead in a gentle restraint.

His pace gradually increases, each thrust competing for depth as I press myself into him, as if my body could somehow manage to take any more length.

If deeper were possible in any way, I would let him fuck the very depths of my soul.

My husky moans become frantic and my legs squeeze him into me, silently begging for more as I attempt to stave off the pleasure threatening to erupt from my body.

As if sensing my orgasm nearing, Darian freezes and releases my arms. Supporting my back, he hooks his hand around my knee and rolls, positioning me on top.

A gasp escapes my lungs at the movement as he grips both of my hips tightly and thrusts up, pulling me deeper onto him.

I pause with my hands braced on his chest, giving myself time to adjust. He's deep enough that when he throbs it tenses against my stomach.

With one hand on his abdomen, the other on his thigh, we move in sync as I ride him, shamelessly chasing the pleasure.

My eyes flutter open as he grips my hips tightly, getting the perfect angle on his deep thrusts.

"Darian, it's too intense, I-" I'm interrupted as he repeats the action and my orgasm crests, and I've buried my nails in his skin, still trying to fend off the pleasure as long as possible.

"Darian," my voice is thick with desperation, and my back arches as he drives into me again, causing me to gasp.

"Don't you dare fucking come yet."

Leaning forward into his chest in a failed attempt to change the intense angle, my moans grow louder, and my pussy clenches as I desperately fight to hold off my climax.

"Please, I can't..." I pant out, my hair slicked against my forehead.

He keeps his pace and wraps his hand around my throat, pulling me to him as he growls, "Come for me. Now."

He expertly meets my movements, circling my clit with his other hand and I lose control of my own body as the most intense orgasm I've ever experienced rips through me.

With his name on my lips, my vision goes completely white, speckled with dancing silver stars, and within moments of my orgasm Darian tenses as his cock throbs, filling me with his own release.

I continue to grind against him through the waves of euphoria, and my pussy grips him of its own volition, determined to get every last drop of pleasure before my limbs become heavy with fatigue.

Resting my head against his strong chest, our breaths mingling in the air as we both pant for a moment before my gaze lifts to meet his.

"You did so well, Sunshine. You took me so fucking well." Darian's deep voice reverberates in the stillness of the tent, his words sending a delightful shiver down my spine as he tenderly presses his lips against mine.

He withdraws and tugs me into his side, nestling me against his chest. His arms encircling my shoulders in a tender embrace with his lips planting sweet kisses against my temple.

"Darian?" Exhaustion has its claws sunk deep into my body and mind, but there's one curious question burning in my head that I've never thought to ask.

"Hmm?"

I yawn, "What's with the nickname?"

Darian chuckles softly, "You're the brightest light I've seen in in centuries. I thought the nickname was fitting."

I respond with a content hum, my eyelids growing heavy with the soothing rhythm of his rumbling laughter and I surrender to the embrace of sleep in the security and warmth of Darian's arms.

Chapter 38

I slowly wake to the gentle caress of fingers tracing circles on my skin and a smile tugs at the corners of my lips.

My eyes flutter open, squinting to adjust to the brightness in the tent, and I let out a contented yawn, stretching my body luxuriously like a cat basking in the morning sun.

"Morning, Sunshine." I can hear the faint smirk in his sleep laden voice, making it sound deeper than usual.

I prop myself up, my face inches from Darian's with his tousled hair framing his features. His lips curve into a gentle smile and the light filtering through the tent accentuates the captivating colors of his eyes.

It strikes me that I've seen the difference in them before but never had I looked.

And I mean really looked.

His green eye is a mesmerizing variety of shades, with vibrant hints of emerald and jade as they blend toward his iris. They're reminiscent of the lush forest near the lake or his nightclub. If you gathered hundreds of thousands of leaves from either place, layering them together in intricate patterns, it still would not do the color justice.

In contrast, his white-blue eye glimmers like glacial ice in the mid-day sun. As if containing a multitude of glistening shards that seem to intensify with the reflection of light.

It's breathtaking.

My heart flutters in my chest, "Morning, my liege." I echo Lor's teasing nickname from the nightclub.

He laughs softly, and I can't help but mirror his grin, "I guess it's time to get up, isn't it?" I cock my head, and Darian lets out a deep, exasperated sigh.

"As much as I would prefer to spend the rest of my days in this tent, I'm afraid so." Darian sits up, peppering me with light kisses, but hesitates and pulls back slightly, his gaze fixed on my eyes.

The flash of desire across his features is the only warning I get.

His chest rumbles with a low growl, and before I can react, he deftly pulls me over, rolling us until he's leaning on top of me again. The kiss is all consuming as his tongue trails against mine lightly, and I open for him.

The world around us begins to fade away as his hand finds the nape of my neck, tugging my head back to deepen the kiss.

Our bodies mold together in a perfect fit, his weight pressing onto me, igniting desire in my core. He pulls back, watching my reaction with a heated expression as he presses the hard length of his erection against my clit. The sensation sending my still sensitive nerves haywire, and whatever he sees darkens his features as if he's about to pounce on his prey.

The air crackles with electricity, but as Darian leans in to kiss me, a loud, exasperated and annoyed huff sounds from outside the tent.

We both freeze, panting as we're torn between desire and reality.

Darian sighs, "I suppose that's one way of telling us to start packing."

We spend the remaining hours of the day hiking through picturesque landscape until the sun descends on the horizon.

As we emerge from the small hiking path, the sky becomes a canvas of pastel orange and pink hues painted across a stunning canvas overhead.

Darian holds the door to the SUV open for me, yet another small gesture that fills me with warmth and makes my chest swell. The peaceful two-hour drive back to the apartment takes us through winding roads, and the fading daylight casts a serene glow upon the world.

Lost in the exhaustion of the recent events, I must have dozed off at some point, only to be gently awakened as we arrive in the dimly lit parking garage.

Stepping into the familiarity of the area, a deep sigh escapes my lips.

"I can't wait to shower." Val's ears perk forward, and he huffs as his playful gaze fixates on me.

My eyes narrow at him.

"Are you saying that you also cannot wait for me to shower?"

His canine eyes glimmer with amusement, and his ears remain perked forward.

I toss my bottle of water at him, and with a quick dodge, he skillfully evades it as it clatters to the ground.

"I do not stink! Not all of us have canine noses. Besides, at least I don't smell like a wet dog."

Darian's laughter echoes from behind me as we near the apartment door, and Val bristles with a canine shake before moving toward me, rubbing his fur on my legs.

Holding the door open, Darian shifts to let us inside.

"Oh, no. You did not just rub your dog smell all over me!" I feign exasperation and Val darts away, his nails clacking against the floor.

I haul my duffel bag to the master bedroom and plop it down next to the door, taking my phone out and turning it on.

Claire: Hi Lara. Just checking in, it's been a couple of weeks and Candace says you're still on vacation. How's it going?

Lara: Hello Claire, thanks for asking. I'll be on vacation for a while longer. Went to the west coast, and won't be back for a bit. It's going well, nightmares have subsided for now. I'll let you know if that changes.

I flick over to the group chat with Candace and Henry.

Candace: Hey Lara. Wanted to let you know Claire's gotten antsy about the radio silence from you and nothing I say is easing her mind. You'll likely hear from her soon if you haven't already.

That explains it.

With a soft chuckle, I continue to scroll through the missed messages.

Henry: There was a group of guys that were hanging around the parking lot, they seemed to be focused on your reserved spot. There were five of them with motorcycles. When Candace and I went out there to confront them for snooping around, they took off. Not sure what they wanted, but they didn't seem like good news.

A shiver runs down my spine as I recall the people they were referring to. Thankfully, they are no longer a concern for us.

Candace: None of the samples are displaying meaningful results, and we've started seeing the flora from the lake wilting now that they're removed. The samples transplanted to the lake are showing major positive impacts. We're back to square one.

Henry: Sorry Lara, we will keep testing, but there's nothing big to report yet.

I exhale deeply, knowing that the explanation I have to offer may not be easily accepted by those who rely solely on scientific evidence and I struggle to put my thoughts into words, typing and erasing my response multiple times.

Just send it Lara. Henry believes in Big Foot for goodness' sake.

Lara: The tests are going to be inconclusive because it's remnants of magic causing the anomalies. It is nothing we can test or recreate on our own.

I stare at the message for a brief moment, feeling my heart pounding in my throat.

They deserve to know.

My finger hits the send button and I watch the message bubble pop up and show delivered.

Candace types a response instantly.

Candace: HA! I KNEW IT! Henry owes me $20.

Relief floods my veins.

Henry: Ugh. My money was on aliens, honestly. Damn.

Lara: You are both incorrigible.

Candace: Well, we'll keep running tests until you return anyways. Hope your time with hot stuff has been long, hard, and fulfilling!

Candace sends a series of emojis ranging from an eggplant, to a cat face and an excessive amount of wink emotes.

I can hardly suppress my eye roll and chuckle at her shenanigans, but guilt weighs heavy on me that they have no idea who I'm with and that Caspian was the danger I needed protecting from.

Lara: It's been something. Of that, I'm certain. I'll fill you in when I see you. Not sure how much longer it'll be. I'm guessing at least another week or two.

Candace: Sounds good, hun! Talk to you soon and be safe!

Henry: Talk to you later, Lara!

I connect my phone to the charger, grab a fresh set of pajamas from the dresser, and make my way to the shower before finally settling into bed.

I startle awake to the sound of gentle knocking, my body curled around Val's form.

We both lift our heads, turning our attention to the door as it slowly swings open. The room is cloaked in darkness, the heavy blackout curtains creating deep shadows that stretch into the corners as Darian's silhouette fills the doorway. He leans casually against the frame, the soft light of the hallway making his face shadowed from where I lay.

Despite his repeated acts to protect me, there's an underlying sense of unease that lingers in the air between us. It's akin to the anticipation before a storm, where the dark clouds gather and distant thunder rumbles, yet the wind and rain have yet to arrive.

"What is it?" My voice is barely a whisper.

Darian laughs softly, "You mean other than time to get up, sleepyhead?"

"I haven't slept that long, have I?" My attention shifts to Val, who shoots me a sidelong glance before redirecting his gaze back to Darian.

The lack of response furthers my unease.

"How long have I been asleep?" My brows furrow in confusion. There's an unspoken tension in the air as my gaze shifts between them.

"Two full days," Darian presses the button on the blinds, bringing a flood of light into the room, "I've come in here a few times to check on you. Do you not remember?" Darian's voice is soft, but the concern in it clear as day.

My gaze lowers to the floor as I desperately try to recall anything but come up empty-handed. "Nothing. I remember showering and laying down to sleep."

I rub my temples, attempting to massage away the slight headache that has settled in my skull.

"Well, I'm glad you're awake. Hungry?" he asks, his tone deceivingly light.

As if it has a mind of its own, my stomach makes a loud gurgling sound, and Darian tilts his head back to bark a genuine laugh.

"I'll be right there, I have 2 days' worth of bathroom breaks to make up for." I say, as my bladder suddenly feels like it could explode.

Scrambling off the bed, I rush to the bathroom, hearing Darian's laughter trailing behind me as he makes his way to the kitchen.

Joining him in the kitchen, I notice him setting a plate filled with a delicious assortment of breakfast sausage, hash browns, scrambled eggs, toast, and bacon on the floor for Val. He slides a plate over to me, adorned with the same mouthwatering spread and my stomach rumbles in anticipation.

Darian, with a knowing grin, pushes a full glass of orange juice across the countertop toward me.

I might be in love.

This has to be love.

The thought comes through jokingly, but a small voice in the back of my mind tuts at me for falling blindly as if knowing that I'm already wrapped around Darian's finger.

"Has anyone told you that you're the best recently?" I smirk at him and take a bite of sausage, the flavors exploding in my mouth and I drop my forehead against the back of my hand in an effort to savor the taste.

Darian laughs softly, "No one that isn't covered in fur and can't currently speak English. Since it's you, however, I'll take the appreciation with particular gratitude."

My cheeks burn as I raise my head, avoiding direct eye contact.

Without missing a beat, I reach out and snag a crispy strip of bacon, reveling its smoky flavors.

"So have we gotten any more info on any more amulets?"

Darian finishes chewing his bite of food slowly, before finally meeting my gaze.

"We did." He offers, his voice low as he takes another bite of his food, creating a brief pause in the conversation.

"And?" I press.

"And… it's around an hour's drive from here." His evasive response raises my blood pressure.

I narrow my eyes at him.

"Darian, just tell me."

He lets out a resigned sigh, "It's in a cemetery. A large one. We will go tonight and see if we can find it."

There's a pause, and I feel his intense gaze fixed upon me, "I don't know what to expect there. We may be there for at least a few hours once we know where it is."

The explanation seems to be enough at the surface but suspicion tugs at my mind, nagging at me that there's something he's worried about that has nothing to do with the cemetery.

He's been acting strange since I woke up.

With a nod, I return my attention to the breakfast in front of me, my mind racing.

That's one of the few silver linings of anxiety and overthinking. If you're imaginative and proactive, it allows you to anticipate various scenarios before they unfold.

While many people view it as a negative trait, I've developed a silent appreciation how prepared I've been when situations align closely with my envisioned outcomes.

I suppose some might refer to it as intuition, but regardless, it's always been a superpower in my eyes. Personally, I've always craved explanations to make sense of things and just going off gut feelings requires little to no logic. If you can't rationalize what's happening then you're either wrong or uninformed.

That's why magic has been a source of frustration for me.

Magic isn't tangible, something you can examine under a microscope. You can't hold it in your hand or perceive it with the naked eye.

And if you haven't experienced it, you rely on theory to rationalize it.

Darian stays occupied for the next few hours before loading the SUV with a shovel and retreats into his office. I can faintly hear his hushed conversation on the phone, growing increasingly tense and curiosity gets the better of me. I peek through a crack in the door, catching a glimpse of him with his gaze fixed on the computer screen before he starts typing.

What is he not telling me?

Chapter 39

As the daylight wanes, casting a golden glow on the horizon, the tension radiating from Darian is palpable.

He appears on edge as if a single misstep could throw him into a tailspin.

His restless movements send my own anxiety swirling as I approach the apartment door.

"So, what's the plan?" I cringe internally as my voice cracks.

"We will enter normally. If security stops us early on, we'll say we're visiting your great aunt, Liza." I raise an eyebrow, waiting for him to continue. "If all goes well, we should be able to retrieve the amulet within the next six hours."

I eye him warily, picking apart his wording. "And, if it doesn't go well?"

His gaze meets mine as he pulls the door open, his expression unreadable. "Let's hope it goes well." he replies, his tone tinged with a touch of apprehension and I suppress a nervous shudder.

We arrive at the cemetery in just under an hour and an eerie sensation washes over me as we pass the weathered steel front gates.

Rows upon rows of burial sites stretch out before us, various marked headstones and simple plaques adorning the ground. Vases with flowers in various stages of decay stand beside many of the graves.

Venturing deeper into the vast cemetery at a slow pace, the gates soon fade from view, and a familiar sensation tugs at my core.

Taking a deep breath, I extend my hand and point to my right, "This way" I whisper.

Darian steers the SUV in the direction I indicate, and I'm soon bracing against the dashboard, panting heavily. The pull from the amulet is like gravity itself, if I were a meteor plummeting toward the earth. As Darian slows down near a fork in the road, I twist in my seat to reduce the discomfort and point in the direction with the least resistance.

Darian cautiously navigates the vehicle, his face filled with concern. The pressure shifts as we crawl at a snails pace down the road and I let out a whimper, unable to suppress it as Darian slams on the breaks.

Desperate to get relief, I open the door and abruptly step out, feeling a surge of weakness coursing through me as I struggle to remain upright.

"Shit" I hear the trunk open and shut before Darian appears beside me, shovel in hand and a tense look gracing his features.

He hooks his arm around mine, providing support and patiently awaits my guidance. With the slightest twist of my body, I point straight ahead into the darkness as Darian keeps me steady.

Normally, a cemetery would be illuminated by lights or lamps, guiding visitors along the pathways. This place seems too large to keep track of since many of the lights are out, plunging us into the dark of night as we continue our slow walk.

I come to a halt, my gaze fixed on a small tombstone before us.

"Nina Schleronov" I mutter under my breath, stealing a glance at Darian who stands rigid beside me.

He remains fixated on the tombstone, his brow furrowed. I clear my throat, shifting my gaze between him and the headstone.

"Do you know her?" I ask softly as he drags his hand down the side of his face and shakes his head.

"No, but she died the day magic disappeared from this world."

I blink and turn my attention back to the grave site.

The tension from Darian hasn't lessened as he drives the tip of the shovel into the solid ground, its impact reverberating slightly beneath my feet.

It never fails to astonish me, witnessing such displays of Darian's sheer strength. While being held by him is one thing, observing the raw power he possesses during moments like this sends shivers down my spine.

It suddenly dawns on me that I have no true measure of Darian's full strength.

The swiftness with which he moves has consistently caught me off guard, as with the seemingly effortless way he ended the lives of the would-be kidnappers in the forest.

So far, I have yet to witness him face any real challenge that would push him to his limits. It leaves me wondering just how much power he truly possesses, and if there are any bounds to it.

It makes me question whether he has to use restraint with me, and what his strength will be once magic is no longer bound from the world.

I watch with renewed fascination as Darian skillfully maneuvers the shovel, scooping the soil aside. Each thud of the tool driving into the ground echoes in the silence of the cemetery.

The minutes turn to hours as he tirelessly continues to dig deeper, not even a drop of sweat on his brow as I peer into the large hole around him.

Suddenly, a sharp impact jolts through his shovel, causing him to flinch and pause as the clatter sounds out into the stillness of the night. The shovel hit something solid, a hard wooden surface peeking out from the dirt, as Darian's gaze tilts upwards to meet mine.

A small look of relief flashes across his features as he gives me a single nod before carefully shoveling the soil around the casket inch by painstaking inch.

The minutes stretch into what feels like an eternity, accompanied by the sounds of the shovel striking the ground when finally, Darian begins to break the rusted clasps apart with his bare hands.

I blink, once again surprised by his effortless display of strength.

Darian's muscles ripple along his arms as he lifts the heavy lid of the casket, the worn hinges protesting the movement with a loud snap. He forces the lid open, and the rattling sound reverberates around us, echoing through the cemetery.

My pulse races.

It feels like we're in the final sprint, an excited apprehension fills my veins at the relief in sight once we get the amulet.

My excitement is muted as the putrid scent of decay and rot fills the air, causing bile to rise in my throat.

My eyes are drawn to the decomposed corpse resting in the center of the casket. Its skeletal frame ravaged by time, with remnants of decayed flesh clinging to the bones. Nestled in the gap between two of the higher ribs, just below the sternum is the rounded top of the amulet.

In the distance blue and red lights flash in my peripherals, accompanied by the growing sound of an approaching engine.

"There's someone coming," I whisper urgently, and my heart pounds faster in my chest.

Darian quickly bends down, retrieving the amulet as the chain tears through brittle fragments of neck bone before striding to the side of the hole.

With minimal effort, he pulls himself over the edge and extends the object toward me. My fingers fumble as I rush to unclasp my necklace, adding the newest amulet to my collection, letting out a relieved sigh.

As I clasp the chain back around my neck, the flickering lights draw closer to the spot where we left the SUV and dread pools in my stomach.

The engine abruptly cuts off, plunging the area into silence until voices echo through the air from the opposite direction and my heart nearly stops in my chest.

There's no way out.

My pulse races, and I look to Darian in desperation.

He has a plan, right?

He must have a plan.

His jaw pulsates as he scans the area, his eyes flicking back and forth in search of a solution before addressing me, "Lara you need to go. They won't know anyone was helping me because there's only one shovel."

He gestures toward a shadowed section of the cemetery, his grip firm on my arm as he guides me with a sense of urgency.

"Head that way until you find the fence, follow it until you find the back exit."

Shouts from behind us and the sound of a barking dog grab Darian's attention, but he doesn't pause as he continues, "The exit will be locked but there's headstones near the fence that's might be tall enough to climb over the gate. I'll get their attention to buy you time."

"But-" I start to voice my protest, the rush of adrenaline making my heart thump in my chest as he interrupts me.

"Go, Lara. Go!" He demands and shoves me gently into the darkness, the abrupt movement nearly causing me to stumble. I watch with wide eyes as he jogs toward the approaching police and K-9 Unit.

The shouts grow louder as they undoubtedly spot Darian, and I watch their flashlights illuminate his form as he bursts into a sprint, leading them away from me.

My heart lurches in my chest but the barking spurs me into motion.

I scramble to my feet, running in the direction he originally sent me.

I refuse to let Darian's efforts be in vain.

My leg muscles turn to jelly and my chest heaves with exertion by the time I reach the fence line and the barking fades away.

No one seems to be following me as I cautiously make my way in the darkness until I stand before a small closed gate, just wide enough for a riding mower to pass through. Just beyond it are headstones, some over a foot taller than the others, positioned right next to the fence.

Standing next to the most imposing headstone, it appears almost insurmountably tall, but it will give me the best chance to get over the 12-foot fence.

I make three failed attempts to hoist myself on top, losing grip each time and sliding roughly to the ground as the fatigue from the hike days ago echoes in my arms.

Whether it's determination or desperation fueling my movements, I manage to drag myself over the edge, panting from exerting strength I didn't know I possessed.

My momentary triumph fades as I realize that the top of the fence looms a whole foot above my head. A flourishing tangle of rose bush vines cascade over the side of the barred fence, and I take a deep, cleansing breath.

Positioning myself atop the headstone a few feet away from the tall rose bush, I swallow audibly.

I close my eyes.

You can do this, Lara. Darian believed you could do it.

Taking another deep breath, I exhale slowly, and position myself at the back of the headstone, putting some distance between me and the intimidating fence.

Leap of faith, Lara. Just do it.

I hurl myself forward, my final step off the tombstone hurtling me into the air toward the rose bush. I collide with the thorny vines, sending crimson petals falling to the ground while countless sharp barbs pierce my skin as I grip the vines like my life depends on it.

Despite the excruciating pain in my limbs, I muster every ounce of strength to grasp onto another bunch of vines higher up. The thorns dig deeper into my skin, drawing fresh blood, but I cling on tightly, dragging myself toward the top of the fence.

By sheer force of will, I shove the pain from my mind and repeat the action, dragging myself upward. My palms become slick with blood and sweat as I haul myself over the top of the tall fence, before dangling my body on the other side.

Just a little bit further.

The initial adrenaline that once fueled my actions starts to fade with the finish line in sight, leaving me with a tightness in my chest and a growing awareness of the injuries to my body.

Each section of vines send renewed pain shooting through my hands, while rogue thorns scrape the rest of my body as I carefully ease myself down. My teeth grit together as I force my limbs to continue to work amidst the constant pain.

When my feet finally touch solid earth, I nearly sob with relief and clutch my injured hands to my chest.

Wandering along a deserted, dimly lit street, my gaze fixates on the gas station we had passed earlier, and hope surges through me as I head that direction.

My hands still covered in blood, and I'm sure I look like a mess as I tug my jacket off, wincing with every movement in my arms and drape it over them, before making my way inside.

I need to clean myself up.

My mind focused on that as I enter the gas station, heading straight for the back where the restroom is located.

The musty smell and flickering light does nothing to ease my mind as I secure the door behind me before turning to face the sink.

My skin is flushed and with splatters of blood and numerous scrapes scattered across my arms.

It's my hands and forearms that bear the brunt of the damage.

The cuts and gashes vary in severity, with some shallow and superficial, while others still continue to bleed and deep enough to require stitches to heal properly.

After rinsing away the blood and fighting off waves of nausea, I create makeshift bandages by tearing the sleeves from my jacket to wrap around my injured hands. Retrieving my phone from my back pocket, I call for a cab, praying the exhaustion holds off long enough for me to get to the apartment.

I enter the apartment with a weariness that permeates to my very core. With a click, I lock the door behind me, my movements unsteady as I stagger to the bathroom to retrieve the first aid kit.

Or rather I hope there is one.

During the ride home, crimson had begun seeping through the makeshift sleeves, and I knew the blood loss I faced was significant.

Every minute feels like an eternity in a constant battle to maintain consciousness.

The clatter of Val's nails against the tiled floor catches my attention, as he rushes into the bathroom. His concerned gaze meets mine before my strength wanes, my knees buckle beneath me and I to collapse onto the floor.

Shit.

I'm losing my grip, and I know it.

I've been on death's door before and made it out alive, but it's not a fear of dying that's keeping me clinging to consciousness.

It's the promise of a future, one filled with precious memories with Darian and Val and all the possibilities that could bring.

He releases a low whimper, his hazel eyes flick to my hands and wrists, and he quickly moves to the cabinet under the sink to retrieve what appears to be a first aid kit, holding it firmly in his mouth.

My shaky fingers open the clasps and I start cleaning the wounds methodically, crying out when the peroxide fizzes against my injuries. Val observes me for a brief moment I pant through the burning pain searing into my skin. As my breathing calms once more, he disappears from the bathroom, only to return with a container held carefully in his mouth.

"What's this?" I murmur, fumbling as I open the lid and peer inside.

To my surprise, it contains a series of needles for stitches and medical-grade sutures. I blink at Val in astonishment, then turn my attention back to the kit.

I swear sometimes I forget he's not an actual wolf.

"Erm, thank you for this."

I take a deep breath in an effort to steady my trembling hands and begin threading the sutures through the needle. As I position it against my skin for the first incision, I steal a glance at Val with apprehension.

Just do it, Lara.

I close my eyes and picture Darian standing next to me, drawing on his silent strength as I mentally prepare for what I'm about to do.

It takes a few attempts before I get the hang of sewing my

own skin shut, and I nearly vomit twice as blood slowly seeps from the deep wounds.

With each careful stitch, my eyelids grow heavier, and my head droops with every slow blink. Finally, I snip the excess material after tying the last knot, and lean my head back in relief.

Val releases a quiet whimper at my side and I encircle my arms around his thick, furry neck and use his strength to pull myself to my feet. I sway where I stand, lightheaded on weak, shaking legs as we cautiously make our way to my bedroom.

A few times I almost stumble and fall, but Val remains steadfast by my side, offering support as we move step by step.

Finally, as we reach the bed, I collapse onto it.

From where I lay face tilted to the side against the pillow, a curve of gold catches my eye and I examine the newest amulet in the collection.

The intricate depiction of a hawk peering back at me with remarkably detailed eyes at the center of the globe.

I can only hope this amulet was worth the trouble, and that Darian gets home soon.

Chapter 40

I rouse from a heavy, dreamless sleep. My body aching as if it had been run over by a truck, while the scent of forest rain assaults my senses.

As my mind sifts amongst the events of the previous day, they seem distant and hazy, as if viewed through a foggy lens.

I force myself upright, pain spearing within my limbs at the movement overpowered by the surge of hope coursing through my veins as I recognize my surroundings.

I vaguely remember collapsing into my bedroom last night after tending to my own wounds, but somehow I've awoken in Darian's.

Val is nestled beside me in the bed, wide awake. His eyes are fixed on me with an emotion I can't pinpoint.

"Is he back?" My voice escapes my lips in a whisper, barely audible even to myself.

Val's ears pin back as a pang of sadness resonates in my chest, and my heart sinks.

"So how did I-" I catch my open-ended question before rephrasing, "Did I move here of my own accord last night?"

Val blinks, his ears perking forward, and he rests his head gently against my leg. Anxiousness and dread start to grip my mind as I obsessively run through every imaginable scenario from the previous night.

With a heavy sigh, I rise to my feet and prepare breakfast for both of us as I consider what our next steps are in Darian's absence.

I flick on the TV from where I stand in the kitchen, the local news starts to play and my heart stops in my chest. The egg in my hand slips from my grasp, splattering on the ground as Darian's bruised and battered face appears on the screen, accompanied by the reporter sharing his recent mugshot.

Scrambling to the living room, I quickly crank up the volume.

"After an anonymous tip, a man was arrested in the Highpoint Cemetery last night under the suspicion of body snatching. The grave site of Nina Schleronov was unearthed and her final resting place was disturbed after twenty-five years. The local police department has the suspect in custody, but no charges have been filed yet as he's being detained for attempting to evade the police and fleeing from a crime."

Rage surges within me as I fixate on Darian's handsome, yet brutalized face on the screen. I turn to Val, whose gaze is still fixed on the TV, and I wonder what's going through his mind.

"We need to get him out of there, Val." I say, my pulse raging in my head.

Val's ears perk forward, and he lets out a low huff before trotting to the kitchen. While I prepare breakfast, my mind races through various scenarios -each more desperate than the last- to free Darian from the clutches of the police.

I catch myself spiraling as darker thoughts creep in, my mind straying to brutal methods that involve causing harm to others.

For taking him from me.

For hurting him.

I shake my head, pushing those thoughts away as I sit down to eat, reminding myself that there must be a better way.

I need to find a solution that doesn't involve causing pain to others, even if it means taking a risk or exploring unconventional avenues.

Regardless of how many paths I conjure in my vivid imagination, they all seem to lead to scenarios where either Darian or I end up injured or dead in the chaotic escape.

The realization dawns on me that there's only one remaining path left to consider.

As I weigh the options in my mind, apprehension fills my thoughts.

This is risky.

Darian would shout at me until he's blue in the face for considering it, but it seems to offer the best chance of freeing him without causing harm to anyone involved.

The only life at risk is mine.

I resign myself to asking for help from the one person directly responsible for all of this. The only one who deserves to face the consequences of their actions.

Caspian.

Anger, resentment, and other various emotions I can't place coat my veins.

The more I piece together my plan, the clearer it is that Caspian is likely the culprit behind the tip that led to Darian's arrest in some sick or twisted way to take him out of the equation.

The realization tightens the knot of anger in my chest.

By dinner time, my panic and dread have turned into stubborn determination. The paused image of Darian's bruised face on the TV screen fueling me as I meticulously go over every detail.

My heart races.

I'm going to give Darian one more day to come home before I put my plan into action.

By the time night has fallen over the city I've checked all the locks, ensuring everything is in place. Strategically hiding knives in various locations, ready to be accessed if needed.

I position a bat near the headboard, slide a knife between the mattresses, discreetly hidden as a last resort. The apartment which was once a peaceful sanctuary for Darian and I, now feels like a battlefield awaiting a silent clash.

Anxiety tugs at my mind as I crawl into Darian's bed with Val, who snuggles close to me as my arms snake around his neck.

"I miss him, Val." I whisper, my voice barely audible.

A lone tear escapes, tracing a path down my cheek as my emotions surge within me as my arms tremble involuntarily.

"I can't lose either of you, you know. It would destroy me." My throat tightens, "I haven't cared for many people in my life, but I refuse to lose you or Darian. I would sooner throw my own life away than lose either of you."

Val watches intently as tears stream down my face, and I can no longer suppress the wellspring of emotions that have been building within me.

The weight of everything I have been holding back, the pain, the fear, and the uncertainty rises to the surface and I squeeze my eyes shut, attempting to contain the tide of emotions.

But the floodgates have been opened.

The raw, unfiltered emotions surge through every fiber of my being. It is though a dam has burst, releasing a torrent of pent-up feelings that I have kept tightly sealed for years.

I reminisce about the mornings when Darian would prepare breakfast for us, going out of his way to ensure that the amulets we sought caused me minimal discomfort.

Every memory flows through my mind, and I am struck by the countless small interactions that brought me peace and calm amidst the chaos that surrounded us. Whether it was a shared smile, a reassuring touch, or a simple act of kindness.

The bed shifts beneath me as Val's forehead gently presses against mine, his nose angled down in a comforting gesture. Unable to contain my emotions any longer, a sob escapes from deep within, causing my entire body to shudder.

Val nudges me gently onto my back as he positions his weight on top of my chest, constricting my breath but anchoring me until my anxiety subsides.

I open my eyes to Val peering down at me, his ears perked forward. He tilts his head to the side, his gaze flickers to my tear-stained cheeks where another solitary tear descends.

My eyes flutter closed, and I draw in a ragged breath as Val's warm tongue glides gently along the path where my tear had just trailed.

His body goes rigid as if he's taken aback by his own display of affection.

My arms shift against his weight, and he adjusts his position to free their movement, and I wrap them tightly around his neck, stroking his fur.

"Thank you, Val." I whisper as the tension eases from his body, and he leans into my touch.

I'm abruptly awakened, startled by a cold sensation against my cheek.

My initial reaction is to flail and swat at the source, my heart racing with a mix of confusion and alarm.

My frantic motions are met with a loud huff, and I still, registering the warm fur at my fingertips.

"Val?" My throat feels dry and scratchy.

Squinting in the darkness, I turn the switch on the bedside lamp. As the soft glow illuminates the room, my eyes instinctively shut tight, struggling to adjust to the sudden change.

When I finally manage to open my eyes, Val's watching me with a wild look. The intensity of his gaze sends a wave of concern over me, and my brows pinch together.

"What is that look for?" I ask, my voice still hoarse.

Concern is plastered on his face as his gaze drops between us.

Following his line of sight, I glance down to my hands where crimson seeps through the bandages.

Shit.

"Did I do this in my sleep?" I question and Val's ears perk up slightly as the unease within me grows.

"I don't even remember anything." I whisper softly, letting out a frustrated sigh.

Gently disentangling myself from the bed, I remove the makeshift bandages from my wounds, examining the stitches with the hope of finding them intact.

More than a few have fully reopened somehow, and it's a short while later that I gently reapply the bandaging overtop to protect the stitching.

One more night of terrors and I might just become a nurse.

Moving to the kitchen, I reach for a glass to pour myself some orange juice. The citrus aroma fills the room as memories of Darian effortlessly surface, intertwining with the present moment.

Gazing down at the glass in my hand, I can almost see the faint reflection of his smile, as if the memory is etched deep within my heart.

Resolve settles heavy in me as I gulp down the remnants of liquid, making my way to the bedroom to check my phone for the millionth time.

No missed messages or calls.

Gritting my teeth I navigate to my contacts list, scrolling through the familiar names until I find the one I'm searching for.

My finger hovers over the green call button, trepidation coursing through me as I press it.

It rings once before his voice sounds out from the other line, breaking the silence that had enveloped the room and my breath catches in my throat.

"What can I do for you at this time of night?" My jaw clenches at the teasing tone of Caspian's voice.

It's hard to forget the better moments between us, regardless of the things he has done. I find myself at war once again trying to reconcile the Caspian I saw versus the one everyone knows him to be.

The silence stretches between us before Caspian chuckles quietly, and I once again consider the possibility that I am stepping into an impossible trap.

"You called me for a reason, Lara. I'm not known for my patience."

I suck in a breath, "You're a detective, correct?"

Caspian hums in curious amusement, "Are we asking obvious questions tonight?"

I ignore the dig.

"Darian was arrested and is being detained at Highpoint Police Station. I need to see him."

The line is quiet for a moment, "Fascinating." He says, and I frown when he sounds genuinely surprised, "I may be able to help with that. In fact, that might actually work out to your advantage."

"What? Why?" I try and fail to hide the annoyance in my tone, sick and tired of the secrets and minimal truth answers.

My conflicting emotions war with one another, torn between the desperate need for help and the nagging suspicion that I might be playing right into Caspian's hands.

I can hear Caspian's grin as he answers and my heart drops, "Because there's an amulet at the Highpoint Station and you're going to retrieve it."

As the early morning light filters through the curtains, I stand before the mirror, adjusting the stolen uniform and badge that Caspian had delivered to the apartment.

The fabric feels foreign against my skin, and I take a deep breath, reminding myself of the plan that has been meticulously replayed in my mind before heading out the door.

Instructing the cab driver to drop me off a block away to avoid suspicion or prying eyes, my heart races in my chest as I exit the vehicle, adjusting the leather gloves on my injured hands nervously.

I can't imagine many detectives would take a cab to the station.

With each step toward the side staff entrance my heart races, and an uneasy lump forms in my throat.

Two officers stand near the adjacent parking lot, idly chattering. Completely unaware of the imposter in their midst.

With bated breath, My hands tremble imperceptibly as I swipe the access card across the scanner, my pulse thundering in my ears as the other officers approach from behind.

My anxiety heightens with every passing second before a decisive beep and a green indicator grants me entry. A wave of relief crashes over me, momentarily dispelling the knot in my stomach.

Before the two officers can make their way inside after me, I turn to face them, maintaining a facade of purely false confidence.

"You didn't scan." My tone is composed and flat as I silently commend myself for it.

I really should have gone into acting.

Missed opportunity I suppose.

The first officer rolls his eyes in annoyance with a sigh, reluctantly scanning his own badge while the second officer snickers.

"Who is going to try to sneak in here?! So stupid we even have to scan and can't just come in."

If only they knew.

They brush past me without giving me a second glance, and I shake my head with relief as they disappear around the corner, oblivious.

That was way too easy.

I continue walking with purpose, maintaining the facade as I pass by two more officers and an administrative clerk, giving them a curt nod, keeping my focus on the tug in my body.

As I move past the door to the evidence room, a sudden surge of pain radiates through my chest, causing me to suck in a sharp breath to suppress any audible reaction.

My gaze briefly shifts to the window providing a glimpse into the room before scanning my surroundings.

I don't need to remind myself of the risks and potential consequences involved in breaking into a police station and impersonating law enforcement.

It's not lost on me that this is a federal crime.

Part of me wonders if Caspian would bail me out or if he'd simply use his authority to force me to help him while in federal prison.

Logic tells me it's the latter, but there's a small voice in my head hoping otherwise.

With a racing heart, I swipe my badge on the scanner next to the evidence room's entrance and a fresh wave of relief washes over me as the light flickers green.

2–0 so far, Caspian.

I push the door open and slip inside, letting it slide closed quietly behind me as I look around.

I pivot my body gradually, acutely aware of the twinge of pain, intensifying in response to the amulet's proximity. Gauging the discomfort and positioning, I estimate that it's situated on the opposite side of the room, concealed around the corner from where I stand now.

With deliberate movements I slowly move closer, taking care to minimize the strain on my body. An assortment of boxes and bags filled with evidence line the shelves along the walls and I start by examining the bottom section.

To my dismay, the boxes on the first two rows are filled with things, but I come up empty. I grasp a box from the third row and pull it close to my chest, the intense tug subsides and excitement rifles through me.

Squatting down, I delve into its contents, sifting through them methodically. Eventually, my fingers come across a bag that holds a weighty, round object that clatters lightly with the sound of metal and glass. Coupled with the palpable relief in my body, it becomes evident that I have found what I came for, and I tear open the bag.

The amulet portrays clouds with lightning bolts emanating from them submerged in the same liquid as the others. I carefully conceal them beneath my shirt as footsteps echo down the hallway, and as they grow closer, my heart pounds relentlessly in my chest.

I quickly tuck the empty evidence bag into my bra and return the box to its original position on the shelf just as the door on the opposite side of the room swings open.

"I just need to put this away real quick." a male voice reverberates from the hallway.

Ducking behind the rows of shelves, I freeze. Listening intently as the footsteps enter the room. I mimic their movements to keep distance, shifting away as they walk down an aisle. As the person reaches a nearby shelf, I hear evidence bags being shuffled and the distinct sound of an envelope being placed down.

The footsteps recede to the hallway, accompanied by the soft click of the door closing. Finally, I allow myself to exhale.

I need to get out of here and find Darian.

I cautiously approach the door, glancing out of the window to quickly assess the deserted hallway. Taking a deep breath, I mentally brace myself for what lies ahead, knowing that the most challenging part of this is yet to come.

I stride purposefully toward the admin reception, determined to maintain my authoritative demeanor as I reach the front desk. I hand over my badge to the officer on duty, my expression neutral yet confident.

I introduce myself with a flat tone, "Detective Klensa."

The receptionist scans my badge and offers me a warm smile, asking, "What can I do for you today, Detective Klensa?"

I deadpan my response, "I'm here to speak with an individual you have detained. The cemetery body snatcher."

Surprise briefly flickers across her face, but she quickly regains her composure. "Uh, I-I'm sorry, Detective. I wasn't aware we'd have any questioning today for that suspect. He's currently in isolation for resisting officers and being uncooperative."

A simmering anger rises within me, and I grit my teeth as I lock eyes with her.

"I'll have him gathered for questioning-" she begins, but I interrupt her.

"I'll do it myself. Make the necessary arrangements." I retort, cutting her off.

Without wasting another moment I pivot, striding purposefully down the corridor toward the isolation tanks, mentally thanking Caspian for sending me the layout of the building.

Each step fuels the burning rage coursing through my body.

The gates beep as I approach the holding cells, and I breeze past the guard, my anger smothering any fear of being caught. As I reach the isolation tank, I swipe my badge on the scanner, but my heart sinks as the display flickers red accompanied by two low beeps.

The guard standing before me trails his eyes down my body in an uncomfortable manner and I fight the urge to squirm. He turns slightly, pausing for a moment knowing I'm waiting for him to swipe his own badge on the scanner.

"What does a detective want with a grave robber?" he asks, a hint of suspicion in his tone.

"Alleged," I correct him firmly, holding his hard stare.

His tone turns callous and his eyes narrow as he responds, "What?"

My heart pounds.

"As far as official records are concerned, he is an **alleged** grave robber," I retort, "Unless there has been a conviction that I am unaware of." As if to emphasize my confidence, I raise a brow at him.

The guard sneers at me, his voice dripping with disdain. "If you had witnessed how he nearly escaped us, you would know that he is far from innocent."

I maintain my composure, despite the anger simmering inside me that feels as if it could produce visible smoke.

"That remains to be seen. Swipe. Please." I assert with more authority than before.

The guard's lip curls with barely contained rage as he reluctantly complies, swiping his card against the scanner which responds with a green light and a chirp.

Not bothering to wait, I pull the door open, my gaze falling upon Darian on the ground with his head bowed.

I muster every ounce of self-control to resist rushing to his side. Instead, focusing my anger and attention to the guard and locking eyes with him.

"Those bruises look fresh," I remark.

Darian's head jerks at the sound of my voice, and he lifts his gaze to meet mine.

My heart thunders in my chest.

The guard shrugs nonchalantly, "He ran into the wall a few times. They tend to go mad in here by themselves if they're here long enough. Seems he has less stomach for silence," the guard replies callously, smirking with cruel amusement.

I fix my gaze on the guard, my voice cloaked in a deadly calm I didn't anticipate. "If I review the surveillance footage and discover any mistreatment prior to a conviction, it will be your responsibility and your job that's on the line."

The guard stammers, his eyes widening in shock, unable to find words to respond.

It's all I need to confirm my suspicion.

In my peripherals, I catch Darian leaning his head back against the wall, a slow smirk spreading across his face.

Handsome even when beaten to shit.

I turn my gaze to Darian, "Come on, alleged grave robber. I have some questions for you."

Then, I shift my attention to the guard, whose face has turned as red as a tomato, "And you, bring food and water to the room within the next 10 minutes."

Darian's smile turns into a wince as he hauls himself to his feet limping slightly as he follows close behind me to the interrogation room. Once inside, he reaches out to flick the button for privacy, and I rip the camera plug from the outlet.

"Are you alright?" Darian's voice is barely above a whisper, and my attention immediately shifts toward him.

Me?

The man was beaten to all hell, and he's worried about me?

"You're seriously asking me that?" My voice trembles with frustration and I take a deep breath.

Darian nods, his hair shifting loosely with the movement. "You're right. I shouldn't have. I got caught, I'm sorry."

My chest constricts, and I raise my hand, "Stop"

Darian pauses, locking eyes with me.

I can't help but take in the sight of his battered face. His split lip and the bruises trailing down his neck and arms send a fresh wave of anger through me.

It takes a conscious effort not to consider burning this fucking building to the ground with everyone but Darian in it.

"I am fine. What did they do to you?" I ask but Darian shakes his head.

"That doesn't matter." he says, glancing to the door, "They're trying to plant evidence to get me convicted. It seems there's someone pulling strings behind this, someone who doesn't want me to be free," he says, his jaw feathering.

Caspian.

I pull out my phone and dial, he answers on the first ring.

"Lara. Get everything you need?" Darian's eyes narrow at his brother's voice.

"Cut the shit, Caspian." I seethe.

There's been enough lies and games.

I'm fucking done.

There is a brief pause on the other end of the line.

"What's wrong?" Caspian's voice remains steady, devoid of his usual cocky amusement, and I can't decide if this newfound seriousness is preferable or not.

"Darian needs to get out of here, today." I say with a low tone, desperation leeching into my words.

"No-can-do, little one. He needs to await trial before he can leave. That's what happens when you evade the police," Caspian dismisses my plea, and frustration surges through my veins.

I lower my voice, moving to the far side of the room, away from the door, in case the guard arrives with the food I requested earlier.

"Caspian, if you do not get him out of here and release Tammy, I'm done. No more finding these fucking amulets. You can hunt them down your damn self and these ones will sink with me to the bottom of the fucking Atlantic."

Darian's eyes widen like saucers as he listens to my words, his gaze shifting between me and the phone as if he hardly recognizes me.

I suppose in some sense he might not.

"Stop playing, Lara," Caspian's voice remains flat on the other line, but there's a flicker of uncertainty in his tone that emboldens me.

I channel my anger into the words I speak, letting the venom seep from my lips.

"Listen to my voice and tell me if I'm fucking playing Caspian. I'm done. Either you put a stop to this little game you're playing to take your brother out of the equation or your entire plan to get back home goes to shit right before your eyes."

There's a moment of silence on the line, and I wonder if I've pushed him too far. Then Caspian's cold tone breaks through the speaker.

"Consider it done. He'll be released tonight."

I hesitate for a moment, contemplating the extent of my leverage. "And Tammy," I add.

Caspian's dark chuckle echoes through the phone, causing conflicting emotions that I would rather smother to wash over me.

"Sure. But if you do not gather the remaining amulets, Lara, your dear friends will be the ones who pay the price."

I abruptly disconnect the call and blow out a breath.

"That was..." Darian starts to speak, but his voice trails off as the door swings open. The guard enters the room carrying a bottle of water, a sandwich, and a bag of chips, tossing them lazily onto the table.

I shoot a glare at the guard, but he simply shrugs, before exiting the room without a word.

Darian takes a seat, immediately cracking open the water bottle and gulping down half of it before biting into the sandwich.

Darian swallows with a wince, "You seem different," he says quietly, "You seem like you're on the edge." he adds hesitantly.

I meet his gaze, and all the walls I had erected around me crumble as I see the concern in his mismatched eyes. The hardness I had been projecting fades away.

I nod, acknowledging both.

"I feel like I'm going to snap," I confess, my voice soft.

Darian tilts his head, chewing thoughtfully on another bite of the sandwich. I remain silent, hoping he won't press for further explanation about the reasons behind my fragile state.

"Val?" he asks, attempting to shift the focus to another topic.

"He misses you." My response is curt, and he lets out a deep sigh.

"I'm sorry, Lara. I truly didn't mean to get-" he begins to apologize, but I interrupt him by raising my hand, signaling for him to stop.

I don't want to hear his apologies or explanations.

I'm not interested in that.

He promised he wouldn't be far from me and nearly drove me right into his brother's hands when he couldn't keep that promise.

But that's not the reason I'm angry.

I'm furious with the police within this station. Their misconduct and abuse of power infuriate me.

I'm seething with anger toward those who harmed Darian and believe they're immune to consequences.

I'm frustrated because it took this ordeal to finally secure Tammy's release.

It shouldn't have taken such extreme measures.

"It's not your fault. It's the fault of whoever called in the tip about us being there." I say finally, and Darian nods thoughtfully, downing the remainder of his water before moving to the chips.

"Thank you," Darian says softly after throwing his garbage into the trash can.

I'm quiet for a moment as I hold his gaze.

My heart wrenches in my chest knowing that I'm going to have to leave him here.

I glance to the door and back before speaking, "We need you to come home. I'm not sure what Caspian has planned to get you released but, come home right away okay?" My voice is only a whisper, barely audible, as I struggle to keep my emotions in check.

I take a step closer to Darian, the longing on his face mirroring the torturous ache in my body, but the moment is interrupted by a loud knock on the door.

We both freeze in place.

I compose myself and forcefully swing open the door, irritation lacing my words, "What?" I bark.

The guard's face remains impassive as he meets my gaze, unaffected by my tone.

"Time's up. We're taking him back to his cell. He's scheduled for release this evening."

That was incredibly quick, Caspian.

I blink, trying to conceal my surprise and offer a brief nod in acknowledgment.

Turning to Darian, I subtly tilt my head, mustering a hint of a smile. "Seems luck is on your side, sir."

Chapter 41

Leaving Darian in that station has my gut twisted into a million pieces.

I slide in the backseat of the cab, quietly providing the address of the apartment, my mind consumed by thoughts and uncertainties throughout the rest of the journey home.

Val is already waiting in the living area as I step through the door, his ears perked forward. Letting out a weary sigh, I kick off my shoes and join him on the couch, leaning against his side, I press a gentle kiss on his shoulder.

"He looked worse for wear in there, Val. Caspian said he'd pull strings to get him released tonight but, unless Caspian was the reason Darian was put there in the first place, something's not right."

Val responds with a subtle head tilt.

With a heavy sigh, I make my way to the kitchen, determined to distract myself from the unease gnawing at me. Cooking dinner for the two of us becomes a welcome respite, if only temporarily.

Midnight comes and goes, and my anxiety intensifies as Darian still hasn't returned. I reach for the phone and dial the police station, my heart pounding with each passing second.

The officer on the other end confirms that he was released at 11 PM, providing a small sense of relief.

There's still plenty of time for him to make his way home. Despite my self-reassurance, unease lingers in the back of my mind, refusing to be silenced.

Sitting on the couch with Val, I find myself drifting off, my eyelids growing heavier with each blink.

Glancing at the clock, it's been hours since Darian was supposed to return. My heart skips a beat as a fresh wave of worry hits me, jolting me fully awake.

I reach for my cell phone and quickly dial Caspian's number, desperation fueling my trembling fingers.

I resent having to rely on Caspian at this moment, but he is Darian's own brother.

Surely, he wouldn't go against our agreement, would he?

With these thoughts swirling in my mind, I press the call button.

"What is it, Lara? Darian not satisfying you or did you just miss my voice?" Caspian's voice is thick with sleep, and his dig only fuels my anger.

Every well-thought-out plan crumbles in the face of my mounting impatience

Impulsiveness sinks its claws into me, overriding any rationality that may have remained. "We need to talk," I state firmly, "Come to the apartment. Alone."

Without waiting for a response, I abruptly hang up.

Twenty minutes later, a knock reverberates through the apartment.

Using the peephole, I confirm it is him before unlocking the door and holding it open.

His wary gaze briefly flicks to Val, who remains settled on the couch.

With his focus on Val, I quickly move toward him from behind the closing door, pressing the edge of my dagger against the sensitive skin of his neck, applying just enough pressure to make my point.

"Lara," his voice is laced with confusion, clearly not expecting this to be a trap.

"Caspian," I utter, my voice laced with a lethal edge as a torrent of accusatory thoughts floods my mind.

I maintain my grip on the knife, refusing to back down.

"Put the knife down, Lara," Caspian retorts, his tone deceptively light, but I hear the underlying threat beneath his words.

He thinks that I lack the resolve to hurt him.

Challenge accepted.

I tilt my head and meet Caspian's gaze.

"I'd rather not." I retort.

He chuckles darkly, and I curse my body for having any reaction to it.

"Someone is going to get hurt." he says, adding, "Do you even know how to fight with daggers?"

I do, but I'm not about to tell him that.

"I'm a quick study," I reply, my voice laced with annoyance.

"I thought you said you wanted to talk?" Caspian gestures between us, his brow raised in curiosity.

"We're talking." I state angrily, "I thought you were going to release Darian."

His brows furrow. "I did," he responds, his tone genuine.

I press the blade further against his neck, my anger seeping into my voice.

"Bullshit, Caspian," I seethe, forcefully pushing him toward a kitchen chair and making him sit. "Where are you keeping him? Where did you move him to?"

His jaw feathers as he snarls back at me, his voice filled with frustration. "Lara, I don't know what you're talking about. I had him released, and that's it."

Unbridled rage surges within me, refusing to accept his words at face value.

But the anger within me continues to swirl, like the molten lava inside a volcano on the verge of erupting. Simmering just beneath the surface, a destructive force that threatens to consume everything in its path.

That's the thing about rage.

You can suppress it, bury it deep down, and try to ignore the triggers that fuel it.

But once you reach that breaking point...

Once you let it consume you, it becomes a force that's difficult to rein in without creating a massive, destructive fucking mess.

I release the blade and straighten as relief floods Caspian's features, and within seconds a cry escapes from my throat as I drive the dagger into his thigh.

The pain registers on his face as he blinks at his leg and then to me, struggling to comprehend what has just happened.

With my free hand, I tighten my grip around his throat and a manic, dry laugh escapes my lips.

Caspian's eyes widen as he stares at me in disbelief.

"Right." I say sarcastically, "Next, you're going to say you had nothing to do with the hunters at the grocery store or when we hiked to the mountains. Hell, you might even try to deny that you hired people to pretend to be my parents. Maybe after that you'll even try to deny that you hired the piece of shit who fucking raped me." I shout, tears of pure rage trail down my cheeks.

His eyes flash with a mixture of confusion and anger, but I dismiss it.

I hold my grip on Caspian's throat, my eyes locked onto him, as his calm and collected voice cuts through my rage.

"Lara I need you to listen to me very carefully," he says, low and steady. "I was responsible for hiring your parents and the hunter who-"

His words hang in the air, and for a moment, I hesitate, a flicker of uncertainty sparking within me.

"I know you do not believe me, but I'm telling the truth. Neither the mountains nor the grocery store were my men and I had no idea Cain was going to fucking assault you. If I knew I would have killed him myself." He finishes with a lethal edge to his voice.

My heart thunders in my chest.

If he isn't responsible for the hunters and Darian's disappearance, then who is?

"Explain," I manage to say, my head swirling.

His expression becomes guarded, "You were collecting the amulets," His eyes flash with anger, "I can't jeopardize that. I may be an asshole, a manipulative bastard, and a villain. But of all the terrible things I've done and will do in my life that make me the monster, I'm not willing to risk you."

My pulse rages and I release my hold on his throat entirely, taking a step back to create some distance as I stare at him, searching for any hint that he's lying.

Caspian rises to his feet with a wince, pulling the dagger from his thigh, "You don't have to believe what I'm saying, but at least give me the opportunity to prove that my brother's disappearance wasn't my doing."

His emerald eyes capture mine for a moment and I nod, ignoring the heat within my body, taking another tentative step back.

I despise having this visceral reaction to a man responsible for much of my pain and suffering in my life.

Directly or indirectly.

Unfortunately, my body doesn't seem to get the memo that this is not the time or the place.

The silence stretches between us, and I watch as Caspian's fingers move over his phone screen, his expression tense.

"What are you doing?" I ask Caspian bluntly. My suspicion and curiosity getting the best of me. I can't help but feel wary of his sudden change in demeanor.

"I'm finding out who is behind this." He murmurs, and I move to join Val on the couch as Caspian eases back into his seat.

Minutes later, he dials a series of numbers in his phone and raises it to his ear. His murmurs gradually escalate in volume, tinged with frustration and anger.

"Find out where the fuck it is!" he seethes, slamming his finger against the end button, he abruptly stands from the chair as sways unsteadily.

Animosities forgotten, I quickly move toward Caspian. We both glance down at the deep crimson liquid staining his jeans and pooling under the chair.

"Shit," I breathe.

Swallowing the panic that I've stabbed the person here to help, I guide him back into the seat. "Stay. I'm going to take care of this."

I call out to Val, urgently instructing him to fetch the first aid kit, while Caspian lets out a chuckle.

"I guess you did know how to use it after all," he remarks with a hint of amusement in his voice.

"I'm full of surprises," I retort dryly.

Caspian's phone chimes and his eyes scan the message before him.

I turn my attention to the stove, igniting the flame and carefully placing the blade of the dagger over it.

"Have a team surround the building," Caspian relays, his voice filled with unspoken threats, "I want her alive and I'll get her myself."

His words send a shiver down my spine, and a sense of dread settles in my stomach. Val pads into the room with his ears pinned back as he carries the first aid kit over.

I can't help but think that he heard the same ominous tone in Caspian's voice that I did.

Caspian presses the end call button on his phone and lifts his gaze to meet mine.

It's then that I notice his washed pallor. His skin now ashen, and a thin layer of sweat coats his forehead.

Fuck.

"We found Darian," he manages to say, his voice strained as he takes a deep breath. "It seems Dolly has gathered a substantial force of guards since she's no longer under his protection. She has taken matters into her own hands to seek revenge."

Oh. That's who 'She' was.

"We have been tracking her movements after she surfaced. Finally after years of hiding behind my brother's protection..." His words are slow as he continues, "I was wondering what she had up her..."

But his words fade into silence, and I notice a sudden change in his demeanor. His head dips downward, and my heart skips a beat at the fluttering of his eyelids.

"Fuck" I repeat out loud, urgency lacing my voice as I rush to Caspian's side, kneeling in front of him to set out the peroxide, "I need to get to the wound." I glance up at him, and to my relief, his focus seems to sharpen, albeit with a hint of amusement in his eyes.

"If you wanted my pants off, my dear Lara, all you had to do was ask." he drawls, his speech slightly slurred.

My cheeks flush and Caspian stands once again, unbuckling his belt deftly with one hand.

I help tug his jeans to the floor as the fabric tugs on the injured skin around his wound, a fresh surge of crimson blood gushes out, the sight making my stomach churn.

He lowers himself into the chair with a heavy thud, his shoulders slump, and I can see the exhaustion clear on his face.

I need to move fast.

My heart pounds in my chest as I quickly retrieve Caspian's belt from the floor, folding it and placing it gently between his teeth before darting to the stove. I grip the red-hot dagger in one hand and snatching the hydrogen peroxide from the kit with the other.

Returning to Caspian's side, I lock eyes and warn him, "This is going to hurt."

Without giving him a chance to prepare himself, I pour the hydrogen peroxide over the wound.

Caspian's chest heaves but to his credit he makes no sound as the liquid fizzes and foams upon contact. His knuckles turn white as he grips the counter and the side of the chair.

Before he can protest or halt my actions, I steel myself and press the red-hot blade against his wound. I focus on angling it in a way that will effectively cauterize the injury and help stem the bleeding.

The scent of burnt flesh fills the air, mingling with the metallic tang of blood.

Caspian's grunts escalate into a deep, throaty moan, the sound reverberating in the room. The pungent odor hangs heavy in the air, and I swallow against the bile rising in my throat.

I move with purpose, carrying the hot blade to the sink and running it under cool water for several minutes. The hiss of steam fills the room as the heat dissipates, and I drop it to the sink with a clatter.

Turning to face Caspian, I find him sitting in the chair, his chest rising and falling with each labored breath as his pallor begins to return to normal. The realization that both Caspian and Darian are far from being typical humans sends a chill down my spine.

Seeing Caspian's recovery gives me hope for Darian's, recalling his state at the police station as my thoughts turn to Dolly.

"The anonymous tip to the police department... was that your doing?" I tilt my head, studying his expression.

His gaze meets mine and my heart flutters.

"No," he finally responds, and I'm surprised as he continues, "I had no prior knowledge of Darian's arrest until it was reported on the news. Someone else must have called it in, and I was informed afterward."

This honesty is refreshing, but incredibly dangerous.

Part of me wonders if it's a trap.

Some clever way to hook me in again into trusting him, even if just tentatively.

The other, much more foolish part of me wonders if this is him.

The room falls into a brief silence, interrupted by the sound of my footsteps as I approach him once more.

My mind races to rationalize the warring thoughts and emotions within myself as I clean the blood off his bare legs and carefully wrap his wound.

I finish tending to his injury, my eyes drop to his torn and blood-soaked pants before I tilt my head to look at him, only to find him already staring at me.

There's a raw intensity in his gaze, a mix of vulnerability, awe, and something akin to pride. The air between us crackles with unspoken emotions as he breaks the silence.

"You stabbed me." his voice laced with amusement and curiosity.

I blink.

Is he just realizing this, or is this a symptom of the blood loss?

Slowly, I nod, unsure what to think, "I did," I say softly.

His head cocks to the side, his emerald eyes searching mine.

"Then you took care of me," he continues, "Why?"

My cheeks flush.

I find myself momentarily lost for words, my mind scrambling to articulate the complex web of emotions. I reach down to lift each of his legs, gently freeing the ruined pants from under him, careful not to jostle his injury.

I know exactly the reason I'm tending to him with such care.

Deep down, I'm conflicted about who Caspian truly is and his motivations. Despite the chaos and pain, I hold onto the belief that there is goodness within him.

But there are other reasons that I refuse to admit out loud, even to myself, for why I'm taking such care in tending his wound. As much as I despise him for the part he has played, the people he's hurt...

The tangled web of emotions between us, that lingering spark refuses to extinguish.

I'm not ready to confront those reasons and I don't know that I ever will be. The bandages, the gentle touch, the hidden concern—each gesture reveals a truth I'm not yet ready to acknowledge.

I choose to offer him a safer explanation, carefully choosing my words, "I'm doing this because you're willing to help me rescue Darian and despite the turmoil you've brought into my life between foster care and Cain, I acknowledge that you weren't responsible for the recent attacks. It also seems that you harbor a deep dislike for this Dolly person, possibly even more than I do. And you know what they say about the enemy of my enemy."

Caspian's jaw tightens at the sound of her name, "I didn't know, Lara." Regret and guilt flicker in his eyes as our gazes meet, and he opens his mouth to speak. "If I had known what was happening to you with Cain and in foster care, I–"

I hold my hand up between us signaling for him to stop, and he abruptly goes quiet.

Surprise rifles through me that he listened.

"We can't change the past, Caspian. All we have is the future, and it's up to us to shape it into a future worth living for." I say, moving to discard his tattered jeans as his gaze drops to the floor before padding to Darian's room.

In his dresser, I locate a pair of his pants and compare their size and fit. They're similar enough to Caspian's physique.

Darian's slightly broader and more muscular chest might pose a small difference, but overall, the pants should be a good fit.

Entering the kitchen again, I hand the jeans to Caspian but give him privacy to put them on as I go to get the mop to get the blood off the floor.

Time passes slowly as I meticulously clean the area, allowing Caspian to recover.

In the following hour, Caspian outlines the steps required to retrieve Darian, his fingers swiftly dancing across his phone's screen as he communicates with his team.

Val and I are tasked with locating Darian.

Caspian's own team will handle the confrontation with Dolly's hired guns.

But Dolly herself? She's to be subdued and kept alive.

Caspian's command for that was chilling, to say the least.

Engrossed in putting away the dishes, my hands jerk involuntarily when a sudden knock on the door startles me.

The glass I hold slips from my grasp, crashing against the floor and shattering. A mix of hope floods my thoughts at the possibility that it could be Darian returning home.

Caspian walks to the door with a slight limp as he checks the peephole.

He opens the door revealing a woman with sleek black hair and dark voids for eyes standing in the doorway. Her gaze shifts between Caspian and me, and I can't help but feel a chill run down my spine as her eyes rake down my body.

Val's growl reverberates from the couch, his fur standing on end. Taking his warning, I find my voice, "I don't want anyone else in here, Caspian. It's already challenging enough having you around."

His lips curl into a smirk, and he tilts his head in acknowledgment. "Very well. I'll text you the location we'll be heading to tomorrow evening."

"Tomorrow evening?!" I snap.

He cocks his head and sighs with annoyance, his asshole demeanor fully returned. "Yes, tomorrow evening. I need time to plan and gather my people, who are currently scattered across the country. Unless you want to go in half-cocked and risk getting captured as well?" His piercing gaze makes me swallow, and I nod reluctantly.

"Very well, now that we have that settled. I'll be in touch," he remarks with a casual wave over his shoulder as he limps out of the door. I find myself once again locking eyes with the woman standing in the doorway.

She looks at me as if I'm delivering a meal she's been eagerly waiting for, her black eyes gleaming with anticipation. It sends a shiver down my spine, and I instinctively reach for the dagger on the counter.

"I'll be seeing you soon, *vrenlon dyrtia*" She grins, a wicked amusement dancing in her eyes, before allowing the door to slide shut.

I exhale the breath I've been holding and shake my head, trying to process the whirlwind of information from the past few hours.

I need a drink.

Chapter 42

The following hours drift by in a haze. I clean the kitchen, take a much-needed shower, and put on fresh clothes.

I retreat to Darian's bed for a nap, and when Val wakes me up from a nightmare, I stumble into the kitchen to prepare breakfast.

I find myself crawling back to the familiar embrace of Darian's bed, longing to feel his presence in some way and I linger there for hours. I'm lost in my thoughts until Val interrupts by tugging at the blankets with an attitude and I swat at him to stop.

Impatience gnaws at me as I wait for Caspian's text with the location. Each passing minute feels like an eternity, and my mind races with anticipation and anxiety. I check my phone repeatedly to no avail.

The waiting game is agonizing, and I find myself growing restless, yearning for some semblance of direction.

As I picture the potential horrors Darian may be facing, I know I can't afford to waste any more time. Propelling myself out of bed and into the bathroom, I gather the necessary supplies for a first aid kit to bring with us.

Bandages, antiseptic, and other medical essentials find their place in my trembling hands. As I organize the kit, my thoughts are consumed by Darian, but there's one sentence I repeat over and over as if to will it into existence.

He will be alive.

Carefully selecting the necessary supplies, I gather enough materials to address a range of injuries, from burns to cuts and even suturing items. Including two adrenaline shots, hydrogen peroxide

They sprint away clearing the path before us as Val and I proceed further into the heart of the compound. We move cautiously to the building, and I tighten my grip on my daggers, grasping one in each hand with the blades angled to my elbows for quick, effective strikes.

That's assuming my semi-healed injuries from days ago don't get in the way.

Keeping low to the ground we dash past the entrance and across the lawn to the door of the building, blending with the shadows along the walls.

Adrenaline surges through my veins as I twist the cool metal of the knob with caution, tugging it open as Val and I slip inside. Stepping into the dimly lit marble corridor, I scan the surroundings to find it surprisingly vacant. I motion for Val to follow as we head deeper into the building.

The chaotic symphony of distant shouts and gunshots echoes in the distance and as we turn a corner I halt abruptly at the two armed guards in our path. They stand tall, blocking access to a set of stairs that descend toward the basement.

With a surge of adrenaline, I make a split-second decision. Taking a step forward to catch their attention hoping Val remains hidden in the shadows.

As the barrel of their guns swing toward me, time slows down as my body taps into speeds I didn't know I possessed. I launch myself to the side of one guard and spin on my heel, parrying his gun away from my body.

With a single, precise stroke, I bring the sharp edge of my dagger across the guard's neck. The air fills with a brief, startled gasp as his eyes widen in shock. The crimson line deepens on his throat, splattering in my face as he gargles.

The guard's gun slips from his grasp, falling to the ground with a clatter as he clutches his neck in an attempt to stop the bleeding. Val dispatches the second guard quickly as his powerful jaws find purchase on the man's throat in a sickening crunch.

Within seconds, both guards are heaps on the ground as we move to descend the staircase, our footsteps echo in the empty space.

We get into two more skirmishes, leaving the broken bodies of armed men in our wake as we continue our advance. The air around us crackles with an electric tension that builds with every step.

The mere thought of Darian being at Dolly's mercy ignites a raging inferno of raw fury that drives me forward.

Finally, we arrive at the bottom of the staircase, facing a large set of doors and my heart pounds frantically in my chest.

Val and I freeze as a woman's voice sounds out, accompanied by a pained, muffled groan.

Darian.

A deadly calm washes over me as I adjust the blade in my right hand, the metal is cold and reassuring against my palm. We stand at the threshold, our eyes locked on the door and I embrace the stillness within me.

The urge to get to Darian grips me as I hear his muffled groans again, and I can't wait any longer as I push open the doors.

My heart sinks at the sight before me.

Darian hangs suspended from a chain, his head bowed. Blood, bruises, deep cuts and blisters cover his skin from beneath his tattered clothes and I can't even begin to imagine the torture he's been through.

Dolly stands before us with some kind of device clutched in her hands. Her blonde hair is unkempt and disheveled. Her cold, blue eyes are bright with disdain as she sneers at him with a level of malice I'd reserve for only my worst enemies.

Grasping a device from the table she walks closer to him, oblivious of our presence until I take a step toward them.

The movement catches Dolly's attention as she twists. Her gaze flicks where we stand in the doorway, and the device clatters to the ground.

I take another step toward Dolly, her rage mirroring my own as she shouts, "How the fuck did you two get in here?"

With a snap of my wrist, her eyes dart to my hand a split second before my dagger is airborne. She narrowly avoids it with shock painted on her features, but not without paying a price.

Gotcha, bitch.

The blade grazes her shoulder, leaving behind a crimson trail down her unmarred skin. The sight of her blood stirs something within me.

If she can bleed. She can die.

And if there's anyone in this world that I want to kill without a shadow of a doubt, it's Dolly.

I surge my body forward before she can fully comprehend it, and we collide with a resounding thud, crashing onto the unforgiving floor. The impact sends waves of pain through my being, but I refuse to yield, my grip on her tightening as we grapple for purchase on one another.

Her eyes widen in shock as I expertly maneuver myself, -thanks to years of training- and within the blink of an eye I'm straddling her chest.

The world around me fades to a haze of red as I unleash rage upon her, my knuckles slamming countless blows into her face.

If there's pain in my hands or arms, I don't feel it.

My relentless assault becomes a frenzy, and I lose count of how many times I've laid into her. It's not until a firm grip suddenly encircles my wrist, that my assault stops in its tracks.

Caspian.

"No!" I shout, struggling against his grip, "I'll fucking kill her!"

My chest heaves and my awareness gradually sharpens but the crimson hue in my vision refuses to fade, and I realize that's because it's Dolly's blood splattered across the surroundings.

"Leave her to me, little one," Caspian's voice quietly cuts through the chaotic air and calms the storm raging within me enough that I stop fighting him.

"Caspian, let me fucking kill her." I snarl.

His touch is surprisingly gentle as he wraps an arm around my waist, lifting me away from Dolly's broken form and turning me to face him.

"You might want that blood on your hands now, Lara. But trust me when I tell you that death would be a gift for her in comparison to what I have in store."

I can hardly hear him as my teeth grind together, fixated on her groaning form on the floor as Caspian grips my face, pulling my gaze to his.

He presses his forehead to mine, and my heart stutters, as if catching up real time.

"I may be the villain, little one. But in this, allow me to be the monster for both of us." he pulls back to search my face and I concede.

"My brother needs you." he whispers, and all the fight drains out of me as my attention flicks to his chained body.

Caspian releases me and I dash toward his limp form, rage forgotten as my heart pounds in my chest. Unsure where to grasp him to avoid causing pain, I wrap my arms around his large torso. To my relief, Caspian helps remove the chains as they slip off the hook, crashing to the ground with a deafening clatter.

Darian's arms fall limp over my head, and we both collapse backward with a heavy thud.

With my body pressed against his, I feel the rise and fall of his weakened breath, and relief overwhelms me.

He's fucking alive.

"Darian." I choke out, my chest crushed beneath his weight.

Although Darian stirs, his eyes remain rolled back in his head, and it's clear she drugged him. Panic sets in as I try and fail to push him off me as my chest tightens, expanding my lungs nearly impossible as I fight for breath.

I catch a glimpse of Val's dark fur out of the corner of my eye as he rushes to my side, slightly rolling Darian over and relieving a small amount of the pressure on my chest.

Caspian appears above me with a hard look, helping Val shift Darian's crushing weight fully off of me.

"Thank you," I manage to say between gasps for air.

Caspian nods, his gaze fixed on me as he jerks his head toward the two individuals standing at the door. "Two of my men are going to escort you three to the apartment and help you bring him inside."

I meet his gaze with wariness and as if sensing my hesitation, Caspian lets out a deep sigh, his features softening as he grasps his handgun.

My eyes widen as I blink at him.

"I'll say it again, the attacks against you recently have not been my doing. If you still don't trust that, then take this," he continues, offering me his handgun, "and shoot them if they overstay their welcome or do anything outside of bringing him inside the apartment."

I hesitate for a moment, glancing to the men who blink at Caspian with wide eyes and my fingers find the cool metal handle as I take the offered weapon.

Meeting Caspian's gaze, I nod before returning my focus to Darian.

"What do you think is wrong with him?" I ask, hoping it's something that will wear off soon.

Caspian lifts the lid to his brother's green eye and then his blue-white eye, his gaze shifting between them. "He's been drugged with some sort of tranquilizer," he confirms, "I doubt she would have been able to restrain him for long without one."

"Is there anything we can do to counteract the tranquilizer's effects?"

Caspian's expression shifts to a frown, "Without knowing the specific drug and its dosage, it's difficult to say," he admits, his tone measured. "But for now that may be for the best, since he'll be in a world of pain once it wears off."

I nod, moving to rummage through my bag, retrieving my first aid supplies and begin tending to the larger injuries that haven't stopped bleeding. Carefully studying the wounds scattered across his chest and abdomen, as I clean his injuries. I apply dressings to the deeper gashes, securing them in place. For the burns, I gently dab them with a cool, damp cloth, providing temporary relief from the searing pain before applying a cream to soothe them.

"I've called in a couple of favors and local police won't be on the scene for 30 minutes. I expect you all to be out of here by then." Caspian says, pocketing his phone.

I nod as he turns to leave, "Give her pain, Caspian." He goes rigid, and his intense emerald gaze meets mine, "I want Dolly to pay."

"Do you remember what I said?" he asks, tilting his head slightly.

Cold vengeance flashes in my mind and I nod once, meeting his gaze, "Be my monster."

His eyes flash, and nodding once in acknowledgement before he turns and briskly leaves the room, his footsteps fading down the corridor.

As I gather and pack the medical supplies, my attention is drawn to one of the men near the door, cautiously making his way toward us. My hand instinctively twitches, longing to reach for the handgun as I keep a wary eye on him.

The man notices my tense grip near the gun and immediately pauses, putting both hands in the air. "Woah, it's okay," he says, "We're just here to get you guys home."

I nod cautiously as the man steps closer, casting a glance at Darian, "Is he going to be okay?" he asks.

"He's stable," I respond, my gaze shifting to Darian's chest, observing the steady rise and fall of his breath.

The second man approaches the other side of Darian, speaking in a hushed tone, "We need to move him to the car quickly. We have only a few minutes before the police arrive."

I blink in surprise.

Has that much time truly passed?

Nodding in acknowledgment, I rise to my feet and Val stays glued to my side.

"Please be careful with the sutures on his chest, if you can. I'd prefer not to have to redo them when he wakes up," I say quietly.

With careful coordination, they lift Darian's limp body into their arms, following Val's lead as we make our way out of the compound. As we reach the awaiting car, the cool night air hits me and I feel a weight lifting off my shoulders.

We did it.

I don't know if this would have been at all possible if Caspian hadn't helped.

The drive is accompanied by a peaceful silence, interrupted only by the sound of Darian's labored breathing in the backseat. The rush of adrenaline finally dissipates, leaving behind an overwhelming exhaustion.

As we arrive at the parking garage, my shoulders sag with relief. The men carefully carry Darian into the apartment, gently placing him in his bed, and before I know it, they're gone.

I suppose the threat of being shot is enough to send them running.

As the hours pass, Darian's breathing becomes steady, and a hint of color returns to his face.

I change into comfortable pajamas and slip in bed alongside him, taking care not to jostle his injuries which is harder than it seems.

But I'm desperate, and even if it takes me 30 minutes to ease into his presence, I'll do it.

My overwhelming need to be close to him overrides any other thoughts or concerns as I sigh deeply with content.

I stir from sleep as a gentle hand brushes against my cheek.

My eyes flutter open, instantly meeting Darian's gaze, and I release a breath of profound relief.

"You came for me," he whispers softly, his eyes searching mine.

My throat tightens with emotion.

"I didn't do it alone," I whisper back.

"But you were still there. I remember hearing your voice," he says, his brows furrowing as if struggling to recall.

Looking into his eyes, I prepare myself for him to think differently of me with my confession.

"I called Caspian when you didn't return, assuming he was responsible. Caspian came to the apartment... and... well, I sort of stabbed him. He agreed to help locate you and Dolly, but he wanted to take her alive. Most of the planning to get in was his, and I almost ruined everything when I nearly killed her myself."

Darian searches my face, and my voice is no more than a whisper as I continue, "You once told me you'd always find me. You said you'd kill anyone who tries to harm me," I hold his gaze and my confession pours out of me, "I admit I am not as resourceful as one may need to be to make these kinds of proclamations, but I will always find you too, Darian. I will always find you and anyone who brings you pain will live to regret it or die slowly. That is my own promise to you."

Darian's eyes widen as he stares at me for a moment, processing the information. "You... you stabbed Caspian?" he asks, his voice filled with surprise and concern. "And you're still here, alive?"

His face bears no judgment, regret, or shame at my loss of control. Instead, he examines me with what I can only describe as awe.

I see the gratitude in his exhausted eyes, but more than that, I see the pain and trauma.

I recognize it well from all the days I looked in the mirror at school. Hidden beneath the mask I'd concealed over my features, my eyes were the lone indicator of the toll the abuse was taking.

Darian shifts next to me and winces, his tranquilizer clearly having worn off some time ago. Carefully, I slide off the bed and retrieve painkillers from the medical kit then a glass of water.

Returning to his side, I offer it with a gentle smile, "Here, take these," I say softly.

He nods gratefully, his hand tremors slightly as he takes the pills and swallows them down with a sip of water. He settles back into a more comfortable position, and I crawl in bed alongside him, curling onto my side, facing him.

I whisper softly, my voice carrying a soothing tone. "Our problems will still be there tomorrow. Rest and let your body recover."

His hand intertwines with mine beneath the covers and I close my eyes, savoring the familiar scent of forest rain that brings me peace.

Chapter 43

The next morning, I am gently roused from my slumber by the soft whirring sound of the blackout curtains lifting up. The room gradually fills with light as I open my eyes.

Darian stands by the door to the bathroom, a towel in his hand. There's a softness in his eyes as he watches me that makes my heart swell in my chest.

The bruises on his face have noticeably faded, their vibrant colors now muted and yellowed. The swelling that once marred his features has significantly subsided, allowing his natural contours to reemerge. The pallor of his skin, which was grey before, has regained a healthier hue overnight.

While the cuts and blisters still cover his body, they too show signs of healing. The angry redness has diminished, replaced by the early stages of the body's reparative process.

It's remarkable to witness how his wounds have begun to mend in such a short span of time.

"Good morning, Darian," I greet him with a warm smile.

"Morning, Sunshine," he whispers back with a slight wink before disappearing into the adjacent room.

The sound of the shower running becomes faintly audible, accompanied by the gentle rhythm of water splashing and cascading.

It's like everything feels right again.

I rouse myself from the comfort of the bed and make my way to the kitchen. Aware that he may not have had a proper meal in a while, I set out to create a hearty breakfast, gathering the ingredients and start the preparation as Val watches me attentively.

As I assemble the food onto three plates, pausing as the sound of the bedroom door catches my attention. Darian's silhouette emerges, dressed only in a comfortable pair of baggy grey sweats. His damp hair cascades loosely around his face, droplets of water still clinging to the strands.

With a gentle smile, he takes a seat at the counter, and moves to set one of the plates on the floor for Val, but freezes as I squeak, "Wait!"

I swing open the fridge, rummaging through its contents, a triumphant smile on my face.

Retrieving Val's food, I pour a generous amount of maple syrup over his dish, ensuring that every piece is coated. I steal a quick glance at Darian, whose face is painted in pure amusement.

He chuckles softly before diving into his plate of food.

"So," I say quietly, placing the dirty dishes in the dishwasher and turning to face Darian.

"So," Darian echoes, a smirk playing on his lips as he meets my gaze.

"Can you tell me what happened to you?" I inquire gently, knowing full well how much I hated being on the receiving end of this conversation.

Darian's expression shifts, his face falling and his eyes growing distant.

I watch as his walls rise with maybe too much understanding.

Silence hangs in the air, stretching out for what feels like an eternity, and I'm about to tell him never mind when his voice breaks the stillness.

"They came to my cell to release me. I remember stepping out and feeling a sharp pain on the side of my neck. It was like my entire body went numb within seconds. When I came to, I was chained up, and Dolly was there. She injected me with some substance again and started asking questions about Caspian."

Anger simmers within me, its flames licking at my thoughts. "I should have killed her," I whisper through clenched teeth.

But Darian's response catches me off guard.

He shakes his head, "No," he says firmly. "Whatever my brother has in store for her, it is likely something worse than death."

Chapter 44

Caspian

I scan the counter before me, meticulously taking inventory of my instruments.

The room is filled with an eerie silence, punctuated only by the faint hum of fluorescent lights overhead. My gaze shifts toward the metal table that dominates the center of the room, where Dolly lies restrained. Thick leather straps bind her wrists and ankles to the cold, unforgiving corners of the table, rendering her completely immobilized.

Dolly's body appears tense, her eyes filled with a mix of fear and defiance. Her attempts to struggle against the restraints are futile, and her muffled protests barely register.

As I approach the table, a myriad of emotions swirl within me.

The path I have chosen, the path of retribution, is one saturated with moral ambiguity.

Yet, I cannot deny the visceral satisfaction that courses through my veins as I stand face-to-face with the embodiment of cruelty and malice.

My lips curl into a grin.

I have waited too fucking long for this.

"Some say that revenge is a dish best served cold," I remark with a chilling calmness in my voice.

I grab a nearby bucket filled with ice-cold water and without hesitation, pour the icy water over Dolly's face.

The shock causing her to convulse and gasp for air. Her body contorts in a desperate attempt to escape the onslaught, but the restraints hold her firmly in place.

The sound of her labored breaths and choked sputtering reverberates in the room, drowned out only by the steady dripping of water onto the unforgiving floor.

It's music to my fucking ears.

The assault continues until the bucket is emptied, leaving Dolly drenched, shivering, and utterly drained. I release the bucket, and it clangs against the floor loudly.

"But those who said that were human after all, and they had a human lifespan to get revenge. Hundreds of years is a long time to consider the ways to exact revenge. Don't you think?" I remark, the corners of my lips curl into a cold, calculated smile.

"You see, Dolly, time has been my most trusted ally. While your actions may have brought pain and suffering to countless lives, they have also sown the seeds of your own destruction. Revenge, in its truest form, requires patience and meticulous planning," I explain, relishing in the power I hold over her.

Her breath hitches, a tremor coursing through her restrained body.

This is it.

This is the moment when she realizes that her death will not be quick or merciful.

It will be a slow, methodical descent into the depths of her darkest nightmares.

"Revenge is not a race, Dolly," I conclude, my tone cold and final. "It is a meticulously choreographed symphony of suffering, and I am its conductor. Your time has come, and I assure you, the wait has only sharpened the edge of my vengeance."

She glares at me with her icy blue eyes. "I did what needed to be done, Caspian," she retorts defiantly.

"Ah, ah, ah," I wag my finger back and forth, my smile widening at her feeble attempt to justify her actions.

Her lips snap shut, a flicker of fear crossing her face, and I chuckle softly to myself. The sound echoes through the room as I retrieve the bucket, purposefully moving toward the sink.

With deliberate movements, I turn on the faucet and let the water rush in, filling it to the brim.

"You see, Dolly," I continue, my voice dropping to a whisper. "Actions have consequences. The choices we make can shape the lives of others, for better or for worse."

With deliberate slowness, I turn back toward her, the bucket of water held firmly in my grasp. On the way to the table, I snatch the cloth on the counter and her eyes widen into saucers. The struggle within her intensifies, and her attempts to free herself become more frantic.

The air in the room feels heavy with anticipation, and I can sense her mounting terror.

Good.

This is a good start.

With a firm grip, I hold her jaw, ensuring that she remains still. The cloth hovers atop her face, and I hear her take a deep breath before I slowly pour the water over her mouth.

The stream is barely a trickle while she holds her breath. After a long minute, I see and hear her exhale. Without a second thought, I increase the flow, and she chokes before desperately flailing against my grip.

The sound of her muffled gasps fills the room as the water fills her lungs. Her struggles intensify, a deeply instinctual, desperate fight for survival, but the cloth remains firmly in place.

I continue until her attempts to evade the drowning lessen, becoming jerky movements before I allow her to breathe freely. The water slowly trickles to a stop, and I withdraw the cloth from her face.

Her gasps for air fill the room, and I watch as her body trembles.

Whether it's from the cold, adrenaline or fear, I don't know. Nor do I care.

"I had to do it." Dolly says between her coughing fit.

My gaze meets hers, and the words slip from my lips, laced with a raw intensity, as I confront her with the truth.

"I don't want to hear your excuses, Dolly," I say firmly, "You knew exactly what you were doing when you handed me over to her."

Releasing my grip on her jaw, I place the cloth onto the workstation next to the remainder of the tools.

"She was going to kill me," she gasps between breaths.

I laugh and Dolly's eyes widen, another flicker of fear crossing her face.

I pause, my laughter fading into an icy stillness. "And it would have ended there," I say, my voice cutting through the silence, "instead, you handed me over as a mere child, and look where we are now."

The room seems to shrink, the walls closing in around us as the tension rises. I meet Dolly's gaze, my eyes are cold and unyielding, mirroring the steel that has encased my heart.

The heart that only has one fucking weakness.

"If you think your death will be a fast one here, Dolly," I continue, my voice dripping with an edge of menace, "you are sorely mistaken."

There is a palpable shift in the atmosphere, and Dolly's defiance falters, her bravado crumbling. Turning to the table with a syringe in hand, I hold it up and cock my head, my gaze fixated on Dolly.

"You're still dead either way, Dolly," I say, my voice laced with lethal finality. "The difference is that you fucked with my entire life, and countless others in the process."

Dolly's gaze flickers between the syringe and my unwavering expression. Fear dances in her eyes, mingling with a sense of resignation and my lips curl.

"One thing I have wondered... How **did** you keep the truth a secret, Dolly?" I ask, my voice dripping with curiosity and disdain. "You must have spun some extravagant tale to gain my brother's protection. What was the dramatics you used? I never was able to get any intel on your sob story."

Dolly's lips curl into a sneer, a twisted expression of defiance. There she is.

With a sudden burst of rage, she spits in my face, her contemptuous act meant to provoke me. But instead, it only fuels my amusement.

As I clean the spittle off, a dark chuckle escapes my lips.

My mind wanders to Lara as I pour liquid into the syringe.

She would have loved this.

"This next part is going to hurt," I state coldly, my voice devoid of any sympathy. "If you have anything important to say, I suggest you do so now while you're still coherent." I position myself by Dolly's restrained hand, my gaze fixed on her.

Her chest heaves in dreaded anticipation. "She will kill you when she finds out what you did to me,"

I stare intently as the needle pierces her flesh, unyielding in my resolve and with a purposeful thrust, I inject a small amount of acid into her fingertip, indifferent to the agony that follows.

A piercing scream escapes her lips as the searing pain takes hold. Her face contorts in anguish, her body writhing against the restraints.

The acidic solution begins its relentless journey coursing through her veins, propelled by her heart. It is not a lethal dose, but it'll hurt like hell.

A cold smirk curls at the corners of my lips, undeterred by her feeble threat. I lean in closer, my voice dripping with disdain. "She would," I nod my head in agreement as her shrill cries echo throughout the room, "But she won't ever learn what happened to you."

After a few minutes, it becomes apparent that the acidic torment has taken its toll. Her screams gradually subside, replaced by labored breaths and the eventual loss of consciousness.

I frown.

This won't do.

Smacking her cheek a few times, she jerks awake and groans hoarsely. "M-make it, s-stop p-pl-please." Her skin flushes and I watch her tremble as the acid burns its way through her body.

A smirk tugs at the corner of my lips and I shake my head, "This only ends with your death, Dolly. I have years of pain to inflict on you in the coming days."

Her eyes flutter before they weakly meet mine. Her blond hair clings wetly to her cheeks, and her pale skin has taken on a fiery red hue.

I hum to myself, picking up two four-inch nails from the table and walking over to the small stove in the corner of the room. Twisting the knob, a flame bursts to life, and I carefully position the nails in the fiery heat.

A whimper sounds from the other side of the room and I grin. She knows what's coming.

"Please." Her hushed voice is barely audible as she pleads.

Her desperate pleas go unheard, her words lost on deaf ears. She dug her own grave when I was young.

Hell, in all likelihood she dug it long before that.

No, if anything, her begging simply makes me enjoy this more.

My hand grips the nail firmly with a pair of metal tongs as I make my way back to the table, the hammer already in my other hand.

Her eyes widen and her screams pierce through the air, bouncing off the soundproof walls around us.

"I don't think I need to say this one will hurt, right?" I cock my head to the side, smirking as I ask her, "Actually, I guess I just did." I add with a chuckle before pressing the tip against her thigh. As a brutal sizzling sound echoes through the room, and I decide in that moment to forego a quick insertion. I hold the head of the hammer against the top of the nail and press in slowly, using steady pressure as the metal digs deep into her thigh.

Her face contorts and her jaw drops open in a silent scream while tears stream down her cheeks. Without a word, I retrieve the second nail, mirroring the placement to her other thigh.

Dolly's eyes roll to the back of her head, and she goes limp, eliciting an exasperated sigh from me.

This will be a long few days if she keeps passing out.

Grabbing a syringe off the table, I jab it in her hip and inject the liquid into her body. It's not a high dose of adrenaline, but enough to bring her to consciousness again.

Within moments, she gasps for air and emits a pained groan, her gaze darting around frantically before finally settling on me. "You're sick." She growls, and I shake my head.

"I'm a product of your decisions, Dolly. You simply weren't prepared to meet the consequences of your actions, and I mean that in the most literal sense."

Dolly whimpers again as I drag over two long wires from the wall, cautious not to touch the metal and risk electrocuting myself. I hook one wire to the head of the nail protruding from her leg, securing it with an electrical grade clamp before moving to the other.

"Please," she whispers desperately. I lock eyes with her and give a slight nod.

"Alright, I'll release you," I respond.

Her eyes widen with hope, and she nervously licks her lips. "R-really?"

A mischievous grin slowly spreads across my face as I let out a snort. "Absolutely not."

Dolly's head dips back in defeat and tears well up in her eyes as she stares at the ceiling.

Connecting the second wire, her entire body goes taut, twitching and convulsing as the electricity surges through her torso.

I let it continue for ten seconds before breaking the circuit and giving her a moment.

Her body goes limp as she passes out again, and I sigh.

By the time she comes into consciousness, I've attached her limbs to a machine on either side of the room.

When the lever is cranked, it increases the tension, resulting in painful extension of the limbs and if you wind the machine enough it will fully dislocate joints.

Hell, it could completely dismember someone.

She glances at me with pure terror, and for a moment, Lara's face flashes through my mind.

I forcefully shove those haunting images aside, reminding myself that the nightmares from the past that Lara endured and Dolly's current reality are not the same.

"I would recommend for you to pray to the Gods for forgiveness, but if they banished me for my actions, I wonder if they would even hear your pleas," I remark, a tinge of bitterness lacing my words.

She sobs and I crank the lever of the machine attached to her right leg enough for it to be uncomfortable.

As her pleading eyes meet mine, I feel no remorse as I wind the bar twice more and her shrieks resonate in the air.

The next few days are going to be fun.

Chapter 45

Lara

A week passes without a word from Caspian, but I'm grateful for the opportunity to let Darian recuperate from his physical and emotional wounds.

Surprisingly, his recovery has been remarkably quick.

Despite the absence of magic on Earth, his body retains a fraction of its resiliency.

We find ourselves immersed in the captivating world of Pompeii, engrossed in every scene unfolding on the screen.

Darian sits upright on the couch, while I nestle into him, using his lap as a pillow. Val sprawls alongside me, his head gracefully draping over my waist, his gaze is fixed on the movie as much as ours are.

Having gone so long without hearing from Caspian, the unexpected chiming of both mine and Darian's phones startles me.

I tilt my head to meet Darian's intense gaze that sends shivers down my spine.

Val adjusts himself to make room as I sit up, while Darian leans forward to retrieve his phone. After a long moment of palpable tension, his voice finally breaks the silence.

"It appears we're making our way back home," he announces.

A blend of apprehension and exhilaration courses through my veins at the prospect of returning to my house, and seeing Candace and Henry.

We spend the next few hours packing before arriving at the executive airport. As we step onto the tarmac, the familiar sight of Darian's private jet awaits us.

With ease, Darian lifts both our carry-on bags up the steps of the aircraft and neatly stows them in compartments close to the sleeping area as Val finds a comfortable spot on one of the chairs.

As if on cue, the flight attendant makes her way toward us, the clicking of her heels resonating through the cabin.

"Good morning, Mr. Cathorn and Ms. Ray," she greets us with a warm smile. "Would you care for a glass of wine or any other beverage?" She clasps her hands together sweetly.

"Pinot, please. Thank you, Heather." Darian replies for both of us. Heather nods and promptly leaves to get our drinks.

As the engine roars to life, we fasten ourselves into our seats.

Heather kindly hands us our glasses of wine before retreating to the front of the aircraft. With a gentle hum, we taxi along the runway, gradually accelerating until we take to the skies.

It's not long before we've reached our cruising altitude.

My ears have popped on a million times through the ascent, and Heather thoughtfully replenished our wine as soon as we were free to move about the cabin.

I must have fallen asleep at some point, as I awaken abruptly, jostled by a bout of minor turbulence. Despite the possibility of seatbelt signs, I seize the opportunity to stretch my legs.

Unfastening my seatbelt, I push to my feet and take a few steps, indulging in a long stretch akin to that of a cat, extending my arms gracefully into the air.

The confines of the cabin melt away as my body revels in the freedom of movement.

Noticing the subtle shift of Darian's seat, I glance over my shoulder, only to meet his intense gaze as he stalks toward me.

Heat radiates from his darkened expression, sending a thrilling shiver down my spine.

Turning fully to face him, I find myself backed against the counter where the wine is stored. My lungs constrict momentarily as he gently lifts my chin, tilting it upward, and leans in closer, his proximity electrifying.

"Darian," I breathe, as his lips gingerly brush against mine sending a shiver through my body

His free hand roams, fingertips trailing up my arm to my shoulder, leaving goosebumps in their wake as he presses his muscular chest into me.

Someone could come in at any moment.

Would they ground the plane if we were caught?

"Lara, stop thinking so loudly." His breath skates over my skin, he forces a knee between my legs, grinding his thigh against my core. I give myself to the feeling and exhale a ragged breath, my limbs trembling.

Every inch of my body is hyper-aware of the contact with his.

Each movement he makes, although subtle, my being seems in tune in with.

I melt into his warmth, feeling his heart beat steadily, its tempo increasing the longer we're this close in proximity.

He releases my chin to grasp my hips with both hands, tugging me flush against him, and rocking me back and forth. The jolts of pleasure with each movement makes my pussy clench as he moves my body rhythmically.

My thighs squeeze him tightly as I whimper with a desperate request for more.

His grip tightens and his fingertips dig into my skin as if he's trying to grind me against his very being, "I could come from the sounds you make alone." He groans.

He quickly lifts one of my legs over his hip and leans his hips heavily against mine, grinding his erection into my clit.

Oh my god, right there.

My eyes flutter as they threaten to roll to the back of my head at the sensation and Darian takes the opportunity to devour my mouth.

Our lips meet in a feverish and urgent kiss, the intensity of his emotions radiating through every touch.

It's a kiss filled with a mixture of longing, desperation, and the raw desire that burns between us.

The pressure of his body bends me backward over the counter, the edge biting into my skin through my clothes. The pain of it is quickly drowned out as he lifts my remaining leg for me to straddle his hips while he holds me up by my thighs.

I'm lost in his body, his kisses, and his need as he towers over me, enveloping my senses.

When we finally break apart, we're both panting with hooded eyes but when I pull back to set my feet on the ground, he holds me in place against him.

My eyes widen in surprise as he swiftly retreats from the counter, holding me effortlessly in his arms.

With purposeful steps, he carries me toward the bedroom, his movements strong and steady.

I hold on tight, my heart pounding as the world around us fades away. We reach the threshold of the bedroom, and he carefully maneuvers us onto the soft expanse of the large mattress.

As we settle on the bed, still entwined, a surge of emotions sweeps over me

This man being gentle, caring and kind could easily break me.

He knows my vulnerabilities, my insecurities and strengths, and accepts them all because they're part of me.

This man who I almost lost.

I can feel the warmth of his body against mine, the electric connection that ignites between us.

My heart races, desire and excitement pulsing through my veins.

"There are still hours remaining on this flight, Lara." he murmurs huskily, his lips brushing against mine in a trail of searing kisses.

The desire in his voice sends shivers down my spine.

"I intend to spend them very wisely."

Darian's large frame towers over me, his kisses are long, passionate and filled with emotion he doesn't say as his hands roam my body.

It's as if he's committing every inch of my skin to memory, savoring the moment as he tugs my pants down.

The cool air of the plane gives me goosebumps along my bare skin as he angles forward, his fingertips trailing from my ankles to my hips.

My pussy aches and throbs with anticipation as he kisses up my stomach to my neck, lifting my shirt over my head and tossing it to the side.

He kisses and nips at my collarbone, his one hand cups my breast through my bra, the other glides up my inner thigh and gently circles over my soaked underwear.

"You're already so wet for me," He groans, leaning his forehead against my chest as he uses both hands to tear off my panties.

Chapter 46

Darian

Seeing her stretch her lithe body broke what little resolve I had to let her enjoy the flight peacefully.

Having spent so much time receiving pain, all I've wanted to do since recovering is crawl between Lara's legs and sink myself into her repeatedly.

I wanted to give her time to recover from what happened too. It was traumatic enough for both of us to go through what we did.

I thought sex would have complicated matters.

Now, I'm only thinking of every uncomplicated reason to fuck her until she can't walk.

Laying over her, tasting her on my tongue, feeling her skin against mine and how her body responds to my touch–I have all the reasons I need.

I'm fucking desperate to be close to her.

I lean in to take one of her taut nipples into my mouth and suck hard.

She writhes beneath me and inhales a sharp breath, her back arching in a silent demand for more. Taking the queue, I slide a finger into her pussy and swallow a groan as she clamps down around me.

I've never fucking needed someone this much in my life.

My cock throbs and pulses in response, painfully tight against my pants as my thumb circles her clit.

She grinds her hips into my hand, and whimpers between breaths.

"Darian," She begs, her back arching off the bed as I slip another finger inside her.

The heat of her pussy is scorching, and the way she's riding my hand tells me that her orgasm is close.

"That's it Sunshine, you're doing so well." I murmur into her skin, and her pussy clamps down again as I force it to stretch to accommodate more. She inhales sharply as I squeeze a third finger in.

Her entire body trembles and she cries out as I curl them to hit the right spot.

"Oh my god," She chokes out as she soaks the bed beneath us and I lean in to taste her.

Fuck. I could eat her for breakfast, lunch and dinner.

She's an entire 4-course meal.

The moment my tongue makes contact with her clit and I flick it, an orgasm shudders through her.

Her legs flex, her toes curl, and she arches off the bed, grinding herself against my face, riding it out as my tongue keeps a steady rhythm.

My dick strains painfully.

I could come from making her orgasm alone.

"Darian, please." Her voice is hoarse as she quietly pleads.

Giving her some reprieve, I trail kisses along the inside of her legs and stomach while I wait for her to come down from the waves of ecstasy coursing through her body.

As the twitching in her thighs ease and her breathing levels out, I sit back and remove my pants before crawling over her body.

She instantly leans in, her silver hair falling forward as she pulls my face in her hands, and kisses me deeply.

My aching cock throbs again as she wraps her legs around my

hips.

"I need you," She murmurs against my lips, and hearing the unspoken plea behind it makes my chest ache.

I swear she could ask for the world and my soul. I'd hand it all to her on a silver fucking platter.

My fingers weave through her hair, gripping it more rough than intended, "You have all of me, Sunshine. I'm yours in every fucking way." I say before eagerly returning her kisses.

I tilt her head back, and her lips part in response. Our tongues dance together, and I lose myself in the heat of the moment, while she grinds herself against my dick.

I've never been so fucking hard in my life.

Each sliding movement her soaked pussy makes against my cock brings me closer to coming, and it's only a matter of time.

I think I can get another orgasm from her before then.

She glides herself up to the tip and I loop an arm around her waist, holding her in position and breaking our kiss for a moment.

"You're going to have to use your words if it's too much, Sunshine. I'm not sure how much control I'm going to have once I'm inside you." I murmur against her lips before leaning my forehead to hers.

Her entire body shudders and as her piercing blue eyes meet mine, I see a reflection of my own insatiable longing that transcends all else.

In the centuries that I've been alive, witnessing the ebb and flow of life, the rise and fall of civilizations, and the inevitable fading of memories, it was as if an ember within me lay dormant.

Yet, through meeting Lara, and with every intimate moment we share, it stirs inside me, as if she's the catalyst to ignite its flame.

Chapter 47

Lara

Darian stares at me with his mismatched gaze that feels like it speaks to my soul as his throbbing cock sits notched at the entrance to my pussy.

In all my life, I've never come so hard and I find myself struggling to comprehend the sensations that are consuming me.

This longing I feel for him goes beyond mere physical attraction.

It resonates deep within the core of my being, on a fundamental level.

"Words, Ray." Darian's voice is thick as he brings me back to reality.

"Words. Right." I echo breathlessly, and he chuckles, sending more heat to my core.

"Lara-" He starts, but I cut him off as he throbs against my soaking wet pussy.

"Darian, I swear to god if you aren't inside of me in the next ten seconds, I'm going to lose my goddamn mind." I interject with a sense of urgency as every moment that passes sends my body into overdrive, desperate to feel him move inside of me.

He grins mischievously and tightens his arm on my waist, securing me to him as he stands up.

I let out a shrill sound with my eyes wide, squeezing my legs around his hips as he carries me to the side of the room, alongside the door where Heather and the pilots are.

"But-"

"I want them and every other person on this damn planet to know who brings you pleasure. I want them to know that this body I have, belongs to you as much as it is mine. Every fucking person on this earth will hear you scream my name until your voice and body give out."

A shudder trembles through me, as he pins me against the wall, the thick head of his cock still nudging my pussy with every throb.

He pushes the tip in slowly and my head falls back as I groan. The feeling of his dick stretching me is a mix of pleasure and pain as I breathe through every inch he gives me.

"Eyes on me, Sunshine." He says as he wraps a hand around my throat.

My eyes snap open to meet his gaze, as he tightens his other arm on my waist.

As he slowly buries himself inside of me, the angle and pressure only increase the burning feeling as he presses in deeper.

By the time he's fully seated, I'm completely impaled on his cock and the gravity of being held against the wall squeezes my clit to his pelvis, edging me closer to another orgasm.

"Fuck, Lara." He breathes out between whimpers and damn if that's not the hottest thing I've ever heard.

He pulls out slightly before sliding in again, squeezing the arm on my waist as if he wasn't deep enough.

If Darian could fuck my soul from within my body I think he'd have found a way with how deep he is.

He withdraws halfway, but instead of going slow, he slams in making me cry out and my back presses against the wall behind me.

"That's it. Be as loud as you need to, sweetheart. Let them know how well I fuck you."

The sheer size of his cock overwhelms my body as he slams into me repeatedly, his brutal rhythm is animalistic as if he's given himself over to madness.

My cries and moans are completely involuntary with each thrust, it's as if branding the inside of my being for the rest of time.

I'm hardly aware of the banging and pounding my body makes against the wall as another orgasm crests from the intense concoction of ecstasy and pain.

Darian must feel it as he fucks me because he keeps his pace but squeezes his fingers on either side of my throat, cutting off the blood supply to my head.

If I thought my orgasm earlier was the most intense I'd ever experienced, this climax now holds the record.

Within seconds I'm dizzy and feel light just as he releases the pressure on my neck and another earth-shattering orgasm takes over my body.

My vision goes white and my nails dig into his back as I scream his name.

He continues to fuck me through each wave of pleasure until my limbs go numb and tremble.

Chapter 48

Darian

I feel the moment the orgasm takes over her body because her pussy becomes a vice grip on my dick. It requires all my concentration and effort to hold back from following her and filling her to the brim.

I know I'm just edging myself but fuck if I don't give her more of this feeling before I unload. She deserves to enjoy this for everything she's gone through.

Men can be selfish, and cruel. Evil.

I'll be damned if I'm ever considered as part of the generalization.

Her body stops twitching as I ease her off the wall while kissing her gently, and she whimpers in protest as I pull out, if not only to keep myself from coming.

I lower us both onto the bed, leaning back against the soft pillows as I bring her with me.

Instead of remaining straddled over me, she moves to sit between my legs and a mischievous but shy smile creeps across her stunning and flush face.

Oh, fuck.

I watch with rapt attention as she wraps her hands around my cock, one over the other, and leans in to lick the tip. My hips buck up involuntarily at the warmth of her mouth, and I grab a fistful of her hair as she drops down, wrapping her lips around the tip.

"Lara..." I warn.

I don't even know what the warning is for.

Maybe it's because I fucking worship this woman and here she is with her lips around my dick.

She swirls her tongue over the head, working the base with her hands before sliding her mouth down further until I hit the back of her throat.

She gags against my dick and I groan, my hand tightening in her hair, holding her in place as the muscles in her throat work to fit my cock. I ease her head back slightly, and she inhales a deep breath, with tears streaming down her face.

I worry in the moment if I hurt her, but that fear is quickly diminished as she slides my cock down her throat again deeper this time while breathing through her nose.

"That's it. Just like that." I grunt out, as my fist pushes her head further toward my pelvic bone. Her grip on the base of my cock squeezes as she gags, but she continues to hollow her cheeks and suck as she works through it.

"You take me so fucking well." I say, moving some of her hair out of the way, captivated by the sight before me. She squeezes her thighs together and sucks with renewed enthusiasm at my praise. "This beautiful fucking mouth was made to take my cock."

My thrusts get more erratic and I feel my balls tighten. I'm not going to last much longer. I pull her head back by her hair, withdrawing my cock from her mouth with a 'pop' sound, and she glances at me with concern.

As if she could ever do something wrong.

Using my fist tangled in her hair, I tug her head back, tilting her face to meet my gaze, "I'm going to come, but when I do it won't be in your mouth. I'm going to fill that filthy fucking cunt that has been soaked the entire time you've been sucking my cock."

Her eyes flash with desire, and I drag her up by her arms until she's straddling me. Placing both hands on her waist, my throbbing dick pulses at the entrance to her pussy and buries inside of her with one thrust.

She cries out at the sudden intrusion and the momentum bucks her forward before I pull out to the tip and slam up into her again.

Soon, she's gyrating on my dick in rhythm with my thrusts and I reach a hand down to circle her clit with my thumb.

One more.

With every caress, her movements become more frantic as she chases her own release, and she starts to chant my name between breaths, each one with more urgency than the last.

Leaning forward, I grab her by the nape of her neck, pulling her ear to my lips as she grinds into me with desperation, "Come for me, Ray. Come all over this fucking cock. It's all yours." I growl as my free hand continues to encircle her clit.

Her pussy squeezes my dick so tight that my vision blurs, my balls tighten, and I come so much that it leaks down my cock still firmly lodged inside her.

She collapses against my chest, and we stay like that for a while, letting our breathing even out.

I wrap my arms around her small frame and place kisses on the top of her head as she melts into my embrace.

"Did you mean what you said earlier, or was that just part of the dirty talk?" Her voice is quiet and soft, almost inaudible as if she's unsure she should be asking this at all.

I frown deeply, tracing circles on her skin with my thumb, "Did I mean what?" I ask softly before pressing a tender kiss against her hair.

"When you said.... about you being mine." Her voice is almost a whisper now, and my heart wrenches in my chest, to think that she worries that the intimacy between us would remain solely for sex.

If only she knew the lengths I would go for her, it would frighten her.

Hell, truth be told, it should scare me, too.

But it doesn't.

I tighten my grip around her in an attempt to meld her closer into my body. "I meant it all, Sunshine. There is no part of me that doesn't belong to you, and that fact will remain long past the day when my soul no longer resides in my body." I whisper softly, and my heart nearly shatters as I feel her tears fall to my bare skin.

Her slender arms wrap around my body as she snuggles into my chest, and we remain this way until sleep takes us both.

Chapter 49

Lara

We retrieve the truck from the satellite lot at the airport, and on our way home, Darian makes a stop at a nearby grocery store. He returns with several bags filled with items, piquing my curiosity as I watch him.

Upon arriving at his house, we unload our carry-ons in the entryway, and a sense of relief washes over me with a deep sigh.

"I was beginning to think we would never return to this place," I say softly, casting a sidelong glance at Darian as he secures the door behind us.

Absorbed in my own thoughts as I move toward the spare room, my steps come to a halt when his fingers encircle my wrist.

"Stay with me tonight. Please," he says softly, a flicker of emotion I can't quite place in his eyes and I nod.

My gaze tracks Darian's movements as he carries our bags into the master bedroom, carefully placing them by the door.

We both take much needed showers and slip into clean clothes.

Caspian had provided us with specific instructions to attend an annual two-week long event taking place at our local convention center, where we could potentially find the next amulet.

The festival reconvenes tomorrow, giving us some spare time to ourselves this evening.

Darian enters the bedroom with a mischievous smirk on his face. "Hungry?"

I respond with a nod and trail behind him to the kitchen where he's arranged items on the counter, accompanied by several bottles of wine.

"What's all this?" I ask, stepping closer to what looks like ingredients laid out on the counter.

Darian grins, "Pizza and our very own wine tasting,"

I blink in surprise, then glance back at the counter as I mirror his grin, rubbing my hands together excitedly.

"Here are the rules. We each select five toppings, and then we'll draw the toppings randomly from a hat. We'll be allowed three toppings each for our pizzas. Once they're cooked, we'll rate the pizzas we tried. The winner will claim the prize" he explains, pausing for added dramatics, "The $300 bottle of tequila from the fridge."

Oh, it's on like Donkey Kong.

"Did I ever tell you that I'm hopelessly competitive?" I tease, reaching for the flour to make a thin-crust pizza.

It's not long before I set the smooth dough ball aside, letting it rest as I jot down a list of toppings from the ingredients Darian purchased.

Pepperoni, mushrooms, peppers, sausage, and olives.

I place each folded piece of paper with different variations of toppings into the large white bowl.

Darian leans forward to drop his own in with a smirk, his dimples on full display as a blush creeps across my cheeks, heightened when he moves to stand behind me.

His hands cover my eyes, and his lips brush the shell of my ear, his breath caressing my skin as he whispers, "Choose well," his baritone voice sends a shiver down my spine.

Aware of Darian's chest pressed against my back, I reach into the bowl, swirling my hand through the small folded pieces of paper.

My senses are alight with his proximity and my pulse rages in my ears as I draw one before placing it on the counter. Delving back into the bowl to select two more, I gather the three chosen toppings.

Darian's hands lower on my shoulders and my pulse hikes up.

He guides me to the side, moving in my place to select his own ingredients.

I reach up to cover his eyes, having to stand on my tiptoes to comfortably cover them with more than just the tips of my fingers and Darian chuckles softly.

Once unable to see, he mirrors my earlier actions, shuffling them around before choosing one and setting it aside. Repeating the process until he has all three.

I unfold my first paper and read it out loud, "Sausage."

Next, I open the second one, "Pepperoni."

A chuckle escapes my lips as I flick open the final paper, "Bacon."

Darian grins, "Meat lovers," he says suggestively, and I punch him lightly in the shoulder, feigning outrage.

"Always so violent now, hmm?" Darian chuckles, nudging me with his elbow. I shoot him a mock glare in response.

"Oh, I was violent long before you came along," I retort. "Remember when you left the window open? I did roam around the house with a baseball bat."

He bursts into laughter as he unfolds his own papers, his humor turns to a groan. "Olives... Peppers," he peers the final piece and tosses it to the counter, "And mushrooms," he laments, and I grin widely.

"Seems like the universe is telling someone to become a vegetarian." I tease, tossing the papers into the recycling bin.

Darian's jaw drops, pressing a hand to his chest dramatically as if I had just insulted him and his entire lineage. "I would sooner die than give up meat."

I blink at him before we both erupt into laughter as I fling a single mushroom in his direction. He jerks back, snatching the pack of bacon to use as a shield.

With a grin, I turn my attention to getting started on assembling my pizza.

I steal a quick glance at Darian, observing as he arranges the olives onto his pizza, preparing to place it into the oven alongside mine. As both pizzas cook, the mouthwatering scent wafts through the kitchen and my stomach growls hungrily.

Darian pours us each some red wine, raising his own glass as he hands me mine.

"Here's to us." He says with a soft smile and I can't help the swell in my chest.

Our glasses clink together, the sound resonating through the air before taking a healthy sip.

I hum with satisfaction as I continue to tilt my glass until the last of it disappears.

Darian's eyes are saucers as he stares at me.

I raise an eyebrow, "What's with the look?" I ask innocently, a smile tugging at the corners of my lips.

"Note to self, stock up on Pinot," Darian mutters under his breath, his gaze fixed on me as I refill my glass, nearly to the brim.

I chuckle and teasingly add, "And Tequila."

He lets out a sigh, feigning exasperation and we both smirk.

It's not long before I remove the perfectly cooked meat lovers' pizza from the oven to place it onto a large cutting board.

My eyes narrowing at Darian, "Squares or triangles. There's only one right answer,"

He blinks, "Triang-" he begins to answer, but I quickly interrupt him with a buzzer sound as if we're on a game show.

I raise a finger into the air, pointing it assertively.

"WRONG! The correct answer is squares. One shot of tequila for Gryffindor!" I cheer.

He bursts into laughter as I begin cutting the pizza in squares with the round cutter.

Halfway through the first slice, I pause and fix my gaze on him, my expression suddenly serious as he raises his glass for another sip of wine.

"Did you think I was joking?" I ask my tone deadpan.

His laughter erupts again, and he chokes on his wine, quickly placing the glass down and coughing in surprise before looking at me with disbelief.

"The tequila is the prize for the best pizza, Lara," he manages to say between coughs.

I narrow my eyes, "Fine, but mark my words, when I win this contest, I'm claiming my shot of tequila." I state with a nod, as if reaffirming that I'll win.

Darian places his pizza next to mine, proceeding to cut it into unappealing triangles and my nose scrunches.

"Well, I have half a mind not to try yours now," I retort.

His chuckle fills the air as he retrieves plates from the cupboard, arranging a selection of pizza slices on each one. Meanwhile, I refill our glasses with wine and dispose of the empty bottle.

With everything in place, I set one plate on the floor for Val, who eagerly sniffs each slice before diving into the meat lovers' pizza.

"Well, let's try yours first, team triangle." I say teasingly, gesturing toward his questionably cut pizza in front of him.

Biting into the slice, I can't help but admit that his pizza is well-made, and I suppress a groan of satisfaction, determined to maintain my facade.

"Alright, now it's my turn. But first, a palette cleanser," I declare, taking a long sip and Darian laughs softly as he follows suit, polishing off his wine and placing his glass down.

We both grab a square of the meat lovers' pizza, and a satisfied grin spreads across my face as I look confidently at Darian.

The meaty toppings deliver a savory, salty burst of flavor that melds with the crisp thin crust. The pizza hasn't lost its texture or become soggy, and the balance of meat to sauce to dough is perfection.

I steal a quick glance at Darian, who has already taken a second piece of the meat lovers and bites into it.

He freezes as he looks at me, his mouth still filled with pizza, and I catch the hint of a smile tugging at the corners of his lips as he struggles to hold it back.

"I think it's time for that Tequila now," I declare with confidence, raising my chin slightly.

"I actually preferred the veggie one," Darian states after swallowing his bite, and I scoff in disbelief.

"You've got to be kidding me! After you devoured another piece of mine? No way!" I exclaim, incredulous.

Darian shakes his head, "I was just saving the best for last."

My eyes roll, and I let out an exaggerated huff in protest. "Well, it seems we'll need a tiebreaker!" I declare, gesturing toward Val lounging on the couch, his ears flattening backwards.

"Val, it's your time to shine," I beckon to him.

Darian chuckles, teasingly claiming, "Clearly, he enjoyed mine more."

I shoot a playful glare at Darian before softening my expression as I turn to Val. "It's up to you. Who gets the tequila?"

Val huffs and strolls into the kitchen, his gaze fixed on the counter where the two pizzas await. He lifts his upper body, leaning over to get a closer look.

With a glance at both of us, he finally points his nose at the meat lovers and in that moment, his ears perk forward.

I erupt in victorious cheers. "Steaks for Val tomorrow!" I exclaim, as Val saunters back to the couch.

Darian, on the other hand, pinches the bridge of his nose in feigned exasperation, "Betrayal. Absolute betrayal." he muses.

I cackle, tearing the fridge open, retrieving the tequila and unscrewing the lid.

Darian slides two shot glasses over to me with a wide grin. Downing one, I feel hardly any burn as it travels down my throat before immediately refilling the glass.

"We do have places to be tomorrow, you know," Darian reminds me, blinking at the liquor.

I meet his gaze and raise an eyebrow, "But tonight, we are free." I declare before throwing back the tequila shot and clinking the glass onto the countertop with a satisfying thud.

We tidy up the remnants of the pizza contest and indulge in another bottle of wine before we settle in front of the TV.

The TV turns on to breaking news on the screen: a local museum has been burglarized, and authorities scrambling to identify the thief or what they took as Darian flips the channel to the streaming app to choose a movie.

We doze off on the couch at some point during the movie, and I awaken to find myself in the comfort of the master bedroom.

Darian is wrapped around me tightly with Val peacefully nestled at my other side. Waking up sandwiched between these two men is a scenario that has become all too familiar.

I squirm against Darian, feeling the unmistakable hardness pressing against my back.

"Keep doing that and we won't be going anywhere today, Lara." His voice, laced with a hint of playful warning, sends shivers down my spine.

"Well, you may want to move because I need to use the bathroom," I choke out as I roll onto my side, trying to relieve the pressure on my bladder.

Darian chuckles, and gracefully slips off the blankets, standing up to make way for me. "At what point is Val going to be the one that moves?" he muses.

My hands instinctively move to my chest in feigned shock before I point toward Val peacefully sleeping like a big furry angel on the bed. "Just look at how cute he is, snoozing away," I remark, unable to hide the affection in my voice.

Val's ears twitch ever so slightly, though his eyes remain shut. I imagine he's silently laughing at our exchange, and the corner of my lips twitch as I try and fail to suppress a smile.

"Cute? You do realize he's a red-blooded male under all that fur, right?" Darian raises an eyebrow.

I turn back to face him. "Oh, believe me, I haven't forgotten," I reply, my voice thick with amusement. "But that doesn't change a thing, does it?" Darian's face flashes for a moment, but my attention is distracted by my bladder.

Unable to put it off, I hurry to the washroom as Darian skillfully prepares breakfast and we both get ready for the convention. Opting for a bold and confident look, I slip into a pair of jeans that accentuate my curves, with a form-fitting black tank top. The ensemble is completed with sleek black wedge heels, adding a touch of elegance to the outfit.

I catch a glimpse of myself in the mirror, appreciating the inch of skin revealed at my waist and the tank top.

The drive to the convention center is peaceful.

That's actually how I could describe my time with Darian and Val since we rescued him.

It's as though I'm on a cloud, floating through the sky, lifted by the very air I breathe.

Part of me wonders if he feels the same.

As we approach our destination, Darian smoothly parks the car in the VIP section and I turn to him with a raise brow.

Meeting my gaze, his lips twitch.

"Caspian pulled some strings and managed to secure VIP tickets for us," he explains, "And with VIP tickets come VIP parking privileges."

My jaw drops.

How much influence do both of these men have?

We step out of the car and toward the entrance. I can feel the weight of the attention from the surrounding crowd as eyes track our every move. The flashes of cameras are blinding, and I avoid looking. It's as if we were celebrities.

It's an unusual and exhilarating experience, if only for the duration of this event.

"Mr.Cathorn!" As the crowd's attention turns toward Darian, I blink. Among the sea of faces, a young woman's enthusiastic greeting stands out, addressing Darian by name.

He acknowledges her with a friendly wave, flashing his charismatic smile to those around us. I'm lost in my own mind as I scan through the faces of people snapping photos, waving excitedly in our direction until a gentle tug on my hand pulls me from my reverie.

Darian interlaces our fingers comfortably, and I follow his lead.

"Are you this well known because of the building you own on the coast?" I ask.

Darian meets my gaze, his expression relaxed, "Among other things. I've just gotten used to it honestly."

I set aside my line of thought and focus on the present as we explore the bustling kiosks showcasing beautiful clothing, art, and model items.

The pop-up food shops catches our attention, and we snag a bag of popcorn as we continue our search.

An hour slips away, and a flicker of doubt starts to creep in.

We had been relying on Caspian's guidance but what if he was wrong?

Suddenly, I come to a halt, the familiar sensation tugging at my senses. Darian notices my abrupt stop and turns, his eyes scanning the surroundings with growing realization.

The pull intensifies, its force gradually increasing as I remain rooted in place. The sensation becomes almost tangible as if an invisible thread is dragging my very being toward it.

I adjust my stance, shifting my weight ever so slightly to alleviate the mounting pressure.

"I think someone is wearing it or has brought it here." my voice barely audible as I press my palm flat against my core in a failed attempt to calm it.

The all enveloping pull takes an abrupt turn, causing a surge of pain to ripple through my body and I gasp.

Fuck. They're moving away.

Clutching onto Darian's arm for support, my words are thick with desperation. "We have to head in that direction. If they keep going further, I won't be able to walk."

His arm loops securely through mine, as I guide us toward the source. The pain subsides, leaving behind a lingering pressure, pointing me in the direction I need to go.

As we push through the crowd, I scan peoples attire and accessories, and searching for any sign of the amulet or even a chain around someone's neck.

My eyes widen as they lock onto a cosplayer, their appearance reminiscent of a robot from an anime or a Transformer.

The details of their costume and the way they carry themselves draw my attention like a magnet, as if the amulet's presence is intertwined with their every move.

Squeezing Darian's hand to grab his attention, I tilt my head in the direction of the costumed individual. Following my line of vision, he releases my hand and strides purposefully toward the person in question.

I hold my breath as I witness the two exchange words. The cosplayer, their face partially obscured by the mask, lifts the front of it.

My heart thunders as they reach for a chain hanging around their neck and begin to unclasp it, revealing the amulet before holding it out.

Darian flashes a charming smile, pulls out his wallet and carefully counts out a banded stack of bills, folded neatly, and passes it over to the cosplayer who simply looks shocked.

With the amulet secured in his grasp, and a grin lighting up his handsome features, he passes it to me with a wink.

Relief coats every inch of my body once the cool of the metal and glass is in my palm. My gaze drops, curious by the detailed depiction of a majestic three-headed dog at its center I wonder what the images inside mean as I carefully clasp it alongside the others on my necklace.

The rest of the day unfolds in a surprisingly normal manner as we continue exploring the various kiosks and the vibrant energy of the convention.

We indulge in snacks along the way as we people watch,

pointing out fun costumes and enjoy the thrill of the event.

Chapter 50

Caspian

I sit at my desk in the confines of my study fully engrossed in my thoughts as a familiar buzz rings out from my pocket.

It's been hours since Lara and Darian were seen at the convention. I can only assume that they have successfully retrieved the key.

Yet, as my focus settles on the last remaining pieces of the puzzle, an undeniable weight rests upon my shoulders.

My gut twists knowing we're near the finish line.

There is a lingering issue casting a long shadow over my thoughts and has given me pause for days.

The museum break-in that resulted in the disappearance of the final key, recovering it would demand another sacrifice. That knowledge gnaws at my gut with a disquieting unease.

Blair's dismissive fucking attitude whenever I broach the subject eats at the corners of my mind.

It is not just her aloofness that troubles me. It is the underlying tension that has permeated our interactions since the incident involving Tamara's release from the warehouse weeks ago.

There is a growing sense of discord.

This development deepens my paranoia, leading me to question the integrity of those within our inner circle. Furthering my suspicion that Blair, or someone closely associated with our trusted group, is being dishonest.

Considering the circumstances surrounding the keys, it's evident that the knowledge of them extends beyond our immediate circle.

Hell, Cain knew about the keys because I foolishly told him, he just didn't know they were amulets.

I'm certain others, for whatever reason, may be pursuing them.

Yet, when I consider the limited number of individuals aware of the amulets' existence—myself, Blair, my brother, and Lara—it becomes increasingly clear that the answers lie within our own ranks.

I had yet to disclose the key's location to Lara and Darian.

This narrows the pool of individuals who could be responsible for the theft even further.

Checking my phone, I notice a message from Blair, and a frown creases on my brow.

It has been some time since we last communicated, once I completed my arduous sixty-seven-hour play session with Dolly, finally putting an end to her suffering.

Blair: Need your help in the garage, have cargo.

I rise from my desk, stretching my limbs to alleviate the stiffness that has settled after hours of work. Exiting the study, I move through the hushed corridors of the house, my footsteps the only sound breaking the silence.

With a push, the heavy garage door swings open, where stacks of nondescript boxes clutter the space as they always have. Confused by the lack of the cargo, I frown, turning my head to scan the area before darkness engulfs me.

~

As consciousness returns my mind is fogged and hazy.

I become aware of my body resting on a bed as I sit up and reach for the blindfold covering my eyes. As it slips off, my gaze sweeps across the room, and confusion washes over me.

I'm in my bedroom?

How did I end up here?

What happened in the garage?

I recall getting a text about cargo, but nothing more.

Blair wouldn't be that foolish to have betrayed me, not with the force that binds us both together.

Frowning deeply, I rub the soreness at the back of my skull before pushing to my feet unsteadily as my legs tremble beneath me. Approaching the door. I grasp the handle and twist, only to find it locked.

My jaw clenches.

Thoughts of Blair, once again, creep into my mind.

She wouldn't have done this, would she?

The uneasy feeling that had been simmering in the back of my mind intensifies, fueling suspicions that I had tried to push aside.

Turning my attention to the room, and my eyes scan the surroundings, landing on a piece of paper placed deliberately on the dresser.

I approach it and carefully pick it up.

Unfolding the note, I read the words scrawled across the paper.

Caspian,

I apologize for the manner of which I deceived you. I dutifully accept the honor of releasing you from your banishment and freeing you of the burdensome act of restoring magic to this world. I will take this final task upon myself thereby sparing you from the weight it carries. Please forgive me, and know that by the time you read this, it shall be done.

Blair

A sense of dread and horror courses through my veins as I absorb the words scrawled on the paper.

With no immediate way to gauge if magic has been restored a foreign sense of panic sends me sprinting toward the door.

I grip the handle tightly, twisting and wrenching with all my strength.

Despite the resistance, fueled by panic and sheer will, I manage to break the knob, forcefully swinging the door open.

One singular thought echoes in my mind.

Lara.

Chapter 51

Lara

The day after the convention passes in silence, with no communication from Caspian.

If Darian worries he masks it well, as he seizes the opportunity to teach me how to ride a motorcycle in deserted parking lots nearby.

With each passing day that Tammy doesn't respond, doubts begin to creep in regarding Caspian's commitment to releasing her.

The radio silence from both has concern nagging at the back of my mind.

I retrieve my phone and power it on, feeling a frown form as I discover a missed message from Claire.

Claire: Hi Lara. I'm beginning to get concerned that we still haven't met recently. I'd like to put something on your calendar soon to catch up. Let me know, thanks.

I let out a weary sigh, my fingers hesitating over the keyboard as I type out several messages, only to delete them. Finally, I settle on a vague response, hoping it will suffice for now.

Lara: Hey Claire. Appreciate that you're reaching out again, but I'm still taking some personal leave. TBD on my availability to meet, I've been busy recently.

The message is instantly marked as read, and my phone begins to ring. I let out an exasperated sigh before swiping my finger across the green answer button.

"Hello?" I respond, my tone laced with a hint of annoyance.

"Lara! I hope I'm not catching you at a bad time," Claire chirps cheerfully.

I inwardly roll my eyes.

She didn't even bother to ask if it was convenient for me to talk.

"Nope, I have a minute to chat. What can I do for you?"

"Well, I was hoping to catch up on how the past few weeks have been for you. What have you been up to?" Her voice is cheerful, but there's an undertone of concern that I don't miss.

Shit. I can't tell her upwards of 90% of what has transpired recently.

"Uhh well, I went to see Tammy and I've been on the coast since. Nothing really new, just needed some R&R."

Claire remains silent for a moment, as per usual before she finally hums in acknowledgment.

"Well, perhaps you could give Henry and Candace some time off soon too. They seemed quite busy when I called the office last week, and now my calls aren't even being answered, so they must be swamped." she suggests.

I nod, even though she can't see me through the phone. "Yes, they definitely work hard. I'll make sure to give them some time off once I'm back," I assure her, knowing full well that their sudden unavailability was likely due to her persistent calls.

Her caller ID is saved on every phone we have, after all.

"Good, good—" Claire's drowned out by Darian's loud voice from the hallway as he calls out, "Hey Lara! Any idea where the ibuprofen is? I looked in the bathroom and—"

My head snaps toward the door, startled by Darian's sudden entrance. He stops mid-sentence as he sees me on the phone.

The tension in the room becomes palpable as his eyes narrow on my cell phone.

"Lara, who is that? Is that why you've been taking time off?"

Claire's persistent questions ring through the phone without a beat, and I lean forward, rubbing my temples in an attempt to soothe the building headache.

"There's just a lot going on, and it's a long story. I really have to go now."

"But we haven't talked abo-"

"Goodbye!" I chime, pressing the end button with more force than necessary.

I toss my phone aside, having no desire to read the disappearing text from Claire's name that momentarily appears on the screen.

"Ibuprofen was by your side of the bed, last I saw," I respond, and he snaps his fingers in a triumphant manner, a classic "Aha!" moment, before disappearing down the hallway again.

I can't help but chuckle at the sight of the slightly domesticated version of Darian I just interacted with.

My phone buzzes once more, and with an angry sigh, I assume it's Claire and grab it, seeing 'unknown number' on the message ID.

A wave of horror washes over me as I open the text to images of Tammy, Candace, and Henry, tied up against a tree and bearing numerous bruises. Their disheveled appearance, torn clothes and bowed heads fills me with a sickening feeling in the pit of my stomach.

Unknown Number: Come to the following coordinates immediately. Come alone. Their lives depend on it.

A second text message comes through with a location that I quickly input into the GPS on my phone.

The destination is a mile away from the area where I've been conducting my research and not too far from where I am now.

It's close enough to walk.

My mind races as I attempt to gather my thoughts and analyze the situation.

Who could be behind these messages? What do they want from me?

Yet, as I glance back at the image of my friends, my resolve hardens.

I refuse to let fear paralyze me.

Whoever this is, they're hurting my friends.

If I tell Darian, he will insist to come or send Val, and I can't risk that.

No.

I won't take the chance for them to be more hurt than they already are.

I quickly change into work clothes. I choose a pair of sleek dress pants with a vibrant red blouse before slipping on a pair of sturdy heels, and carefully tuck my runners in my purse.

I move toward the door, feigning nonchalance while Darian and Val watch an episode of Cops as a suspect attempts to evade arrest. Darian's gaze briefly shifts to me, and he does a double take, his brow raised.

"Where are you off to?" he asks, genuinely surprised.

I steady my pulse, and reach for the keys to Darian's truck. "I'm heading to the office to meet with Claire and check in on Candace and Henry," I reply.

The lie slips from my lips, leaving a bitter aftertaste in my mouth.

Val's eyes flicker and Darian, though still uncertain, nods, "Okay, want Val to come with you?" He asks, presenting the option as a question, but I can tell he is mentioning it because it's his own preference.

Waving my hand dismissively as I make my way toward the door, I inject a hint of boredom into my voice. "No, there's no need.

I'm confident there won't be any trouble. I'll be back before you know it."

I offer a half-hearted smile and deep down, I know I can't involve Val or risk anyone else's safety.

I need to face this alone.

Without waiting for his response I briskly walk out the door, letting it close behind me.

My steps quicken as I throw open the garage door and climb into the truck, my heart pounding in my chest.

The engine roars to life, filling the air with its powerful rumble as I pull out of the driveway coolly. My eyes flick to the rearview mirror every few seconds, just in case.

Using the GPS directions, I drive for ten minutes down the main road until I reach an unused service path. The dense forest narrows on either side, making it impossible to continue with the truck. I park it safely and swapping my heels for runners to make the rest of the journey on foot.

For the next two hours, I navigate through rugged terrain, my legs growing weary with each step.

The GPS buzzes, indicating that I'm getting closer to my destination and my heart races.

As I approach, the symphony of crickets dominating the air gradually gives way to the gentle crashing of waves against the shore. The familiar, peaceful sandy ground beneath my feet eases my anxiety if only for the moment.

And then, that's when I spot them.

There, tied to a tree near the shore, are Tammy, Candace, and Henry. My heart sinks at the sight of their bruised and battered forms.

My body acts without permission as I bolt forward to rush to their aid but my knees buckle, and I stumble over a root.

Before I can dash the rest of the way to my friends a black haired woman steps closer, holding a long dagger that glints in the fading light, and I freeze.

My breath catches in my throat as recognition washes over me.

It's the same woman from the apartment the night I stabbed Caspian.

Fear grips me, holding me in place as I realize the danger I'm in.

"I'm so glad you were able to make it, vrenlon dyrtia," she says, her black eyes darting around before a sinister grin spreads across her face. "I'm pleased you followed my instructions."

I square my shoulders, trying to muster confidence that I don't have. "Release them," I demand, and the woman's eyes narrow.

She clicks her tongue and shakes her head mockingly. "I'm afraid I cannot grant your request just yet. If you comply, however, they will remain unharmed."

Her eyes flash with a mix of excitement and satisfaction as I take a cautious step closer.

My brows pinch together as a familiar sensation in my body halts me in place, and my hand instinctively goes to my abdomen, feeling an inexplicable pull.

Here?

The woman's gaze tracks my movement like a predator stalking her prey and her grin widens, revealing gleaming white teeth.

She reaches into her pocket, producing an amulet as she holds it between us, "Ah, yes. I believe this is something of great interest to you. I took the liberty of retrieving it from that dusty old museum."

My eyes widen in disbelief.

"That was you? Why would you steal the amulet? What do you want?" My voice gets stronger as my fear and confusion melt into frustration.

She throws her head back and lets out a chilling cackle.

"Oh, vrenlon dyrtia, our desires align. I want the same thing as you. My purpose is to see that magic returns, and you are the key to making it happen," she declares with a wicked gleam in her eyes.

"What is vrenlon dyrtia? Why do you keep saying that?" I demand, grinding my teeth together.

There's the anger.

Her grin widens, as if she's excited to educate me.

"Have you never been told the prophecy? My, my. Vrenlon dyrtia still has so much to learn but so little time." she says, taking a step closer.

The pull inside me intensifies, and I shift to maintain my balance.

Her smile widens, and she begins to recite words that flow effortlessly from her lips, each sending shivers down my spine.

"Born of sun and moon, will reveal the keys.
To unlock source's power, once sealed away.
But darkness lurks, seeking to deceive.
And one must sacrifice for magic to be freed."

She takes another step closer, and I instinctively move a pace back, but a sudden jolt of pain tremors its way through my chest and core.

Panic coats my veins when I realize I won't be able to run from her if she has the amulet.

"Beware the one who pulls the strings,
A deceiver with blood magic's control
For the banished seeks to return
With a thirst for power, his heart a black hole."

I shudder as she takes another step, further closing the short distance between us, and my legs begin to quiver beneath me.

> *"In the water where realms collide,*
> *Her body will break the final seal.*
> *Great sacrifice to unleash great power,*
> *But darkness rises, with essence it shall steal."*

My knees buckle under her final step, and she seizes my hair, forcefully dragging me behind her. The relentless pull of the amulet renders my resistance useless as we wade deeper into the lake, the water rising to our waists.

> *"Only she alone can save their fate,*
> *And with magic's return, a new dawn awaits.*
> *A future world of wonder, free from fear,*
> *But with rampant darkness, the future's unclear."*

Agony forces a cry from my lips as she rips the chain from my neck, holding the amulets before her with a manic smile on her face.

My arms brace against my trembling thighs as I struggle to maintain my balance, panting heavily as horror coats my veins. I steal a quick glance at my friends, still safely unconscious on the shore.

At least her attention is fixed on the amulets.

"I will accomplish what Caspian failed to do. I will succeed in breaking the seal and restoring things to the way they were long ago," she declares, her words echoing in my ears.

Time seems to slow down as she pulls her arm back and thrusts the blade through one of the amulets. The glass shatters, releasing the shimmering liquid contents into the lake.

A violent tremor rips through me and the water around me pulsates with energy.

She shatters another amulet and I gasp for air, feeling as if the very oxygen has been sucked from my lungs.

With each successive strike she smashes the remaining amulets, and I fight to stay standing, clinging to every ounce of strength I have.

If I can just hold on until she's done with the last one, I may have a chance to escape. But as the knife pierces through the final amulet, the one with a stunning sun disk at its center, I can no longer fight the force dragging me down.

My legs give way, and I collapse into the water onto my knees, the chaotic lake rising over my ears and threatening to pull me under. Gasping for breath, I desperately keep my face upturned to avoid drowning.

After she drops the last shattered piece into the water, she turns toward me, her grin stretching from ear to ear.

"Vrenlon dyrtia, in my native language of ancient Servilian, means chosen daughter. You see, you are the one born of the sun and moon, of day and night. Born of the gods themselves. You are the key, the one destined to break the final seal. Your life essence, the blood within your body, shall be the offering that I will deliver."

Her words echo in the air, sending chills down my spine.

She tilts her head back and laughs maniacally as she slices my wrist with her dagger, quickly bringing it to her lips and greedily drinking my blood.

I'm paralyzed. Unable to move or make a sound as I feel the life force draining from my veins.

My strength slowly wanes, and I'm uncertain how long she continues to drink or how much of my blood she consumes.

Eventually, she withdraws, a stream of deep crimson staining her chin and neck, leaving me weakened and on the brink of unconsciousness.

My thoughts turn to Darian, the sense of safety and protection I felt in his arms floods my memories.

I think of Val, the subtle twitch of his ears whenever I asked him a question, and the playful humor in his eyes during our banter with Darian.   I think of how both of them consistently showed up to protect and guard me.

To find me when all hope seemed lost.

My mind lingers on Caspian next.

Despite his coldness, there were rare moments of vulnerability he displayed, glimpses of someone who possessed kindness beneath his hardened exterior.

I remember the gestures he made in our little time spent not hunting amulets, finding May and Rose a loving foster family, sparing me from killing Dolly in cold blood.

Those are not typically the acts of a heartless villain.

No, those were the actions of my monster.

In this moment, I sadly long for more time with them, realizing that these three men — Darian, Caspian, and Val — have become an unexpected necessity in my life.

It's a realization that catches me off guard.

I never anticipated my greatest regret would be not seeing them again.

I suppose life has a way of surprising us when we least expect it.

With a tight grip on my hair, she yanks me to my feet until the water reaches my waist.

I flex my limbs, trying to make any movements to free myself, but they remain frozen, as if paralyzed completely from my body's commands.

Her eyes lock onto mine, determination on her face as she raises the dagger, and quickly drives it into my stomach.

A guttural shriek claws its way from my throat with raw intensity as the blade pierces my abdomen.

White-hot searing pain radiates from my stomach and my gaze drops as the lake around my body darkens with my blood.

She suddenly pushes away from me, quickly turning to face the shore, where a shouting and commotion erupts.

As chaos unfolds, the water surrounding me ripples and surges, gaining momentum with each passing moment.

The once calm lake that only moved with the wind now churns and swirls of its own accord, echoing the turmoil within me as the numb feeling in my limbs spreads through my body, making it increasingly difficult to stay upright.

This is it, this must be what dying feels like.

As my vision blurs I strain to make sense of the chaos unfolding around me.

The woman who had shattered the amulets is now nowhere to be seen, replaced instead by a colossal, shadowy serpent writhing in the grip of a massive, jet-black panther.

The snake's scales shimmer with an otherworldly iridescence, while the panther emanates an aura of strength and primal power that sends a shiver through my chest.

I blink rapidly, desperately trying to regain focus as the serpent contorts, morphing before my eyes into the very woman who had attacked me, her black hair cascading around her face, and she smiles.

"It's too late!" she screams, as the air crackles with energy, and the ground beneath us trembles violently as if the very foundation of the earth is being shattered.

The tremors beneath my feet make it even more difficult to stay standing, and if my swaying by itself is any indication, I won't be upright much longer.

My vision flickers, and amidst the chaos, movement catches my eye as a man sprints through the churning water toward me.

His long black hair flows down to his shoulders, and his bright hazel eyes are filled with a mixture of desperation and fear as he fights against the chaotic lake.

My heart skips a beat as I recognize the familiar features are Val, running toward me in his human form.

Time seems to slow as I observe the raw power in his muscular frame, each stride bringing him closer. His full lips and chiseled jaw move as if he's shouting, but the sound reaches me muffled, as though I'm submerged underwater.

My weakened legs finally give way and I fall forward, collapsing toward the water. In that moment my gaze meets the terror etched within Val's eyes, and our connection transcends words.

That's when the dark waters envelop my vision entirely.

Strong arms encircle my limp body as Val cradles me to his chest, lifting me from the water. I'm unable to move or speak as he carries me to the shore, catching a glimpse of Darian's hurried approach, his expression mirroring Val's.

I feel nothing as Darian puts pressure on my abdomen, and deep down I'm painfully aware that it's near futile for them to try to stop the bleeding.

The anguish on their faces as our hands intertwine tells me that they know too.

Peace and serenity engulfing my very being as I realize this is it.

The corners of my vision start to fade, darkness creeping in, but I find that I'm not afraid.

Instead... I feel only a profound sense of gratitude.

Gratitude, that in these final precious moments, I have been granted the gift of seeing them one last time before I succumb to the dark.

Acknowledgements

I have to first say a huge thank you to Amanda Dumky for the insanely gorgeous cover and for putting up with my chaos. This was a learning experience I will remember forever, and I cannot express enough gratitude for all your hard work.

A huge thank you to my husband, who supported my rather abrupt fixation on reading that turned into a passion and hobby. I'll never be the same now that I've started, but I'm so excited that we're on this ride together. There's no one I'd rather have by my side, my own personal book boyfriend.

I'd like to extend a particularly special thank you to my friends and family who read this... See ya'll at Thanksgiving...

But in all seriousness, I'm nothing without those I love and care about. Your support has meant the world to me, and I'm so deeply thankful to have such amazing people by my side.

Lastly, thank you to all the readers who decided to give my book a chance.

I can't promise it's the most well written, or well written at all... but I, as with many authors, put a piece of myself into my work, and taking the time to read it... well that may be the best gift of all.

It's just my hope that you enjoyed it, even if only for a moment before you move on to your next adventure.

Table of Contents